A TOUGH MAN'S WOMAN

DEBORAH CAMP

AVON BOOKS ◆ NEW YORK

AVON BOOKS
A division of
The Hearst Corporation
1350 Avenue of the Americas
New York, New York 10019

Copyright © 1997 by Deborah E. Camp
Published by arrangement with the author
Visit our website at **http://www.AvonBooks.com**
Library of Congress Catalog Card Number: 97-93177
ISBN: 0-380-78252-9

First Avon Books Printing: November 1997

AVON TRADEMARK REG. U.S. PAT. OFF. AND IN OTHER COUNTRIES, MARCA REGISTRADA, HECHO EN U.S.A.

Printed in the U.S.A.

WDC   10 9 8 7 6 5 4 3 2 1

"Monroe's got his spurs in a tangle over you," Drew said.

Cassie nodded calmly. "That's right."

"He means to win you over, maybe even marry you."

"He'll have to get in line."

Drew craned his neck, trying to glean something from her serene expression. "What's that mean?"

"It means that I have half the bachelors in the county wanting to court me."

"Other men have been snooping around you?"

Cassie gave him a chiding glance. "What do you think?" Batting her lashes and flashing a smile, she pitched her voice to a seductive purr. "Take a look at me and tell me if you don't think I'm easy on the eyes."

Holy hell, it was a good thing he had a sound head on his shoulders! He figured she had *all* the bachelors in the county vying for her attention. All except him. He knew what she was after, and it wasn't what was inside his trousers; it was what was outside his front door—land.

To Ellen Edwards, who has expended so much of her time and talent for my benefit. Yes, I know it's your job, but thanks for doing it so well.

Second-hand gold is as good as new.

—Cowboy saying

Chapter 1

April 1886
Near Abilene, Kansas, and the Chisholm Trail

He sat his horse like a king overseeing his holdings. Peering through the spyglass at the solitary rider, Cassie Dalton noted the proud span of his shoulders, the straight back, and the ease with which he commanded his spirited mount. He was still too far away to make out his features under the brim of his hat, but she could see him turning his head, examining the land, taking inventory.

Probably another vulture coming to pay a call on the widow and steal her land out from under her, Cassie thought, lowering the spyglass. Yesterday she'd had trouble chasing a couple of them off her land. At dusk two men had ridden up and invited themselves to supper. Cassie had tried to get rid of them without raising a ruckus, but she'd been scared. If one of her ranch hands hadn't checked in on her, things might have gotten ugly.

The men had taken their leave, but she worried they

might be back and try to get the jump on her. For sure, they were up to no good.

She glanced down at the baby she cradled, no longer suckling, fast asleep. Her angel.

A young Mexican woman came out onto the porch, her steps mincing, her demeanor subservient. "Who is it?" she whispered, staring at the rider in the distance.

"Don't know." Cassie tucked the spyglass into her skirt pocket. "Take little Andy, Oleta, and go inside. I'll handle this. Get me my hat and gloves."

"Which hat?"

Cassie considered her choices for a moment. "The one with the red feather. My buckskin gloves will do."

The girl brought the items to her. "There won't be shooting, will there?" Oleta asked in a hushed voice, taking the sleeping baby into her arms.

"Only if he gives me trouble." Cassie set the broad-brimmed hat onto her blond hair and pulled on the sturdy gloves. Even if he was trouble on horseback, she didn't greet anybody without dressing proper. Ladies, even those owning ranches, had to keep the sun off their face and their hands as soft and white as a baby's bottom. "I'm tired of cocky men who think they can bully, threaten, or flatter me enough to get my ranch." She withdrew a Colt .45 from the folds of her skirt. "Stay inside until I tell you different."

"*Santa María!*" Oleta's eyes rounded with worry. "T-Bone and Gabe probably saw him and are coming."

"I doubt it. They're mending fences out south, and King of the Prairie is riding in from the north."

"Then there is no one to save us!"

"Go on inside," Cassie said, trying on a smile to comfort the excitable girl. "Everything will be fine."

Clutching Andy, Oleta went into the house, leaving Cassie to await the rider.

Cassie rolled her eyes and wondered if Oleta Rodriquez would ever quit being afraid of every shadow, every frown. She'd hired the sixteen-year-old three months ago in Abilene. Oleta lived with a drunken father and was desperate to get away from him. Cassie, who knew all about wanting to break out, run away, get shed of bad people and bad pasts, had taken pity on the girl. Besides, after her husband's death six months ago, Cassie had needed someone to look after little Andy while she worked alongside her two remaining ranch hands.

Staring intently at the rider in the middle distance, she took comfort in the gun she held. Something about him caused the hairs on the back of her neck to quiver. Raising the spyglass again, she examined his horse. Not the usual cow pony. Nope. He was riding a coal-black, blazed-face stallion with white stockings. A high-stepping, sure-footed cutting horse, she surmised, observing the gait and stride. Bred for perfection and purpose. Such an animal would bring a hefty price, so the rider either could afford him or had stolen him.

But if he was thinking he could buy or steal her ranch, he would be disappointed or dead. She'd sooner sell her soul. She hadn't endured A.J. Dalton's mean mouth and stingy heart for two years to turn over her hard-earned inheritance to some flashy cowboy on a fancy horse.

No siree. She had big plans for the Square D. Once she sold part of her herd, she meant to fix up the house, which was falling down around her ears. A.J. had never allowed a penny to be spent on it, so windows stayed broken, shingles lay where they fell after a storm, wood rotted, and only specks of paint remained on bleached boards.

She could see the stranger's face now in the spyglass, and her breathing grew shallow. My, my, he was one handsome *hombre!* Sort of hard-looking ... tough ... but mighty pretty, all the same, with a wide, full mouth and a square, smooth-shaven jaw. His eyes were in shadow, but she could see that his nose was strong and straight. His clothes looked new—dark-blue shirt, leather vest, dark trousers, concha-studded chaps, boots with shiny spurs, dark-blue hat with an Indian bead band. A long rifle rested in a sling behind him and he wore a gun belt.

She tightened her hand on the Colt .45 and lowered the spyglass. He was close enough now that she didn't need it, so she slipped it into her pocket. Fixing a scowl on her face, she stood, hiding her gun in the folds of the split skirt she wore when she worked with T-Bone and Gabe. She'd ridden back to the house to nurse the baby, but as soon as she finished with this uninvited prospector, she'd rejoin them to stretch barb wire and straighten fence posts.

She knew the moment he saw her because his head jerked and she actually sensed his gaze sharpening. A strange feeling sizzled through her. Not fear or anything unpleasant. In fact, she stepped down from the porch and into the sunlight to make it easy for him to get a good look at her.

He reined the snorting stallion to a canter. The saddle, she noticed, was fitting for the animal—hand-tooled leather and big silver conchas. Expensive rigging for a special horse.

He jerked on the reins, and the stallion reared up, then

set its front hooves back down and stood quivering a few yards from the porch. She could see the man's eyes now. Sky-blue and inquisitive.

"You the housekeeper?" he asked, his gaze drifting over her, missing nothing.

"I'm the owner. State your business." She made her voice hard-edged and matched him scowl for scowl.

One corner of his mouth kicked up. "Owner? The hell you say. Where's old man Dalton?"

She bobbed her head to the west. "In the bone-yard. I buried him six months ago. You knew him?"

He looked toward the white fence that cordoned off the small burial plot. "I knew him." A few moments passed before he yanked his attention back to her. "Where'd you get into your head that you—"

The baby cried inside the house and was hushed by Oleta. The man stared at the front door, and Cassie could sense his mind spinning, piecing together a puzzle.

"State your business," she repeated. "If you've come to buy my land, you're wasting my time and yours. It's not for sale."

"Your land." He screwed up one eye. "*Your* land." One side of his mouth inched up again. Any other time, she might have appreciated his lopsided smirk, but right now she didn't much cotton to being laughed at.

"My land, stranger, and you're trespassing on it." She brought the gun out from the folds of her skirt.

He glanced at the weapon and shook his head at her as if she were a precocious child. Cassie's blood began to boil. He crossed his wrists on the saddle horn and leveled those blue eyes on her.

"You're not thinking clear, little lady. This place doesn't belong to you. You're squatting on it. There's a big difference. What did you do—keep house for him, doctor him while he was sick?''

''I did all of that and more,'' she assured him.

''That's right Christian of you, but you're still a squatter and squatters have no rights.''

''Hold up—'' she began hotly.

''No, you hold up.'' He straightened in the saddle, making the leather creak, and surveyed the land around him. ''I don't mean to throw you off the place overnight. You can stay until you find yourself a room in town.''

''Oh, is that right?'' Cassie said, sarcasm dripping from each word.

He nodded. ''Was that your baby I heard squalling?''

She stiffened, her jaw firming to rock. ''He's a good baby and he's mine.''

''You can find somewhere in town to stay, even with the baby. I imagine you can hire on as a housekeeper or—''

Save your breath and your advice,'' she cut in. ''I'm not leaving.''

He squared his impressive shoulders. ''Look here, I'm trying to be fair.''

She laughed, amazed at his cockiness. ''You take first prize in male arrogance. I can tell you think you're mighty special, what with your pretty duds and prancing horse, but I'm losing patience with you, stranger.'' She raised the gun, aiming for his head. ''You get now while you're still handsome and you've got all your parts. I'd sure hate to have to spoil your goods.''

Her threat didn't seem to trouble him any. He twisted in the saddle and sized up the place. ''Where are the hands?''

''They're around,'' she assured him.

"Is T-Bone still here, or did you run him off?"

She lowered the gun. "How do you know T-Bone?"

"What about Bob Millstone?"

"He's gone to Texas. Left a year ago."

"Gabe Brindle?"

"Gabe's on my payroll," she said, regarding the stranger warily. He knew too much about her. Way too much.

"Who's in the house with your baby?"

"None of your business."

He surveyed the sagging roof, the gray, unpainted boards of the porch and railings. "This place is in a sorry state. You're not much of a housekeeper."

"I'm the boss lady, not the housekeeper, and A.J. is the reason this place ain't fit for rats." She huffed out a breath, peeved at herself for coughing up excuses to this cock of the walk. "But I have plans for this place. Big plans."

"Is that right?"

"That's right," she assured him. Rising dust in the distance snagged her attention. She squinted, spotting two riders. One rode a palomino—the men from last night! Her gaze snapped back to the fancy rider. "Are those your friends coming to join you?"

He twisted around to have a look. "Never saw them before."

"They were here last night. Funny they should return at the same time you show up in my porch yard."

He faced her again. "I told you I don't know them."

She moved backward and up onto the porch. "Stay in there," she whispered to Oleta through the screen door, "and stay low and out of sight." She pulled shut the wood door.

The stranger glanced from her to the approaching horsemen, and Cassie felt a change in him. He sensed the danger, same as her. Although he made no threatening moves, she could tell he was coiled for action.

"Hey, there, ma'am," the man on the palomino greeted her, touching the brim of his dirty white hat. "Thought we'd visit you again and see how you be faring." He eyed the blue-eyed newcomer. "This one of your ranch hands?"

"I'm the foreman," Blue Eyes said before Cassie could answer.

She started to call him a liar, then decided to keep quiet. If he wasn't with these two varmints, then he was with her, and she'd use that to her benefit.

"The foreman, huh? I'm Reb Smalley and this here is my partner, Dan Harper. We're looking to buy us a ranch and we're hoping your boss lady here will sell us this one."

"I told you this place ain't for sale," Cassie said. "You go on about your business and don't come sniffing around here anymore."

"You got expensive clothes for a foreman," Dan Harper noted. He ran his tongue over his yellow teeth, then spit brown tobacco juice in the direction of the jittery stallion.

The black horse snorted, but Blue Eyes held him in check. "She pays me well," he said, glancing at Cassie, eyes dancing for a moment. "From the looks of you two, I don't reckon you could buy yourself a one-hole outhouse."

Reb threw out his chest. "Can't tell a book by its cover." His gaze shifted to Cassie again. "We been over t'the Hendrix ranch and heard that your man done died and left you more than you can handle.''

"Did Monroe Hendrix send you over here?" Cassie asked.

"After last night we figured we'd come by in the light of day and look the place over," Reb continued, ignoring her question. "Maybe make you an offer. Ain't that right, Dan?"

"That there's right," Harper agreed, shooting tobacco juice through his teeth again.

"The Square D is not for sale," Cassie stated again, gripping the gun handle while trying to keep an eye on all three riders. "Y'all be on your way. I got work to do."

"You ain't heard our offer yet," Dan said. "You got to hear us out first."

Reb grinned, showing off surprisingly white teeth and pink gums. "A lady listens when a man talks to her. So shut your trap and open your ears. We're trying to do you a favor."

Anger closed off her throat and seared her insides at being told by yet another man to shut up and do as she was told. Cassie meant to raise the gun and threaten them with it, but before she could move a muscle, Blue Eyes had filled both hands with his lethal .44 Winchester rifle. He levered a round into the breech and aimed the weapon between the men, ready to blow holes through both of them.

Reb and Dan stared at the Winchester, and their fingers and eyes twitched.

"Don't be stupid," Blue Eyes advised, his voice deep and full of confidence. "Take my advice and make tracks, boys. You don't want to draw on me. I'd kill you before you could clear your guns."

"Hey, hey!" Reb glanced nervously at Cassie. The

red whiskers on his chin almost bristled. "What's this? You gonna let your man here threaten us? We weren't doing nothing but trying to do some business with you."

"You heard him," Cassie said, nonplussed by having Blue Eyes referred to as "your man." "Make tracks. And don't come back!"

When they still didn't move, Blue Eyes raised the rifle and fired a round into the air. The stallion, although seemingly skittish, braced itself, ears laid back. The other two horses reared and pawed the air, ready to run. Blue Eyes waved a hand and shouted, sending the two horses racing for the horizon and their riders grabbing at reins and trying to stay on board.

Cassie couldn't suppress a giggle, which brought those blue, piercing eyes back to her.

"They won't give up as long as they think you own the place," he said, slipping the rifle into the sling. "You're not safe here. You'd better pack your things and head for town as soon as you can."

"You don't hear too good, do you?" Cassie asked, moving forward into the sunlight again.

The front door opened and Oleta stuck out her head. "Did somebody get shot?" she whispered, her voice trembling.

"No." Cassie flung her a frown. "Get inside."

"Who else is in there with you, *señorita?*" Blue Eyes asked. "Besides the baby."

"Just me, *señor,*" Oleta answered, batting her big, brown eyes at him.

"Oleta, hush up!" Cassie hissed. "And get back inside. And you . . ." She stepped onto the porch step. "I appreciate your help, but I don't appreciate your questions or your advice."

"Does Roe Hendrix have his eye on this place?"

"Yes." She regarded him, catching the familiarity in his question. "You know Monroe Hendrix, do you?"

"Yes. Better than you do, I reckon."

"Did he tell you I was looking to sell?"

"Haven't seen Roe in almost three years." He ran a hand through the horse's ebony mane. "How did you aim to keep this land all by yourself?"

"I'm *not* by myself."

"You have a couple of ranch hands and a nanny for your baby. This is a big spread. Eight hundred and eighty-five acres. What have you got—four or five hundred head of cattle?"

"More like five or six," she said proudly, then scrutinized him. Damn if he didn't know her holdings down to the last acre! Who had given him all this information if not Monroe or one of her ranch hands?

"As far as you can figure," he drawled. "Hell, you haven't done a head count. Don't even know how many calves have dropped this week or last, do you?" He chuckled with derision. "No wonder Roe's thinking he can make off with this ranch."

"I know what he's up to," she said hotly. "He's not pulling any wool over my eyes. Monroe Hendrix thinks he can flatter and charm and woo this land from me. He thinks I'll get all gooey in my heart and marry him, but I won't!"

"Marry him?" He blinked his sky-blue eyes and removed his hat. Sunlight swam over russet waves of thick hair that curled at his collar. "Shoot, he's got twenty years on you."

"Yeah, well, A.J. had fifty. That didn't stop him any."

He dabbed at the sweat on his forehead with the cuff of his shirt, then froze and stared hard at her. "What's that? Are you saying that old man Dalton was your *husband?*"

"Yeah. What of it?"

He looked heavenward and laughed harshly. "Well, I'll be a son of a bitch! That dirty old fox, hitching up with a girl like you."

"I'm not a *girl*," she corrected him. "I'm a woman and the boss of this spread."

His blue eyes measured her from the jaunty hat to the toes of her boots. Interest sparkled in those eyes before he averted his gaze and cleared his throat.

"What's your name anyway?"

"Cassandra Dalton. Folks call me Cassie."

"You must have wanted this place mighty bad to hook up with the old man."

"I've got work to do." She waved the gun at him, not liking his tone or his views. "Be on your way, mister."

"That's how you thank someone for chasing coyotes from your door?"

Justly chastised, Cassie delivered a stiff smile. "Thanks for your help, but I could have handled them."

"Sure you could," he said with undisguised disbelief. "Like you can handle this ranch? You're dreaming, sweetheart."

"I ain't your sweetheart!" She raised the Colt again. "You get!"

"I'm not going anywhere."

One of the herding dogs burst from the bushes and yapped noisily when it spotted the stranger, then bared strong teeth and raised the blond fur along its spine.

"Is that you, Lasso? Hey, girl, it's me. You remember me. Have you been swimming in the cow pond?"

The dog's growl changed to a whine. She sat on her haunches and beat her tail on the ground, caking her wet fur with dirt.

"How do you know this dog?" Cassie asked, her curiosity seized.

"I belong on this spread more than you do."

"Is that so? A. J. Dalton left this ranch to A.J. Dalton Junior—my baby. Seeing as he's only ten months old, I'm overseeing the place until he's grown," she informed him. "I don't mean to sell it, give it away, or have it stolen from me. If I have to shoot every vulture that lights on this land, I'll do it. Don't you doubt it, mister."

That crooked grin was back, making her feel funny inside, distracting her. "A. J. Dalton Junior, huh?"

"That's right. I call him Andy, but his full name is Andrew James Dalton Junior. Named after his pa."

"Uh-huh." He threw a leg over and slipped from the saddle, landing with animal grace and a jingle of spurs. Lasso trotted forward to lick the back of his hand. He patted the dog's head, but his gaze stayed on Cassie. "Boss lady, you're on the horns of a dilemma."

"Oh, how's that?" Cassie asked, propping one hand on her hip and leveling the gun at his stomach.

"Because *I'm* Andrew James Dalton Junior, which makes *your* whelp A.J. the Third." The other side of his mouth lifted in a full-out smile that dazzled her even as his words devastated her. "This ranch is mine. All mine."

Chapter 2

He had to hand it to her. She was tough.

From his stance near the porch steps, Drew Dalton admired the pint-sized female. There sure wasn't much of her, but what was there was put to good use. Plus she had spirit and courage. For her to stand before him, brown eyes sparkling with defiance after he'd snatched her baby's inheritance from her took backbone.

"A. J. never said anything to me about any other children," she said, her kittenish voice containing an underlying growl. "Funny to me he would insist on naming our son after him when he already had one walking around."

Drew glanced toward the burial plot again, his insides knotting and his heart crusting over. "It's not funny to me at all. Sounds just like something the old devil would do."

She lowered the gun. "Guess you knew him, but that don't mean you're related to him."

"I don't have to prove anything to you, Shorty. All you have to do is ask T-Bone or Gabe. They'll tell you who I am and that this ranch is rightfully mine."

She puffed out a sigh and swept a long strand of white-blond hair back from her face. "I'm not standing here on the porch, jawing with you all day." Throwing a glare at his horse, she made a dismissive gesture. "See to that big stud and come on inside. I'm gonna grab something to eat before I join up with the hands again. You're welcome to partake."

"You calling me a big stud, or Dynamite here?"

She cast him a long, speaking glance. "You figure it out, Junior." Then she flung open the door and sashayed inside, her split skirt hugging her backside and making his mind quiver.

"Holy damn," he muttered as he led the stallion to the shade of a tree. After loosening Dynamite's saddle riggings, Drew sauntered into the house where he was born and raised.

Things were different. First off, he didn't smell stale body odors, chewing tobacco, and whiskey. Sniffing, he identified the soft, unmistakable smell of a well cared for baby. He recognized other aromas: fresh coffee, yeast bread, prairie flowers, and lye soap. Smelled like a real home, he thought, surveying the combination parlor and kitchen. He remembered the furniture, but now it was shined up and spread with doilies and lace. Vases of flowers perked up dark corners. Plump pillows of bright yellow and green lay scattered on the old sofa and the two big rockers sat by the fireplace. He looked down at the floor. God Almighty, it was clean! He'd never known the boards to shine, and he sure hadn't known they were wide planks of knotty pine.

"Take off your hat," she said, already sitting at the kitchen table and tucking into a bowl of stew. Her hat and gloves lay on a low table near the sofa. "I didn't have much breakfast this morning," she explained between spoonfuls. "Got to keep up my strength for little Andy. Oleta, slap together some sandwiches for the boys. I'll take them with me."

"*Sí, sí.*" The dark-skinned girl hurried to obey, but sneaked a few fearful glances at Drew.

Hanging his hat on a peg by the door, Drew searched the horizon for any signs of Dan and Reb. Seeing nothing, he joined Cassie at the table. She pushed a bowl of stew at him. "You want water or coffee?"

"Coffee."

"You want it black?"

"With sugar, if you have it."

"We've got it. Oleta, pour him a cup."

"*Sí, sí.*"

"The word for 'please' in Spanish is *por favor*," Drew said, giving the Mexican girl a smile when she set the coffee mug in front of him. "And the word for 'thank you' is *gracias.*"

"I know that," Cassie snapped.

"Oh, so you're rude and snappish on purpose."

"Oleta and me get along fine." She glared malevolence at him. "It's you and me I'm worried about."

He blew on the steaming coffee. "Oleta . . . what?" He raised a brow, waiting for the girl to answer.

Oleta blushed. "Rodriquez."

"You gonna eat or flirt?" Cassie demanded of him.

"Both," he rejoined, smiling. "This place looks better on the inside. It's clean. I've never seen it clean before."

"Now that A.J. is gone, I'm going to paint the outside. I planted a flower and vegetable garden out back already. He wouldn't let me while he was living."

"Why not?"

She shrugged. "Because he was down deep mean and he wouldn't let me do anything I had my heart set on."

"That's my old man." Drew saluted with his mug and took a sip. The coffee was strong and sweet, sort of like the two women flanking him, one strong and one sweet. "How long were you married to him?" he asked the strong one.

"Two years."

"Did he find you in Abilene?"

"No, he found me through a mail-order advertisement."

"A *what?*" He swallowed the half-chewed mouthful of savory stew, best he'd tasted in years. "He placed one of those ads?"

"Yep."

"And you answered it?"

"I did." She stared hard at him. "Something wrong with that?"

He examined her features—lushly lipped mouth, milk chocolate eyes, flawless skin, pert nose, streams of pale blond hair that she'd plaited into a long braid down her back. Her breasts were small, but round and inviting, and her hips were heart-shaped, like her face. He'd noticed that right off. All in all, she was fetching.

"Looks to me like you wouldn't have much trouble catching you a man."

Her brown eyes melted a little. "Oh, I don't have trouble with that a'tall," she assured him, her voice going whispery and seductive. "Never had much trouble striking up a man's notice."

Something in her voice and in the gentle glitter in her eyes shot fire to his loins and fogged his brain. He gulped at the coffee and tried to stop his blood from pooling between his legs.

"Catching a husband with something to offer," she went on, "now that's another story. I wasn't about to settle down with some hard-luck cowboy and ride from handout to handout on a broken-down pony with nothing to show for my life but a passel of starving children. That's how I was raised up, and I want better for my offspring."

"So you lassoed my old man and thought you'd earned yourself a ranch for your baby son."

She pushed away the empty bowl and dabbed at the corners of her mouth with a napkin, ladylike. "A.J. got as good as he gave. I'll tell you this, Junior. I didn't put up with A.J. Dalton's stinking hide and his nasty mouth for two years to end up with nothing for my son but a bad name."

Oleta placed a gunnysack on the table. "Food for T-Bone and Gabe," she said, then backed into the bedroom and sat on the bed. Her eyes were huge and fearful.

"She's a fidgety thing, isn't she?" Drew observed.

"Her pappy beat her regular. He's a drunk." Cassie grabbed the neck of the sack. "You can ride out with me if you want."

"Tell you what . . ." He stood and stretched from side to side to work out the kinks in his muscles. It had been a long ride from the federal prison. "I'm going to pay a call on Monroe Hendrix and I'll catch up with you later."

"Fine by me." She pulled on work gloves and her wide-brimmed brown hat with a red feather stuck in its band. "See if Monroe sent those men out here to bother me." Taking the gunnysack with her, she marched out of the house without bothering to say good-bye.

He watched the single braid swing across her back, perfectly timed with the swish of her hips. Gussied up in satin and lace, she'd probably put a man's eyes out, she'd be so bright and pretty. Shaking his head, he tried to imagine her with his old man but couldn't. That coupling must have been as unnatural as a fox taking a shine to an opossum.

The snuffling sounds of a baby drifted from the bedroom. He peered into the shadows and saw Oleta gather the babe into her arms and whisper for him to be quiet.

"How old is he?" Drew asked.

"Ten months."

Drew moved forward, sensing the girl's recoiling. "I'm not going to hurt you, I just want to see the baby. He's my half brother, I reckon."

Oleta stood and stepped into the sunlight that poured through the window. The baby flinched and waved tiny fists. Drew touched a fingertip to the button nose.

"Hey, little man. You're a chubby thing, aren't you?"

The baby opened his eyes. Blue, just like his. Just like his own mother, God rest her soul. The old man's eyes were gray and shifty. He never looked anybody square on for more than a few seconds. Not like this little cowboy, who stared hard at Drew, clearly puzzled by the sight of him.

"Looks healthy," Drew observed.

"*Sí, señor.* He's a big boy. She told me she had a hard time getting him out."

"I don't doubt it. She's a slip of a thing." He peered intently at the girl. "Where's she from?"

Oleta shrugged and backed into the bedroom. "Here, I guess."

Well, he'd get nothing from this Mexican mouse, he surmised, dipping his head and taking his leave. He stepped outside, rocking his hat back onto his head, whistled to Dynamite, and received an answering whinny.

"Hey, there, son," he murmured, stroking the horse's neck and shoulder, remembering the night he'd helped this squirming ball of horseflesh pop out into the world. "Do you recall this place? You were born here. Right over there in that dilapidated barn. Your mama was one of the finest mares I ever rode, and I paid two months' wages for the privilege of having your sire mount her."

That investment had been the beginning of his reputation as a noted horse breeder. With Dynamite, he knew he'd have a golden opportunity to breed some of the finest horses in Kansas and the surrounding territory. That was also the hour his old man had turned on him for good. Theirs had always been a competitive relationship, but for the first time, Drew had accomplished something A.J. couldn't equal. The old man knew cattle, but he didn't know spit about breeding and training cutting horses.

Cinching up the saddle and whispering in Dynamite's ear, Drew pondered his own magic touch with the equine. He'd always been able to cajole horses, coax them, sweet-talk them, get the most out of them. He could remember his mother sitting him up in the saddle—way, way up—and telling him to hold on and trust the animal. She'd loved horses, too. He couldn't have been more than three when she'd placed him on his first saddle pad. She'd let him ride an old pinto she called Dumplin. Those had been his happiest days, and they had ended with her death when he was seven.

Settling into the saddle, he rode Dynamite west, past the barn and graveyard and toward Monroe Hendrix's Star H Ranch. He owed it to Monroe to let him know that he'd been acquitted and was home again. Roe had been the only person to speak in his defense at his trial for cattle rustling nearly three years ago.

He looked back over his shoulder at the white cross marking his father's last resting place. Backstabbing old coot. He'd heard that A.J. Dalton was ailing and near death, but he'd expected to find him alive. He certainly hadn't dreamed that his old man would have taken himself a young wife. Must have gotten lonely without his son around to browbeat and bad-mouth, Drew thought with a twist of malice.

The black-hearted lout hadn't offered one word of support during Drew's trial. He'd wanted to see Drew thrown in prison because he couldn't stand it that Drew had won respect among the cowboys and ranchers around Abilene. Jealous old fool. God, how he hated the bastard!

But he respected him, too, and had spent most of his life trying to win the old man's respect in return. That's what had knotted his gut and bruised his heart. Striving for the favor of a sworn enemy ate at a man's confidence and sanity.

Two and a half years in prison had been hell but had afforded him plenty of time to think and sort through his life and separate the chaff from the grain.

For the first time in years he saw things clearly, knew what he was about and where he wanted to go. The only wrinkle in his plans was Cassie Dalton and her baby. But he could iron that out. He'd make her see reason, give her some seed money and escort her to town. Might even buy her a fetching dress and bonnet to entice her. Once she saw the advantages of living in town, she'd be eager to leave the ranch to him.

Pleased with the scheme, he decided to ride into Abilene after his talk with Roe. He'd get one of the shop girls to help him pick out a dress and stylish bonnet. Hell, he'd throw in a bottle of perfume, too. That would do the trick. One whiff of French perfume and his pa's widow would be dreaming of dances and dandies instead of longhorns and lassos.

Approaching the ranch house of the Star H, Drew lifted a hand in greeting when the front door popped open and Monroe Hendrix strode out onto the wraparound porch.

A man of medium height and build, Monroe was dressed in buff-colored pants, mustard-yellow shirt, and brown boots. A green and red bandanna was tied at his throat. His brown hair was streaked with white, and his eyes were black and glittery, narrowly spaced and heavy-lidded. Some would find him handsome, but most would agree he fell short of that mark. He'd gained some weight since Drew had last seen him. His midsection was thicker, his face fuller.

Hanging his thumbs in his belt loops, he peered through the dust at Drew, and his mouth fell open.

"Is that Drew Dalton?" he called.

"Sure is."

"Did you escape from prison?"

"Nope. I was sprung, thanks to a right smart lawyer I hired. He got me a new trial, and I was set free."

"Isn't that something," Monroe said, holding out a hand to Drew. "Put 'er there, son. Good to see you again."

Drew dropped from the saddle and shook Monroe's hand. As he remembered, the grip was too strong and too energetic. Monroe Hendrix had a way of over-stepping.

"I thought you were my new man. I hired a fella and he's supposed to be here any day."

"Another wrangler?"

"More like an overseer. You just get back?"

"Yeah, but I stopped by the old homestead." Drew slanted Monroe a sardonic look. "Pa took himself a wife, huh?"

"Yes, that's right. You didn't know?"

"I didn't know anything while I was in prison. My lawyer said he'd heard that Pa was sick, but I figured he was too mean to die."

"He had something wrong with his innards," Monroe said. "Couldn't keep anything in his stomach there after a while, and stuff was running out of him at both ends. He wasted away. It was hard on Cassie."

"She thought her baby had inherited my ranch. I set her straight, but she's dug in and won't budge."

"You're aiming on staying here?" Monroe was clearly surprised. "I thought you'd be glad to see the last of this place, seeing as how it brought you nothing but trouble."

Removing his hat, Drew walked his fingers along the brim. "I've had my share of troubles, that's true, but the land is my heritage. It's all I've got."

"It would bring a nice price. Hell, I'd even buy it from you to help out. You could go anywhere in the country and live the good life." He winked. "Buy yourself a little cantina in Mexico and a pretty whore to warm your bed."

"Have you made an offer on the land to Pa's widow?"

"I might have mentioned that I'd buy it. I feel sorry for her, strapped with that baby and all. A.J. was mean to her like he was to you." He stared in the direction of the Square D, and a sour expression came over his face. "She can't run that place by herself, not even with T-Bone and Gabe helping her."

"That's what I told her, but she doesn't listen too good."

Monroe waved him onto the porch and into one of the big, white rockers. Sitting in one beside Drew, Monroe gave him a big smile.

"Drew Dalton, damn if it ain't good to see you again. What are your plans, besides sticking around here for the time being?"

"I'm thinking of raising horses, picking up where I left off."

"That lawyer you hired must be a firecracker."

"He is," Drew agreed. "He believed in me—like you did—and he wouldn't rest until he sprung me."

"I should have kept in touch with you . . ." Monroe shook his head and his face seemed to sag into wrinkles. "Lord knows I thought about you, rotting in prison and all. Guess you're anxious to kick up your heels." His expression brightened. "Or have you already been in town and picked yourself out a pretty gal?"

"I'm more interested in getting settled on the ranch again."

Monroe glanced toward Dynamite. "I see you kept that stallion. Where'd you stash him while you were in prison?"

Drew grinned. "A fella named Ice took care of him

for me. I met Ice shortly before I was arrested, and my gut told me I could trust him. He could see that Dynamite was one of a kind and offered to take him to his family's spread in Texas and keep him fit while I was locked up.''

''And he did, huh?''

''He sure did. When I got out of prison, I went straight to Texas, and Ice was right where he said he'd be. So was my horse. Ice will be here in a couple of weeks.''

Monroe sat back, his black eyes shielded by his droopy eyelids. ''Sounds like you've got some big plans.''

''I do. That's what kept me going while I was in prison.''

''You getting rid of your cattle?''

''No, I need the cattle to train the horses on.''

''So, you're going into the horse business.''

''That's right.''

''Yep, I should have visited you in that prison, but I couldn't get away from these cows. A.J. was close-mouthed and never even mentioned your name after you were gone. When he called that baby Junior, we all thought it was strange, but nobody said anything. We figured it was his way of telling folks that you were dead to him.''

Drew nodded. ''He told his widow he was leaving the place to A.J. Junior.'' He schooled his features against the burning hatred in his heart. ''His plan backfired, I reckon. He didn't count on me ever getting out of prison.''

''Where'd you find the money for your lawyer?''

''Stud fees paid for Dynamite,'' Drew said. ''Ice handled all of that for me and wired me the funds. I asked around in prison and heard about a slick lawyer, so I hired him. Before I knew it, I was standing before a new judge and I was a free man.'' He shook his head, still a little shocked to be walking around without leg irons weighing him down. "Now I can do what I want with the Square D and nobody can stop me.''

"What about your new mama?''

For a few moments Drew didn't know who Monroe was talking about. When he figured it out, he turned his head and spat the bad taste from his mouth.

"She's my father's widow, not my new mama. I'll deal with her. I'm going into town and I'll buy her some pretty things, then send her on her way. Her and her baby.''

Monroe chuckled. "I'd pay to see that.''

"To see what?''

"You sending her on her way and her going meek as you please. You aren't the only one with big plans, you know. She thinks she's going to be a cattle rancher, a wheat farmer, and a rich, respected lady, all rolled into one. Until she discovers different, she won't be willing to leave the Square D behind.''

Drew shrugged. "I'll let her stay for a few days, maybe a few weeks, then she'll have to move on. She'll see what's what soon enough.'' He stood and wedged his hat onto his head. "Just wanted to drop by and say howdy.''

"Well, hell, it's good to have you home.'' Monroe stood and slapped him on the back, then pumped his hand again. "Don't be a stranger. Come by for a game of cards one night.''

"I'll do it,'' Drew promised. He went down the steps

and crossed the yard to where he'd left Dynamite.

"Don't be surprised if your other neighbors don't welcome you home."

Atop Dynamite, Drew cocked his head to the side, struck by that remark. "Why? I'm innocent."

"I always knew that, but folks around here might think different. We haven't had any cattle missing since you've been away." Monroe sent him a hard wink. "If anybody gives you any trouble, you be sure and let me know. I'll set 'em straight right quick."

"Is Carlsbad still the sheriff?"

"No, it's Amos Nelson now. He's a good man. Tries to be fair."

"So you think the folks around here won't trust me? Even though I was released from prison?"

"People are funny, Drew. Until they're sure about you—well, just watch out for yourself."

"I don't have to prove anything to anybody." Drew jerked on the reins and spun the stallion around. "Be seeing you." He set in his spurs, and Dynamite broke into a wind-slicing run across the flat land.

He hoped there wouldn't be any more trouble. He'd had himself a bellyful of it.

"Just why didn't y'all ever tell me that A.J. had another son?" Cassie demanded of T-Bone and Gabe.

The two men stood under the boiling sun and wiped their sweaty faces with grime-streaked handkerchiefs.

"Truth to tell, we didn't neither one know whether Drew wanted anybody to know he existed," T-Bone said. "He ain't had a rosy life and he mighta wanted to disappear. The old man sure never mentioned him after he left."

"Only in his dagburned will!" Cassie huffed and threw the sack of biscuits and sausage at Gabe. "There. Something for y'all to eat."

"And about time, too." Gabe looked around. "Let's go grab some shade under that there oak tree and gobble this down, Tee."

"Sounds like heaven to me."

Cassie followed the two bow-legged men to the shady spot, where they hunkered down and swallowed the sandwiches. Gabe was the taller and as thin as a rail. He had a boyish face full of freckles. T-Bone was older. Cassie figured he was at least fifty, while Gabe was around thirty. T-Bone's beard and mustache were grizzled, but he was spry and quick when he wanted to be.

"Does Drew aim to stay awhile?" Gabe asked.

"He aims to take over the ranch," Cassie answered crossly. "But I won't let him."

"How you gonna stop him?" T-Bone asked, wiping sausage grease from his mustache.

"By digging in my heels," Cassie retorted. "He might be bigger and meaner, but I'm not moving off this land. I earned every last acre of it."

"But the old man willed it to Andrew James Dalton Junior and—"

"And who is to say that A.J. didn't mean *my* Junior? You said yourself that he never mentioned his firstborn, so why would he think to leave his ranch to him? A.J. named Andy, not me."

Gabe scratched at his chin stubble. "She's got a point."

"Maybe, but I don't think a judge would see it that way," T-Bone said.

"Judge? Who says we're going to court?" A tingle

of alarm feathered through Cassie. Lord God, if Blue Eyes took this to court, would she have a leg to stand on? She felt the world wobble underneath her. "There won't be any judge deciding *my* future. It's in my hands and I'm staying put. Seems to me that Blue Eyes isn't too interested in the place, or he would have showed up months ago. Where's he been all this time anyway?"

Gabe and T-Bone exchanged a long glance that made Cassie take notice.

"You two know where he's been?"

T-Bone ducked his head. "I reckon you should ask him."

"I reckon I will." Cassie smoothed the work gloves over her hands.

"How come you call him Blue Eyes?" Gabe asked.

The question brought her up short, and she felt her cheeks heat up. "'Cause his eyes are blue," she said, trying to make the least of it.

Gabe grinned. "So are mine."

Cassie whirled toward her horse. "Let's get to work, men. Daylight is slipping away from us."

"Is he staying at the house?" T-Bone asked.

"If he is, he's staying in the bunkhouse or the barn, not in *my* house."

"Lordy, lordy, lordy," Gabe moaned.

"What?" Cassie asked, eyeing Gabe's mournful expression.

"Oh, nothing. I'm just dreading all the fussing and fighting. It's been so peaceful since A.J. died."

"There won't be any fighting," Cassie assured him. "If he gets too ornery, I'll pull out my .45 and plug him."

"Lordy, lordy, lordy," Gabe moaned again, while T-Bone shook with laughter.

"What's so dagblamed funny, besides Gabe's belly-achin'?" Cassie demanded.

"Nothing, nothing," T-Bone said, still chuckling as he waved aside the question. "You tickle me when you get all puffed up, that's all. You remind me of a little old horny toad."

Cassie reached out and tugged at the brim of T-Bone's floppy brown hat. "If that isn't a fine thing to say to a lady! No wonder you've never married, Tee. No woman wants to be called a toad."

"She makes me think of one of them spread adders," Gabe spoke up, his round blue eyes growing even rounder. "You seen one of them snakes? They're little, but when they get scared, they spread out and make themselves look bigger."

"A toad and a snake," Cassie said with a grin. "It's good to know what you men think of me."

"Aw, now, boss lady, we were just poking fun at you," T-Bone said. "Ain't that right, Gabe?"

"Sure nuff," Gabe agreed. "Besides, I think some snakes are right pretty. 'Course, I wouldn't want to pet one or have it in bed with me—" He broke off and his face flamed a bright red. "I-I . . . that is, I wasn't saying that I'd want you in bed with me . . . that is—aw hell, quit laughing at me, Tee!"

Cassie grabbed a shovel and sent the business end down into the crusty earth. "Let's get to work, fellas, before we talk ourselves into even more trouble."

Chapter 3

They were unsaddling their horses in the dying light when Blue Eyes rode up on them out by the barn, his stallion prancing and snorting and showing off. Cassie glanced at T-Bone and Gabe to gauge their reactions and was stunned to see them both break into huge smiles, thrilled to see him again.

Her two wranglers pulled Blue Eyes from the saddle and slapped his back and pumped his hand and grinned like monkeys.

If that don't beat all, Cassie fumed. *Them treating him like the returning king, glad to be shed of their sitting queen!* She stood to one side, arms folded, a stony expression fixed on her face. After a minute or two, they felt her granite-hard glare and turned toward her. T-Bone and Gabe hung their heads and kicked at tufts of grass. Smirking, Blue Eyes opened his saddlebag and removed a parcel wrapped in white paper and tied with twine. He extended it toward her.

"Got something for you."

She eyed the parcel but made no move to take it. "What is it?"

"Something for you," he repeated.

"Where'd you get it?"

"In town."

She regarded him warily, wondering what trick he was playing now. Her curiosity piqued, she took the parcel from him and untied the twine.

"You might want to wait until you get inside before you open . . ." His voice trailed off as she lifted the frilly hem of a petticoat.

"What have we here?" she said, cold fury changing her voice to a dangerous purr. "Why, if it ain't a new set of petticoats and a new town dress! Oh, and looky here. A lacy hanky and a bottle of perfume." She looked toward T-Bone and Gabe, who were both shifting uneasily from foot to foot, their faces turning red. "Ain't that something, boys? He thinks he can buy me off with a dress and some underclothes." She seared Blue Eyes with a smoking glare. "Mister, I've been offered a helluva lot more for this place. You insult me. You think I've never had pretty dresses and perfume?" She tipped back her head and let loose a harsh laugh. "There was a time when I'd use this here garment as a polishing rag!" She tossed the parcel back at him and he caught it against his chest. "And I've got no use for perfume on a cattle ranch. No, thanks." She stalked to the house.

"You're welcome," he called after her before she could slam the door against his voice.

"That peckerwood," she grumbled, tossing her hat and gloves onto the table.

Oleta was stirring a pot of beans on the stove. "Is that blue-eyed man back?"

"Yes." Cassie dropped into a chair, feeling depleted and defeated. She hated Junior for making her feel that way. "You were watching out the window, so don't pretend like you don't know what happened."

"What was in the package?" Oleta asked, abandoning any pretense.

"A dress and perfume. Can you believe that? He thinks he can buy me some clothes and I'll get all giddy-headed and hand over my ranch to him."

"His ranch, he say. He is Junior."

"He is out of luck if he thinks he's going to run this ranch while I head for the nearest town in my pretty new dress." That he would treat her with such frivolous regard made her blood thicken to molasses consistency. "Where's he been all this time anyway? Off gallivanting, that's where," she answered for Oleta. "He's been whoring and gambling while I dealt with his ornery old pappy. He probably heard that A.J. died, so he came back here and expects me to hand over the ranch. Ha!" She shot up from the chair and began to pace furiously. "I'd rather eat a mile of dirt than turn over one acre to him."

Oleta pulled a bitter face. "Eat dirt? Phwu-ee! Why do that? Why not talk to him and maybe he can help you with this place?"

"I don't need his help."

"You need somebody's help."

"Who says?" Cassie challenged, stopping to glare at the girl, then regretting it when Oleta ducked her head so that a black curtain of hair fell along either side of her face. "Don't hide from me." Cassie laid a hand on the girl's shoulder. "I'm not yelling at you. I'm just—just yelling. Shouting at the Devil. I don't mean to frighten you, Oleta. Now, why do you think I need somebody's help? I'm getting this place into shape. It's better than it was before A.J. died.''

Oleta shrugged. "I wasn't here when he lived. All I know is that a woman cannot work a ranch by herself. She needs a man."

"I've got two."

"T-Bone is getting old, and Gabe, he is getting lazy. That man—that Junior man—he is strong and young. If he feels that this is his ranch, he will make sure it runs good. He could help you."

"I don't want him thinking that this ranch is his."

"But it is his," Oleta said, her simple statement slicing through Cassie like a hot knife. "He was raised up here."

"But he doesn't care about it like I do. Otherwise, he would have stuck around."

The door opened and the object of their discussion strode inside. Dropping his bedroll, and the parcel containing the dress and petticoat onto the floor at his feet, he then hung his hat on a peg—the one usually reserved for Cassie's hat—and pulled off his gloves.

"What's for supper?"

"What's f-for—?" Cassie stuttered in frustration. "You're expecting to stay for supper, are you?"

"Sure, don't mind if I do, thanks." He sniffed the air. "Beans and cornbread?"

Oleta giggled and turned her back to him to remove a round pan of yellow bread from the oven. He glanced around and his gaze came to rest on the loft.

"What's up there now?"

"I'm going to make it my office."

"Office?" He arched a brow. "You going into business? Maybe opening a bank?"

"I'm putting my office up there," she said, bristling. "Haven't had time to arrange things yet, but I will. My desk is up there, and I'm going to build shelves for my records and other paperwork. Then I'm going to—"

"Yeah, well, for now I'll make use of it as my bedroom, seeing as how Oleta and you have hogged up the others." He moved toward the ladder, bedroll tucked under one arm, but Cassie blocked his path. "You got something to say about that, too, I guess," he added.

"You bet. If you're staying, you can bunk with T-Bone and Gabe."

He shook his head. "Not a chance, sugar britches. Now get out of my way. I don't want to tangle with you."

She tried on a smirk of her own, but she was no match for him. Besides, that "sugar britches" remark had her mind reeling like a drunk on Saturday night. "You don't want to tangle with me, huh?" she repeated. It was the best she could do at the moment, however lame.

"Not if you aren't lying stretched out with me on top of you, no."

Oleta gasped, and Cassie had to hold her breath to keep from doing the same thing. Her face heated like a stove lid, and she wondered why she was so flustered, so embarrassed. After all, this wasn't the first lewd proposition she'd heard. He seized the moment and sidestepped her. Before she could recover, he was already halfway up the ladder, agile as a mountain cat.

"You can't stay in here with us," she said, wincing when her voice came out plaintive instead of forceful. "It's not decent. We don't know you."

From the loft he looked down at her. "I don't know you either, but I'll take my chances. I guess we'd all better sleep with our guns under our pillows just to be on the safe side." He turned and disappeared from sight.

Listening to the *clump-clump* of his boots on the floorboards, Cassie fumed as her mind raced to find an escape from this trap he'd pushed her into. She looked toward Oleta but found no help there. The girl was busy setting the table—three places. Moaning, Cassie conceded, suddenly too weary to keep up the fight. When Andy cried softly from his cradle in her bedroom, she went gladly to him, eager to hold him and find peace in the blue depths of his eyes and in the sweet scent of his soft skin.

Cuddling her baby, she sat in the rocker and spoke nonsense until he stopped crying and watched her intently. What had she done to calm herself and make her troubles go away before she'd had her baby? she wondered, jiggling him so that he'd smile. Her gaze skittered to her bed and the rag doll resting there. Ah, yes. She had held Miss Tess. Her doll was showing wear from the years of being hugged and squeezed and cried upon. Andy jabbered happily, and Cassie imagined the day when he would speak his first real word and not just papapa or mamama or googoogoo.

"Gapahdah," Andy said, then gurgled and spit up milk.

Cassie grabbed a diaper and wiped his chin and lips. Wouldn't it be her luck if his first word was "Papa"? That would be another thorn in her heart, for her little son had no pa, and she couldn't ever see herself giving him one. Men were trouble. Yes, they had their good points—like spurs—but she sure didn't need a permanent one in her life. She liked being her own boss and not having to please someone else or ask permission to do something or go somewhere. All her life she'd been asking. She enjoyed doing the telling now.

Standing up, she placed Andy on the bed and changed his diaper. She kept her ears tuned to the other rooms, hearing the scrape of chair legs on the floor, the squeak of wood, the clatter of dishes.

"Supper, *señora!*" Oleta called to her.

"Coming." Picking up a quilt and Andy, Cassie entered the main room again. As she suspected, *he* was sitting at the table, fork in one hand, spoon in the other. Cassie arranged the quilt on the floor and sat Andy in the middle of it. She scattered toys around him— wooden blocks, a cloth horse, a rag doll, and his favorite, a gourd that made discordant music when he shook it. "You play while Mama eats, then I'll feed you," she told him.

"I will take the food out to the men," Oleta said, carrying a tray loaded with two big bowls of beans, four pieces of bread, and half a blackberry pie.

"I'll wait for you," Cassie said, taking her place at the other end of the table from her unwanted guest. "*We* will wait for you to get back."

Drew smiled and made no move to serve himself. "You make them eat out there, do you?"

"They like their privacy. So do I."

"What happened to all the horses? Are they out to pasture?"

"Other than the ones we ride, there are only two, and they're grazing along Two Forks Creek, I reckon."

He lowered his dark auburn brows. "Did you sell the others?"

"There weren't any others."

"Hell, there were twenty here when I left."

"Well, there were five here when I came." She rested

her elbows on the table and leaned forward. He was scowling, thinking hard about what she'd said and obviously not pleased. "Just where have you been all this time, Junior?"

His eyes became blue steel. "The name's Drew."

She looked at the bowl of beans, his gaze too harsh for her to bear. "So where have you been?" she repeated, tempering her sarcasm.

"Down south."

"Yeah? Doing what with who?" She met his gaze through the veil of her lashes and saw that he resented her question. Being a woman with secrets, she recognized them in others. "Something you don't want to share? Something you're ashamed of, maybe?"

He jerked his head toward the front door. "Gabe and T-Bone haven't been talking about me?"

"Not a word. They didn't think you'd ever show your face around here again."

"I can understand that."

"Good for you. Now, how about letting me in on it? What have you been doing while I've been working this ranch?"

"Yeah," he said. "You've been working the ranch, marrying an old man, having his baby. You've been mighty busy."

"Yes, I have," she agreed. She noticed his relieved smile when Oleta came back inside.

"Can we eat now?" he asked.

"After Oleta says her prayer," Cassie said. "She was raised up Catholic and she won't take a bite until she thanks the Lord."

He smiled warmly at the girl as she joined them at the table. "Go right ahead."

While Oleta said grace in Spanish, Cassie swore at herself for feeling snubbed by Blue Eyes. She didn't like the way he turned on the charm for Oleta while he treated her like a bad habit he wanted to shake. Ladies' man, she thought. When he spots a green girl, he can't help but move in for the deflowering. She'd have to protect Oleta from him. "Amen," Oleta said to signal the end of her prayer.

"Amen," Drew said, his voice sounding deep and strange in the female household.

Oleta spooned beans into his bowl, then Cassie's, while Cassie scowled at her. The girl was a fool for a handsome face.

"Our . . . supper guest was getting ready to tell all about his adventures while he's been away from the Square D," Cassie said, smiling to herself for making him grimace. "Go ahead and tell us—Drew." She expelled his name, her lips puckered as if she were sucking on a persimmon.

Studying those petal-pink lips, Drew suddenly wanted desperately to kiss them. *That's what happens when a man goes years without a woman,* he told himself, tearing his gaze from her mouth and mentally slapping chains on the beast raging within him. He dragged his napkin across his lips, giving himself a few more seconds to bring his rampant lust under control. The first chance he got, he'd go into town and hire himself a woman for an hour or two, he promised himself. That would cure what ailed him.

"So where have you been, Blue Eyes?" she asked again, a smug smile curving her lips.

Those lips . . . those sultry bedroom eyes . . . Blue Eyes? He cocked an eyebrow, encouraged that she'd noticed his eyes. Hell, what was wrong with him? He didn't want the woman's attention. He wanted her to leave!

"Mexico? Texas?" she probed, prodding him as if he were a stray bull. "Maybe you spent your days on a gambling boat or panning for gold?"

"Gold? You find gold?" Oleta asked, eyes shining.

Drew shoveled food into his mouth and methodically chewed and swallowed it, making them wait a while longer. Like a dog with a bone, the woman just wouldn't let go, he thought, glaring at Cassie. Maybe she already knew. T-Bone or Gabe might have told her, and she was doing this to get under his skin.

All right, then. He'd tell her, and it wouldn't change a thing. This ranch would still be his, and she and her baby would still be squatters.

"I haven't been looking for gold and I haven't been traveling on the river," he said, keeping his gaze trained on Cassie's face to gobble up every twinge, every quirk. "I've been in prison."

Only the slightest narrowing of her eyes gave her away. His admiration for her grew. Oleta, on the other hand, gasped and clapped a hand over her mouth. Her eyes were large and frightened.

"Prison," Cassie repeated. "Did they let you out or did you break out?"

"They let me out. My sentence was overturned."

Her brown eyes tested him, measured him, pieced him together. "What were you in for?"

"Cattle rustling."

That sent her backward in her chair. Her spoon clattered to her plate. "Whose cattle?"

"Neighboring ranchers. They were found on the Square D, but I didn't take them."

"So who took them?"

"Damned if I know. Maybe your husband did, hoping I'd get thrown in prison."

"Your own pa thought you were guilty?"

Drew pushed aside his plate, his appetite withering. "He knew better, but he didn't open his mouth to speak in my favor. His silence was enough to make the folks around here believe I was guilty."

"So you're a black sheep in these parts?"

"I don't know what people think about me and I don't give a good goddamn. I'm innocent, and I'm picking up my life and getting on with it."

She folded her arms and settled more comfortably in the chair. "Why would you steal cattle when you've got a ranch full of them?"

"We'd lost cattle and the old man blamed me. He said they got through a fence I was supposed to repair. Anyway, he was madder than a wet hen, and we had one helluva fistfight over it." He noticed her lowered brows. "Once I got big enough, I traded him punch for punch. When I was little, I had to take his blows. You're lucky he died on you or your son would have been his next punching bag."

She shook her head, looking at the baby, who was waving his arms and gurgling happily. "If he'd laid one finger on my child, I would have packed our bags and left him." She cleared her throat. "So you two had a fight."

He nodded, picking up his story. "And then prime cattle started turning up missing from the neighboring ranches. They were found in that gully out by Two Forks Creek.''

''I know it,'' she said, picturing the secluded area in the far southern portion of the ranch.

''When the sheriff questioned the old man about it, he turned on me and yelled that nobody told me to go stealing cattle to replace the ones I let get away.'' The memory scorched him, and he gritted his teeth against the bitter anger. ''I was arrested, and I swear the old devil was grinning when the sheriff took me away.''

''Nobody spoke up for you?''

''Monroe did.''

''He never mentioned you to me either.''

''Folks figured I wouldn't ever show my face here again, so they put me out of their minds. I was sentenced to fifty years, so I was as good as dead to them.''

''Fifty years!'' She ran a finger across her lips in thoughtful repose. ''How long you been out?''

''A few weeks. I collected my horse first.''

''Where did you board him?''

''Texas, near the border.''

''He's a beauty.''

''He's the future of this ranch.''

''This is a cattle ranch.''

''You sound like the old man.'' He nodded when Oleta offered him a wedge of pie. ''I've got a way with horses. I know them. I can make money off them. Cattle have never sparked my interest.''

''Well, me and cattle get along just fine.''

He grinned. ''I don't doubt that. They're stubborn and not too bright.''

She flung down her napkin, her eyes blazing. ''You calling me stupid, mister?''

"Nope, but I'm wondering how smart you are to be hanging around out here when you could take your baby into town and find yourself another husband to help you raise him. I don't mind giving you a little money to get you started."

"And I don't mind shoving your money and your advice right back into your face!" When Oleta whimpered, Cassie shot the girl a quelling look. "Calm down," she told her. "She's always afraid someone's going to get hurt once voices are raised. Quit your trembling, Oleta, and cut me a piece of that pie." She redirected her gaze to him. "Speaking of not being too bright, have you noticed that we seem to be talking in circles?"

"I noticed."

"The only way you're going to make me leave is in a pine box. I've got as much right to be here as you do. I'm Mrs. A. J. Dalton, like it or not."

He couldn't resist. "Did *he* like it?"

Color stained her cheeks and her eyes darkened. "Yeah, Junior, he sure did. He liked it just dandy." She ran her hands down her sides, flaunting her feminine shape. Defiance glinted in her eyes, shaming him. She stood, leaving the pie Oleta had sliced for her untouched, and picked up her baby.

"I'm going to bed," she said, not looking at either of them. Striding to her room, she stopped at the window by the front door and released a whispered oath.

"What is it?" Drew asked, rising from his chair.

"Somebody's out by the corral. That fire-breathing horse of yours is racing around like he's holed up with a swarm of hornets. It's probably the same vermin who dropped by earlier today." She spun around at the sound of a rifle being readied. She hadn't sensed him moving, but he was across the room and had taken down the Winchester from above the fireplace. "What in the hell do you think you're doing?"

His eyes were cold, blue steel. "I'm going to shoot me some vermin, skin them, and nail their hides to the fence posts to warn off any other scavengers."

He strode past her and ducked outside before she could stop him. Shoving the baby at Oleta, she tried not to surrender to the panic billowing inside her.

"Hell's afire," she complained bitterly. "All we need is a trigger-happy convict around here. Take little Andy and keep low, Oleta."

"Where are you going?" the girl asked, her voice shaking.

"Outside to get shot, probably." Then, in a crouch, Cassie left the house, and the darkness swallowed her up.

Chapter 4

Running from cover to cover, Cassie made her way across the porch yard toward the barn. She passed near the bunkhouse and could hear the strumming of Gabe's guitar and his wavering tenor. No wonder they hadn't heard anything with Gabe wailing like a cat in heat!

Ahead of her she thought she saw a figure slinking near the skittish stallion. The horse reared and pawed the air, eyes rolling to show white. A shrill whistle, two short notes, pierced the air, and the stallion immediately placed all four hooves on the ground. He lowered his head, ears laid back, and went as still as a statue. Another whistle, lower and longer, and the horse whirled and trotted to the opposite side of the corral.

I'll be shuck, Cassie thought, impressed with the horse's training. Maybe Blue Eyes wasn't all brag when he said he had a way with horses.

Peering through the darkness, she saw a shadow move and lengthen across the corral. Her ears picked up the rattle of pebbles and the scrape of boots.

A rifle barked and spewed a ball of fire, lighting the

45

darkness for a split second, long enough for Cassie to see a ragged hat fly off a balding head. The now hatless man in the corral yelped and dropped to his haunches.

"Christ! Put down yer gun! Whatcha tryin' to do, kill me?"

"No, but the next bullet will pull you up lame."

Cassie stared in the direction of that unruffled, deep voice. She could see nothing except the big stallion standing in the corner, quiet as a mouse.

"We was just watering our horses."

Cassie could see the man—she thought it was the one called Reb—duckwalk backward, probably toward his buddy. She began to ease her way around the corral, intent on surprising the other varmint. By the time she spotted Dan Harper, he was astride his horse and Reb was leaping onto the back of his. The rifle flashed again from across the corral. Reb shouted and grabbed his leg, while his partner returned fire and whirled his horse around for a quick getaway.

Raising her gun, Cassie squeezed off a shot, aiming high. The bullet whizzed past Harper's head, and he yowled in pain and clapped a hand to his ear. Cassie grinned, glad to have taken a piece off the mangy coyote.

"Good shooting."

She nearly leapt out of her skin when the voice sounded right behind her and warm breath fanned her cheek. Blue Eyes grinned at her jumpiness, then calmly pushed aside the gun she had unintentionally pointed at him.

"Don't go sneaking up on an armed woman unless you're looking to get plugged," Cassie said, angry and shaken. "I think I hit the other one."

"Yeah, you took off some skin. I was thinking of chasing after them, but it's not worth the trouble."

"What's going on out here?" T-Bone shouted, stuffing his shirt into the waistband of his pants as he jogged toward them.

"Who you shooting at?" Gabe asked, bringing up the rear, his shirttail flapping in the breeze.

"We're shooting at thieves," Cassie told them. "And they would have taken every horse we have while Gabe sang off-key love songs to you, T-Bone. That stallion was having a fit, but y'all couldn't hear a dagblamed thing over Gabe's howling."

"Those weren't love songs," Gabe said. "Them are church hymns. I only know a couple of love songs and I ain't gonna waste them on Tee."

T-Bone grinned and shadow-punched the younger cowhand. "You try singing love songs to me and I'll—"

"It was the same two skunks who were here earlier today," Cassie interrupted, exasperated with them. She glanced at Drew, wondering why he was so quiet, and caught him examining a wet spot on his sleeve. "What the—Hey, you're bleeding! Were you shot?"

"Looks like it," he acknowledged without a hint of concern or discomfort. "I think the bullet went right through the meat. Lucky shot. He sure wasn't aiming."

"Let's go inside where I can take a look at it," Cassie said, more upset by the sight of his blood than she cared to admit. "You two keep your eyes and ears open," she told Gabe and T-Bone. "Wouldn't hurt if you made sure everything's locked up tight."

"We'll do," T-Bone said, already making for the barn along with Gabe.

Cassie led the way back into the house. She motioned toward a kitchen chair, silently ordering Drew into it while she took down the metal box of bandages and medicines from the kitchen cupboard. Oleta hovered on the threshold of her bedroom, holding Andy on her hip.

"Everything's fine," Cassie assured her. "Drew managed to get himself shot, but he's not hurting or anything."

"Shot?" Oleta shifted her big, round eyes toward him.

"Yeah, somehow I stepped right into the path of a bullet. It's all my fault. But at least it doesn't hurt—or so I'm told."

Cassie bit her tongue as she set the metal box on the kitchen table and flipped it open. Her gaze wrestled briefly with his before she concentrated on tearing off a length of white bandage. She poured hot water from the kettle into a shallow pan and added a dipperful of cool water to bring down its temperature.

"Well, does it hurt?" she asked, eyeing his soaked shirtsleeve.

"Not much. I reckon I'll live."

"Roll up your sleeve and let me have a look."

"You won't faint?"

She arched a brow. "Andy was eight pounds and two ounces, and I pushed him out all by my lonesome. When I was done, the sheets were crimson. I didn't faint then, so I doubt I'll faint now."

His Adam's apple bobbed, and he started rolling up his sleeve, but it was rough going, since the fabric was torn and stiff with blood. Cassie waved aside his hand, grabbed the shirt at the shoulder seam, and neatly ripped the sleeve free.

"Damn it all, woman!" he bellowed, as if it were his arm instead of his sleeve she'd torn off. "That was a new shirt!"

"It's an old, ragged one now," she calmly informed him. Bending closer, she squinted at the seeping wound. "You're right. The bullet went in and out." She angled her head to see the exit wound better. "Clean. That's good. It's not a free bleeder either."

"You a doctor?"

"I'm *your* doctor for the time being," she informed him archly. "Unless you want to dress this yourself."

He firmed his jaw and stared straight ahead. "See to it."

She wanted to give him a good kick in the shin but restrained herself. Instead, she cleaned the bullet hole and wrapped his upper arm in clean, white strips of cotton gauze. He was as tough as a leather whip, she concluded, scrutinizing his muscled arm. Sure didn't look like a man who'd been corralled in a prison. He'd be right handy on the ranch, providing he wasn't all talk and no work.

When she was done, the water in the bowl was pale pink and her patient was chalky white.

"I guess you ought to go to bed," she advised. "You'll be sore in the morning but on the mend."

He nodded. "Thanks." Then he made his way to the ladder.

She started to tell him he was headed in the wrong direction, that the bunkhouse was outside, not up in the loft, but she clamped her teeth together and held her tongue. Shouldn't kick a man when he's down, she counseled herself. Besides, she was grateful for his help tonight with those two mangy rascals. She watched his slow, steady progress up the ladder and listened to his shuffling footsteps. He grunted a couple of times in pain while he undressed and let out a groan when he settled onto his bedroll. No more than a couple of minutes passed before she heard his soft snoring.

"He is sleeping in here with us?" Oleta asked.

Cassie sighed. "Tonight, yes." She dumped the water outside and washed and dried the bowl. "I'll worry about him and everything else tomorrow." She held out her arms for Andy and Oleta gave him to her. Cassie carried her baby into the bedroom and shut the door.

Sitting in the rocker by the window, she let the baby nurse until he fell asleep. Then she did what she loved to do best. She just looked at him. She never grew tired of admiring her child, his round face, curly blond hair, long sandy lashes, delicate skin, and dimpled elbows and knees. She imagined what kind of man he'd be—big and strong, but a gentleman, a man of his word, and a man of faith and heart.

Not like his father.

She thought of the man up in her loft. If he was like his father, it was no wonder he'd ended up in prison. She harbored no doubt that A.J. hadn't vouched for his son's innocence. It would be just like A.J. to stand by passively while his only son was sent off to rot in prison, especially if he felt that Drew was a better man than him. Better at anything. The old devil wouldn't tolerate anyone challenging his authority, sassing him, or besting him. She'd discovered that the first day she'd met A.J. and revealed that she loved to read. That night he burned her books and letters, even her Bible. She received a few pieces of mail, but she never got to read them because A.J. collected them in town and tore them into tiny pieces right in front of her.

After he died, she'd written her two best women friends, Doris McDonald and Adele Gold, and explained why she hadn't been writing. She'd recently received letters back from them, expressing relief and happiness for her present circumstances. Everything had seemed so rosy.

But now she had another Andrew Dalton in her life. She settled Andy in his cradle, smoothing a hand over his soft hair and trailing a fingertip along his dewy cheek. Her baby. The time she'd spent with A.J. had been worth it because she now had her son, her beautiful son. Bending down, she kissed his sweet-smelling cheek, then tiptoed to the other side of the room to undress. Glancing occasionally at the closed door as she removed her clothes, she realized she was tense. *What foolishness!* she chided herself. Blue Eyes was sound asleep. Still . . . maybe she should sleep with a gun under her pillow. He'd been joshing her about that, but she thought the suggestion might be wise. After all, he'd been in prison. He might awaken during the night with women on his mind.

After slipping into her cotton nightgown, she quietly left her bedroom and retrieved the handgun and tucked it under her pillow. She shoved a trunk against the closed door before getting into bed.

Even with those precautions it was hours before she drifted off to a restless sleep. When the rooster crowed shortly before first light, she was already up and dressed, anxious to face the day and the man who had come to ruin it.

Oleta was stoking the fire in the cookstove. Cassie

smelled freshly brewed coffee and spotted a mug on the table. She glanced at it, surprised to find that it had been used. Usually she was up half an hour or more before Oleta.

"Looks like I'm not the only early riser," she said, selecting a clean mug for herself from a collection by the stove.

"I don't know how long he's been gone."

A few seconds passed before Cassie gleaned meaning from Oleta's statement. She whipped her gaze to the loft. "You mean he's not up there asleep?"

"No. I looked. He is gone. I did not hear him even when he made coffee."

"He brewed the coffee?" Cassie stared at the dark liquid she'd poured, then crossed the room to stare out the window. "His horse is gone," she noted. The bunkhouse windows were dark. "T-Bone and Gabe haven't stirred yet. Wonder where Blue Eyes is off to so early? I suppose it's too much to hope that he decided to hit the trail and leave us be."

"This is his home."

Cassie spun to glare at Oleta. "No more than it's my home." She set down the chipped mug, sloshing coffee onto the table, and went to wrench open the front door. "I'm going to milk Daisy."

Crossing the yard and making for the barn, she examined the hoofprints leading from the corral. He had headed east, not toward Abilene or Monroe's spread, so where the devil was he so early?

As she pulled the milking stool to beside the mooing Jersey cow, Cassie tried to put Drew Dalton out of her mind, but he kept barging in. All day long he barged in.

*   *   *

He came barreling toward the house like a rider shot from hell. Cassie lifted a hand to shade her face from the barrage of the setting sun and thought Drew Dalton looked like he rode in the center of that bright orange orb, surrounded by it, empowered by it. Shaking off the fantasy, she braced herself for another confrontation with him. He'd been gone but not forgotten throughout the day, too often the subject of her snatches of conversation with Gabe and T-Bone, both of whom were itching to know how she was going to handle this new burr under her saddle.

She would have told them if she'd known herself. For the life of her, she couldn't figure out what to do with the man, what to say to him, or how to treat him. All she could tell T-Bone and Gabe was that she wasn't budging.

Drew's black horse gleamed with sweat, the mane streaking backward in the wind. Before the stallion could come to a complete stop, he was out of the saddle and striding toward them, his face set in angry lines beneath the brim of his midnight blue hat.

"I've been riding the fences," he growled at her, barely sparing a glance for T-Bone or Gabe, who were unsaddling their horses. "And I found three places that were down. You've lost at least fifty head from the looks of the tracks. Is this how you run a ranch? I could hire in a twelve-year-old boy to manage it better."

"You could do squat," she shot back at him, "because you're *not* the boss man around here. I am." She jabbed a thumb between her outthrust breasts and wished she hadn't when his gaze locked on them. "Boss woman, I mean," she amended, again wishing she'd left well enough alone.

Some of the anger bled from his face. "Yep, you're a bossy woman, all right, but you don't know spit about running a ranch. I bet those cattle are mingled in with the Star H, and Roe's men won't weed them out unless I ride over there and say something about it."

"Roe will bring them back here," she informed him. "He's done it before." She turned away from him.

"What do you mean, he's done it before?"

"He's brought some strays home, that's all."

"Ever wonder how many he *didn't* bring home?"

"I thought you liked Roe," she charged.

"Liking someone doesn't make him a saint."

She made a sour face. "Tell T-Bone where the fence breaks are, and we'll fix them come morning."

"I fixed them *today.*"

She stopped and turned slowly back to him. "By yourself?"

"By myself," he said forcefully.

"With what?"

"Wire and nails and sweat."

And bulging muscles, she added, eyeing his physique. "Guess that gunshot wound isn't troubling you any."

"Not enough to keep me from work." He led his horse to the water trough. "Me and you are going to have to get a few things square over supper tonight," he told her. "You call yourself a cattlewoman, but you let your herd trample the fences and wander wherever they want, and you wait for other ranchers to round up your strays and bring them home to you?" He shook his head. "It's a wonder you've held onto this place for as long as you have."

She caught T-Bone's eye. "How many fences you reckon we've fixed this week?"

He scratched at his short beard. "At least a dozen broke places," he answered. "I betcha them fences wasn't broke on our side, but on Roe's side. He's got himself a couple of randy young bulls with a penchant for butting fence posts. Them places you found busted up were close to the west windmill, weren't they?"

Drew loosened the saddle on the stallion. "Some were," he answered, chagrin creeping into his voice.

T-Bone nodded. "Figured as much. That's them bulls of Monroe's. He says he's selling them off this spring. Can't sell them quick enough to suit me."

"Me neither," Gabe chimed in with a wide grin. "I think somebody ought to tell Monroe Hendrix that he should fix the fences since they're torn down by his bulls. But shoot, Hendrix is lazy about things like that. He don't mind if his cattle chomps on our grass or tramples our fences. He probably sees this land as his already."

Cassie's temper surged at that suggestion, and she noted that Drew's face flushed red, too. *Hmm, maybe he could be a friend instead of a foe,* she thought. Two fighting to keep the land would be better than one, especially when the one was a woman with a baby.

"He knows better now that I'm home," Drew said, leading his horse toward the corral. "He's always had a hankering for this land, but he'll get it over my dead body."

Cassie watched him walk. She liked to watch him walk and found it hard to tear her gaze away from him. She heard his voice, soft and whispery, as he spoke to his treasured horse. She didn't have to wonder how that silky voice would affect a woman. Having him whisper like that into her ear—why, even the coldest of women would melt around the edges!

She jerked her mind from that trap before she could get caught up into thinking of him as anything more than a possible partner. Seemed like he knew his way around a cow, a horse, and a ranch. Didn't seem to be the lazy sort either. She might offer him a partnership. Maybe. If he backed her into a corner. What she *could* offer him was a compromise for now. She wouldn't ask him to leave if he would quit expecting her to pack her things and head for Abilene.

She sighed with relief, happy with the sound of that agreement. Over supper tonight she'd present it to him, and then they could both breathe easier and get on with the task of living—living with each other.

A frown creased her brow. Now, if only she could get him to move his bedroll out to the bunkhouse . . .

"I'll move into that bunkhouse when pigs fly!" Drew slapped the napkin down beside his empty plate and folded his arms against his chest. "As for letting you stay here for now, I don't have any quarrel with that. Your baby, after all, is my little brother. I'm not so hard-hearted that I'd render him homeless."

His little brother. Her Andy? Cassie glanced toward the high chair, where Andy beat his fists on the tray, anxious to be fed another spoonful of mashed peas and potatoes. Smiling, Oleta obliged, and Andy smacked his lips.

"If only you would stop being so stubborn and go into town, look around, find yourself a room or maybe even a small house," Drew said, his voice taking on a placating note she didn't like. "Wouldn't that be better for your little one? There are upstanding gentlemen in Abilene who would appreciate the attention of a lady like yourself.''

She blasted him with a fiery glare. ''For your information, I've spent most of my life in towns scattered from here to the California coast, and I've met my share of upstanding gentlemen. I want to give my son what is rightfully his. Andy is a Dalton and this is the Dalton ranch. A.J. told me he was leaving this place to my son. He willed it to him.''

''He willed it to me,'' Drew said, arms still folded. ''And by doing so, he had the last laugh on both of us.''

''How do you figure that?''

''He left me the ranch and he left me a brother I have to fight for it. A baby brother.'' He looked at Andy, and his expression softened. ''And I imagine the old man knew you'd fight me tooth and nail, too.''

Witnessing the softening around his eyes and mouth when he looked at Andy, Cassie took a different tack. ''You sleeping under the same roof with your little brother's mother ain't right. Folks will talk.''

His blue eyes slid to her again, and one corner of his wide mouth kicked up. ''What folks?''

She shrugged and made an expansive gesture. ''Folks.''

He glanced around at Oleta and Andy. ''Oleta here will keep quiet, and not many people can understand Andy's jabbering. I'll take my chances.''

Cassie released a huffy sigh. ''Neighbors will talk. How can I face the preacher and the congregation this Sunday at church with you living under the same roof with me?''

"The gossiping folks around here will have plenty to talk about without worrying if I'm staying here in this house with you. Hell, I'm a hardened criminal who's been released from prison to spoil and plunder this land again." He widened his sky-blue eyes and hunched his shoulders. "Lock up the women and children! Guard your families and your herds! Dalton is back, and that means trouble."

She wasn't impressed with his histrionics. "I doubt if anyone is shaking in their boots at the news you're riding the range again. Maybe they'll keep a sharper eye on their cattle, but that's all the bother you'll cause."

He leaned forward, resting his folded arms on the table, and the light went out of his eyes. "Don't underestimate me or what I've been through. If I didn't leave here a hardened man, I assure you I've come back one. My old man and two and a half years in prison turned my heart into a chunk of rock. I've got one aim, to make a name for myself as a horse breeder. That's what I care about—my horses and the reputation I'll build from them. Anyone who gets in my way gets run over. Anyone who messes with me gets bloodied."

Oleta swallowed a shriek and stood up. "I will go to my room. I will clean the dishes later." She left the table, quick as a frightened rabbit.

"Well, you've got her running scared," Cassie allowed. "But me and Andy are standing our ground." She leaned toward the baby and chucked him under his chin. He grinned and blew spit bubbles. "Ain't that right, big boy?" Cassie said, laughing at her son's antics. "We won't tuck tail and run. No siree. We love this land, and heaven knows I've earned my right to oversee this place."

"Why, because you've got a 'missus' before your name?"

She straightened up from the baby. "No, because I put up with your foul-smelling, putrid-mouthed, ornery old pappy and bore him a pretty son. I tried to be a good wife to him, but he didn't want a wife. He wanted a slave girl he could boss, who wouldn't talk back or cry or complain. We've both been in prisons. Yours had bars, mine didn't, but I was stuck, same as you."

"You could have left him."

Smiling, she shook her head. "No, I married him. I don't welsh on my word."

He stared at her for so long that she grew uneasy and had to busy herself by picking up the dishes and stacking them on the drain board.

"I don't welsh on my word either," he said from behind her, his voice suddenly huskier. "We'll share the damned ranch, but I'm not giving up on my plans to make the Square D known for its horses as well as its cattle."

Her heart boomed so loudly that she was sure he could hear it as she turned around to face him again. For a hard man he sure had heavenly eyes. Celestial blue. Angelic, almost.

"I appreciate that," she said, finally finding enough breath to fuel her voice. "You can stay in the loft, I guess."

He grinned lopsided, rakish. "Why, that's right sweet of you, ma'am."

She grinned back, knowing full well that her permission meant nothing to him, but enjoying the playfulness of the gesture.

Andy squeaked and gurgled, drawing their gazes.

"Did A.J. want the baby?" he asked.

She bit her lower lip, worried about how he would react. "The first day I arrived, he told me he wanted a son."

He nodded slowly, almost sadly. "Yep, if he's not roasting in Hell—which I hope to blazes he is—then he's laughing his ass off, the old goat."

"He's not laughing now," she told him, wanting to lessen the bitterness and anger she sensed in him. "We've struck a bargain, you and me, and I bet that's something A.J. Dalton didn't expect from us."

"Not so soon anyway." He tucked his thumbs under his belt and was quiet, lost in thought.

Cassie heated water for the dishes and washed Andy's face and hands. After a few minutes Drew stood and stretched his arms over his head.

"I'll ride over to the Star H tomorrow and have a talk with Monroe about his rowdy bulls. You want to go with me?"

She nodded. "Right after breakfast?"

"That'll do. I'll take a turn around the place before I crawl into bed."

"Here." She held up an apple and tossed it to him. "It's got a bruised place. Give it to that show-off horse of yours."

He examined the apple, and a smile poked at the corners of his mouth. "He'll like this." Touching two fingers to his forehead, he fashioned a salute. The light was back in his eyes, twinkling, tempting. "G'night . . . Cassie."

"G'night . . . Drew."

She turned back to the stove, where the water was boiling and steam blasted her in the face. She hardly felt the heat. Her skin was already hot, her temperature spiked, her interest on the rise.

Damn, if the man didn't have a right fetching smile when he chose to use it.

Andy released a string of vowels that ended with a high-pitched screech.

"I know, baby," Cassie said, leaning down to drop a kiss on top of his head. "You're the only male I should be thinking about." But in the next moment, she found herself hoping that Andy's eyes would stay blue, and turn that heavenly, star-sparkling shade.

Chapter 5

Monroe Hendrix stood on his expansive front porch and wore a big smile that showed off his straight, white teeth. Morning sunlight slanted over his pepper-and-salt hair and glinted off the silver handles of the guns strapped around his waist. His clothes were wrinkle-free, and his snakeskin boots had been polished to a shine.

"Good morning," he greeted Cassie and Drew. "You two haven't shot each other yet, I see."

Drew laid a hand on his injured shoulder, feeling the bandage under his shirt. "As a matter of fact, I *was* shot, but by a couple of drifters who were snooping around our horses, looking to steal them. You know them. Reb Smalley and Dan Harper."

Monroe lifted his dark brows. "Yes, they were here looking for work, but I sent them on."

"To the Square D?" Cassie asked.

"No. I just sent them on their way. They tried to steal your horses, did they? Thanks for coming out here to warn me. I'll keep an eye out for them."

Drew strode up the porch steps and into the shade.

"We came by to talk to you about some other trouble we're having."

"Trouble?" Monroe ran a finger under the white and black checked bandanna tied around his neck. "Already?"

Cassie took her place beside Drew, not wanting it to appear that he was the boss man now and she was along just for the ride. She stepped forward, angling for the upper hand but feeling like a sapling between two towering oaks.

"We've had a rash of fence breaks," she said, fixing a scowl on her face. "Some of our cattle might have wandered off."

Monroe gave a scoffing laugh. "Hell, that ain't trouble, girl! Your cattle are always wandering onto my land."

Drew placed his hands on Cassie's shoulders and unceremoniously pushed her aside. She would have told him off right then and there, but he was talking before she could think of a comeback.

"That's going to change. Now that I'm back, I'll make sure the fences are kept up. Of course, I'll expect you to do your share. I hear you've got some young bulls that are butting posts and knocking them over."

"Yeah, that's right," Cassie said, wedging herself between him and Hendrix. Monroe smiled at her, but she felt Drew's cold glare on the back of her neck. "We can't keep spending all our time shoring up the fences bordering your property, Roe. You've got to do something about those randy bulls of yours."

Monroe laughed and rested a hand on her shoulder. "So that's what this is all about. My young bulls? Why, I'd do anything for you, Cassie. You know that."

Cassie felt her face heat up and was agonizingly aware of Drew's scrutiny. Any fool could see that Monroe Hendrix was sweet on her, and from what Cassie had seen, Drew Dalton was no fool.

"If some of the Square D cattle are mixed in with yours, you don't mind if we round them up today, do you?" she asked.

"I imagine you've got more than you can handle," Monroe said affably. "I can a spare a man or two to round up your strays. I'm expecting a new ranch manager to arrive here any day now to keep a better eye on my place."

"Have you been having trouble around here?" Drew asked.

Monroe waved off the question. "Nothing serious."

Drew leaned his good shoulder against a porch support. "Since you have men to spare, why don't you send them out to patrol the west border and repair your own fence breaks for a change?"

Cassie ground her teeth, watching the friendly light dim in Monroe's eyes. She believed in being a good neighbor, so she placed a gloved hand on Monroe's forearm and offered him a smile. Pleasing men and smoothing ruffled feathers were second nature to her.

"I'd be much obliged, Roe. Say, are you going to offer me something cold to drink or send me away from here parched and pouting?" She felt both of the men's keen gazes, but she was more concerned with Drew's. She knew he thought she was a tart for flirting with Monroe, but she had learned long ago how and when to use the few gifts God had bestowed on women.

"Where are my manners?" Monroe rested his hand on hers and gave it a squeeze. "How about a spot of tea? Drew and I will have a slug of whiskey. Sound good to you, Drew?''

"Sure." Drew's eyes laughed at her.

Liquor was something she had no taste for, but she knew a challenge when she heard it. "Whiskey's fine for me, too.''

"W-what?" Monroe sputtered.

"I'll have a slug of whiskey, too," she repeated.

Drew eyed her but kept quiet.

Monroe shrugged. "Well . . . If you're sure . . .''

Cassie sat in one of the rockers while Hendrix went inside for the liquor.

"You're a whiskey drinker, are you?" Drew asked, one corner of his mouth kicking up as he sat in the rocker next to her.

"I'm being neighborly. Wouldn't hurt if you'd try it. You're snapping at Monroe like he's your sworn enemy. I thought he was the only one who stood up for you when you were charged with cattle stealing.''

"Don't you worry about me and Roe. We don't pussyfoot around when we've got something to say. Me and Roe have always been straight with each other.'' His smile became cynical. "You two been courting?''

"No!" The word exploded from her just as Hendrix rejoined them on the wide front porch. He carried three shot glasses and distributed them.

"There you go." He lifted his high. "To women of good breeding and men of guts and glory.''

Cassie removed her work gloves and brought the glass to her lips. Women of good breeding . . . Was he telling her that she wasn't one for indulging in this whiskey ritual? To hell with him—and with smirking Drew Dalton! She flung the whiskey to the back of her throat and swallowed it. The liquid fire scorched a path to her stomach, but she didn't cough, didn't choke, didn't gag. It had been a long while since she'd indulged in the Devil's brew, but not so long ago that she couldn't hold her own with it.

She smacked her lips and spoke in even tones. "Not bad. It's got a nice kick to it. Did you still it yourself, Monroe?"

"No, I bought it off a moonshiner in the next county."

Monroe regarded her warily, as if he expected her to turn green any second.

"You know your whiskey, huh?" Drew asked.

"I know it well enough to leave it be most of the time," she rejoined. "That's something most men can't ever get through their thick heads. Your pappy, for one, couldn't drink without getting pie-eyed."

"I'm not him." His voice mirrored his expression—granite-hard. He swallowed the whiskey in one gulp and didn't even blink.

Monroe cleared his throat. "You should let Drew help you, Cassie."

"Oh, I aim to," Cassie replied evenly. "I'm letting him help me run my ranch."

Monroe sat forward, looking from one to the other. "You two are partners now?"

"Not exactly," Drew allowed. "We're looking out for our own interests in the ranch. She's not my boss and I'm not hers. That's why we both came around this morning to talk to you about the fence breaks."

"I see." Monroe set his empty whiskey glass down beside his chair and essayed a helpless gesture. "I'll do what I can."

"Thanks." Cassie drew on her gloves again, ready to get back to her own side of the fence.

"How does it feel to be free again?" Monroe asked, rocking gently in the chair, smiling at Drew.

Drew smiled back, but offered nothing more.

"What was it like, being locked up?"

Cassie swallowed the tangle of nerves in her throat. Although she could see by the tightening of Drew's jawline that he didn't appreciate the nosy question, she found she wanted to hear his answer.

"It's like being dead, but you're still breathing," Drew answered. "Every day seems like a year."

Monroe looked away from Drew's unwavering gaze. "Must have been awful. Are you sure you want to hang around here now that you're footloose?"

Drew's smile turned sly. "Roe, if I didn't know better, I'd say you aren't glad to see me. You want me to vamoose so you can sweet-talk Cassie here into joining the Square D with the Star H?"

Cassie sputtered with speechless fury, but Monroe laughed and slapped his thigh.

"Like I need more land to worry with," Monroe said between chuckles. "No, no, I was just thinking that you deserve something better than breaking your back over a bunch of stubborn cows. I'm glad you're home, Drew. I sure don't want to see that ranch neglected, sectioned off and sold. That wouldn't be good for anyone around here."

"Who said it's being neglected?" Cassie asked.

Monroe sent her a placating smile. "You're doing the best you can. I know that." He sat forward, directing his attention solely to Drew again. "Of course, I wouldn't mind expanding my herd. My bloodline could use some improvement, I reckon.'' He removed a flat, silver tin from his shirt pocket and extracted a pinch of chewing tobacco from it. He offered some to Drew, who shook his head. ''I'm going into Abilene next week to sell my bulls and a few older heifers. I hope to find some quality cattle there to buy. I don't suppose you'd be interested in selling me some of your herd?''

Although he'd been talking to Drew, Cassie chimed in to field the inquiry. ''Like I've told you before, I'm keeping what I've got.''

''She's the cattle baroness,'' Drew drawled. ''Horses are my concern.''

Monroe stuffed the tobacco between his teeth and bottom lip. ''You ought to come with me when I go to Abilene. They usually auction off some mighty good horseflesh.''

''Maybe I will.'' Drew got to his feet. He swept his hat off his head and whacked it against his leg to dislodge the dust from it, then he wedged it back on over his russet hair. ''Glad you'll be taking care of that bull problem.''

''Anything I can do to head off trouble.'' Monroe's expression was suddenly grave. ''Those days are behind us. Am I right, Drew?''

Drew cut his eyes at Hendrix, and Cassie felt the snap and crackle of tension. Again she stepped between the men, giving Drew a shove toward the steps.

''Don't be a stranger, Roe,'' she said, herding Drew off the porch. He jerked away from her, resenting her interference, but swaggered to his horse and swung up into the saddle, much to her relief. She grabbed Sweet Pea's reins and stepped into the stirrup. Once she was settled in the saddle, she waved at Hendrix before turning for home.

They rode side by side for a while before Drew broke the silence.

"Roe's got his spurs in a tangle over you."

Cassie nodded. "That's right." She felt him scrutinizing her, but she didn't give him much to work with.

"He means to win you over, maybe even marry you."

"He'll have to get in line."

Drew craned his neck, trying to glean something from her serene expression. "What's that mean?"

"It means that I have half the bachelors in the county wanting to court me and not just because my son will inherit the Square D."

"Other men have been snooping around you?"

She gave him a chiding glance. "What do you think?" Batting her lashes and flashing a smile, she pitched her voice to a seductive purr. "Take a look at me and tell me if you don't think I'm easy on the eyes."

Holy hell, it was a good thing he had a sound head on his shoulders! He figured she had *all* the bachelors in the county vying for her attention. All except him. He knew what she was after, and it wasn't what was inside his trousers, but what was outside his front door: Land.

He didn't want to look, but he couldn't help himself. She pushed her hat off her head and it dangled against her back, held on by the chin string. Sunlight glistened in her white-gold hair, and her brown eyes were warm and liquid, like melting chocolate. A fetching blush bloomed in her cheeks, and her mouth formed a slight pout that fired his blood and made him want to kiss her, press those lips flat against his and separate them with a thrust of his tongue.

"Well?" she murmured, those plump lips barely moving.

"You'd look better to me from a distance," he said, trying to be gruff.

Her sultry smile slipped away, and she jerked her gaze forward. "You're rude."

"That's right," he agreed proudly. "And I'm not some greenhorn kid who will be suffering Cupid's cramps over you, so get that out of your head."

She grinned. "Cupid's cramps?" Then she laughed, carefree, like a girl in pigtails. "I should be mad at you, but I'm not. I don't need you to tell me that I'm pretty. Men have told me that my whole life. What's more important is that I'm smart and I know when a man's being truthful and when he's just airing his lungs."

She set her spurs to the gelding and rode ahead of him, letting him watch her hair flow back from her and her backside rise and fall in the saddle.

She didn't have to look over her shoulder to make sure he was watching. She knew it.

A few days later Drew went with Monroe into Abilene to the auction and returned the next morning with three mares. One of them was already pregnant. Cassie sat on the top rail of the corral fence with T-Bone and watched as Drew and Gabe went over each of the new horses.

Dynamite whinnied from his stall in the barn, and T-Bone chuckled.

"Your stallion smells female," he shouted to Drew.

"It was all I could do to keep him off them on the way back here," Drew said, pausing to wipe sweat from his brow. ''I'm going to breed him to the gray mare first.''

''Ought to get a right nice foal from them,'' Gabe said, stroking the gray's sleek neck.

''This chestnut will foal by next summer.'' Drew scratched between the mare's ears. ''She was bred to an Arabian. You ever see one of those? A full-blooded one?''

''Nope, can't say that I have,'' Gabe confessed.

''They're beautiful. Regal-looking. But for my money, there is no better breed than the quarter horse. They've got good dispositions and they're smart. Smarter than a lot of cowboys I've known.''

He turned to the third horse, a dark-brown quarter horse with black points, mane, tail, and legs. Lifting a hand, he frowned when the horse skittered backward.

''She's head shy,'' Cassie said. ''Probably been mistreated. Whipped in the face.''

Drew murmured, his voice musical and husky, using sounds instead of words. Cassie felt something inside her respond, unfurling and circling around her heart. The horse must have felt something, too, because she stood still, letting Drew rest a hand between her laid-back ears.

He massaged her ears and whispered into them. Cassie edged forward on the rail, her legs and torso tense, as she strained to hear the soft murmurs and watch the gentle stroke of his hands on the horse's ears, blazed face, and quivering neck. Something quaked deep inside Cassie, and she realized her breathing had grown shallow.

What was it about this man? Maybe it was his voice— so deep and compelling, but soft and husky. Or maybe it was his looks. That ornery glint in his eyes, those full lips that said so much without forming words. He was dreamy handsome, and his muscled body had stamped itself on her mind's eye. At the oddest times she caught herself thinking about how the muscles in his arms flexed when he lifted Andy high into the air and about how he walked with that strutting swagger, his long legs eating up the ground.

But it was more than his looks that captivated her. It was his manner. Quiet and controlled, he kept himself on a tight rein.

During the past few days she'd noticed that he was careful with a dollar. He'd gone over their money ledgers and had allotted a meager sum to use on fixing up the house, but he'd explained that more funds would be freed up after they'd built their nest egg. Cattle would be sold in the spring, and they'd budget to last the year. No luxuries, nothing but necessities, he had cautioned.

She'd been impressed by his way with a dollar. His father had wasted too much on whiskey, smelly cigars, and betting on card games. While he had refused to spend any money on fixing up the house or buying new clothes, he squandered money on his vices.

But not Drew Dalton. In fact, she wasn't sure he had any vices other than his prancing, high-spirited stud horse. Might be fun to find out, she mused, watching him run his hands all over the skittish mare's head. Over her eyes, her nose, her ears, her wide face. The mare settled, almost as if she were in a trance, and closed her eyes. Actually shut her eyes, giving herself over to the feel of those hands.

Hell, who could blame the nag?

Cassie slid off the fence and walked toward Drew. "What are you doing to her?"

"Getting her used to my feel," he said, almost in a

whisper. "Making her trust me. Once she understands that I won't hurt her, she'll calm down. Won't you, girl? Pretty, pretty girl." His voice was honey-dipped. "There, there, pretty girl. Settle down and let me show you how much I think of you. That's it. Relax, darlin'. You're in good hands now."

Cassie shifted from one foot to the other, suddenly feeling hot and moist. Her skin felt prickly and her heart galloped like a colt. She found that she was watching his hands—his good and steady hands—stroking and caressing the mare. If one could judge a man by his hands, then Drew Dalton was strong and tender, sensitive and knowing. After a night with him, a woman probably couldn't get the smile off her face for days.

Giving herself a mental slap, Cassie drew herself up and cleared her throat of any huskiness that might be there. "What I want to know is if any of these horses will make good cow ponies."

Drew slanted her a look. "I didn't buy them with that in mind, but yeah, they're quarter horses, so they can cut cattle with the best of them."

"What did you buy them for if not to ride?"

"Breeding," he said, and the word coming off his tongue and lips struck a tuning fork deep inside her. "Dynamite needs some mares to mount. You're looking at this ranch's future. In ten years the Square D will be known for its horses."

"In the meantime, cattle is our money crop," Cassie reminded him. "Dreams have to wait—as usual."

"It's not just a dream anymore. I'm making it happen."

She arched a brow, displaying her skepticism. "But you *will* ride the range with us lowly cow handlers, won't you? Dynamite won't be needing much help connecting with these mares, so you should have a lot of time on your hands.''

One side of his mouth kicked up. ''I didn't think you needed any help around here.''

''What I don't need is someone to feed who doesn't carry his load.''

''Don't worry, Shorty. I've never been accused of that.'' He returned his attention to the mare, rubbing her ears before gliding a hand over her back. The horse quivered from head to tail. He laughed softly. ''That's right. Feels good, doesn't it, girl?'' His eyes met Cassie's across the mare's sloped back. ''What are you all red-faced about?''

Her mouth had gone dry, so she shook her head and walked back to where T-Bone perched on the fence. She propped her elbows on a rail and leaned back to contemplate Drew and his way with the mares.

''Is he tweaking your tail feathers?''

She swiveled her head to glare at T-Bone. ''What's that mean?''

T-Bone shrugged and chewed on a hangnail. ''I figured by the way you two are pecking at each other that he's ruffling your feathers, that's all.''

''Oh.'' She pulled a hand down her face, trying to wipe away the prickly heat that crept over her skin like a fever. ''Yeah, I guess so. He irritates me . . . like a damned rash.'' Absently she scratched at her arm, then her neck.

''Hey, turn around here,'' T-Bone said, grabbing her shoulder and spinning her to face him. He squinted at her. ''You ain't just talking, boss lady. You best go look in the mirror.''

"Why?" She pressed her hands to her hot cheeks.

" 'Cause you're breaking out in red freckles!"

With a cry of alarm, Cassie raced to the house, while her memory returned her to a patch of vines and weeds she'd strode into to retrieve a lost calf earlier that day. Poison ivy! Just her rotten luck.

Chapter 6

When Drew entered the house at dusk, he could tell by Oleta's frazzled appearance that things could not be much worse. The Mexican girl stood before the stove and jiggled a wailing Andy while she tried to pull a pan of biscuits from the oven.

"Here," Drew said, drawing off his gloves and tossing them and his hat into the nearest chair. "Let me have him while you finish up supper." He took the baby from her and examined Andy's red, damp face. "What's all this ruckus?" he asked both the baby and Oleta. He felt the babe's diaper, but it was dry. "Is he hungry?"

"His teeth are coming," Oleta said, backhanding a trailing black curl off her forehead. "He has the fever."

"What about his mother? Does she have the fever, too?"

"She is trying to rest, but *sí,* she is sick. She itches and tries not to scratch."

"If she scratches, she'll make it worse." He knew that much about poison ivy rashes but little else. Looking toward the closed bedroom door, he hesitated only a moment before rapping against it with the toe of his boot. "You decent? I'm coming in."

"Don't!" Cassie yelled.

But he was already filling the threshold. She sat bolt upright in bed, the covers thrown askew, her hair unbraided and falling like a veil over her shoulders. She wore a chemise and underpants that reached her knees. Her arms, chest, neck, and face were covered in bright pink spots. A rag doll sat next to her, propped up by pillows. The murderous glare Cassie delivered struck him funny, and he laughed. Andy stopped crying for a few moments and stared at him, startled by the happy sound.

"What are you doing with him?" Cassie demanded crossly, glancing from him to her red-faced son. "Where's Oleta? Oleta!"

"She's got her hands full," Drew said, glancing sideways and shaking his head to ward off Oleta, who had moved to answer Cassie's call. "Your baby is cutting his teeth and yowling like a cat in heat. What should I do for him?"

"Give him here." She held out her hands, which he noted were covered with soft cotton gloves, probably to keep her nails from digging into the rash. Most of the time she wore gloves just to be wearing them. Hats, too. Like she wasn't fully dressed unless she had them on.

"No. I asked you what *I* could do for him. You'll rub that poison all over him if you aren't careful."

"No, I won't. I washed."

"I've heard of folks passing it to everyone they touched. You want to take that chance?" He noticed the bowl of white paste on the bed. "What's that?"

"Something I stirred up to put on my rash. It should ease the fire and the itching." She flexed her gloved fingers as if she wanted to claw at her skin but was barely refraining. Andy sucked in a big breath and released a howl of frustrated agony. Tears welled in her eyes. "Poor baby. Wet a rag with cold water and bathe his gums with it. Let him chew and suck on it. Make sure the rag is clean and keep it soaked in as cold a water as you can find."

He nodded and started to leave.

"Wait." She hitched herself higher in the bed. "I'm not finished. Tell Oleta to boil some catnip seeds into a tea and give Andy three spoonfuls. Four if he'll take it."

"Catnip? What the hell will that do?"

"It will calm him."

"Catnip will make him crazy. I've seen cats jump as high as jackrabbits when they get a whiff of it. Why, even a horse will get a little looney if he wades through a swath of that stuff."

"It works different on people," she said, beginning to spread the paste over her arms. "I give it to Andy when he's colicky, too." She flashed him a slicing glance. "I know what I'm doing."

He arched his brows. "He's your baby." He backed out of the room and shut the door. "Oleta, you know anything about brewing up catnip tea?"

"Ah, *sí!*" Her dark eyes lit up. "I forget. That will help the little one." She reached up into a cupboard and drew down a metal container.

"You see to that first, and then we'll worry about supper. I'll take the tray out to Gabe and Tee and eat out there with them."

Oleta smiled shyly. "*Gracias, señor.* With the *señora* ill and the baby having his teeth fever, I am not working so good."

"You're working fine." He smiled fleetingly, then

jostled Andy against his shoulder, trying to appease the bawling bundle, while he found a clean rag and dunked it into a bucket of fresh well water. The liquid was bracing and cold. He wedged the soaked cloth into the baby's mouth. Andy spit and coughed and complained, but then the cold met the fire of his gums and his cries diminished. His eyes rounded, and he grunted and let Drew slide the cloth across his beet-red gums.

"There, there, little man," Drew whispered to him, smiling at the babe's blissful expression. He could feel the bumps of emerging teeth under the baby's gums. "That must hurt like a son of a bitch, but you'll live. Pretty soon you'll be biting the hell out of your mama, and she'll be taking you off the breast."

Mentioning Cassie's breasts sent a shiver of awareness sluicing through him. He steeled himself against the reaction and told himself that as soon as everyone was on the mend, he had to get into Abilene and bed himself a lusty female.

After midnight Cassie left her bed to check on Andy. Since Oleta hadn't placed him in his cradle, Cassie assumed the girl was letting Andy sleep with her so that he wouldn't bother Cassie.

Stepping into the main room, Cassie saw immediately that she was wrong.

Seated in one of the rockers in front of the empty fireplace was Drew Dalton. Sleeping in his arms was her son. Cassie tiptoed forward and realized that Drew, also, was sleeping soundly, his breathing regular and deep, near to snoring but not quite. She stopped to appreciate this sight. Two Daltons. Half brothers. Her gaze moved over the elder Dalton's face in repose. He was undoubtedly a handsome man with his wavy russet hair and tanned skin. Rugged, she thought. Rugged and rangy. Her gaze slid down his long body to the length of his muscled legs. He still wore his dusty work pants, but his belt was unbuckled and his wrinkled shirttail spilled out. Unbuttoned, his shirt hung open, revealing his gleaming chest. Auburn hair grew in an inverted pyramid, the point disappearing under his leather belt with its big, silver buckle glinting in the moonlight.

Cassie tore her gaze from him and was about to take her baby from his arms, but then thought better of it. They were both sleeping peacefully, so what was the harm in allowing them to continue?

She returned on tiptoe to her room and lay awake for several hours, her fevered skin in perfect unison with the feverish thoughts flitting through her tired brain. What was a woman to do when she had such thoughts and no suitable man around to vanquish them?

Turning onto her side, she bowed her back and made her body into a ball, and for the first time since she'd arrived at the Dalton ranch, she thought about getting drunk. But that wouldn't help. After the liquor finally left her bloodstream, the wanting would still be there and the wild, carnal thoughts of Drew Dalton's gleaming chest and how it would feel to run her palms across it and down, down past that shiny buckle to where a woman's delight awaited. Moaning, she reached for her rag doll and clutched it to her breasts.

The next day she continued to cover herself with the paste she'd made from aloe vera plant juice, oatmeal, and soda. The poultice was doing the trick, drying up the rash and cooling her skin.

Drew went out with the other men, leaving her at the house with Oleta and Andy. Standing at the door and looking at her land, Cassie cursed her bad luck. If only she'd noticed the poison ivy, she could have located its antidote—either jewelweed, plantain, or gumweed—which usually grew nearby, and rubbed it over her exposed skin. That would have stopped the rash, and she wouldn't be marooned in the house like somebody's wife. She wasn't a wife anymore, she was a rancher, the boss lady, and she should be out there with her men.

There was work to be done. Real work. Not dusting and mopping and kneading dough. She'd had as much of that as she wanted. Waiting on an ungrateful man who lorded it over her was not her idea of a useful life. It was one thing to *offer* to wait on a man, to *want* to see to his needs, but it was quite another to be *expected* to jump when he bellowed and hurry to him whenever he crooked his finger.

"I hate being indoors," she complained.

"I like it," Oleta said behind her. "The sun, he is so hot today, it's good to stay inside. Andy is better, *si?* He loves sucking on the wet cloth."

"Yes, it eases him," Cassie said, her mind wandering to last night when she'd found Andy asleep in Drew's arms. "What do you think of Drew, Oleta? Do you think he is the type to steal cattle?"

"No, *señora.* He wears honor like a coat."

Cassie smiled at that image. "Like a coat, hmmm? Yes, I suppose he does. A heavy coat. I've rarely seen a more prideful man. He bristles with it. I can't imagine a man like that bringing shame upon himself or his kin. Even if he hated that kin."

"I don't think he hated his papa."

"He says different."

"*Sí*, but I don't hate mine, and he was bad to me. It is not easy to hate one who fathered you. A piece of your heart keeps hoping that your papa really loved you and could not show it."

Cassie thought of her own father, his head stuck so far into the clouds that he couldn't see that his children needed him. Papa Little dragged them from place to place, from stake to stake. They lived in tents, in wagons, sometimes even out in the open. When her mother died, any sense of stability died with her, and the Little children were left to their own devices. Many nights they stole or begged for food. Other nights they went to bed with growling bellies and salty tears drying on their cheeks.

Fathers. Good ones were often in short supply.

Turning slowly, she looked at Andy where he played on a quilt on the floor. He lay on his back and rolled from side to side as he gummed the damp cloth. He made humming noises, then caught her eye and grinned around the cloth. Cassie's heart constricted with intense love, and she dropped to her knees and gathered him close. She kissed his curly head and rocked him, swaying with the love shimmering through her.

Who would have figured she could love someone this much? she mused, and not for the first time. She liked people—her friends Doris McDonald, Adele and Reno Gold—and she felt connected to some—her own siblings, for instance, though she hadn't seen any of them in years and years. But love. She'd never loved anybody, except her mother and father. But the love she'd felt for them was a speck compared to what she felt for Andy. The moment he'd kicked in her womb, she had been seized with an overpowering devotion, which had grown with the child in her belly and had increased tenfold since his birth.

She wanted to give him everything. Did everything include a father to love him?

"Why are you crying?" Oleta asked, bending at the waist to peer into Cassie's face.

"Crying? Am I?" She felt the tears on her cheeks and tried to laugh them off. "I'm being sentimental, like an old lady at the end of her years." Laying the baby on his back, she began changing his diaper. "Oleta, do you ever wish you'd never had a father?" She cocked her head to look at the girl. "You ever wish that?"

Oleta considered the question, then shook her head. "No. I would not wish that, *señora*. Even when he was contrary, which was most of the time, I still would want to know him. Know what he looked like. What he sounded like. After my mama died, who would have kept me if not my papa?"

Cassie sighed. "Yes, it was the same with me. For all his faults, my father didn't completely abandon us. We all left him as soon as we were big enough, but he never turned his back and left us."

"I am glad to be here," Oleta said quickly. "I would not want to go back to my papa's house. But to never know him? To never have a papa? No." She shook her head more vehemently now. "That I would never wish."

Guilt weighed heavily on Cassie until she straightened her shoulders and shrugged it off. She had nothing to feel guilty about. After all, poor Andy's father had up and died. She'd tried to doctor A.J., but he'd been too sick and too old for her meager medicine. Even the town doctor had said there wasn't anything anybody could do for A.J.

If he'd lived, he would have been a sorry father for her Andy. He'd sired the boy, but he wouldn't have had a hand in raising him, other than trying to beat him into submission. It was a wonder Drew had a decent bone in his body or a tender spot in his heart, being raised by the likes of A.J. Dalton.

But Drew was decent, and although he couldn't be called soft-hearted, he had a gentleness about him. With his horses. With her Andy.

"You thinking about *Señor* Drew?"

Cassie's head came up and she narrowed her eyes. "No," she fibbed. "Why'd you ask that?"

Oleta's lips curved into a cunning grin. "No reason. I just saw you smiling a little and I thought . . ." She lifted one shoulder in a graceful gesture of dismissal.

"You thought wrong." Cassie stood and went to the door to look out, wishing again to be in the saddle and involved in something other than her own silly mean-derings about fathers and husbands and the like. The rash on her arms and neck began to itch, and she resisted the urge to scratch. Time for more poultice. "Oh, I hate being cooped up in here!" She swung away from the door and stomped into her bedroom.

At two o'clock in the morning, Cassie paced with Andy in her arms and waited for the catnip tea to brew. The stove's fire had died to embers, and she'd had to replenish it with wood and stoke the coals into flames. Meanwhile Andy fretted and whined and sobbed, be-deviled by his swollen gums. "Hush, baby," Cassie whispered, when Andy's cries grew louder. "Don't wake the house. Once we get this tea down you, you'll feel better. Suck on this cloth.''

But he wouldn't. He shoved the wet rag aside and cried, his little chin quivering and glistening with drool.

The squeak of a floorboard alerted her, and she turned to see Drew climbing down the ladder from the loft. He'd pulled on his trousers and an old shirt, left unbuttoned. His hair stood up in back, mussed by his pillow. He must have seen her eyes on it because he smoothed the unruly hair with the flat of his hand.

''I tried to keep him quiet so he wouldn't wake you,'' Cassie said.

''Is it his gums again?''

''I think so. I don't think it's colic. When this tea boils . . . Ah, finally!''

''Let me take him while you do that,'' Drew said, already removing Andy from her arms so that she could strain the catnip tea and let it cool in a saucer.

''You don't have to trouble yourself,'' she said.

''No trouble. He can't help it, can you, little fella?'' Cradling Andy in one arm, he walked the length of the cabin and spoke as softly to him as he did to his precious horses.

Cassie blew at the tea, transfixed by this man who could be so gentle with her baby, who reached out and plucked him from her arms as if it were the most natural thing in the world for him to care for her son. She wondered what he'd been like as a boy.

''Before you were sent to prison, did you have yourself a girl?'' she asked, speaking before giving thought to how the question might sound to him.

He stopped in his tracks and regarded her intensely

until she felt blood heat the remaining rash patches on her neck, her arms, and her forehead.

"A girl?"

She cleared her throat. "Yes, you know, a lady of your own. Were you courting someone?"

He scowled. "I don't remember."

"Just tell me it's none of my business. That's better than a lie."

"I'm not ly—" He pressed his lips together, interrupting his own denial. "There was a girl. Name of Rosy. But I hear she married a preacher and moved way off to New Hampshire."

"Rosy. Was she pretty like her name?"

"Yeah, I reckon. Pretty enough for a jughead like me." He shifted his gaze to the saucer of tea. "That ready?"

"Yes. Bring him over here." She sat down at the table and took Andy into her lap. Carefully, patiently, she spooned the tea into his mouth and made him swallow it. He fussed and fidgeted, but his cries diminished to grunts and sniveling. She rested him against her breasts and shoulder and rocked back and forth with him. "Thank you," she mouthed.

Drew shrugged, dismissing his acts of kindness.

"You're not a jughead, but you must know that." She wrinkled her nose and pitched her voice to a whisper. "It's called mock vanity. I figure you face yourself in the shaving mirror every morning and see a good-looking man staring back at you. I bet you had more than Rosy trying to catch your eye."

"I don't stare at myself in the mirror. I've got better things to do with my time."

She rolled her eyes. "Speaking of that, I'm riding

with you tomorrow, if I can get this baby to sleep in the next hour.''

"Tomorrow or today?''

She smiled. "I mean, today. Wonder what time it is?''

"Close to two-thirty, I reckon.''

Cassie stretched her neck wearily. "It's going to be another long day.''

Andy raised his head from her shoulder and blinked owlishly at her. Then he looked up at Drew and grinned.

"Hey, there, cowboy. Feeling better?'' Drew placed his hands on his knees and leaned down until his face was level with Andy's. "No more crying? No more . . . Hey! What's that shining in your mouth? Is that a tooth?''

"What? Where?'' Cassie pulled back to get a better look at her son.

"Right there in front. That white spot.''

Cassie eased a finger between Andy's lips and felt his gums, which were noticeably cooler to the touch. The bump was sharp. "A tooth! It's a tooth!'' Smiling happily, she looked to Drew to share the moment of triumph. "His first.''

"The first of many,'' Drew said, smoothing a hand over Andy's blond curls. "Way to go there, little man. Bet that feels better, doesn't it?''

"I can't believe he's growing up so fast,'' Cassie said wistfully. "He's got his first tooth and he's trying to walk. He pulls up on everything so he can stand.'' She caressed her baby's dimpled knees. "Pretty soon he won't need me.''

"Aw, hell, that's a long way off,'' Drew said, scoffing at her sentimentality. "That boy's going to need you when he's got gray in his hair and a bow in his back.

Sons don't get shed of their mamas so quick. If my mama hadn't died, I figure she'd be here with me and I'd be asking her good opinion on just about everything and everyone.''

"Really?" Cassie asked, her heart softening toward him.

"Why, sure." He looked down at his bare feet, and a shy expression crept over his face before he clamped down on it. He brought his head up, his eyes frank, bold. "You think a man like me couldn't love his mother?"

"No, I didn't mean that," she protested, then Andy grabbed a handful of her robe and squealed with delight. She blinked at him and laughed at his antics. "Are you happy about your tooth, baby?"

"He seems to be," Drew observed. "Maybe he'll drop off to sleep before sunrise."

"I hope so."

A crease appeared between Andy's eyes and Cassie knew the sign. He wanted nourishment so that he could fall asleep. Strangely, she found she didn't want to leave Drew's company, although she always had before when she fed Andy from her breast. With her heart anchoring her to the chair, she shifted, angling her back to Drew as she eased open the parting of her robe to let Andy suckle. His lips locked around her nipple, and the pull made her womb tingle and her blood heat. She closed her eyes for a moment, enjoying the pleasant sensations. Looking down into Andy's face, she saw her own milk bubble at the corners of his mouth and his eyelids begin to droop.

Standing behind her, Drew scarcely breathed. He knew he should go back up to the loft and give Cassie privacy while she fed her babe, but he couldn't make his feet move. He gazed over her shoulder at the slope of her breast and the melding of the baby's hungry mouth to her nipple. Soft sucking noises filled the silence, punctuated by an occasional satisfied grunt from Andy. Drew thought he might die. All the blood in his body swam to his loins and stiffened his member.

Shame was what he should be feeling, he knew, not unyielding lust. But there it was, grappling with his mind and overtaking his better judgment. Lust. He wanted to take his father's widow right there, right then. On the floor, the table, in the chair with her baby nearby. He didn't care anymore. The wanting was so immense it squeezed the life out of all reasoning.

Cassie glanced over her shoulder to find that Drew had not moved from his stance near her. Shadow bathed his face. "He's already getting sleepy," she whispered.

Drew's nod was his only response, so she turned back to Andy, watching peace settle over his face. Gradually his lips grew slack and he let go of her nipple. Cassie adjusted the sides of her robe and shifted Andy to lie against her shoulder. Smiling, she looked up, then froze when her gaze connected with Drew's. He had distributed his weight from one foot to the other, and light from the fire in the cookstove now slanted across his face.

Her womb tingled again and her blood heated, but this time for an entirely different reason. She knew that look of longing in his eyes, and her body responded hungrily. Her nipples tightened, and tendrils of sweet sensations flowered in her belly and spread between her thighs. Good Lord, she wanted him to kiss her. No. She wanted far more than that!

As if reading her mind, he leaned down, his face coming closer and closer until his lips were but a fraction of an inch from hers. She could feel his breath upon her face, could see a pulse beating below his left ear. Cassie let her lashes fall and gave herself over to fate.

His lips brushed hers, incredibly warm and soft. With a mewling sigh she leaned into him. His hand cupped the back of her neck and steadied her while his lips opened over hers, sucking gently, making hers slick. She wished she didn't have her baby in her arms so that she could have raked her fingers through his hair and pressed her tender breasts against his bare chest. She couldn't remember the last time she had wanted so much from a man . . . if ever.

Undone by the unconditional surrender of her kiss, Drew took time to explore her taste and the incredible gentleness of her seductive mouth. He curled his fingers at the nape of her neck beneath the soft fall of her hair and breathed in her particular aroma—milk and honey, leather and greening earth. And soda and oatmeal, a corner of his mind registered, making him smile against her lips. The poison ivy rash was nearly gone from her sweet, heart-shaped face, but the scent of the healing paste remained on her skin.

His heart thundered while his mind filed away every detail of these moments. His mouth mated with hers, and his body swayed closer, yearning for a more complete coupling. He sent the tip of his tongue over her lips, and she parted them, wanting to taste him, to fully experience him. Moaning, he took more, but withheld his tongue because he knew if he deepened the kiss, he would be helpless to stop himself. And there was still a sliver of caution left in him, reining him in, scrambling for control.

His mouth continued to court hers, lifting and pressing, one kiss quickly followed by another until her lips tingled and throbbed. *More, more*, she chanted to herself. She wanted more than kisses. *Needed* more.

"Drew . . . oh, Drew . . ." The sound of her own voice emerging in a husky, lust-laden whisper brought her back to herself. She stiffened away from him, suddenly ashamed to be kissing him ardently with her son held between them. "I-I—uhmm." She looked down at Andy. "I can't do this." Not now, she thought. Why did he start this when she was holding her baby? His timing left much to be desired.

"You're right." He shoved himself away from her and walked backward until he bumped into the sofa. "I shouldn't have. But, well . . ."

"Don't apologize," she implored him, not wanting to end this sweet session on that sour note. And did it have to end? Couldn't he suggest that she put the baby in his cradle and come back to him, up to the loft with him? She trembled, shocked by her own wanton thoughts. This was the man she hadn't trusted, the man who wanted to take all that was hers, except for her son.

"Nothing to apologize for," he said almost angrily.

"That's right. We're both grown."

He nodded, looking awkward for the first time since she'd met him. "But it's wrong. 'Night." He turned and climbed the ladder, his movements uncommonly jerky.

"Good night." She stood slowly so as not to awaken Andy and went to her bedroom. After placing Andy in his cradle, she covered him with a light blanket. What had Drew meant about it being wrong to kiss her? Was he simply taking what she'd blurted out and agreeing with her, trying to appease her? Or did he think it was wrong to kiss his father's widow?

Cassie sat on the edge of the bed and twisted the cotton spread in her hands. It *was* wrong, she told herself sternly. Wrong, wrong, wrong to be entertaining notions of kissing and caressing a man like Drew Dalton. A man who lived right under the same roof with her and was hell-bent on taking over her ranch and running it as he saw fit.

Yes, his kisses were a soothing balm to what ailed her, but they weren't worth the ranch and her future, her son's future. No man's kisses were worth that.

Oh, but his lips had been so soft . . . and arousing.

She fell back on the bed with a tortured groan and stared at the fly-specked ceiling until dawn crept across it, coloring it coral and then gold. Her head and heart hammered, but she rose up, determined to join the men today, determined to look Drew Dalton in the eye and not flinch, and determined to act as if nothing had happened between them.

Chapter 7

⟡

Throwing down the bale of wire, Cassie glared at the crown of Drew's dark-blue hat. "You know, we can't go on acting as if nothing happened between us."

He whirled on the balls of his feet and peered up at her. "Why not?"

"Because that's what kids do. We kissed and that's that. We should own up to it."

"I never disowned it." He swiveled back to the fence he was mending.

"The hell you say! You've not said a word and hardly even looked at me. When I said I'd ride with you today and leave T-Bone to ride with Gabe, you almost choked. Don't be grumbling and swearing under your breath, Drew Dalton. I saw you gulp like you'd swallowed a bug."

"Maybe I did swallow a bug. Maybe my mood this morning has nothing to do with you."

"Oh? Then why are you as sore-tempered as a broke-tailed cat?" she challenged, hands on her hips.

"Because so far this morning I've spied six of our

cattle grazing on Monroe's land, that's why." He straightened and pulled taut the wire he'd strung to repair the fence. "I reckon we should wait for his hands to weed them out and bring them to us, but it galls me to see the Square D brand mixed in with the Star H cattle."

She jutted out one hip and her lower lip. "Cattle on your mind, huh?"

"That's right. Should be on your mind, too."

"Oh, they are," she assured him, looking past him to the cows lowing in the distance. "Roe will bring ours back to us. He's been nothing but fair with me."

"Yeah, I noticed."

She frowned. "If you're going to fume about every man who looks walleyed at me, then you're going to be in a perpetual sod-pawin', horn-tossin' mood."

He cocked his head and examined her from beneath the deep brim of his hat. "I don't believe I ever met a woman who set a greater store on herself than you."

"I just don't cotton to acting like I don't know how I look or how men look at me. Unlike some others, who pretend they don't admire their reflection and pretend they haven't lifted a few skirts in their time."

"You talking about me?" He arched one brow.

"You going to keep acting like you're stupid?"

The brow lowered to join its mate and form a dark bridge of displeasure. "Are you spoiling for a fight this morning, Cassie?"

"I'm trying to clear the air. We're going to have to work together, and it's plumb silly for us not to talk about us locking lips last night."

He narrowed his blue eyes. "Call me stupid once more and . . ."

"And what?" she sassed, angling up her chin, making it a target.

His gaze didn't linger on her chin but on her mouth. Memories of that mouth had cost him sleep last night and fogged his brain this morning. Kissing her had shattered his previous notion of what constituted a good kiss. Hell, kissing her was better than the sex he'd had! But he didn't like these feelings he fostered for her because they were damned dangerous. He'd come back to stake his claim on the land, not on his old man's young widow.

Although he badly wanted to crush her mouth beneath his, he shoved her aside with rough disregard and strode to his horse. Swinging up into the saddle, he looked down at her flushed face and fisted hands.

"Are we going to jaw all day or work?"

"Coward." She stomped across the ground to her horse and almost sprang into the saddle.

Drew issued a grunt of derision and swung Dynamite around to follow the fence line. He heard Cassie's horse behind him but kept his mind focused on the land and his place on it.

"It's been so dry lately, I'm going to check the creek level," she announced, then spurred her mount toward a thicket of trees.

Drew released a long sigh of relief. The woman was a trial. Of course, he hadn't made things easier for himself by lovin' up on her. But he'd suffered for it, lying awake most of the night thinking about her mouth, its heat and seduction. Lord God, the woman could kiss! He'd wanted to plunge his tongue into the simmering pool of her mouth, but he'd known he would drown there, sucked into the whirlpool of longing.

For a gal who had men lining up for her, she sure was quick to spark. Maybe she'd been waiting for the right man—

"Whoa up there, son," he said to himself, and Dynamite stopped in his tracks. Shaking his head and chuckling at his own mutterings, he spurred Dynamite on. "Sorry, boy. I should get my mind on my work, I guess." He focused outward instead of inward and immediately saw a wide depression in the grass ahead of him. Frowning, he examined the area, not liking the story the flattened grass told him. What the hell—?

He slid off Dynamite and walked the fence, looking for any sign of damage. He'd not taken twenty strides when he discovered a wobbly fence post. Testing it, he determined that the post was merely propped into the ground and could be lifted and set aside to make a wide gate for cattle to run through. He followed the beaten path toward the fringe of trees that bordered a creek. He found Cassie there.

She squatted at the edge of the creek and used her hat as a bucket, bringing it to her lips for a drink. Glancing toward him, she nodded at the chewed up earth around her.

"Something funny here," she remarked.

He dismounted and examined the evidence of a herd being watered. The Square D cattle had several watering holes and didn't converge on just one. "Back there I found a loose fence post. Somebody's driven a herd across here." He looked around, trying to see where the tracks led.

"The tracks go up that way," she said, reading his mind and pointing south. "But they fade out. The ground is dry and the grass scarce the farther you get away from the creek. The prints turn to dust. We don't let the herd graze much in that section. At least, not until we get a rain. The soil there is too poor and needs to lie fallow this year. Maybe next. You think Roe would let a herd in here to graze?"

"Roe? Why would he?"

"Some of his grazing land is getting bad, and he doesn't put aside sections for wheat and hay fields like we do."

"Since when does he not have hay fields?"

"He hasn't since I've been here. He told me it's too much trouble and he'd rather buy what he needs. I think he might have one hay field, a small one."

"Well, I guess he knows what he's doing." Drew shrugged. That's not how he liked to run a ranch, but he and Monroe had never seen eye to eye on that. Monroe spent too much money on silly things like red buggies and brass- and gold-fitted bridles. To buy all the hay needed on a cattle ranch seemed purely ignorant, but since he didn't know how much money Monroe had, he couldn't judge the man fairly. Maybe Roe had too many cows and not enough grazing land for them, so he had to let them into the fields he would normally use to grow hay or wheat. It was a thought.

Cassie straightened and stretched, swaying from side to side to work out the kinks. "So what should we do?"

"They must have crossed Roe's land, too," Drew said. "I think I'll ride over and ask him if he knows anything about it."

"Let me." She replaced her hat on her shimmering hair, which she'd gathered into a tail that swung down her back. "You'll bark at him like a mad dog."

He stepped closer and nudged the underside of her

chin with his forefinger. "I told you before, Roe and me go way back. I don't have to bat my eyelashes at him and make my voice like honey to get his attention, but I assure you that I can discuss this with him without riling him."

She edged away, her eyes snapping. "Go ahead, but don't go telling him that you're the boss man around here."

"Is that what you're worried about?"

"I'm not worried about nothing. I just don't want you spreading tales behind my back."

He mounted Dynamite again. "I don't have to fill Roe in on my place on this ranch. He already knows I'm my father's son and rightful heir. You're the only one in this county who isn't clear on that." He tugged the brim of his hat and swung Dynamite around, spurring him into a gallop to drown out any retort she might have made.

Drew returned to the ranch a couple of hours later. He had engaged Monroe in a companionable conversation but had learned little about the cattle crossing. He and Monroe had ridden to where the tracks were visible, and Monroe had been puzzled by the discovery. They had agreed to keep each other informed of any other strange activity in the area.

Reining in Dynamite, Drew caught sight of a spotted horse tethered to the hitching post near the house. He recognized it.

Giving a whoop, he leaped off Dynamite and was heading for the porch when he heard a familiar voice call out to him. Spinning about, he grinned at the long-legged, long-haired *hombre* striding toward him.

"Ice! It's about time you got here, you ornery polecat.'' He reached out to shake the younger man's hand and pull him close for a quick hug. "Damn, if it's not good to see you! How's your family in San Antonio?"

"They're fat and fit," Ice said, a blazing white smile splitting his dusky face. His midnight hair, brushed rakishly back from his forehead, fell to his shoulders, and his silvery gray eyes sparkled with mischievous lights. He reached out to finger Drew's leather vest. "You didn't get this in prison, my friend."

"It's one of a kind. Made by a saddle maker I know. You like it?"

"*Sí, gracias.* How much you want for it?"

Drew batted away his hand and laughed. "You don't have enough money on you, pal." He traded grins with Ice. "Damn, if you aren't a sight for these sore eyes!"

"This is some fine place you have here. And your papa's widow!" Ice shook his hand as if he'd burned it. "Woowee! You lucky coyote." Giving a wink, he added, "The young housekeeper isn't bad either."

"You took your sweet time getting here."

"Ah, my mama wouldn't let me go. She loves her youngest son." He laughed. "One of my sisters got married, and I stayed a few extra days to attend her wedding. There was much news, too. Seems I have some relatives who are landing in prison and getting shot for stealing cattle and robbing stagecoaches and trains out by Laredo. They are giving the Perez family a bad name." He chuckled. "I had to swear to my mama that I would not take up with them, that I would be a good little boy."

"I envy you your family ties," Drew said, admitting something he usually kept to himself. But he'd formed a quick and lasting relationship with Pedro "Ice" Perez since their first meeting in a saloon in Abilene a few months before Drew had been charged with cattle rustling. When word had reached Ice, Drew had already been judged guilty and sentenced. Ice had visited him in jail only a few hours before Drew was to be transported to prison. In his hour of need, Ice had come through for Drew, taking Dynamite to his family home in Texas for safekeeping.

"And I envy you your fine taste." He eyed Drew's vest again. "And *your* family ties," he added with a grin.

"Yeah, you've met Cassie." Drew glanced toward the house. Oleta was standing in the doorway but ducked out of sight.

"*Sí, señor,*" Ice said, laughing a little. "She told me to wait here for you. Then I met the shy Oleta and then I scouted your bunkhouse. How many men you got working for you?"

"Two."

Ice made a choking sound and reared back on his boot heels. "On a spread this size? You're hiring more soon?"

"Not on the money we've got right now, no. I'll have to sell some of the herd this spring before I can allow for extra men. Besides, when I was in Abilene, I was given a cold welcome. I might be a free man, but to most people around here I'm guilty. The only men who have shown an interest in this ranch are those hankering to steal it or its livestock."

"Then it is good I have arrived to save the day, eh?" Ice laughed and wrapped a sinewy arm around Drew's neck. He stood an inch or two shorter than Drew. Four years younger and ten times more demonstrative, he treated Drew like an older, much-revered brother.

The two tussled like boys for a few minutes, laughing and shadowboxing, trading handholds and punching each other in the ribs and arms. Out of breath, Drew pushed Ice away with a grunt of satisfaction.

"You're just what I needed, Ice. I was feeling low as a snake's belly, but now that I've got your ugly face to look at, my spirits have lifted."

"Ugly face?" Ice glanced around. "Who are you talking about, *compadre*? Not me. Oh, not me, because I am one fine-looking man." He puffed out his chest. "I leave ladies swooning and men cursing their bad luck for not being as pretty as me."

Drew laughed, glad for the diversion of nonsense. His visit with Monroe had left him feeling unsettled. Roe was cordial and as helpful as he could be, but Drew sensed that Roe didn't trust him. The feeling was mutual.

Ice leaned closer. "I have brought two fine horses, *amigo*. I bought them off my new brother-in-law, who gave me a very good price. They are fine stock."

"Where are they?"

"In the corral," he said, gesturing in the general direction.

"I don't have the money now to buy them from you. I bought three mares in Abilene the other day and—"

"Did I ask for money?" Ice asked, spreading a hand over the front of his dark shirt and black, silver-studded vest. "You offend me. I have brought them to buy my way into a partnership, my friend. A partnership with you."

Drew narrowed one eye. "What do you have up your sleeve?"

"Nothing. I have a business proposition. I will work

here for you. I will learn from you, and we will become well-known horse breeders. For this I offer the blood-red stallion and gray mare now in your corral. Good breeding stock, my friend.'' A smile inched up one corner of his mouth. ''Quarter horses.''

''You speak my language,'' Drew said, clapping Ice on the shoulder. ''Welcome to the Square D, partner.''

They shook hands, then strolled to the corral to inspect the additions to their herd.

Riding across the flat land, Cassie spotted the two men at the corral. She veered Sweet Pea in that direction. Nearing the area, she studied the dark-red stallion and big gray mare, her irritation mounting. Had Drew bought *more* horses after lecturing her about how they had to cut their spending to the bone until they had sold some of their cows?

She'd met up with Ice on the trail that led to the house. He'd introduced himself and inquired after Drew. She'd wondered then if he was bringing those two horses to Drew, and she figured he would ask a pretty price for them. Had Drew already bought them without telling her, without consulting her? Her blood began to boil. Damn his arrogant hide!

Dropping out of the saddle, she stalked to the corral, barely acknowledging Ice's warm greeting and Drew's quick tug on his hat brim.

''What's going on here?'' she asked, trying and failing to soften her tone.

''Just two partners building a dream,'' Ice answered. ''Good to see you again. Your house girl showed me your son. He is as handsome as a new rope on a thirty-dollar pony.''

Cassie couldn't help but preen with motherly pride, although that stuff about a dream rattled her. "Thanks. He's precious, that's for sure." She eyed Drew with suspicion. "Partners?" She knew she was on the right trail when Drew dropped his gaze. The skunk. She turned to Ice. "You said something about partners?"

"Yes, me and Drew. We are going to raise horses together."

"Oh? Where?"

"Where?" Ice glanced at Drew, worry creasing his brow. "Why, right here, *señora,* on Drew's ranch."

"On *Drew's* ranch," she repeated.

"Now, hold up, Cassie," Drew drawled. "Don't go snorting and kicking like a—"

Sounds good to me, Cassie thought a second before connecting her boot with his shin. She noticed that his new partner took a backward step, distancing himself, and she admired his good sense.

"Ow, damn it!" Drew grabbed his shin and hopped around on one foot. "I ought to shake you till your eyes cross!"

"Just you try it, Junior, and I'll give you what I gave your old man." She balled up a fist and shook it in his face. "I'll shell your teeth with this."

Drew stared at the puny fist stuck in his face and couldn't help but grin. She sputtered, so angry she couldn't form any words, and he grabbed her fist and brought it sharply down to her side.

"You hit my old pa, did you?"

"Knocked out his front tooth," she bragged.

Damn, if she wasn't pretty when she was hot with temper! He still had hold of her fist, and he slid his thumb across the scampering pulse in her wrist. Instantly something changed in her face. Something changed in him, too. He let go of her and beat down the desire rising in him like a gusher.

"Ice brought these horses and is going to work here with us. Yes, we're partners," he said before she could ask it again, "and that's that. It's got nothing to do with my agreement with you."

"I told you I don't want you strutting around and telling folks that this ranch is yours. What did he just say?" she challenged. "He called this 'Drew's ranch.' " She rounded on Ice. "This spread belongs to me, and *I* say who is hired and who is shown the door. You've shaken hands with the Devil, mister, but it won't get you work on this ranch!"

"Damn it all, that's enough!" Drew clamped down on his temper as he seized her elbow and thrust her ahead of him. "Excuse us, Ice. Unsaddle your horse and stow your gear in the bunkhouse while I speak to Cassie. Make yourself at home."

"Sure thing. Don't mind me." Ice tipped his hat at Cassie before Drew could hustle her around the corner of the barn and out of his sight.

Cassie snatched her elbow from Drew's grasp and sent him a smoldering glare. "Don't you start bawling me out about—"

"No, *you* listen to *me*," he said between clenched teeth. "We need another hand on this ranch and you know it. Ice is a good man, and he's working for practically nothing because he's a friend of mine and he's interested in learning all he can about horse breeding." He gripped her upper arms and gave her a shake. "I've let you talk to me like I'm a mangy dog, but I won't let you talk to Ice that way. You got that?" When she didn't speak, he gave her another shake. "Answer me."

"Yes," she hissed, and he let go of her. She backed away from him and rubbed her arms. "You're just like your father. A brute."

"That's right, missy, I *am* my father's son. Ask anybody in this county and they'll tell you that I'm good for nothing, that I'm a cattle thief, that I'm not worth killing. But remember, your own baby was sired by the same old bull, so you might want to hold your tongue about the bad blood flowing in the Dalton veins." He started to turn away but stopped to look back at her. "And I'm going to tell Ice about the situation we have here with the ownership of this ranch. When you rode up, I hadn't had time to say much more than a howdy-do to him." He strode around the corner of the barn to rejoin his friend.

Cassie blew out a breath of frustration and massaged the ache out of her upper arms. That man could fire her temper as surely as he could fire her womanly desires, and that was right unsettling. What was even more unsettling was that he'd been right in everything he'd said to her. She'd jumped the gun, and she shouldn't have torn into him in front of his saddle pal. She'd handled the whole thing wrong.

It wasn't like her. Usually she had a good head on her shoulders and was careful not to trample feelings. Head down, she made her way to the house. Moving dispiritedly into her bedroom, she felt like a child who had been roundly scolded.

Chapter 8

Drew would probably spend the night in the bunkhouse with his buddy and the other men, Cassie thought as she settled in one of the rockers after supper. He'd eaten with them, preferring their company to hers and Oleta's. The evening meal had been inordinately quiet without him, and now the time stretched out like an endless road before her, much to Cassie's consternation.

Andy was fed, diapered, and asleep. Oleta had retired to her room to read and write letters to her aunts and uncles in Texas and Mexico. Cassie thought of going to bed, but she wasn't tired. She'd entered a few items in her journal, noting the signs of a herd crossing the land and the arrival of Ice.

Now she rocked and stared at the empty fireplace grate, her thoughts returning to the quarrel she'd had with Drew. Did he think he was punishing her by not gracing her with his company? She made a derisive sound. She hoped he never ate with her again or slept in the loft! That would suit her mighty fine indeed. She liked having the house to herself, just her and Oleta and Andy. That's how it should be. Wasn't right for him to be staying—

The front door opened, letting in the far-off cry of a wolf . . . and Drew Dalton. He bobbed his head in a greeting and carried a tub full of soiled dishes to the sink.

"Supper was good. That beefsteak was so tender I could have cut it with my spoon."

She nodded but held her tongue. He clattered dishes, and Oleta opened her bedroom door and started out, but Drew waved her off.

"These are soaking in water and will hold until morning."

Oleta smiled and began closing the door. *"Gracias, Señor* Drew."

"Sleep well, Oleta." He turned toward Cassie. "Something got you sleepless?"

She shifted in the chair, feeling antsy and irritable. She'd cut out her tongue before admitting that he was on her mind, so she tackled a less dangerous subject. "I was thinking about the herd that crossed our land. Whoever drove them sure was as bold as brass. You think other herds have been taken across there, what with that fence pole loose and all?"

He sat on the sofa across from her, his long legs bent at the knee but his boots still crowding hers in the space between the sofa and rocker. "Hard to say. Once is enough. We'll have to keep our eyes peeled."

"I forgot to ask—did Monroe have anything to say about it?"

"Nope." He ran his tongue along the inside of his cheek and stared up at the ceiling for a few moments. "I met his new man. Used to work for a big spread in Texas. Calls himself a Regulator, which is a fancy name for a fella who is trigger-happy. Roe says he's planning to increase his herd and improve his stock. Before I went to prison, Monroe Hendrix was more interested in playing cards and chasing women than he was in breeding cattle. He sure has changed his tune.''

"Maybe he finally got shed of his boyhood," Cassie remarked. "We all have to grow up sometime. He's . . . about forty, I guess."

"Yeah, he turned forty last month."

"And how old are you?" she asked, surprised that she wanted to know the answer so badly.

"Twenty-eight. Are you even twenty yet?"

"I will be—in two months."

"That's what I thought."

She didn't care for his droll tone and decided to shift the conversation back to Monroe. "Could be Roe is short on funds, just like us, and he realized he wasn't going to make any money at poker and courting."

Drew narrowed his eyes to blue slats. "Not unless he courts someone who has an adjoining ranch.'

Cassie didn't bother to comment on that. She stared at the fireplace grate and gritted her teeth, refusing to be drawn into another verbal brawl with him.

After a few minutes, he chuckled and stretched out on the sofa, his boots hanging off one end. "So why did your pa let you marry an old man like mine?"

"My pa was dead long before I answered A.J.'s ad for a wife."

"You must have been plenty desperate."

"I was tired of having nothing of my own." She crossed one leg over the other beneath her long skirt and swung her foot. Her past visited her, coated her in melancholy. "My ma died when my family was making its way to the California coast. My pa was a wanderer, a dreamer, always looking to get rich without having to do much in the way of labor. He believed every wild story he heard about gold mines and buried treasure and winning land in poker games. But he was the unluckiest man who ever drew a breath.'' She closed her eyes, seeing her father's thin face. His features were hazy, diminished by the years. "He was handsome and selfish. Poor Mama couldn't keep up with him, so she fell behind. She was real sick, but Papa kept on going, chasing his dreams. I don't even remember where Papa buried Mama. Somewhere between Montana and California. I remember I bawled for days and days. All us kids did. But Papa kept on going. He had gold fever.''

"I guess he didn't strike gold."

"No." She laughed with scorn. "He struck bottom, that's what. The older kids left and I finally did, too, because Papa was never around and I was on my own anyway. I kept house for an old woman for a few months and then I . . ." She shrugged, unable to tell him what she'd done after that to make a living. "I got by."

"Then you happened on this wrongheaded idea to marry a stranger. Didn't you know any better? Wasn't there anybody around with enough sense to talk you out of it?"

She delivered an arch look. "I'll have you know that I know a couple who got together through an ad, and they're as happy as fish in a mountain stream. They're friends of mine, and that's what gave me the idea. *She* ordered *him*."

He frowned. "That's the dumbest thing I ever heard."

Shifting onto his side, Drew felt his initial disgust dissolve when he saw the stars in Cassie's eyes and the beatific expression on her face. Transfixed, he bit back any other caustic comments in favor of her flushed cheeks and dreamy eyes.

"The man is very handsome and a complete gentleman," she said. "His name is Reno. Isn't that a pretty name?"

Drew nodded, although "pretty" wasn't a word he used often—except for now, when he looked at Cassie.

"The woman knew him before, when they were kids. Her name is Adele."

"So they weren't strangers."

"No, but they hadn't seen each other in years. At first they didn't get along, but before many weeks passed, I could tell they were falling for each other. Shoot, I figure they loved each other back when they were children. They just didn't know it."

"So did she send him a letter and propose to him?"

"No. She placed an ad, and he saw it and answered."

"Why? If he was so special, why did he have to answer an ad to get some woman to marry him?"

"I don't know all the particulars." She frowned and cast him a sour look. "All I know is that they're happy and they have a baby girl now. They called her Katy, named after a railroad line. Trains played a big part in bringing Reno and Adele back together." She released a long sigh and slid her clasped hands over her bent knee. Her eyes glowed with romance.

She was a puzzle, he decided, admiring the sheen of her skin and hair, the tilt of her chin, the delicious shape of her mouth. Full of quirks and surprises, she was a woman hard to figure. She never left the house without wearing some kind of hat and gloves, but he guessed that was okay since her skin was flawless and she had the smoothest hands he'd ever felt.

''That doll you've got on your bed. Is that for your baby?'' he asked, suddenly remembering the rag doll he'd seen the night she'd been afflicted with poison ivy.

She shook her head. ''She's mine. Her name is Miss Tess, after the lady who gave her to me when I was a little girl. She wore the prettiest hats and gloves you ever did see.'' A peaceful expression settled on her face. ''Miss Tess . . . I wanted to be exactly like her when I grew up.''

So that's why she wore those gloves and hats! To be like Miss Tess. *That's Cassie*, he thought, strutting about like a great lady sometimes and then working like a man on the ranch. Something she'd said earlier that day continued to nag at him, and although he didn't want to erase that dreamy expression on her face, he had to voice it.

''My old man didn't . . . force himself on you, did he? That's not why you knocked his tooth out.''

As he'd feared, the pleasure bled from her face along with the pink color. Frowning and ashen now, she shook her head.

''He never forced me, but he slapped me. Finally I got enough of it and I hit him back. Made him think twice before hauling off and slugging me again. Didn't stop him, but it slowed him up a bit.''

Drew jerked his gaze away from her, a mantle of undeserved guilt weighing him down. Damn the old man for putting her through even more hell! Seemed like she'd had very few men she could count on for more than fat lips and broken dreams. The little gal had been through tough times, and it was a wonder she wasn't as mean as a desert rattler.

''Seeing as how we're trading stories about our

lives,'' she said, looking sideways at him, ''I was wondering . . .''

He tensed. ''About what?''

''Prison.''

Propping his head in one hand, he smiled faintly. ''I can't recommend it.''

''Did you meet anybody famous there?''

''Famous for what?''

''You know, gunslingers or bank robbers.''

''I kept to myself. Didn't make any friends there.'' He rolled onto his back and laced his fingers on his chest. Talk of prison cast bars of shadow across his heart and shackled his soul.

''Did they feed you? I've heard that they only give you bread and water.''

''They fed us, but it was pig slop. Watery soup, dry bread, stringy meat. We had rice and beans nearly every damn day. Nothing was seasoned. We never had any sweets. I used to dream of pies and cobblers until I'd wake up with my stomach tied in knots.''

''You've got a sweet tooth, huh?''

''I used to, but prison life got rid of it. You learn to stop dreaming of things you can't have. Once the hope is gone, the dreams stop and you're empty inside, but that's better than thinking of getting out and heading for home or wishing for a woman.'' He cleared his throat, realizing he'd trod on a touchy subject and said more than he'd intended. ''Prison life isn't really a life at all. It's just one damned day after another.''

''I guess you were bitter, being locked up and innocent.''

''If it hadn't been for the hate, I would have had nothing to occupy me. I used to devise ways of getting out.

I'd dream about coming back here and beating my old man to a bloody pulp for not sticking up for me.''

"You didn't make even one friend while you were there?''

Dark memories crowded his mind. "No. I tried to stay out of everyone's way. There were men there that''— he swallowed the sour taste in his mouth—"they got pleasure out of taking a man's dignity.'' Unable to bear the sharp memories, he sat up and rubbed his hands up and down his face.

"You okay?'' Cassie asked, her voice small and soft.

"Yeah,'' he said, almost grunting, then he stood and made for the ladder. "See you in the morning.''

"Did you straighten out everything with your new partner?''

"Yeah. His name is Ice and he's a friend of mine, Cassie. He's the only man I trust in this world. I don't know how long he'll stay, but I do know we're damn lucky to have him working here. He'll be more help than four T-Bones and ten Gabes.'' He took hold of the ladder and started up.

"Which woman did you wish for while you were in prison?''

Her question froze him for a second, but then he continued on. "One with two breasts, two legs, and two lips,'' he answered drolly. "And one who didn't talk except to say yes.'' He grinned when he heard her exhale with affront.

But that night, as he lay on his pallet in the loft, he wished for something more than body parts and a pliable will. That night, much to his distress and self-loathing, he wished for Cassie.

*   *   *

That Sunday after church Cassie put Andy in the swing she'd fashioned from an old saddlebag and hung it from a big hook on the porch. He kicked and waved his chubby arms, squealing with glee, as she gave him a gentle push.

"You love this, don't you?" she asked, grinning at him. "You think you're flying, sweet boy?" She gave him another push, then sat in a porch chair and watched her son enjoy himself. She looked around, wondering where the men had disappeared to after church—those who had gone to services, that is. Drew and Ice had sent word with T-Bone that they wouldn't be joining the others in the wagon bound for the Wooden Cross Church, halfway between the ranch and Abilene. When they'd returned to the ranch, Ice and Drew were nowhere to be found.

During church she'd been asked by several people if it was true that Drew was back. Their worried expressions bothered her, making her wonder if her neighbors were going to hold Drew liable for a crime he hadn't committed. Was that why he'd decided not to go to church? Had he already endured their neighbors' cold shoulder?

She spotted a horse and rider in the distance and recognized Monroe Hendrix. He waved and she waved back. He was riding a big roan, which he reined in at the porch.

"Afternoon, Monroe," Cassie greeted him. "Care for some apple cider?" She reached for the pitcher and started pouring before he could answer.

"Don't mind if I do." Monroe dismounted and wrapped the reins around the hitching post. "I looked for you after church, but you'd already loaded up and left before I could get outside."

"Andy was fussing and hungry," she explained. "Did you need to talk to me about something?"

"Not really." He sat in the chair next to hers and accepted the glass of cider. "Thank you, Cassie." He looked at Andy and smiled. "Your little one seems to like that swing."

"Yes, and it's good for him to kick like that. Builds his muscles. He'll be walking soon."

"How is everything around here, Cassie? Drew's not giving you too much trouble, is he?"

"Not too much. We've reached an agreement for now."

"That's good." He settled back in the chair and sipped the cider. "Ah, that goes down good. Nice day, isn't it? That breeze puts me in mind of a day a year or two ago when I took out my new hunting dog and ran into a covey of quail like you've never seen. . . ."

His voice continued, but the words ceased making sense as Cassie's thoughts shifted to Drew. No, he wasn't much trouble. If he'd get it out of his head that she would eventually leave this ranch to him, she wouldn't mind having him around.

Remembering the feel of his mouth on hers, she crossed her arms and gripped her elbows as a tingle raced through her. Sometimes she caught him looking at her, his blue eyes alight with feelings that she was too timid to translate. That kind of attention from any other man would disturb her, but with Drew she was pleased and a little proud to be enticing to such a man. For he was not only handsome, but strong and smart. She wondered if he and Ice had gone into town looking for female company. Jealousy knifed through her.

". . . but I'm boring you with my hunting stories," Monroe said, leaning forward to touch her arm. "Could I trouble you for more of that cider, Cassie?"

"What?" She blinked, her thoughts returning to the man who was looking at her curiously. "Cider? Oh, yes. Let me." She poured more into his empty glass, noticing that a tremble ran through her arm and that her heart was beating too fast. Seemed like she couldn't even think about Drew Dalton without getting shaky. She hated that.

"You know the acorn doesn't fall far from the tree."

"What?" she asked again, trying hard to focus on the man present instead of the man absent. "What's that you said?"

"Something my mother used to tell me when I was running around with what she felt were the 'wrong kind of folk.' " Monroe smiled almost indulgently. "I was thinking of Drew and I sensed you were, too. He has you puzzled, I see."

"He's hard to figure," she admitted.

"Just remember that the acorn doesn't fall far from the tree," he repeated. "He was raised by A.J., and when you give lessons in cruelty to a critter or a person, you shouldn't be surprised when he turns mean." He shrugged. "Some things are learned and others are inbred. A.J. was a bad husband because he had no respect for women. Just remember, Drew's a Dalton."

Cassie ground her teeth and fought to control her temper. "And you might remember that my son is also a Dalton, and I don't believe for a minute that he's inherited cruelty or any other such nonsense."

"Of course . . . I didn't mean . . ." Monroe's face

flushed red, and he pushed a hand through his hair in a nervous gesture. "Forgive me, I didn't mean to insult you. It's just that, well, Drew is a hard man and he's been through a lot. While I think this ranch is too much for you, I don't think Drew has your best interests at heart when he suggests that you move to town and find work there. He only wants the ranch."

"I know that." She eyed Monroe, testy that he'd think she was thick-headed. "But he's a man, Roe, just like you, and the ranch ain't the only thing he's had his eye on lately."

She knew she should be ashamed to tease him, but she couldn't help it. Jealousy blazed in his eyes and tensed his mouth. Served him right to feel the sting of competition. Men were men, no matter what they'd been through or who sired them. She'd learned that early in her life, and it had served her well.

"He's tried something already?" Monroe asked. "You want me to talk to him, set him straight?"

"I can take care of myself," she said, fluffing her skirt and pushing a wispy curl off her temple. "If he needs talking to, I've got words just like you."

"Yes, but I can speak to him man to man."

She smiled. "I appreciate that, but like I said, I can take care of myself. The sooner you and Drew understand that, the better."

"And the sooner you understand that running a ranch this size is too much for a little lady, the better for you. I'm only trying to help you out, Cassie. I count you as a friend and I hope you count me as one."

"You know I do, Monroe." She reached and patted his hand, and he captured her fingers before she could withdraw them. Cassie stiffened, wishing he'd let her go.

Suddenly she felt trapped and anxious, although his grasp was not that confining. He brought the back of her hand up to his lips for a soft kiss before he released her.

Uneasy, she grabbed her glass of cider and faced front, her body language speaking for her. She had to admit that she was flattered to be courted by Monroe Hendrix. He was surely the most admired bachelor in the county, and everybody knew he was smitten with her. Yes, she was flattered, but she couldn't say that she was swept off her feet by him. Try as he might, he just couldn't seem to make her pulse go giddyup.

"Cassie, would you do something for me? One friend to another?"

"What?"

"Go to the barn dance with me."

"The barn dance?" She furrowed her brow, then remembered. "Oh, yes, *your* barn dance this Friday night." The thought of music and laughter appealed to her, but she shook her head. "I can't leave Andy."

"What about the Mexican girl? Can't she watch him?"

"Oleta will want to go to the dance, and I wouldn't think of saddling her with my baby. She's young and pretty and she needs to get out and kick up her heels."

"Then bring the baby," Monroe said, and his offer seemed genuine. "Me and you and little Andy, we'll have a fine time, and you can show off your son. Why, the women will be cooing and making over him something awful."

"I don't know. He's so young. I couldn't stay out late with him. I put him to bed pretty early."

"There will be plenty of laps at the dance," Monroe

said. "You've seen all those grannies and young girls rocking babies at the dances."

She hesitated, then surrendered to the notion. "Okay, I guess I could go. I'd like to get away from this place for a few hours. You know that since Andy was born, I haven't been out much except into town for supplies, and then I've had to hightail it right back here. Of course, once in a while I sup with you, which I enjoy."

"Me, too. I'm so pleased you'll let me be your escort. You'll be my hostess. Won't that be grand?" Monroe finished his cider and stood up. "I'll be getting back to my side of the fence." He sent her a wink. "See you Friday night. I'll be around to collect you and Andy right before sundown. You can help me greet all our neighbors."

"We'll be ready. Thanks for asking, Roe."

"I'll be the envy of every man at the dance."

She flapped a hand. "Monroe Hendrix, you're as slick as a greased saddle rope."

Chuckling under his breath, he moved off the porch and pulled himself up into the saddle. "Good day to you, Cassie."

She waved, her mind already busy with what she'd wear. Now she wished she hadn't thrown that dress back into Drew's face. Had Blue Eyes taken it back to town? If not, she might be able to buy it off him. Oh, it would be wonderful to be the hostess at Monroe Hendrix's annual barn dance. Everyone in the whole county would be there. She wondered if Drew could step to the music, or if he owned two left feet. Guess she'd find out soon enough!

* * *

Cassie moved up behind Drew, bent over a wash bucket, dunking his arms in up to the elbows. Splashing water into his face, he scrubbed his skin and wet his hair. She cleared her throat, and he reeled around, throwing water droplets into her face. Blinking, she backed up.

"Sorry." He ran a shirtsleeve down his face. Drops of water clung to his long lashes. "What can I do for you?"

"Uh . . . uhm . . ." She pushed the toe of her boot into a clump of dandelions. "How come you didn't go to church?"

"Didn't want to."

"Did you go into town?"

"No. Me and Ice rode out to Two Forks Creek and fished."

"Catch anything?"

"Nothing but mosquito bites."

"Oh . . . umm . . . Drew, you know that dress and those petticoats you bought for me?"

"The ones you threw back in my face? Yeah, I know them."

She pursed her lips, wondering how to ask without infuriating him. "Did you take them back to town?"

"Nope."

"Did you give them to somebody else?"

"Like who? Gabe? Tee?"

She laughed and reached out a hand to skim her fingers down the front of his shirt. He went still, watching her hand drop away from him. Suddenly distrust glinted in his eyes. She knew she had tripped up.

"What do you want, Shorty?"

She hated it when he called her that! "The dress,"

she said bluntly. "I'll buy it. How much did you give for it?"

"It's not for sale. Why do you want it back all of a sudden?"

"Because I need it."

"For what? You planning a party?"

"There's a barn dance Friday."

"A barn dance, huh?" A smile kicked up one side of his wide mouth. "You're wanting to go to it?"

"Yes."

His smile widened. "Well, if you want—"

"Yes, I do want the dress, Drew. You see, it's Monroe's barn dance, and he was here earlier and he said he'd take me. I'm going to be the hostess."

Drew's mouth straightened into a thin, hard line. "The hostess?" he repeated with a sneer. "Well, I'll be damned!" He turned his back on her and plunged his head into the trough. Sputtering and growling like a bear, he brought his head back up in a spray of water. "I'll be a son of a sidewinder! Somebody kick some sense into me before it's too late! Better yet, get a gun and put me out of my misery!"

"What are you jawing about?" she asked, confounded by his behavior. "Will you let me have the dress or not?"

He faced her again, his lips peeled back in a snarl, his blue eyes mere slits. "You can have the damned dress! Now get out of my sight before I—I—aw, hell!" He stalked away from her, shoulders hunched and fists swinging wide at his sides.

Cassie released a long breath, glad to have that particular chore done. She'd figured he wouldn't like her asking for the dress, but his reaction baffled her. After all, she'd offered to pay him for it.

Men! If she lived to be a hundred, she wouldn't be able to predict their moods. Just when she thought she had them all figured out, she found herself bamboozled. Take Drew Dalton . . .

Would have been nice if he had been the one to ask her to the dance.

But he wouldn't ask, of course. He wouldn't do something like that, something that would make her happy as a lark. Oh, no! He was too much of a *man* for that!

Men!

Chapter 9

D rew saw Cassie sauntering toward the corral. He bent over the big gray's newly shod hoof and ran a thumb over the shiny metal, making sure it was a secure fit.

"How does that look?" Ice asked, wiping sweat from his brow as he walked over to Drew. He'd been forging horseshoes all afternoon, and he and Drew had finally outfitted all the newcomers and given them a thorough examination. They were healthy, except that the mare had a sore on her right inside hock.

"This one's a good fit," Drew said, sliding the hoof off his thigh and rubbing a hand down the horse's leg.

"What about that raw place?"

"I put some medicine on it. Looks like she got nipped by another horse or maybe by a dog or coyote."

Ice noticed Cassie's approach and pushed his hat back on his forehead. "We just shod the last one," he told her.

Drew scowled at her, feeling more out of sorts with her than he knew he should. Ever since she'd asked him for that dress, he'd been agitated and wanted to bawl her out every time she got near him. It didn't make sense, he knew, but that didn't stop the angry words that rose in him like bile. Even now he wanted to yell at her, to frown at her, and make her lash out at him. He guessed it had something to do with her wanting to pretty herself up for Monroe Hendrix.

What kind of game was she playing, leading Roe on like that, when she'd said she wouldn't entertain the notion of him gaining control of this land? He figured it was a female thing, messing with a man's hopes. Wasn't right, he thought, watching her as she ducked through the fence rails and came closer.

Her clothes were dusty, as if she'd been rolling in the dirt, although he thought she'd been fixing the roof on the henhouse.

"The windmill's broke," she said, tucking her hands inside her belt and staring pointedly at Drew. He stared back at her.

"Well, I didn't do it," he said, when it looked like she had nothing further to say on the subject.

"I wasn't accusing you," she said, scraping her boots in the dirt and refusing to look him in the eyes. "But I can't seem to fix it. I thought that you . . ." She glanced at him, lightning-quick.

Drew brushed his hands together to dislodge dust from them. He knew what she wanted, but she was going to have to ask him, or that windmill could stay broken.

"Well?" she asked.

"Is the well broken, too?" he asked, barely able to keep from grinning, especially when Ice let loose with a bray of laughter and slapped him on the back.

"I hope you two jackasses get stitches in your sides

from laughing.'' She turned away, but Ice reached out and grabbed her by the sleeve.

"Don't be mad,'' Ice cajoled. "We mean nothing by our jests.''

"Maybe *you* don't,'' she said, giving Drew the evil eye, "but don't speak for your partner there. I just thought I'd tell you about the windmill. Thought you'd want to know.''

"That's not why you told me,'' Drew said.

She narrowed her eyes. "What's that mean?''

"You told me because you want me to repair it.''

Cassie looked away from him and stared off into the distance. After a few moments she kicked at a stone, sending it skipping across the corral. "What if I do?''

"Then ask me. Don't come to me dropping hints like you're dropping hankies and expecting me to pick them up and play your silly female games. I'm not Monroe Hendrix.''

He wished he could have taken that back when her gaze bounced up to his and she smiled like she'd drawn a winning poker hand.

"I would never mistake you for Roe,'' she assured him. "And I'm not playing any game. I didn't think I'd have to ask you to help me fix the windmill, since this place is partly yours, or so you keep telling me.''

He saw that Ice was watching this exchange with a sense of puzzlement. Hell, he couldn't blame him, Drew thought, because he didn't know what they were talking about either. Whipping his hat off his head, he ran a hand through his damp hair.

"I'm done here, so I can look at the windmill.'' He strode toward the contraption, and she was right on his heels. When he got there, he stopped and turned toward her. "I said I'd look at it. You don't need to oversee me."

"I'm going to lend you a hand, that's all," she rejoined, the color rising in her cheeks. "Once you get a bolt loose, I think I can take it from there."

"I'll fix it," he said, then started climbing up the windmill. Halfway up he paused to look down and cursed under his breath when he saw her scrambling up behind him. The woman was getting on his bad side right quick, and she was either too stubborn or too thick-headed to know it.

When he reached the mechanisms, he saw the tools scattered around it and a few fresh droplets of blood soaking into the bleached wood. She joined him on the narrow platform, and he noticed the cut on the tender skin of her forearm.

He pulled his red handkerchief from his back pocket and handed it to her. "You're bleeding. Better wrap this around it until you can see to it proper."

Much to his surprise, she accepted the makeshift bandage. "That bolt is too tight. I couldn't get it to budge. That gear there has shifted and the teeth aren't meshing anymore. Needs to be pulled back into place."

"Yeah, the wind and rain beat at this, then the wood shrinks and swells and splits around these metal parts," he said, taking up the wrench and fitting it around the bolt. "Before you know it, the whole contraption is out of whack." He grunted, and the nut on the bolt creaked and then gave way.

She sighed. "I worked on that blasted bolt for nigh on an hour."

"Must really chap your hide."

"What?"

"Having to ask a man to do a job because you can't do it yourself. What with you always proclaiming how you can take care of yourself and don't need anyone around to help you."

"I never said I didn't need help. I just don't need a man around to take over this ranch. I can run it, same as a man."

"You just can't fix the windmill."

"That's why I have hired hands."

He set the wrench aside. "I'm not your hired hand and you're not my boss lady."

She picked up a hammer and battered it against the metal workings before he could wrench it out of her hand.

"Just what in the hell do you think you're doing?"

"Knocking that back into place," she said, huffing.

"You're going to knock it back into Texas, is what you're going to do. This is delicate, these teeth and how they meet and all." He bent over the contraption and tapped it several times with the hammer, made another adjustment, gave it another careful tap, and then reached for the bolt and nut. "There. That ought to work." He glanced up and saw that he no longer had her attention.

She was staring out at the land stretching to the horizon in all directions. Drew stared at her. In profile she was even more stunning, her nose tipping up gently and her lashes curling against the robin's-egg blue of the sky. Her hair, gathered in a long plait, moved gently with the breeze, some strands lifting away from the others and floating in the sea of wind. Sadness quivered around her, that and her shining spirit. He'd never met a woman with more mettle, he thought, recalling how she stood up to him at every turn and how she never sidestepped work, no matter how dirty or backbreaking it might be. She was a gal with a lot to prove to herself, he figured, and wondered why. Hadn't she done enough by coming here and marrying a stranger, then giving him a fine, strong son? Now she was fighting her dead husband's eldest. Guilt tugged at his heart.

Without pondering the outcome, he placed a hand on her shoulder and was shocked when tears built in her eyes and glistened in the sunlight.

"What's wrong?" he asked, his voice emerging huskier than usual, his hand slipping away from her.

She wiped the tears from her eyes. "Nothing. I was just thinking."

"About what?"

"This land . . . how pretty it is and how much it's come to mean to me." She turned to face him. "Excepting for Andy, it means everything to me."

He could see the truth of that in her brown eyes. "Why? Why does it mean so much? This place is nothing but hard work and hard luck. Nobody's going to get rich here."

"Anybody who claims this land is already rich." She sent her gaze far, all the way to where the sky melted into the earth. "I've never had anything and that's why I came here. I wanted to belong somewhere, to call some place mine. I wanted out of towns where people live on top of each other and most of them are just passing through."

He examined the area, the gentle slope of the land, the color of it, the smell of it. "When I was in prison, I dreamed of this place. For some reason I thought a lot about Two Forks Creek. I didn't know the impression that place had made on me until I couldn't see it anymore. Then that's all I thought about—not the house or the outbuildings, not the acres of grain and wild flowers or the fishing hole—just Two Forks Creek and how the banks are mossy and mist hangs over the water every morning like a ghost.''

She nodded and brought her knees up against her body. She looped her arms over them and rested her chin on her knees. Her smile brought dimples to her cheeks.

"When I was a boy I'd go there and hide," he said.

"Hide from what?"

"From my pa. He'd get mad about something, and I'd head for the creek. I'd forgotten about that until I was in prison and it all came back to me. Funny what you remember when you're alone and you've got too much time to think.''

"I think about my ma when I'm scared or worried. I remember her voice. It was sorta soft and high, like a flute.''

"Like yours?"

"Higher than mine. Girlish. She would sing and she sounded like an angel—not of this world. She'd rock me against her and sing gospel songs, and I'd fall to sleep feeling safe and warm. So when I'm scared, I remember that. It's about the only thing I recall about her, other than that she cried a lot.''

"You been scared lately?"

Her face tensed slightly. "Some."

"Scared of me?"

"Of what you might try to do," she admitted.

His chest closed in around his heart. Did she think him a barbarian?

"Force me off this land," she added. "I figure you could go into town and get some of the men there behind you and throw me off this place. A woman alone has nowhere to turn. Men know that. They use that.''

He removed his hat and hung it on his bent knee. ''I won't do that.''

''You won't?'' She narrowed her eyes, scouring him with a hard glare.

''No, I won't. But if you ever want to leave, I'll buy you out. I'm not leaving. That's what I want straight. I was taken from this land once, but now that I'm back, I'm back for good.''

''I know.'' She gave him a tight smile. ''And I hate to admit it, but I could use your help. Seems to me you know a goodly amount about cattle, and I wouldn't mind if you'd teach me what you know.''

He'd been settled on one knee, but now he sat back on his rump. ''Did I hear you right? Are you asking for my help here?''

''That's right.'' She gave an affirmative bob of her head, and sunlight made her hair glisten like pale gold. ''I'm asking.''

He ran a hand over his jaw, and the stubble of his whiskers made a raspy sound against his palm. ''If this isn't a red-letter day . . .'' He slanted her a grin. ''Sure, I'll be glad to impart what I know about cows. First, they're dumb and second, they stink.''

She popped his shoulder with her small, harmless fist. ''They don't smell any worse than a horse—or than you do right now, for that matter.''

He widened his eyes, then buried his nose in his shirt-sleeve. Sweat and dirt and smoke combined to sting his nostrils. ''Damn if I don't. Guess I need to take a dip in Two Forks Creek instead of just thinking about it.'' He exchanged a smile with her, and a ribbon of happiness wrapped around his heart. It felt good. Damn good. His work was done up here, but he was in no hurry to climb down, because he liked talking to her in private. Just the two of them up here close to heaven, where it was quiet and cool and the breeze played with her hair and made her eyes water. "You okay now?" he asked.

"Sure. It's a female affliction," she said, picking bits of grass off her breeches. "Life comes at you, knocks you around a little, and you've got to cry or go crazy. The tears don't mean nothing. They're just drops of frustration rolling out of me. I'm back in working order now." She patted the platform beneath them. "Like this windmill."

"And I didn't even have to take a hammer to you."

She grinned. "No, but you helped. Talking instead of yelling always helps."

He knew that, so why did he fuss at her, shout at her every chance he got? Maybe to keep his distance from her—her and her warm, soft lips? He thought about slipping inside her and letting her envelop him in her softness, in her sweetness. He thought of her breasts and her legs and her hands upon his face and his chest. Everywhere. Was that why he picked fights with her? To keep himself away from her?

"Are you going to the barn dance?"

The barn dance. Why did she have to remind him of that? Of her all gussied up for Roe Hendrix?

"I wouldn't be caught dead at that dance," he grumbled. Then suddenly he couldn't wait to get off the windmill and back on solid ground. He should know better than to stick his head in the clouds and let his mind go fuzzy, he told himself, scrambling down, down, down until his boots hit earth again. He looked up and saw her heart-shaped behind waggling at him, and all his blood swam to the vee of his legs. In an instant he was as hard as a pioneer winter.

"Hey, wait for me!" she called down to him.

"If you can't keep up, that's your problem," he told her, striding toward the barn, his own voice ringing in his ears.

There he was, yelling at her again.

Two hours later, Cassie emerged from Two Forks Creek feeling fresh and cool. She rubbed herself dry with the toweling cloths she'd brought with her and slipped into her baggy breeches and one of A.J.'s old shirts. Sitting down on a big, flat rock, she pulled on her socks and boots, then ran her fingers through her wet hair, combing out tangles while listening to bird songs and the croak of a frog. The creek babbled to her, and she closed her eyes to listen. A jaunty whistled melody rose amid the bird calls, capturing Cassie's attention. She sat upright, her senses sharp and quivering.

Who's that? Immediately she thought of cattle rustlers and other trespassers. She looked toward her horse, where she'd left her rifle in the saddle sling, but then the whistling took on a familiar note and she relaxed. She recognized the tune and the musician. Blue Eyes.

He was upstream from her. Cassie crept in that direction, slipping from tree to tree for cover, a part of her wondering why she didn't want to be seen, another part loving the subterfuge. He was in the creek, splashing and soaping himself, sending sprays of water into the air. The low sun burned on the hill and changed the droplets into rainbows. She could see his body clearly from the waist up, but she'd seen that much of him before. Still, her eyes took him in, the muscled chest and its sprinkling of dark hair, the thickness of his neck and arms. A tingle erupted in her stomach, and she placed a hand there, trying to squelch the sensation of pleasure, of passion.

Shame crept upon her, shaking its finger until she could not tolerate her actions any longer. She stepped out from the cover of the trees and toward the bank.

"Looks like we had the same idea," she said, startling him. "I just climbed out downstream a ways." She flung her wet hair over one shoulder and ran a hand down her oversized shirt and pants. "Feels good, doesn't it?"

"What?" He blinked, his gaze traveling with her hand from her waist to her stomach, her hip.

"The creek water. It's cool."

"Oh." He blinked. "Yeah. Feels good."

"Did you think to bring soap? I've got some back—"

"I brought a hunk," he said, showing it to her.

"Oh. Okay." She looked around at nothing and wanted to stare only at him, at the way the hair grew in a fan design on his chest and arrowed to his navel. "Well, I guess . . . I left my things and my horse and . . . everything back there, so I'll mosey on and let you—" She swallowed, realizing she was making very little sense. "See you back at the house." She shook her head, feeling like a blithering idiot, and turned sharply and left him, melting into the tree shadows again.

What was wrong with her? She felt funny inside, all jittery and fluttery. Like she might break out in giggles or hives at any second. She placed her palms against her hot cheeks and knew her face was red. Blue Eyes was getting under her skin, for sure. Seeing him naked in that creek. Lord, that memory would fuel her dreams for weeks, months to come! She knew it.

Finding a patch of sun, she sat in it to let her hair dry before riding to the ranch house. Oleta would have supper ready by the time she got there. Would Drew eat with them or with Ice and the others in the bunkhouse? Earlier, at the windmill, he'd seemed at once tender and cross with her. He was a hard one to figure. Was that one of his attractions? That she couldn't predict his moods, couldn't pinpoint his feelings for her?

She heard his approach through the woods, but she only had time to rise from the bank and turn before he confronted her. He stopped, his boots sliding on the mossy grass, and pink crept up his neck and into his cheeks. He was dressed now, his shirt sticking to patches of wet skin, the tails flapping. He'd pulled on his pants but hadn't buckled his belt yet. Shoving his fingers through his wet hair, he skinned it back, but dark-russet curls fell onto his forehead again. She realized he must have bounded from the creek and thrown on his clothes. But why?

"Something wrong?" she asked, leaning sideways to look past him. Dynamite picked his way through the brush and trees, coming to his master. "Is something besides your horse chasing you?"

"What?" He glanced over his shoulder. "Oh. No." He cleared his throat. "I just thought . . . You want to ride back together?"

That was it? He threw on his clothes and galloped ahead of his horse to ask her if she wanted to ride back to the house with him? She smiled, knowing there was more to his actions. Maybe he was feeling funny, too. Maybe they'd both caught the same fever.

She sauntered closer to him, leaned in, and sniffed. "You smell better now."

One side of his mouth kicked up. "I reckon so. Do you come here often to take your baths?"

"Hardly ever, but after us talking about the creek, I couldn't get it out of my head."

"Same with me."

She noticed that he was having a hard time looking at anything but her mouth. "Guess we think alike about some things."

"Guess so."

Cassie arched a brow. Did he expect her to rub up against him and get him started? With any other man she might have done that, but not with him. She wanted him to move in her direction first, to show her that he wanted her, then she would be most happy to return his affections. She'd been wondering if he'd been with other women since his release from prison. Now something in his eyes—so vulnerable and naked—told her that he hadn't, that it had been a long, long time since a woman had claimed his body. She wanted very much to be that woman.

"I hope you don't think I was sneaking a peek at you," she said, smiling. "Of course, I was tempted. The devil in me whispered for me to keep quiet and let you stride out of the creek before I let you know you had company, but I figured you'd be madder than a swatted hornet." She shrugged and clutched her hands behind her back, swaying side to side, jutting out her breasts and giving him something else to look at besides her mouth. "'Course, men aren't as guarded with their bodies as women. I guess you wouldn't have squealed and run back into the water if I'd caught you . . . uh, in your altogether.''

A slow grin claimed his beautiful, masculine lips. ''I might have squealed, but I wouldn't have run.''

She laughed, tickled by that incongruous image. ''You've never squealed in your whole life, Drew Dalton.''

His gaze drifted down. ''You look awful cute in that getup, Shorty.''

''Maybe I should wear this to the dance.''

A storm cloud passed over his face. ''Maybe you should.'' He started to turn away, but she caught his shirtsleeve.

''How come you don't want me to go to the dance and have some fun?''

''I don't give a damn if you go dancing or not.''

''Then how come you're growling at me?''

''I'm not—'' He clamped his lips together. ''Now that you're passing yourself off as the hostess at the Star H shindig, I suppose it won't be too long before you take the job permanent.''

She shook her head. ''No, that won't happen.''

''Won't it? Seems like you enjoy being on Roe's arm, playing the role of his lady.''

Cassie tipped up her chin, offended by his tone and his accusation. ''I like being looked up to, it's true. I want folks to think good of me. There's nothing wrong with that. Monroe is placed in high regard in this county, and I'm proud to be called his friend, but I'm only interested in being treated like a lady, not in being *his* lady.''

Drew squinted one blue eye. ''You sure of that?''

She squinted one brown eye. "Positive. Why? You jealous?"

"Jealous?" He almost sputtered, almost choked. He stumbled back a step as if rocked off his feet. "Of Monroe Hendrix? Not in a million years, sweet britches. Get that out of your head, you hear me?" He leaned down, nose to nose with her. "Jealousy isn't in my nature."

She smiled. "Like hell it isn't. It's in every man, woman, and child's nature. Admit it. You wish you were taking me to that dance."

"Bull!"

"And since you can't, you're going to act like a brat and not show up at all!"

"Bull!"

She frowned. "So you've said." She would have spun away, but he second-guessed her intention and gathered the collar and front placket of her shirt in one fist to keep her in place before him. His eyes were stormy blue, his mouth a straight, tense line. Cassie trembled a little, awed by his checked anger, thrilled by the dark flames of desire leaping in his eyes.

"Damn you, Cassie Dalton," he whispered hoarsely. "I don't know whether to shake you or kiss you, hate you or worship you, leave you be or dog your every step."

Suddenly she was afraid. Afraid that if she gave herself to him now. she would be lost forever. She wasn't sure she wanted that . . . could handle that. Cassie placed her hand over his fist and squeezed gently.

"Let me go, Drew. While you still can."

He stared deeply into her eyes, his face taut, his hand still fisted, pinning her to the spot. Finally he released a long breath and set her free. He reached behind him and snagged Dynamite's dangling reins. His gaze never left hers.

Cassie felt strangely empty and near tears. The day had been full of contradictions and puzzles, and she could stand no more.

"You go on," she said. "I've got to gather my things, braid my hair. I'll be right behind you."

He opened his mouth as if to say something, then closed his lips firmly. He sprang up into the saddle, stared down at her, anger clearly on his face, in his eyes, shimmering around him like a heat wave. Pride was there, too, keeping him silent and apart from her. For once she was glad of his stubborn pride. He reined Dynamite around and left her.

Warm tears spilled onto Cassie's cheeks and she brushed them away angrily.

"That man is making me crazy," she said, trying to be furious but failing. She wanted to be mad at him. She wanted to curse him. But all she felt in her heart was yearning and the first tender buds of love.

Staring at herself in the mirror, Cassie was suddenly sad when she should have been brimming with good feelings. But she couldn't help herself. She wished she was wearing this dress to impress Drew tonight instead of Monroe.

Drew had a good eye for fashion, she thought, touching a row of ruffles on the dark-blue gingham skirt. She had added a few tucks at the waist to make it hug her body more snugly, and she had shortened the sleeves, since the cuffs had crept over her hands. Other than that, the dress had fit her like in a dream.

Ebony lace edged the ruffles, the cuffs, and the oval

neckline. Cassie screwed on her best earbobs—teardrop-shaped onyx set in silver—and added a silver necklace with a silver and gold cross pendant. Casting a critical eye on her reflection, she decided she'd knock Monroe off his feet.

But what about Drew? Would he approve? She knew he was boiling with jealousy.

Understanding him was hard, because he wasn't a man who talked much, especially about his feelings. While he could seem as candid as a child, he was in truth a closed book. She wondered if being raised by A.J. or prison had done that to him.

She couldn't accuse him too severely, though, because she wasn't exactly forthcoming about her feelings about him either. She didn't entirely trust him—couldn't, what with his penchant for keeping to himself. And she wasn't sure her feelings for him should be confessed, seeing as how she enjoyed being independent and had decided she wouldn't ever hitch her wagon to one man again. Oh, she would indulge herself in flirtations and maybe even have herself a lover, once her son was of an age when he didn't need her, but she didn't see any point in having herself another husband.

That's why her dream last night had been so upsetting. She had seen herself in this house, cooking a big meal. Andy was eight or nine years old, and she had herself a baby daughter. She was expecting her husband home any minute, and they would share this special meal. It was somebody's birthday, maybe the baby's. Right before she had awakened with a start, her heart puddling in her chest, she'd seen her husband walk into the house. He was Drew.

"Great goose grease!" she muttered, shaking her

head to clear it. "If that don't beat all. Him as my husband. He'd choke on his own tongue if I told him about that."

Running a hand along her neck and tucking a few loose tendrils into her upswept hairdo, she released a small, sad sigh. If only she'd met Drew Dalton in one of those towns she'd lived in. If only they could say what was on their minds and in their hearts.

The squeak and rattle of a buggy pulling up outside shook her free of her melancholy musings, and she scolded herself for being so sentimental over a man who probably saw her mostly as a nuisance. Monroe had arrived and he'd never hidden his feelings about her, although she didn't return them. But it would be nice to spend time with a man who openly admired her and told her so whenever he got the chance. Still, as she left her bedroom and stepped into the parlor, her gaze went immediately to Drew, who was sitting by the fireplace, instead of Monroe, who was standing by the front door.

"Lord God, will you look at this vision," Monroe said, his tone full of awe. "Cassie, you're beautiful."

She afforded Monroe a quick look and a smile before directing her attention back to Drew. He glanced at her, then away, then back with a snap. His gaze swept her from head to foot, and she saw something feral in his expression. He didn't have to say a word. She knew in that instant that he thought she was lovely and that he wanted her more than he wanted his next breath.

Supremely satisfied, she turned toward Monroe and held out her hand to him. He took it, kissed her fingers, then blew out a long, masculine whistle.

"You stop my heart," he told her. "Let me look at you." Still holding her by the hand, he twirled her like a ballerina, making her laugh. "You will be the most fetching woman at the barn dance, guaranteed."

"How kind of you to say so," she said, glancing around. "Has Oleta already left?"

Drew grunted in response. "She and Ice have been gone nearly an hour."

Andy sat on the rug in front of Drew. He gurgled and waved a bright orange gourd, making the seeds in it rattle.

"Come along, baby," Cassie said, moving forward to scoop her son up into her arms. "We're off to the dance, and you, my sweet boy, will be the center of attention. No female there will be able to keep her hands off you."

"Yes, we should be going," Monroe said. "I want to greet everyone as they arrive. It's such a beautiful night, I think everyone in the county will be there."

"Everyone but Drew," Cassie noted. "He refuses to go. He's going to stay here like some puffed up 'possum while everyone else is having fun and being neighborly."

"Is that true? What's wrong? You feeling poorly?"

"I don't feel like dancing, that's all." Drew smirked at Monroe as he stood and walked toward them. "Besides, you couldn't stand the competition, Roe."

Monroe barked a laugh. "Competition?" He shook his head in a scolding gesture. "Drew, look who you're talking to. I'm a fine specimen if ever there was one, while you—well, I think too much of you to tell you the truth." He winked at Drew. "Aw, hell, I hope you change your mind. Give the girls a thrill and show off your handsome face tonight."

"Get out of here," Drew said, shoving Monroe away

even as a grin conquered him. "I intend to enjoy an evening of solitude. I've got me a good book to read and a couple of crisp apples to eat. I'm in heaven."

"Looks to me like you'd be tired of your solitude," Cassie said, sitting Andy in his high chair so that she could pull on her black gloves. "Wasn't that what you hated in prison? Being all alone?"

"Being locked up and spending time by yourself aren't the same thing," Drew said, his gaze following her every move while she stood before a wall mirror to position a perky black satin and lace hat on top of her blond curls.

Sensitive to his attentions, her heartbeats accelerated and her skin tingled. Thinking of being with him at the creek the other day, she wished for the hundreth time that she'd let him kiss her again, let herself go with him. All she could think about was what might have happened. Even in her dreams he haunted her. If she'd given herself to him at the creek, he'd be out of her system. Or would he?

She faced him once she'd secured the hat with two long pins and saw him blink away the naked longing in his eyes. Mule-headed man, she thought, wishing he would go to the dance so that she could take a turn with him. Being in his arms would be . . .

Clearing her throat and her head, Cassie picked up Andy again and then linked arms with Monroe. "Andy and I are ready to go."

"Then let's get that buggy moving." Monroe opened the front door and escorted Cassie and Andy outside.

Cassie looked back once to see Drew's silhouette in the doorway. Regret shadowed her heart. She forced him from her thoughts and threw all her efforts into having a wonderful time with Monroe.

She smiled at him, his face illuminated by starlight, and wished he was closer to her age and that he had one chin instead of two.

Chapter 10

Breathless from dancing, Cassie joined a clutch of women standing near the table laden with cider, lemonade, cookies, cakes, and candy. She reached out for Andy, who was sitting happily on the lap of Ida Nelson, the sheriff's elderly mother.

"Did you wear Monroe out?" the white-haired woman asked, sweeping a hand over the skirt Andy had wrinkled.

"He went outside for a smoke," Cassie said.

"And for a nip of whiskey, no doubt," Mrs. Nelson added with a wink. "The men think we womenfolk don't know about that. They think we'd pitch a fit if we knew they were tasting some home brew." The older lady set her rocker into motion and squinted up at Cassie. "You and Monroe sweethearts?"

"Sweethearts?" Cassie looked around at the expressions of interest and realized she'd been the center of gossip. "No, ma'am. We're friends, that's all."

"But you were standing at the door saying howdy to everyone along with Monroe. I figured maybe you'd agreed to be his wife."

"No, ma'am." Cassie shook her head firmly, wanting to derail this train of gossip. "I like Roe, and he's been mighty good to me, but I'm not interested in marrying him or anybody else, for that matter. Did Andy give you any trouble?"

"That sweet child? Lord, no. He sipped some cider and clapped his hands to the music. I don't mind watching him one bit. You go ahead and dance, honey."

"Oh, I think I'll take a rest," Cassie said, propping Andy on her hip and swaying to the music.

Monroe's huge barn was full to bursting, and the musicians, made up mostly from one of the local families, had everyone tapping their feet and snapping their fingers. Gabe Brindle, dancing with a chubby redhead, came waltzing by and grinned at Cassie.

"You sure look pretty tonight," he called to her, and Cassie smiled her thanks.

Viola Danforth approached from across the barn. She was a bit older than Cassie and had been married for a few years, but her husband had died after getting kicked in the head by a bull.

"Hello, Viola," Cassie greeted her.

"Oh, hello." Viola selected a cookie and a cup of cider. "I've danced so much I've worked up an appetite and a terrible thirst." She eyed Cassie. "I saw that dress in the front window of Miss Hornby's Tailor Shop, didn't I?"

Did she? Cassie glanced down at the garment. Miss Hornby's was the most expensive store in Abilene, and only deep-pocketed ladies could afford to shop there. She'd never for a moment considered that Drew had paid a high price for the dress, although it was clearly fetching and finely stitched.

"Yes, you might have," Cassie answered Viola. "I didn't pick it out."

"Oh?" Viola lifted a thin brow and waited for Cassie to elaborate, but Cassie's attention was now riveted to the front of the barn, where moonlight spilled through the open doors.

Suddenly her chest was so tight she could take only shallow breaths as she stared, almost afraid to believe her eyes, at the man who had entered. Her lips formed his name—*Drew*—and her heart somersaulted with joy. She hadn't realized how much she'd hoped he would change his mind and come to the dance until that moment, when the world seemed to grind to a stop and her heart seemed to burst from her chest.

"Who is *that?*" Viola asked. "He looks familiar, but—"

"Why, that there is Drew Dalton," Mrs. Nelson said. "He was sprung from prison, but I hear-tell it wasn't because he was innocent but because he got together enough money to hire himself a slick lawyer."

"That's not true," Cassie said. "He *is* innocent. He should never have spent one day in prison." Cassie realized that her fervent declaration had attracted attention from the women around her, and her face suddenly felt as hot as an August sun.

Mrs. Nelson chuckled. "If you say so, honey. If you say so." She wiggled her fingers at Andy, then held out her arms to him. Cassie let the older woman take the baby from her again.

"A judge and jury said Drew Dalton was guilty of stealing cattle from around here," one of the other women said. "That's why he went to prison."

"But another judge said the first judge was all

wrong,'' Cassie explained. ''Drew Dalton is innocent.''

''Now that he's out, I sure hope no more cows get took,'' another woman piped up. ''My man said he'll blow a hole through anybody he sees on our land who ought not to be there.''

''My husband swears he'll do the same,'' someone else replied.

''Y'all might ought to let my son handle the law and order of this here county,'' Mrs. Nelson said. ''If'n you don't watch out, your husbands will be the ones in prison!''

That silenced them, but they directed baleful glares toward Drew. Cassie ignored them and dedicated herself to studying the man she'd defended so fervidly. He'd changed clothes, she noted, admiring his black trousers, black vest, and boiled white shirt. His boots were spit-polished and his hair was carefully combed. He held his hat in his hands and searched for someone, those beautiful blue eyes of his moving slowly to take in the crowded dance floor and the clusters of people standing near the food and drink tables.

When his gaze touched her and stayed, she realized she was the one he hunted. He started toward her. Cassie's heart bucked, and happiness arced through her like a rainbow.

Before Drew could reach her, Monroe returned, stepping in front of her and cutting her off from Drew.

''Did you miss me?'' Monroe asked, taking one of her hands in his.

''You weren't gone long,'' she said. *Not nearly long enough.*

''It's crazy to spend time with some ugly men outside when I have a pretty woman waiting for me in here.''

Cassie glimpsed Drew behind Monroe. He hesitated, and she could tell he was trying to decide whether to interrupt or leave them be. She held her breath, hoping, hoping . . . He frowned and turned aside. Disappointment crashed into her.

"Monroe Hendrix," Mrs. Nelson said, "how come you haven't played us a song tonight on your harmonica?"

"Those boys don't need me," Monroe said, looking toward the makeshift stage. "But thanks for asking there, Grandma Nelson."

"Them boys is good, but they don't have nobody playing the harmonica. You brung it, didn't you? Then go on up there and play us a couple of tunes on it." She looked around at the people nearby. "Don't y'all want to hear Monroe Hendrix blow his harmonica tonight?"

Expressions of agreement rose from the onlookers. Out of the corner of her eye, Cassie saw Drew face them again. She squeezed Monroe's hand.

"Go on," she urged him, then pulled her hand from his. "I don't think I've had the pleasure of hearing you play. Won't you do this for me?" She looked into his eyes and placed a sweet smile on her lips. As she expected, his resolve melted.

"Very well. For you, Cassie." Monroe bowed at the waist, then withdrew a silver and gold harmonica from his inside jacket pocket. With a definite strut to his stride, he made his way to the front of the barn, where the musicians were finishing a rousing rendition of "Turkey in the Straw."

With Monroe no longer standing in front of her, Cassie had a clear view of Drew. His eyes locked with hers and he approached her. She realized she was holding her breath again. Forcing herself to breathe, she marveled that Drew could evoke such reactions in her. Why, she couldn't recall ever getting so worked up over a man! She warned herself to rein in her emotions, but it was too late. They stampeded her good sense, and she found herself slipping her hand into Drew's without speaking a word to him and allowing him to guide her onto the dance floor.

A space was made for them. She was vaguely aware of people staring at her and frowns directed at Drew. Did he notice how his neighbors shunned him, disapproved of him? If he did, he paid them no notice. His arm circled Cassie's waist, and the rest of the world slipped away. She looked up into his eyes, shaded beneath his hat brim, and felt the sexual pull of him. She could not see his father in his eyes or in his face or in the way he touched her. She was glad, because she wanted no reminders of A.J. Her time with him had been short but not short enough.

Her tainted relationship with A.J. was something Drew could sympathize with, something he shared with her. She doubted if A.J. had ever had a loving union with anyone. He'd been too selfish, too greedy to view anyone as his equal or as his partner. Not his wife. Not his son.

"I'm glad you're wearing that dress I picked out and didn't make me keep it," Drew said, his voice a husky whisper near her ear as he bent down so that his lips brushed her hair and teased her skin. "It looks so much prettier on you than it would on me."

"Think so?" Impulsively she bussed his cheek.

His brows shot up. "What's that for?"

"For coming tonight."

"I said I wouldn't be caught dead here. Didn't say anything about showing up alive and well."

"Ah." She smiled. "I didn't think of that. Well, thanks anyway. It's high time you showed yourself and let everybody get their gossiping about you over with."

"What are they saying about me?"

"The usual—what have you been up to, who you've been doing it with, what your plans are, if you're innocent or guilty."

He released a quick laugh. "Any man in here over the age of five is guilty."

She laughed with him. "Same could be said of females, too." Smoothing a hand across his shoulder, she felt the crisp, spring-smelling material of his shirt and decided he was the most handsome man she'd ever danced with, and she'd danced with more than her share. When she had worked in saloons, the men had sometimes wanted to dance with her first, like that somehow made what they did with her later more acceptable.

"You having a good time with Roe?"

"Oh, he can be amusing," she allowed and caught the flash of jealously in his blue eyes. He would never admit to her that he wanted to spit green fire every time he thought of Monroe Hendrix putting his hands on her, but he didn't have to admit it. It was written plain as day on his face.

"You must like your men old and ragged."

"Ragged? You mean, rugged, don't you?"

"No, I mean ragged."

"Age don't matter. It's what's in a man's heart that means something to me."

"Then A.J. must have been a disappointment, since he didn't have one to speak of."

She grimaced and wagged her head. "True enough. I was buying a pig in a poke and got what I deserved, I reckon. But it wasn't so bad. I wanted a home and I got one. I wanted a baby and I got one."

"What do you want from Roe?" His jaw looked like it was carved out of bedrock.

"What I've got. His friendship. If I wanted more— which I don't—I surely could get it."

"You certainly are sure of yourself and not the least bit shy about singing your praises."

"The good Lord blessed me with a pleasing appearance, and I realized years ago that I shouldn't ignore it but learn to use it instead."

He chuckled and shook his head. "You are a rare find, Cassie. A woman who sings her own virtues but who can't be called vain. Yes, a rare find."

"Is that a compliment?" she asked, trying to decide for herself. "Doesn't sound like one, but then . . ."

"It is," he assured her.

The music faded and Cassie's pleasure faded with it. She applauded with the others and hoped Monroe would heed the calls for one more tune, but he was already stepping off the bales of hay that formed a makeshift stage and weaving among the dancers, making his way toward Cassie and Drew.

"Here he comes," Cassie whispered, ever mindful of Drew's arms and hands slipping away from her.

"Your knight, your suitor, your Romeo," Drew taunted in a whisper. "The king of the county, coming to claim his queen."

"Oh, hush up!" Cassie stomped her foot squarely on top of Drew's. She smiled at his quick intake of breath and held out her hands to Monroe. "Wasn't that grand!

Monroe Hendrix, you've been hiding your light under a bushel.'' She hadn't the slightest idea what she was talking about, since she hadn't actually listened to Roe's mastery of the harmonica. For all she knew or cared, he had been thumbing his nose.

Monroe grinned good-naturedly. ''So you decided to show yourself after all,'' he said to Drew.

''I figured I'd be neighborly. Your shindigs were always a good time.''

''That's the spirit!'' He clapped Drew on the back. ''Spread yourself around, Drew. There are several young ladies here tonight who are going begging for dance partners.'' He captured Cassie's hand. ''They're getting ready to call a dance, Cassie. Will you do me the honor?''

''Why, certainly, Monroe.'' She delivered him a smile, although she wished it was Drew who had asked to partner her in the square.

Drew turned on his heel and stomped across the dance floor.

''What's wrong with him?'' Monroe asked.

Cassie shrugged, catching a glimpse of Drew's broad shoulders. He had stopped near Mrs. Nelson and was picking up Andy.

''He's hard to figure,'' she said. ''Are we going to dance or not?''

''We are,'' Monroe assured her, beaming, as he took his place on one side of the floor. Cassie stood with the other women, who faced their partners and waited for instructions to dosey-do or promenade.

The caller stepped forward and began directing the dance steps. Watching them from across the barn, Drew's gut churned. Holding Andy, he divided his attention between the sleepy-eyed baby and the babe's dancing mama. That smile of hers was a damned branding iron! She blasted a man with it, and his heart bore her mark from then on. Just look at Monroe making a blessed fool of himself over her! And Drew knew he wasn't mark-free himself. She'd branded him, but by God, she wouldn't castrate him! He wouldn't be led to the slaughter, grinnin' like a drunk cat as Monroe Hendrix was right now.

"... ain't that right, Drew Dalton?" Grandma Nelson's graveled voice invaded his thoughts.

"What's that, Mrs. Nelson?" he asked, turning toward the old woman in the rocking chair.

"I said, that there baby is your half brother, ain't he?"

"Yes, ma'am, he is." Drew noticed that Andy was sleeping, but fretfully. The little sapling was tired out and should be put to bed. "Looks like he's ready to leave this party and head home." Drew shot a glance at the dance floor and saw Monroe's hand sliding up and down Cassie's back. His temper flared like a struck match. "And so am I," he declared, suddenly certain he couldn't stand one more minute in the same room with Monroe without breaking his fingers one by one or kissing Cassie senseless. "Mrs. Nelson, you tell Cassie that I've gone home and that I've taken little Andy with me. You tell her to dance her shoes off and have a gay old time with Monroe and not to worry about her tired little son. I'll take care of him and see that he's settled in his own bed, safe and sound. You tell her that for me, okay?"

The old lady squinted up at him and chuckled. "Sure I will, son. That's right sweet of you, looking after her baby so she can twirl her petticoats."

Drew glared across the barn at Cassie's swirling petticoats—ones he'd bought her. "Yeah," he spit out as
if each word were a hard, round pit, "I'm a peach."

Riding back to the ranch with Andy cradled in one
arm, Drew hummed softly and looked for falling stars
above him. The night sky's canvas was vast, making him
feel like a speck and helping him put the things in his
life in the correct order.

In the overall scheme of things, he knew that a man's
life could be as fleeting as a falling star and that a wise
man lived each day as if it were his last. When he'd left
prison, he had a clear goal in mind: to build a horse-
breeding business on his father's spread. He hadn't bargained on finding his old man already dead and buried
and a widow with a child standing in his way.

What was important then was still important. That
hadn't changed. He loved horses, had a special touch
with them, and he would make a name for himself
breeding quarter horses. Within ten years folks all over
Kansas and beyond would know that the best quarter
horses were bred by Drew Dalton at the Square D
Ranch.

He wouldn't be bothered by Cassie very long, he figured, because she was a beauty and would be married
before another year slipped by. A woman like her
wouldn't stay alone for too many more months. He
sensed the passion in her and knew that she would not
deny that part of herself. Maybe she had convinced herself she would, but he knew better, even if she hadn't
figured it out. Cassie would take herself a husband and
move away. At that time Drew would draw up a will,
leaving the ranch to Andy after Drew had joined his own

mother and father in the family burial plot.

Things would work out fine.

He saw another shooting star and smiled up at it. *Pretty,* he thought, and then found himself remembering how Cassie had looked in that dress he'd bought. Every man at the dance had admired her. He'd felt their eyes on him when he'd held her close. She'd felt like pure pleasure in his arms, all soft curves and smelling like crushed roses.

For a few minutes he had lost himself in her cinnamon-colored eyes. He loved the shape of her mouth and the femininity of her voice. Yes, she was beautiful, and he would never forget kissing her warm mouth and sliding his hands over her white-gold hair. But that's where it had to end. He had big plans and he had no intention of being sidetracked.

He'd also felt his neighbors' hostility tonight. Monroe was right. They didn't trust him, even though he'd been found innocent. In their eyes he was as guilty as sin.

Let them think what they wanted. *They* wouldn't sidetrack him either!

Andy had fallen asleep. Drew had grown fond of the baby, but that didn't mean he had what it took to be a good father. Why, he had no earthly idea how to raise a child, since the only example he had was his own pa, who had been a sorry excuse for a parent. Drew always made it clear to any woman he bedded that he wasn't going to be any baby's papa. 'Course, that was fine with the women, because they weren't looking to be mamas either. Gals in saloons and dance halls might be hunting for husbands, but they weren't in the baby business.

Nope. He wasn't fit to be any child's shining example. Cassie would find little Andy a man he could look up to; a man who hadn't been raised by a heartless, pig-headed bull of a man and who hadn't suffered the horrors of prison; a man respected by his neighbors, not blamed for every shadow and blight on the land.

Dynamite's ears pricked forward and he shook his mane, grabbing Drew's notice. Surveying the area, Drew saw nothing out of the ordinary at first, then moonlight and shadows shifted among a stand of trees, and Drew instinctively tugged on the reins, stopping the horse.

Two riders streaked from the spindly trees that stood at the mouth of a gully, handkerchiefs fluttering across the lower part of their faces.

Masked riders? Something was up. Drew's hackles rose. The men thundered away, making tracks in the direction of the Chisholm Trail and Abilene. Cautiously Drew urged Dynamite forward, noticing that the horse was calm, although his ears were still tilted forward.

He smelled them before he saw them. Cattle. Dynamite walked through the trees and into the gully, where about twenty head of cattle milled about, their coats wet from sweat, their sides heaving from having been driven hard. They weren't Square D cattle.

Easing the big horse closer, Drew bent to examine the brands in the failing light. Hell's afire! They were from the Bar Q Ranch out by Abilene. His stomach clenched and his temper reared up.

"Son of a bitch!" he spat, already turning Dynamite around to give chase. Andy shifted against him and waved a tiny fist. Drew pulled up on the reins. "Damnation!"

He couldn't ride full-out with a baby in his arms. Giving up on that plan, he examined the cattle again and decided they wouldn't be going anywhere soon. He'd ride back to the ranch house, wait for the others to return from the dance, then he and Ice would take these cattle back to the Bar Q. He had to talk to the owner, Will Quentin, and tell him how the cattle had arrived at the Square D. He'd return the cattle personally so that there would be no talking behind his back about how he might have stolen them. A fox didn't return the chickens he'd scattered.

With frustration boiling in his gut, Drew pointed Dynamite toward home and patted Andy's chest to reassure him.

"Go on back to sleep," he whispered to the baby. "Mama will be along soon to feed you and rock you to sleepy-bye."

Sleepy-bye? Now where in tarnation had he picked *that* up? Must have heard it from Cassie. She was always talking foolishness to her baby, and Drew had often caught himself listening with warm enjoyment.

He pushed aside thoughts of her and tried to recall everything he could about the two men he'd seen riding away, but details were scarce. Clouds had moved in to obscure the moon, making the night black as sin. Handkerchiefs and hats had covered the men's heads and faces.

Someone was trying to get him thrown back into prison, but who? Could it be those two scoundrels he'd shot at? Maybe they were still lurking nearby, making trouble. Or maybe they'd been hired by someone else. Perhaps even Quentin was behind them, though Drew found that difficult to believe. Will Quentin was respected and had never impressed Drew as a man of dishonor.

Whoever was trying to ruin him was in for a fight. Drew would spill his last ounce of blood on this land before he'd leave it again.

Chapter 11

When Monroe finally pulled up in front of Cassie's house, it was nearly one in the morning. She knew she should have been home from the barn dance hours ago, but she had hated to see the rare evening end. The laughter, the music, the friendly neighbors had kept her dancing until the last song, "Good Night, Ladies," had been played.

Knowing that Andy was safe at home with Drew and Oleta, who had left for home before midnight, eased her conscience. She figured Drew would fuss about her staying out so late, but she didn't care. He was jealous, pure and simple. He should have escorted her instead of leaving it to Monroe Hendrix. Shoot, everybody there could see that Drew had it bad for her and was pie-eyed with jealousy when Monroe or anybody else danced with her.

Everybody there seemed to have a grudge to settle with Drew, too. She couldn't help but notice that when he left, the people seemed to breathe a collective sigh of relief. She'd heard some of the men refer to Drew as "the cattle thief." Monroe had called them down and defended Drew. It pained Cassie to realize her neighbors

159

were so closed-minded that they refused to give a man a second chance.

The house was dark except for a dim light in her bedroom. Oleta had probably lit a lamp there for her before she'd turned in.

"It was a wonderful evening," Monroe said, setting the buggy brake and turning toward her. "You made it wonderful for me, Cassie. I was proud to have you on my arm."

"That's nice of you to say," she said, uncomfortable because she knew he expected a kiss and she didn't feel like obliging him. He was a nice enough fellow, but he didn't make her the least bit hot and bothered. She gazed past him toward the bunkhouse. No lights there. She wondered if Drew was already in bed in the loft, asleep. She'd halfway expected him to be waiting up for her, ready to scold her for staying out so late.

Monroe leaned closer to her. "You were the most beautiful woman there tonight."

She laughed, feeling awkward. "I shouldn't have stayed out so late."

"You deserve a night out, many nights out. Cassie, you're young and lovely and you should have a man around to heap blessings on you." He took her gloved hands within his and squeezed them a little too hard. "I would like to be that man. I'd try my best to make you happy. I know I could, Cassie. Won't you think about it?"

"Roe, I've got enough on my mind right now. I don't need anything else to think about."

"Yes, you have your troubles, and I could shoulder them. If you'd marry me, I'd make sure the ranch was run properly and that you and your son would be worry-free for the rest of your lives.''

"You can't promise such a thing, Monroe. Nobody can promise that.'' She pulled her hands from his and flexed her aching fingers before patting him, friendly-like, on the arm. "But it's a sweet sentiment. Now, I should be getting inside.''

He wasn't ready to let her go. His arms came around her, preventing her escape, and he dipped his head. His lips fumbled with hers. Cassie didn't struggle. Her body stiffened and she waited for him to finish the kiss. When his fingers groped for her breasts, she captured his hands and pushed them away from her.

"That's enough, Monroe,'' she said firmly. "Let me go inside now.''

With a sigh of regret, he sat back from her. "Think about my proposal, Cassie.''

"I will,'' she whispered, but knew in her heart that his was a lost cause.

Monroe held her by the elbow to steady her as she stepped down from the buggy. She turned and looked up at him, smiling and lifting a hand in farewell.

"Good night and thank you.''

"Sleep well, Cassie.''

He waited for her to slip inside the house before he flicked the reins and set the horse and buggy off toward his own ranch.

Cassie leaned back against the closed door, listening to the departing vehicle. She looked up into the loft, but it was dark and nothing moved up there. A hoot owl called out, then again, sending a shiver over her.

Oleta's bedroom door opened and the timid girl padded out on bare feet in her white nightgown.

"*Señor* Drew and Ice are gone," she announced.

"Gone?" Cassie glanced up into the loft again, frowning. "Gone, where?"

"I don't know exactly. When Ice came home, *Señor* Drew went out to meet him. He had been pacing like a wolf. He told me I should watch the baby. Then he and Ice rode off."

"Just like that." Cassie sighed. What were those two up to now? "Which way did they go?"

"Straight." Oleta pointed north, then northwest, then north again.

Cassie rolled her eyes. "Straight. That's a lot of help." She peeled off her gloves. "Guess all I can do is wait for them to get back."

She moved quietly into her bedroom and checked on Andy. He was sleeping soundly, so she undressed and pulled on her nightgown and robe. While she brushed her hair and then braided it, she listened for the drumming of horse hooves but heard only Andy's rhythmic breathing. Instead of getting into bed, she went to the parlor and sat in one of the rockers. What could have sent the two men out into the night? They wouldn't have gone to town. Not this late and not after a barn dance.

The owl hooted again, and Cassie knew in her gut that this clandestine journey could only mean trouble. Maybe Drew had seen some cattle down and wanted to see about them before sunrise. Or he could have seen a pack of coyotes or wolves roaming about. Maybe those horse thieves were back and he'd caught sight of them. Realizing that she was getting herself worked up, she clutched the chair arms and rocked furiously for nearly an hour before she heard the jangle of riggings and spurs outside.

Jumping up from the rocker, she went to fling open the door and stare up into Drew's startled expression.

"What's wrong?" he asked, looking past her into the house.

"That's what I want to ask you," she said, moving aside to let him enter. She looked out and saw Ice leading two horses into the barn. "Where have you and Ice been at this hour? Oleta said you left without telling her a dagblamed thing."

"I told her to watch over Andy." He removed his hat and hung it on a peg by the door. "From the way you and Monroe were getting on, I figured you might spend the night over at his place."

"If I cared about your opinion, I'd slap your face, but I don't." She spun away from him so that she wouldn't be tempted to change her mind and wallop him upside the head. "So where have you been?"

"Rounding up some strays."

She faced him again. "After midnight?"

"They're from the Bar Q ranch. You know it?"

"Will Quentin? What's his cattle doing way over here?"

"They were herded here by a couple of men wearing neckerchiefs over their faces." He scrubbed his own face with his hands and sat wearily on the sofa. "I saw them when I was riding home with Andy, but I couldn't give chase, what with the baby and all."

"They herded the cattle here on purpose? That's more than a day's ride when you're herding cattle. Why would somebody—?" She pressed her lips together as an answer clouded her mind. "This has to do with you. Somebody's trying to get you in trouble again, get you sent back to prison."

"That's how I see it. Of course, you might see it different. Maybe you think I'm up to my old tricks and trying to lie my way out of it."

She flung her braid over her shoulder. "Don't talk foolishness to me, Drew Dalton. If you were given to lying, you'd do a better job of it. You saw the men? What did they look like? Anybody you—now, why are you staring at me like that?" she demanded, her train of thought derailed by his slowly emerging lopsided grin and the soft, teasing light in his eyes.

"Never mind," he said, shaking his head and looking down at his boots. "You tickle me sometimes is all." He cleared his throat, and when he looked up at her again, the smile was gone and his eyes were dark blue and serious. "Me and Ice herded the cattle into the holding pen. I'm taking them back to the Quentin ranch tomorrow."

"And what will you say to Will? Or are you hoping to sneak the cattle back onto his land?"

"I'm no sneak. I'll tell Quentin what happened, that's all. He'll believe me or he won't. All I can do is tell the truth." He rested his arms along the back of the sofa. "I don't know who the men were who brought them here. Their faces were covered up and it was dark. Now that I know somebody is out to ruin me, I'll be on the prowl and I'll catch them red-handed."

She sat in the rocker across from him. "You think the same ones who got you in trouble before are behind this now?"

"I don't know. Could be."

"Why, Drew? Why would anyone want you to go to prison so bad?"

"Maybe to get me out of the way so they can get this land."

"But that wouldn't get them this land. They would have to get through me first."

"Maybe that doesn't pose much of a problem to them. You don't seem to understand that a widow woman with a baby is no barrier to any man who is determined. Some men might even see you as an added bonus. He gets the land and a good-looking woman to cook and clean for him."

"As if I would!" She folded her arms under her breasts and crossed one leg over the other in a defensive posture. "I'd die first."

"That's the other option," Drew said, his blue eyes as ominous as a stormy sky.

"You trying to scare me?"

"No, I'm trying to make you see reason and quit living in a dream world. You wouldn't have a prayer against any ruthless man who decided he wanted this place for his own."

"I have legal rights."

"Dead people lose their rights. You'd better start using your head, Cassie, and realize you're a sitting duck out here."

"Don't you think I know that?" She shoved up from the chair and paced to the fireplace. "But I'm not going to hand over this ranch without a fight, by gum! And I'm not going to be scared off it either."

"I'm not trying to scare you off."

"The hell you aren't!"

"I'm not," he insisted. "I'm just trying to make you understand that you can't hold onto this land by yourself. You need me." His jaw tightened and a muscle fluttered like a pulse. "And now I need you."

Everything went still inside her, and she looked at him—really looked at him. In the dim lantern light, she could see that he was deadly serious and that this admission had cost him dearly. His mouth was a tight line, and she sensed the crumbling of his pride. She was confounded and bewildered, unsure of how to respond. Finally she took a deep breath and asked him the obvious.

"Why do you need me now?"

"Because trouble's coming. Could already be here if Will Quentin doesn't believe me. I'm going to need you in my corner. Whether you believe me or not, I need you to act like you do so folks around here won't be so ready to lynch me or run me out of the county."

She sat again in the rocker, her knees trembling and an odd little thrill stealing through her. Drew Dalton was asking her to believe in him, to support him. She never thought she'd see the day when he asked her for anything. And now this.

"You're well liked around here and I'm not. That was clear tonight at the dance. If you stand by me, they'll give me the benefit of the doubt for a spell. That might be the time I need to find out who's trying to get me killed or thrown back into prison."

"They might stand by you, too, if you'd let them." She sighed, knowing in her heart it would take more than that. Drew would have to prove himself to their hard-headed neighbors.

He ran a finger under the handkerchief knotted around his wide neck. "Are you with me or against me?"

"I'm not against you. Never have been. Of course, I'll stand with you. Those men who rustled cattle and left them on my land have put me in hot water, too. I'll ride with you to the Quentin place and explain this mess to him.''

''No, you stay here.''

''I will not!''

''There's work to be done,'' he said in a calm voice. ''You stay here and run the ranch. Otherwise, Tee and Gabe will laze around with no boss to oversee them. You know it's true.''

''They're not that bad,'' she murmured, but knew he had a point. The men tended to slack off when no one was around to check on them. ''You go ahead and take Ice with you,'' she said, realizing that she was acting as if this was her idea instead of his. ''I'll stay here and run the ranch.''

''Good thinking,'' he said. His eyes crinkled at the corners and his lips twitched against a grin. ''We'll leave at first light. Should be back in a couple of days.''

''You know Quentin well?''

''We're not chums, but I've known him since I was a boy. What about you?''

She shook her head. ''I heard about him from A.J. Is he a fair man?''

''If you're asking if I think there will be trouble, I don't know. All I can do is show him the truth and hope he recognizes it.'' He glanced up at the loft. ''Did you have a good time at the dance?''

She shrugged, eyeing him carefully. ''It was nice to get out and about.''

''I guess you danced with every man who asked you.''

Cassie balled her hands into fists. ''I reckon I did.''

''I thought you'd want to dance all night with Roe.''

"Why deprive so many men of the pleasure of my company?"

He frowned.

She frowned back at him. "What's wrong?"

"You're talking like a tart."

She flinched, his words sinking like talons into her heart. Was she? Did her way of speaking reveal more to him than she wanted him to know? Or was he jealous and lashing out blindly?

"I'm turning in," he announced abruptly.

He climbed up to his bed in the loft. Cassie shuffled off to her own, her thoughts weighing her down. Maybe she should just tell him about her past. It was stupid for her to hide herself, hoping to be thought of as a lady. Stupid, childish, cowardly.

But she knew she wouldn't confess—especially to Drew Dalton. She'd fought hard for her self-respect and the respect of her neighbors, and she'd fight just as hard for Drew's respect. If she told him about her former saloon work, if she told him that she used to sell herself to men, then he'd never look at her with anything but disgust on his face. And he sure wouldn't want her as his partner.

Groaning, she squeezed her eyes shut as other worries came to the fore. She flung herself onto her bed and snuggled with Miss Tess, her trusty doll. Someone was trying to send Drew packing, but who? She closed her eyes against the beginnings of a headache. Lord, the list of suspects was damned near endless!

Drew was gone before Cassie or the sun had left their beds. Disappointed that he'd made tracks before she could talk to him again, Cassie found herself in a sour mood all day while she worked the herd alongside T-Bone and Gabe. By the time she and T-Bone rode back to the house with the last rays of the sun warming her back, she had to admit that she missed Drew and was worried that he suspected she might not be a decent sort after all. He'd been around his share of saloon tarts, and he probably recognized another one when he saw her.

"He's no fool, that one," she mumbled to herself as she slid out of the saddle.

"You talking to the horse or yourself?" T-Bone asked, giving her a funny look.

"Myself." She handed the reins over to him. "Put up Sweet Pea for me, will you?" Pressing a hand to the small of her back, she twisted from side to side. She felt T-Bone's measuring gaze and faced him. "What's wrong?"

"Nothing. I'm just wondering why you've been so grouchy all day. You feeling okay?"

"I'm worried about Drew, that's all. I hope Will Quentin is a reasonable man . . ." Her voice trailed off as she caught the sound of a galloping horse. She spotted Gabe on his yellow mustang racing toward them. "Wonder what's got him in such an all-fired hurry?"

T-Bone strode forward, reaching out to place a hand on the mustang's sweaty neck and make a grab for the reins. "What's wrong now?"

"You'll never guess who I seen out by Two Forks Creek," Gabe said, breathing heavily, his face red with excitement.

"I don't want to guess. You tell me," Cassie said.

"The sheriff and two deputies! They was looking at the break in the fence—the one you and Drew found and patched—and all them tracks. The fresh ones, too.

The ones made by that bunch from the Bar Q.''

A bolt of alarm rocked Cassie back on her heels. "Did you talk to them? Did you ask them what they were doing on my land?"

"They're coming here to the house to talk to you," Gabe said, still trying to catch his breath. "I think somebody's told them about them cattle being here. That's what I think."

Cassie rolled her eyes. "Well, that's obvious, isn't it? Even baby Andy could have figured that one out." Whipping off her hat, she slammed it against her thigh in agitation. "Who's been shooting off his mouth, that's what I'd like to know."

"Weren't me," Gabe said. "I ain't been anywheres near the sheriff, and I didn't know nothing about them cows until this morning, when you told me and Tee how Drew and Ice was taking them back to the Bar Q."

"I'm not accusing you of anything," Cassie said. "But somebody sent the sheriff here. He wouldn't just pick this ranch out of the blue to look for lost cows."

"Maybe he would," T-Bone said softly. "What with Drew being back here and all."

Cassie turned on him. "You think Drew rustled those cattle? If so, then pack up now. I won't have anyone working for me who is against him."

T-Bone narrowed his eyes in a cagey squint. "Lord, gal, you sure have changed your tune! Did I say I thought he took those cows? Don't you go putting words in my mouth, Cassie Dalton. You'd better simmer down before the sheriff gets here, or you'll make him think you're covering up something. Which you ain't," he added quickly.

Realizing she'd overreacted, Cassie reached out and

tugged T-Bone's shirtsleeve in a gesture of supplication. "Sorry, partner. I didn't mean to jump on you with both spurs. I'm edgy, that's all."

"Looky there," T-Bone said, gazing at the horizon. "Here comes the law."

Cassie ran a hand over her hair, smoothing back wayward strands, then put her hat back on. She tucked her hands in the waistband of her split skirt and walked forward, giving a nod in greeting to the sheriff and his two deputies.

Amos Nelson wore a big brass star pinned to his red shirt. He'd been sheriff for as long as Cassie had been in the county, and he was respected and well liked. A man in his fifties, he sported a luxurious white mustache and long sideburns. His hair was white and curly but thinning at the crown. That's why he hardly ever took off his hat. He touched the brim now, returning Cassie's silent greeting. He was flanked by two young deputies, neither one much older than Cassie.

"Gabe told me y'all were taking a look-see at my land," Cassie said, getting right to the point. "What's the problem, Sheriff Nelson?"

"I got a report this morning that there were some stray cattle on your land."

"Who told you that?"

"Oh, just a couple of cowhands."

"Anybody I know?"

"I doubt it. They're drifters. They told me they saw some men herding Bar Q cattle through a break in your fence. I thought I'd better check it out. I see you have a wobbly fence post out by the creek and some fresh prints in that area." The sheriff pushed his hat back off his forehead to reveal small but probing dark eyes. "You know anything about that, Mrs. Dalton?"

"Sure," she answered easily. "But not as much as I want to know. Late last night Drew spotted some cattle rustlers, but they had handkerchiefs tied across their faces, so he couldn't identify them. Anyway, the cattle was from the Bar Q, like you heard."

"What have you done with the cattle?" the sheriff asked.

"I imagine they're almost home by now. Drew left with them early this morning. He's taking them back where they belong and reporting the theft to Will Quentin."

The sheriff glanced at his deputies. Cassie felt a ripple of surprise pass from one to another.

"Why didn't he report the theft to me?" Sheriff Nelson asked.

"He wanted to be the one who told Quentin what he saw," she said, choosing her words carefully. "Drew has had trouble like this before, you know, and he's rightly concerned. He knows Will Quentin, and he felt he should talk to him man to man about the theft. After all, Drew sure doesn't want Quentin to think he had anything to do with it, although that's what the thief certainly had in mind." She paused, looking from one lawman to the next. "Doesn't take a genius to see that somebody is trying to get Drew thrown back into prison."

"That's what you think, huh?" Sheriff Nelson peered down at her, his broad shoulders blocking the setting sun.

"That's what I know," she retorted, glad her tone was solid and without a quaver. "Ever since A.J. died, I've had vultures circling around me. Everybody wants me to sell my land. Even Drew, at first. But now me and him are partners. That has somebody worried, and that somebody is trying to break up the partnership so I'll be on my own again.'' She didn't like the word, but she spoke it through gritted teeth. ''Vulnerable.''

Sheriff Nelson glanced from one of his deputies to the other, then shrugged. ''As long as those cows are returned, I see no problem here.''

''Except that somebody took them and left them here on the Square D. I hope you sniff them out before they cause more grief for us,'' Cassie said, moving back from the three men on horseback. ''You'll let me know if you catch them, won't you?''

''Sure thing, Mrs. Dalton. If anything like this happens again, you be sure to get word to me.''

''I'll do that,'' she promised.

The lawmen reined their mounts and rode away at a trot, but Cassie figured they'd snoop around a bit more on her land before they headed for Abilene.

''You and Drew are partners, huh?'' T-Bone asked, cutting his eyes sideways at her.

''Sort of. Yeah.'' She shrugged. ''No use fighting over the land when we both deserve stakes in it.''

''You trust him?''

She gave another shrug. '' 'Bout as much as I trust anybody.''

''That ain't saying much.''

''You got that right,'' she rejoined with a smirk.

''Y'all don't think Drew stole them cows, do you?'' Gabe asked, eyes wide and mouth hanging open.

''No, we don't,'' Cassie answered for everyone concerned. ''And if I hear otherwise, I'll be as mad as a wet hen. We've got to stick together on this.'' She looked out at the shadows stretching across the grassy acres, like black stains. ''Somebody wants this land mighty bad, and until we know who, we've got to watch our backs.'' She turned and headed for the house. ''I sure hope Drew watches his,'' she murmured under her breath.

Chapter 12

The next day Cassie worked with T-Bone in the branding pen. By midafternoon she was covered with dirt from head to foot as she wrestled a fat calf to the ground and held it while T-Bone pressed hot iron to its hip.

The stench of scorched hide choked her and her eyes watered as she let go of the bawling calf. The little doggie gave a kick that grazed Cassie's chin before she could duck out of the way.

"Ow, damn it!" She covered her stinging skin and thought for a moment she might cry. Swatting at the galloping calf, she turned away from T-Bone so he wouldn't see her discomfort.

"You okay?" he asked, his voice low and monotone.

"Yes. Dagburned cow kicked me."

"Yeah, they do that if you don't get out of their way. Can't blame them."

"I can if I want," she said, hearing the petulance in her voice and hating it. She looked across the land, something she'd done countless times since yesterday after Drew had left for the Bar Q. She saw a rider and

175

her heart bucked, but in the next instant she recognized Gabe's loose-limbed posture atop his stocky mustang. He was supposed to be herding more cattle to the pen, but there wasn't a cow in sight. "Will you look at that pea-brain? Here he comes riding like he's racing the Devil instead of working cattle, which is what I pay him to do."

"Maybe something's wrong."

Cassie's heart bucked again, this time with fear. As Gabe reined in his snorting horse, Cassie hurried to the fence.

"Is it Drew? What's happened to him? Tell me!" she demanded, her voice pitched high with alarm. She grabbed Gabe's boot in the stirrup and shook it.

"Drew? What about him?" Gabe slid off his horse. "Did y'all hear something?"

"Nope." T-Bone came to stand beside Cassie. He laid a hand on her shoulder and gave it a squeeze. "We thought you might have heard something since you're riding in here like your tail's on fire when you're supposed to be bringing us some more cows to brand."

"Uh . . . oh, yeah." Gabe removed his hat and scratched at his thatch of unruly hair. "I'll go back and get them. I saw Monroe Hendrix and I forgot . . . Anyway, I guess the sheriff told Hendrix about the rustled cows from the Bar Q, 'cause that's all he had on his mind. Told me he's hired a sharpshooter."

Cassie felt T-Bone's scrutiny, but she ignored him. She figured he suspected that she was having certain feelings for Drew Dalton. Her actions just now had given her away, and she wished she had exercised more restraint. Her two cowhands were terrible gossips, and she cringed when she thought of what they might say to Drew about her panic on his behalf.

"A sharpshooter?" T-Bone repeated with a squint. "What the hell for?"

"To kill anybody who tries to take Star H cattle," Gabe said, his eyes round with excitement.

"I wish the sheriff would keep his trap shut." Cassie crossed her arms on the top fence rail and rested her smarting chin on them.

"He's got to let other ranchers know what's going on, so they can protect their herds," T-Bone said, climbing up to sit on the rail and roll himself a smoke. "That's what he's hired to do."

"I wonder if he knows about Roe hiring a sharpshooter and taking the law into his own hands," Cassie said, looking to Gabe.

"Yeah, he knows. Hendrix said the sheriff thought it was a good idea."

Cassie released a groan of exasperation. "A good idea? Well, if that don't beat all. I think Drew and Roe are blustering bulls who should pull in their horns and set a trap instead of pawing and bellowing and shooting everything that moves."

"What kind of trap?" Gabe asked.

"If we'd work together, we could patrol our borders and maybe catch the rustlers some night. Roe's got . . . what, twenty hands?"

"More'n that," T-Bone said, blowing blue smoke from his cigarette. "I'd say he's hired thirty men. Wouldn't you, Gabe?"

Gabe nodded. "He hired four new ones a couple of weeks ago. He's looking for more and says he's going to add to his herd. Wants to be a real cattle baron, like them ones in Texas.''

Cassie nodded, recalling the ride home from the barn dance, when Monroe had told her about the wealth he'd seen while visiting a few ranchers in Texas last year.

''He'll have to change his ways,'' T-Bone said. ''Problem with Hendrix is that he wants to be a cattle baron without raising good cattle. I reckon the past few years his herd has improved some, but they still don't bring top dollar.''

''Yeah, they're mostly scrawny,'' Gabe agreed. ''Comes from years and years of him not paying enough attention to the breeding program. I think that's why he's all lathered up about this rustling business. He's afraid some of his improved herd will be taken and he'll be back to where he started.''

''We're all lathered up about the rustling,'' Cassie said.

''Now, who's that coming?'' T-Bone asked, straightening his back as he stretched to look across the land at an approaching horse and buggy.

''I don't recognize that rig,'' Cassie said. ''It's not Roe.''

''Looks like a woman driver,'' T-Bone said.

''A woman?'' Cassie slipped through the rails in the fence and waited for the buggy to draw closer. She didn't recognize the woman dressed in a light shade of purple until she was reining the old bay horse. ''Oh, lord,'' she whispered. ''It's Viola Danforth.''

''Lawrence Danforth's widow?'' Gabe asked.

''That's her,'' Cassie said. ''Betcha she's come here on a husband hunt.''

That made Gabe and T-Bone both hunch their shoulders as if they were trying to make themselves less conspicuous. Cassie laughed at them.

"Don't worry, fellas. I believe she's here to impress Drew," she said, still whispering, so as not to be heard by the woman who was now climbing down from the buggy. "The widow Danforth would be wanting herself a ranch *owner,* not a ranch *hand.*"

"Guess we'd better round up some more heifers," Gabe said, already moving toward his horse.

"Yeah, guess so," T-Bone said. "I'll ride with you."

"Y'all go on, slinking off with your tails between your legs," Cassie hissed at them, then turned toward Viola and forced a smile of greeting to her stiff lips. "Howdy, there, Viola. What you got there?" she asked, eyeing the wicker basket covered with a checked cloth.

Viola Danforth was a comely woman with her raven-black hair with one large streak of white right down the center of her head. She had green eyes and an aristocratic air. Everyone knew that she'd married Lawrence Danforth for money, not love, just like everyone knew that Cassie had married A.J. because he'd advertised for a wife. Viola's marriage hadn't lasted long and had produced no children when Lawrence was kicked in the head by a bull and died instantly, leaving his ranch to his brother, George, much to Viola's aggravation.

"Oh, I cooked up a little something." Viola glanced around, obviously looking for someone in particular. "Fried chicken, apple pie, honey nut bread."

"Somebody sick around here? Somebody have a baby?" Cassie asked, pretending not to understand Viola's intention.

"What?" Viola focused on Cassie for the first time. "Oh, no. I was . . . This is to welcome home Mr. Dalton."

"Mr. Dalton!" Cassie arched her brows and gave Viola a speculative look. "He'll be sorry he missed you."

"He isn't here?" Viola glanced in the direction T-Bone and Gabe had ridden. "Is he out on the range? I can wait—"

"He's gone on business. Won't be back until late tonight or tomorrow morning."

Viola's face fell like unleavened bread. "Oh." She stared at the basket she held, shrugged, and shoved it at Cassie. "Here."

"Thanks." Cassie took the offering. "I'll tell him you brought him some food. Of course, we feed him regular around here, you know."

"Yes, but . . . well, my fried chicken is legendary." Viola's green gaze moved slowly over Cassie, and her lips thinned in distaste. "What *have* you been doing?"

Suddenly Cassie felt like mule droppings. Looking down at her dirty clothes and knowing that her face was probably grimy, she wished for a tub of water to jump into. Her chin throbbed where the calf had kicked her, and she wondered if it might be turning blue or even swelling. She didn't dare touch the spot, not wanting to draw Viola's attention to it.

"I've been . . . that is, we . . . branding," she finally said, the words sticking to the roof of her mouth. "We're branding today."

"I see." Viola flicked a dandelion tuft from her sleeve. "My ranch hands see to that."

Cassie bristled, resenting Viola's air. "Our situations are different. George runs the Danforth spread, and *I'm* the boss of this one." She tucked her thumbs under her belt as she'd seen men do hundreds of times. "I wouldn't ask my ranch hands to do anything I'm not willing to do myself.''

"Now that Mr. Dalton's home, I should think he'd be running things around here.''

"Him being here hasn't changed anything," Cassie said, but the lie was too bitter on her tongue, and she had to sweeten it with truth. "Except that we're partners.''

"Partners?" Viola arched her perfectly shaped brows. "That's generous of him.''

"What's that mean?''

"This ranch is his." Viola made a grand gesture, her gloved hand graceful and sweeping. "It's generous of him to share it with you.''

"The way I have it figured, this ranch belongs as much to my son as it does to Drew. They're both offspring of A. J. Dalton.''

Viola gave a sniff, dismissing Cassie's reasoning. "I don't approve of how Mr. Dalton is being viewed now that he's home. I say if the court has found him innocent, then he is innocent. I wanted to let him know that he has a friend in me.''

Cassie forced a smile. "I'll be sure to tell him.''

"And tell him I will call again." She moved to the buggy. "I believe in being a good neighbor.''

Cassie pressed her lips together to keep from reminding Viola that she hadn't been interested in being such a good neighbor until Drew Dalton had showed up again.

"Did you know Drew before he was packed off to prison?" she asked as Viola settled herself on the padded buggy seat.

"No. I wasn't raised around here. I lived in Maryland before I came to Kansas to visit my aunt and uncle in the next county. I met Lawrence at a dance during that visit and decided to marry him."

Cassie was struck by a devilish idea that made her fight back a face-splitting grin. "Viola, you should pay a neighborly visit to Monroe Hendrix. He would surely appreciate getting a basket of chicken from you."

From her perch Viola gazed down her nose at Cassie. "Mr. Hendrix doesn't need my attentions when he has yours. Everyone is wondering when you two will marry."

Cassie felt every drop of blood drain from her face. "You can tell everyone that there won't be a marriage. Monroe is a neighbor and a friend. That's all."

Viola's smile was indulgent. "You don't have to get huffy, Cassie. I would think you'd be flattered to have a fine man like Mr. Hendrix sweet on you."

Cassie mirrored Viola's smile. "I'll tell him you said so, Viola. He probably has no idea you set such store in him."

Viola narrowed her eyes and picked up the reins. "I'll be back to speak with Mr. Dalton personally, so that there is no distortion of my friendly and respectful feelings for him. I wouldn't want him to think I sought anything more than his kind regard." She flicked the reins and the buggy set off.

Cassie whirled about and marched to the house. That uppity witch! What gave her the idea that Drew would be the least bit interested in eating her chicken or sharing her company? Nothing worse that a woman running after a man who wasn't even aware she was alive.

She slammed into the house, making Oleta jump with

alarm and so scaring Andy that he released a yowling wail.

"I'm sorry, baby," Cassie cooed, bending close to Andy and kissing his chubby cheek. He sat in his high chair, a few toys scattered on the supper table in front of him. "Hush, now. Mama didn't mean to startle you."

"Is your work done for the day?" Oleta asked.

"Yeah." Cassie sat at the kitchen table and pulled off her boots. Her feet stung inside her damp socks.

"What's in the basket?" Oleta asked, eyeing Viola's offering, which Cassie had dropped just inside the door.

"Viola Danforth brought some food for Drew. I guess she figures if she feeds him, he'll beg her to marry him just to get at her recipes."

Oleta giggled and peeked inside the basket. "Smells good."

"Put it out tonight for supper. We might as well eat it, since Drew can't."

"He should be back soon, *sí?*"

"Tonight or tomorrow." She tried to imagine Will Quentin's reaction when Drew told him about finding the cattle on Square D land. "Hope there wasn't any trouble," she murmured.

"You like each other now, don't you?" Oleta asked.

Cassie frowned. "We're partners."

"T-Bone says *Señor* Drew took Ice with him because he didn't want to leave him here with you."

"What?" Cassie squawked. "That's plumb stupid. T-Bone's mouth is running wild like a river."

Oleta gave a shy shrug. "T-Bone and Gabe think *Señor* Drew has gone soft on you."

Despite herself, Cassie smiled. She turned away from Oleta, embarrassed by her own pleasure. Drew soft on her? The thought sent a wave of giddiness through her that she had to clamp down on before she actually giggled with delight and made an even bigger fool of herself in front of Oleta.

"I've got to wash up," she announced, rising from the chair. "Heat some water for my bath, will you?"

"*Sí.*"

"And quit your grinning," Cassie said, but she was grinning, too.

"*Sí,*" Oleta said, blatantly disobeying.

"Do you think he believed you?" Ice asked as he and Drew rode side by side along a grassy path.

Drew slanted a glance at him. "Quentin, you mean?" When Ice nodded, Drew winced with regret. "There's no way to tell. He didn't at first, that's for sure."

"Good thing we ran into those two cowhands Quentin had dispatched to the Square D. Talk would have spread like wildfire, and you'd be the goat of the county."

"I already am that," Drew said darkly. "You hadn't noticed?"

"I'm new in town." Ice grinned. "So you have to prove yourself an honest man. You'll do it. You'll make them all eat crow."

Drew chuckled at the younger man's optimism and envied him that. The more days Drew lived, the less he believed in hope and justice. "At least I surprised Quentin by bringing his cattle back to him. He couldn't believe his eyes there for a minute."

"You did the right thing, *hombre*. That man will have to adjust his opinion of you now."

"I don't care what he thinks of me," Drew said, his anger firing again. He'd been blowing steam by the time he'd rounded the cattle into a pen near Quentin's ranch house. When his cattle had come up missing, Quentin had immediately sent his ranch hands to the Square D, having heard that Drew Dalton had been released from prison. Even now Drew ground his teeth in fury when he dwelled on that. He wondered if Will Quentin might be out to get him but had trouble believing it. He hadn't known the man that well, and Quentin had never shown any interest in the Square D.

He felt Ice's attentiveness and looked at him curiously. "What are you gawking at? Not my vest again." He laughed. Ice had been coveting his black vest for weeks.

"If you were a good friend, you would give me that vest."

Drew ran a hand down the front of it, fingering the silver disk buttons. "Give it to you, huh? How about if I let you try it on? If it fits, I might trade it for that Apache saddle blanket you've got in your bedroll."

"That's a swap!"

"It won't fit you." Drew took off the vest. "My shoulders are broader. I have a man's chest and yours is still growing."

"That's not what all the women tell me," Ice bragged, grabbing the vest from Drew and slipping his arms into it. It did hang more loosely on him, but he carried it well. Smoothing his palms down the soft leather, he whistled low. "This is one fine garment, *amigo*. I could get any woman I wanted wearing this."

"Is that all you think about? Getting another woman under you?"

"*Sí,*" Ice said. "That and raising horses and getting rich. What else should occupy a man's mind?"

"Good question." Drew fell silent, his mind seized with thoughts of Cassie. He'd thought of her often while he'd been away. He couldn't shake loose of her, not even in his dreams.

"Was your father a good-looking man?" Ice asked, out of the blue.

"Not particularly." Drew shifted his attention back to Ice, wondering what had spawned that question. He spurred Dynamite to catch up with Ice's gelding. "Why'd you ask that?"

"Oh, I was thinking about Cassie."

"What about her?"

"Don't growl at me like that," Ice said with a laugh. "I wasn't thinking about bedding her."

Drew faced forward, shaken by his own raw emotions.

"I was just wondering what she saw in your father. You know, why she decided to marry him. From what you've told me, he was no ladies' man."

"No, and he never tried to be. He usually bought his women. In a way, that's how he got Cassie."

"He bought her?"

"He advertised for a wife and she answered the call."

Ice shook his head. "A pretty woman like her? Why'd she do it?"

Another good question, Drew thought. Why did a woman with Cassie's looks settle for a man like A.J. Dalton? Even if she was nothing but a gold digger, she could have enticed a richer man, a better man. She was always telling him that she'd turned her share of heads, and he believed her, so why had she married A.J.?

"I think you should take the woman into your arms and erase your father from her mind."

"That's your answer for everything. You think that

thing between your legs is a magic wand.''

''Ah, but it is! I wave it and women swoon.''

Drew pretended to choke.

''If you need help romancing that woman, you ask your partner here, and I will come to your rescue. I know it has been a long time since you used your own magic wand, and you might have forgotten—''

''I've forgotten more than you'll ever know about pleasuring a woman, son.''

''You are slow, old man.''

''Maybe I don't want to have anything to do with the lady in question.''

''Your eyes slide over her like a lover's hand, my friend. Anyone can see that you want her.''

''That's bull,'' Drew denied hotly. ''You don't know what you're talking about. Hell, you see romance when a fly sticks to cow dung.''

Ice clucked his tongue, and his horse quickened to a trot, moving ahead of Drew on the trail. ''I think this vest is mine now.''

Drew chuckled. ''What about that Apache blanket? We had a swap, remember? Hey, get back here, you thief!''

Drew saw Ice jerk and pitch backward off his horse before the sound of the shot reached him. For a split second he couldn't comprehend what had happened, then he was on the ground in a crouch, his gun drawn, shielding Ice as best he could.

A quick assessment told him that Ice was conscious and bleeding, but from where he couldn't tell. Drew scanned the area. Trees were thick around them on either side of the trail. He steadied himself and regulated his breathing, trying to make less noise so he could hear any rustling of leaves, any snapping of branch, any click of ammunition sliding into a chamber. Ice moaned, and Drew pulled his hat down over his face to muffle the sound.

A glint in a thicket riveted his attention, and he waited, his skin beaded with sweat, his mouth coated with a thick, copper paste. He felt like a deer in a clearing. To hell with that.

Grabbing Ice under the arms, he pulled him off the trail and into the bushes. Hunkered beside him, Drew watched for any movement around them, his senses quivering. He checked on Ice and saw that he'd been shot in the back, high on the shoulder. Might have shattered bone. Easing the leather vest off Ice, he examined the wound through Ice's torn shirt and saw bone fragments. Not good.

"How is it?"

"Bastard shot you in the back," Drew said, avoiding the real answer.

"Who was it?"

"I never got a look at him. Hell, I don't even know where the shot came from."

"Me neither." Ice tried to sit up. "I can ride."

"You'll have to, because I can't do anything for you here."

After another five minutes or so with no sign of the shooter, Drew whistled for Dynamite. He pressed his bandanna into the wound in Ice's back to try to dam up the seeping blood. He helped Ice up into the saddle and tied the blanket from his bedroll around him. Ice was shaking, and his face had drained of blood.

"Hang on," Drew said.

Ice nodded, grabbing the saddle horn with both hands.

Drew went to look for Ice's horse. Luckily the animal had trotted only a short way down the path. Drew settled him down and climbed into the saddle. He looked back at Dynamite and whistled. Dynamite's ears stood up as straight as tent posts.

"Come on, son. Follow me." Drew took one more careful look around before he set his spurs and made for the ranch. The whole way he felt as if he were being watched, hunted. He expected to be gunned down and didn't relax until he crossed onto his own land. Even then he kept low in the saddle, glancing back from time to time to make sure Ice was still astride Dynamite.

The lights shining in the windows of the ranch house had never looked so good to him, and he sent up a prayer of thanks.

Chapter 13

~~⚬⚬⚬~~

Dressed for bed in a white nightgown, Cassie slipped on her patchwork robe and padded barefoot from the bedroom into the kitchen. She glanced out the window, wishing for Drew. She'd been sure he and Ice would make it back to the ranch by supper time, but there had been no sign of them.

They probably took a side trip to Abilene to drink and gamble, she told herself. Just like men not to consider others back at home who pace with worry all night long.

She shook off her irritation, realizing she sounded like somebody's wife. In Drew's absence she had also realized that she'd grown to depend on his company. It was good that they had found common ground and could get along with each other, but she was a fool to believe that anything more could come from their partnership.

He's decent, she told herself. Decency was conveyed in the set of his jaw, the glint in his eyes, the straightness of his back. A decent man. An honorable man. If he ever found out about her past, he'd have nothing more to do with her. She should just come right out and tell him, be done with it, but she couldn't. If she told him, others would eventually find out, and she'd never live down her past. She couldn't do that to her son either. She wanted everything beautiful for Andy. She wanted her son's respect.

Andy. This evening he'd taken his first steps without holding onto something. She'd been overjoyed, and then in the next instant, she'd been sad. Sad because she wished Drew had been there to share in the joyful moment. Drew would have been so proud. He really did have a soft spot for Andy, and Andy couldn't keep his eyes off Drew. Cassie had noticed how her son watched everything Drew did, how he giggled when Drew showed him any attention, how he waved his fists and kicked his feet excitedly when Drew entered the house at the end of each day. There was a bond between them.

She hadn't been aware of staring out the window until her vision sharpened on dark shapes moving against the indigo sky. Riders? Cassie gripped the sill and pressed the tip of her nose to the pane, her eyes wide and searching.

"Please make it be Drew," she whispered, her breath fogging the glass.

Another minute passed before she was sure she recognized the set of his shoulders. Her burst of happiness was tempered by the slumped figure on the other horse. Either Ice was dead tired or he was almost dead.

She ran out to the front porch to wait for them. They came at a lope with Dynamite carrying Ice instead of Drew.

"What's wrong with him?" Cassie asked when Drew was close enough to hear her.

"Shot," he answered tersely, swinging out of the saddle before the winded gelding had come to a stop.

"Who shot him?"

"Don't know."

In the light spilling from the open door, Cassie saw worry and fatigue etched on Drew's face, and she hurt right along with him. A rumbling came from the north, and a few seconds later lightning streaked across the sky. She touched Drew's sleeve. It was damp.

"You think it was Quentin?"

"I doubt it, but I don't know. I didn't see the shooter."

"You been riding in the rain?"

"We rode through some drizzle. I've managed to stay ahead of the storm, but it's coming. Help me get him inside. Can we put him in your bed?"

"Yes."

He grabbed a handful of the blanket wrapped around Ice and pulled. With no resistance Ice fell sideways off the horse and into Drew's arms. Drew grunted under the man's weight. Cassie went around to Ice's other side and draped his arm around her shoulders. With Ice dangling between them like a side of beef, she and Drew carried him up the porch steps and into the house.

Ice mumbled in his fever, the words running into each other and making no sense. They angled him to the foot of the bed and then let him fall back on it.

Andy roused in his crib, and Cassie patted his tummy until he dropped off to sleep again.

"Maybe I should move his crib out to the kitchen," Drew said. "Ice might make some noise once you start working on him."

She nodded. "The bullet's still in him?"

"As far as I know. I didn't stop to look him over real

good. I figured the best thing to do was to get him here quick as I could."

"Am I supposed to dig the bullet out of him?"

He looked at her with a glint of challenge in his steel-blue eyes. "You seem handy with a medicine kit."

"You have to help me." She examined her patient. "Strip those clothes off him, boots and all. I'll gather up what I need in the kitchen." Turning, she bumped into a wide-eyed Oleta. "Put the kettle on, Oleta, and keep this door shut. He'll probably start moaning and wake up the baby. I'll leave little Andy to you, seeing as I'll have my hands full."

"He was shot?"

"Yes."

Oleta chewed on her lower lip and wrung her hands. She scuttled backward, cowering into the kitchen shadows. "You think whoever shot him followed him here?" She cast a nervous glance at the door and windows.

"I doubt it. Oleta, quit shaking like a leaf and do as I asked." Cassie gave the girl a push. "Get along now and make yourself useful."

Thunder rolled and shook the roof. Oleta let out a squeak.

"It's only a storm, 'fraidy cat." Cassie rummaged through the shelves for her medicine box and some stained tea towels. She located a dusty bottle of whiskey in the back of the potato bin and uncorked it. The fumes made her eyes water. "I knew this would come in handy one day." Armed, she marched back into the bedroom.

Drew had removed Ice's clothing and was pulling a sheet up to his waist. Clothes lay in an untidy pile on the floor. She reached down and picked up the leather vest on top and examined the bullet hole in its back.

"This is yours."

Drew looked over his shoulder at her. His brows met in a scowl. "Yeah, but Ice was wearing it. He fancied it and I let him try it on."

She dropped it back onto the pile. "Maybe the shooter was aiming for you. Maybe he thought he shot you."

"Because of that vest?" Drew asked in a scoffing tone.

Cassie moved to the side of the bed where she could see Drew's face. His expression told her a different story. "You wear the vest most of the time. Anybody who has watched you lately knows it. And nobody else around here has one anything like it."

"What's your point?"

"I made my point and you know it." She held his gaze and he looked away first. "Could be the shooter plugged the wrong man."

"And it could be he meant to rob us and chickened out or maybe he meant to scare us, send us a message. Didn't matter who he shot. The bullet was the message and he delivered it." He looked into her face, his features carefully schooled now. "What do you want me to do, hold him down?"

"For a start, yeah." She lifted the whiskey bottle and took a long drink, then handed it to him. The liquor burned and smoked her insides. Her eyes teared. "Take a swig and then get ready to pour it over the wound when I tell you." Her voice came out gruff, roughened by the whiskey.

"Are you okay? You're not going to pass out on me, are you?"

"I'm not planning on it." She gathered in a deep

breath and moved the candles and lanterns closer to the edge of the bedside table, throwing more light onto Ice. "Flip him over onto his stomach."

Drew's gaze remained on her face, worry etching lines into his. He took a drink from the bottle and coughed. "That's strong stuff."

She nodded. "I learned a long time ago that whiskey's only good for one thing—making the world go away when it gets too ugly." She picked up a knife and passed its blade several times through a candle's flaming heart. "This is gonna get ugly."

Drew emerged from the bedroom first. Oleta had left a lamp burning on the kitchen table. Outside it was still dark, but he knew it was past dawn. Fat storm clouds obscured the new sun. Rain beat frantically on the window panes. Drew glanced toward Oleta's room. Sometime during the night she had taken Andy and his crib in there with her and closed the door. Drew hoped she and the baby were asleep. It had been a long, noisy, bloody night.

But Ice was alive and should keep on living. And he had Cassie to thank for that.

Cassie. Drew sat in one of the rockers near the fireplace and let his head loll back against the cushion. He closed his eyes, and his feelings for Cassie Dalton poured over him, chasing away the gloominess. Cassie the strong, the beautiful. Cassie, the woman of rock-steady hands, of sterling courage, of iron will.

The removal of the bullet from Ice's back had been tedious. The lump of lead was buried so deep in muscle that Cassie had whispered a fervent prayer as she'd extracted the lead. When she held it up, her eyes had shone with triumph and her lips had trembled with relief.

In that moment Drew had realized that not only had he grown to respect this woman, to admire her, to want her, but he was damn close to being in love with her, too. In that crystal-clear moment she was incredibly beautiful to him, so beautiful that his eyes had watered.

He sat forward in the chair now, elbows propped on his knees, and scrubbed his face with his hands.

Damn it, man, get hold of yourself!

The words were spoken sternly in his mind, but they could not penetrate his heart. Had his father ever felt this for her, even an ember of it?

He doubted it. Couldn't imagine it. Not any more than he could imagine Cassie feeling tenderness for A.J. Dalton.

Boots scuffled on the porch and a soft knock sounded on the door. Drew stood and went to open the door, knowing who it was before he peered out into the grayness at T-Bone's craggy face beneath his wet hat.

"Saw your horses."

"We got back sometime after midnight."

T-Bone scratched his beard. "There was blood on your tack."

"Ice was shot in the back. Cassie got the bullet out of him a little while ago. It was tough going, but I think he'll be all right."

"Holy Moses! Who shot him?"

"We didn't get a look at him. The shot came from a blind of trees." He stepped out onto the porch and stretched his arms over his head. "You and Gabe go ahead and do what you can today. Cassie hasn't had any sleep and I won't be fit for much."

"Yeah, sure, you two get some rest. I'll make sure

Gabe breaks a sweat. Between the two of us we ought to finish up the branding and tagging.''

"That's good. How do they look?''

"Better than I thought they would. They're all healthy and fat.''

"Good breeding will do that.'' Drew clapped a hand on T-Bone's shoulder. "After I get some shut-eye, I'll pitch in.''

"Like I said, we can handle it for today.'' T-Bone jumped off the end of the porch and hunched his shoulders against the rain. He ran toward the bunkhouse, dodging puddles along the way.

When Drew entered the house again, he saw the bedroom door open. Cassie slipped out and closed it behind her. Her steps were unsteady, and she braced herself against the kitchen table before lowering herself into one of the chairs.

Drew came toward her. "You okay? How about I make us some coffee? Could you eat something?''

She smiled wanly. "Just about anything,'' she assured him. "And coffee sounds mighty good.''

She cocked her head to one side, and he realized she was listening to the patter of rain on the roof. He was content simply to look at her, to admire the sheen of her hair, the smoothness of her brow, the delicate coloring of her skin. He had never enjoyed the sight of a woman more. While he prepared the coffee and heated up some leftover stew, he glanced at her from time to time, unable to understand the upheaval of his feelings for her. After a few minutes, she sighed and cleared her throat.

"His fever has broken,'' she said, her voice raspy, strained. "I was afraid . . . But he's breathing easy now and his skin is damp. That's a good sign.''

"He'll make it," Drew told her.

"He sure lost a lot of blood."

"But he'll make it."

She nodded. "Yes, I believe so. You think a lot of him, don't you?"

"Yeah. He's had it tough. His family is poor. Some of them are in jail. Some are running from the law. He could have gone that way, but he didn't. He's a good man, a good friend."

"And he took a bullet for you, whether he realizes it yet or not."

"We can't be sure of that." He didn't like that flicker of fear in her eyes.

"How was Quentin with you?"

"Cautious." He set a cup of coffee in front of her, then ladled stew into two bowls. "We ran into a couple of his men who were headed here." He placed the bowls of steaming beef and vegetables on the table and located a hunk of bread in the warmer.

"They were headed here? What for?"

"They were looking for stolen cattle. Quentin said he'd heard I was out of prison, so he figured his cattle would end up on my ranch."

She set her coffee cup down on the table with force. Her eyes flashed with sudden anger. "Why, that mangy, no-good—"

He laughed under his breath and sat down across from her. "I told him what I think of him. He was surprised that I'd brought the cattle back, but I couldn't say for sure that he believed my version of how they got to the Square D."

"I think he sent one of his men after you to shoot you."

''No. That doesn't add up.''

''He didn't believe you. He wanted to make sure you didn't steal any more cattle.''

''The way I figure it, some old boy was going to shoot us and rob us, but he lost his nerve. Or maybe we moved quicker than he expected, and he couldn't get off another clean shot. I don't know. I never got a look at the man. Could have been somebody who thought he was shooting at a deer and found out too late that he'd shot one of the two-legged variety.''

She frowned and ate ravenously for a few minutes. ''I don't like what's happening around here. The sheriff and a couple of his men came by looking for those cows.''

A cold uneasiness settled in Drew. ''How'd he know about them?''

''He said some men told him they saw tracks. He didn't know the men, he said.''

''That sounds suspicious.''

''Don't I know it. This whole business is stinking to high heaven.''

''Maybe I should clear out until—''

''No.'' She set her spoon down and delivered him a level gaze that made his loins burn. ''Don't leave.'' She lowered her lashes and pink color stained her cheeks.

''You've changed your tune,'' he said, wanting to stroke her shimmering hair and draw her gaze back to his. ''Not too long ago you were telling me to clear out.''

''I've gotten to know you since then.'' She shrugged and finished the stew in her bowl, then wrapped both hands around the coffee mug and brought it to her lips. ''You're useful,'' she whispered. ''You're a good . . .

worker.'' Her lashes lifted and her brown eyes were soft and luminous, telling him things her words had not conveyed.

She went to his head like whiskey, and Drew's breathing sped up and he felt himself harden with desire. He told himself he had to move in a different direction, or he'd regret this night for the rest of his life.

But she was the one who moved—in his direction. She set her empty bowl and mug on the sideboard, but she didn't move away. She was within easy reach, and she didn't move away.

He shook his head, forbidding himself the pleasure, but his arm hooked around her waist and she poured herself into his lap like honey. As sweet as sin, her mouth covered his, and he forgot his denials, his promise to keep himself from her, his decision to be a loner and never give his heart to a woman or accept another's heart to break.

''I sure missed you,'' she whispered, lifting her lips from his and combing his hair back with her fingers. ''Andy took his first steps without holding onto anything and—''

''No kidding? Damn, I wish I'd been here to see that.''

''I wanted you to be here, too, Drew. Oh, how I wanted—'' She moaned and pressed her full lips to his again, her arms twining around his neck, her soft breasts flattening against his chest.

Her hair felt like satin, and he buried his fingers in it and crushed her mouth to his. He thrust his tongue inside, and she groaned and touched his tongue with hers, sliding and stroking, advancing and retreating. He opened his mouth wide, taking her in, but still not satisfied. He pulled open her robe and cupped her breasts in his hands. Her nipples hardened under the thin veneer of her cotton gown. There was an instant when he thought about tearing the fabric, ripping it from her body in a mindless act of possession, but then she was kissing his neck and murmuring in his ear, distracting him with sensations that were foreign and delightful.

". . . so strong . . . touching me, yes, yes . . ."

Her words buzzed in his ears. He stroked her back and hips, then her hair again. Her mouth returned to his and she dropped lush kisses there, one after another. He closed his eyes, drifting in the sensations of having her pay attention to him, touch him, caress him, as she had so many times in his dreams.

"Drew . . . Drew . . ." She said his name, making him smile. "I've thought about this . . . about us being to-gether . . ."

He made a humming noise in his throat where her lips nuzzled his skin.

". . . falling hard for you . . . loving you . . ."

The words splashed through him, cooling his ardor. She felt the change, or perhaps the words had the same effect on her. She straightened from him, and her eyes cleared slowly until all passion was gone from them.

Thunder rumbled overhead, and she looked up at the log ceiling, then over at the loft where he slept. She smoothed her hands across his shoulders, but absently, not ardently, as she had done moments ago.

"I . . . I . . ." She smiled briefly and stood up. "I'm glad you're back and I want you to stay. If I couldn't run you off this land, then nobody else should be able to do it." She rearranged her clothes and retied the belt of her robe. "What I said just now . . ."

"I know you didn't mean it."

He couldn't tell what she was thinking when she looked at him, her eyes soft but somehow haunted. Rising from the chair and feeling stiff and swollen, he reached out to touch the bruise on her chin.

"What happened here?"

"I got kicked by a calf we were branding. It's nothing."

"Could have been something, though. You take on too much, Cassie. You should let men do that work and you—"

"Bake bread and breastfeed the baby?" she cut in. "I can do all that *and* help with the ranch."

"But you don't have to," he said, trying not to pick a fight, especially with passion for her still smoking his mind and thickening his blood. "That's all I'm saying. You don't have to. Since you trust me now and you value my work—"

"Yes?" she asked, her head coming up, interest sparking in her eyes.

"You ought to go out more." He almost winced, hating to speak the words, although he knew they were the right ones. Yes, he could take advantage of her now, but he wouldn't. He thought too much of her. She needed a good man, a man worthy of her, and he knew that man wasn't him.

Her brows met in a scowl. "Out where?"

"Out," he said, gesturing toward the front door. "Out to socials or whatever. Out to town."

"Town," she repeated with a snarl. "What is it with you and town? You're always wanting me to go there."

"That's where you're more likely to meet a man."

"Meet a man?" she parroted again, this time with a

short laugh. "I don't have to go to town for that."

"You mean Monroe?"

"Yes. And you."

He shook his head. "You need to hook up with some-one closer to your age. You up and married my father and he was way too old for you, and now you're mess-ing with Roe and he's too old for you, too. You need someone younger."

"Like you?" she persisted with a sly smile.

Drew edged away from her while he still could. She was working on him, chipping away at his defenses, making a mockery of his honorable intentions.

"Someone my age or younger. Like Ice."

"Ice?" She laughed again. "I don't want to take in someone else to raise, thank you."

"You can do better than Roe. You need someone to help you raise that boy and give him brothers and sis-ters."

But you couldn't do that, huh? Something wrong with your equipment?"

He sent her a black look. "No, but I'm not fit to raise any children."

She gave him a once-over. "And why not? You look fit to me."

"In here." He tapped his chest. "Just like my old man, my heart is dried up. He sure wasn't a good father. I grew up with no one to look up to, to fashion myself after. Then in prison . . . Well, what heart I had is as hard as stone now."

Cassie shook her head. "Don't blame A.J. for your reluctance to love anyone, Drew Dalton. If we can't rise above our families, then many of us are lost at birth. You pointed out before that Ice is a good man, but some of his relatives aren't. We all have free will, Drew. Even you.'' She propped her hands on her hips, and the robe opened a little. He jerked his gaze away from her. ''By the way, Viola dropped by to let you sample her wares. She was awfully disappointed to find you gone.''

Drew scratched absently at the bristles sprouting on his cheeks and chin. ''Who? Viola? What are you talking about?''

''Viola Danforth,'' she said somewhat angrily. ''She came by today with a big basket of fried chicken to tempt you. We ate it for dinner. Wasn't all that tasty, although Viola said she was famous for—''

''Danforth? Is she George's sister?''

''Sister-in-law. She's Lawrence's widow.''

''Oh, yeah. I heard about him dying, but I don't recall seeing her—''

''She was at the barn dance.'' Cassie pulled her robe more tightly around her and went into the parlor. She sat on the sofa and hugged herself. ''She's wanting to measure you for a wedding suit.''

He batted aside that notion. ''I'm not the marrying kind.''

''Well, me neither.''

Drew slanted her a dubious glance. ''That's not true. You're a nest builder. You came here to marry a stranger, you wanted a nest so bad. And you had yourself a baby soon as you could. You're the marrying kind, all right.''

''How come you're so dead set against it?'' she asked, combing her fingers through her long hair and working out the tangles he had put there.

''Just doesn't interest me.'' He could see that she didn't believe him, and he didn't know what he could say to convince her. In truth, he had never wanted to marry, but thoughts of a life with her kept intruding on him, messing with his head, his heart. It was damned unsettling. "You'll marry again, though, if you ever get out and about and find yourself somebody worth your while."

She shot up from the sofa, swayed on her feet, then placed a hand to her head and shut her eyes. "I'm too tired for this."

Drew had an arm around her for support before he realized he'd moved. She slumped against him, and it was too late to withdraw his arm, too late to make her stand on her own. With her body against his, her heat mixing with his, his other arm circled her of its own volition. Natural. Right as rain. She sighed and tipped her head back to look into his eyes.

He wanted badly to kiss her again, but he knew he couldn't stop himself again from taking all of her, and he didn't think she'd try to stop him either.

Instead of kissing her mouth, he brought her hand up to his lips. He stroked her slim fingers and ran the pad of his thumb across her short nails. How he loved her hands. These hands she covered with gloves, keeping them soft and unblemished. A lady's hands. He pressed his lips to her middle knuckle and she trembled. Her eyes were luminous, her breath sweet.

"Drew," she whispered, "I swear, if you don't—"

He curved his other hand at the back of her head and brought her face to his shoulder, stopping her words. Her useless, pointless words.

"You should go to bed," he said, and he felt her stir restlessly against him, but he held her even closer, imprisoning her. "You can sleep up in the loft. I'll make do in the bunkhouse.'' He let go of her and strode toward the front door. ''It's raining buckets, so nobody will get much work done. I've already told T-Bone to work without us today. We're both dead on our feet. The way it's raining, though, nothing much will get done.''

He meant to leave then, just leave and not look back at her or give her a chance to call to him, to say one more word to him, but something compelled him to pause, to look over his shoulder at her. She was sitting on the sofa again, her eyes bruised and dark, full of questions.

''When Ice comes to, I know he'll thank you, but I want to thank you, too. We're both beholden to you.''

She blinked slowly, then shook her head. ''I did what anybody would do.''

''I'm not so sure. You did more than just patch him up.'' He smiled, thinking how deceptively dainty she appeared. ''For a little thing, you're mighty strong.'' He dipped his head. '' 'Night, Cassie. Get some sleep.'' Then he opened the door to the wet day and plunged into it.

Cassie reached out, meaning to detain him, but none of the words in her head made it to her throat. Her hand fell back into her lap and she closed her eyes. She was drained. Wrung dry of emotion. Listlessly she made herself rise from the sofa and labor up the ladder to the loft. It wasn't until she was halfway to the bed that it dawned on her she hadn't been up here since Drew had claimed it.

Irritated at his intrusion, she'd refused to mount the ladder even to gather laundry. He'd brought her important papers and ledgers downstairs to her when she'd asked for them. She noted that he had shoved her desk, crates, and the rest of her belongings into one corner and had draped a sheet over them.

His bed was simply a collection of blankets and bedding on the floor. An oil lamp and a box of matches lay atop a crate beside it. She approached the arrangement with trepidation. Could she sleep here, smelling him on the bedclothes, letting the blankets that warmed his flesh warm hers?

Slipping out of her robe, she eased her tired body onto the pallet and found it surprisingly comfortable. It was thick, and the blanket and sheet she pulled up over her were cozy. And they did smell of him.

Cassie inhaled the scent of Drew and cursed him for getting her all fired up over him and then acting as if she'd called him a bad name when she'd forgotten herself and said she was falling for him. What did he expect? Did he think she was the kind of woman who threw herself at a man when she cared nothing for him?

Well, of course he does, an inner voice mocked her. *That's exactly what you did with his father, isn't it? Threw yourself into a marriage when you had barely met the man? Why shouldn't his son think of you as no better than a whore?*

Especially now, after she'd all but asked him to kiss her, to make love to her, would have if he hadn't stopped her.

Her body throbbed with unspent desire, and she clutched at the bed covers and writhed with longing. Oh, the way he kissed her! The way his hands moved on her! Heaven. Sheer heaven. How could she sit back and watch some woman take him, seduce him, win him? Someone like Viola Danforth.

He might not be the marrying kind, but he was the

wanting kind, and he had wanted her—for a few minutes.

She would keep a tight rein on herself and not let herself fall too hard for him. She could do that. Wouldn't be wise to let things go on too long, but a night or two of letting herself go, giving herself to him . . . how could that hurt? And by gum, she deserved it! She deserved to be with somebody who could make her heart gallop. Someone challenging. Drew had said it best. *Someone worth her while.*

Recalling the childhood game of tag, she let her fantasies run amuck in her mind.

"You're it, Blue Eyes," she murmured. "You're *it.*"

Chapter 14

Two days later, T-Bone and Drew helped move Ice from Cassie's bedroom to the bunkhouse. Weak but mending, Ice had insisted on vacating Cassie's sanctuary, insisting that she should be back in her own room with her baby by her side.

Because Ice was showing signs of recovery, Cassie finally agreed. She wanted to sleep in her own bed again instead of taking Drew's. She was tempted enough without having to lie upon bedding imprinted with his big, strong body.

The rain had stopped after soaking the land. Puddles glimmered in the sunshine, evaporating with each passing hour. The land greened up and the cattle were divided, some herded to the south pasture, the others winnowed out for market. They were put in a holding pen and given extra grain to fatten them for the trip the first of June.

Two young bulls were sold at high prices. Cassie heard that Monroe's randy bulls were underweight and had crooked bones. Nobody had been interested. Finally Roe made a deal with Grandma Nelson, selling both for half what one young bull had brought at the Square D.

After getting Ice settled into the bunkhouse, Drew brought the skittish mare out to the corral to work her. Spotting them through her bedroom window, Cassie quickly finished changing the sheets and went outside. Rain clouds scuttled off to the west, and the sun beat down, throwing diamonds into the mud puddles.

She loved to watch Drew work the horses, her fascination with his technique never waning. She'd heard of men, Indians mostly, who could speak a silent language to a horse and make the animal do his bidding, but she'd never seen the practice with her own eyes until she'd watched Drew. He could settle a nervous horse with a whispered word and slip a lead rope on with no trouble at all.

Climbing to the top fence rail, Cassie perched there and lifted a hand in greeting when Drew spotted her. He waved back before concentrating again on the jittery mare. The animal snorted and pranced nervously in the corral, flinging mud and attitude. The other animal in the pen, the two-legged one dressed in dark trousers, boots, dove-gray shirt, and red bandanna tied around his neck, moved with slow deliberation and in sharp contrast to the mare.

Cassie smiled, anticipation coiling pleasantly in her chest as she waited for the show to begin. She had found precious little time to be alone with Drew in the past two days. With Ice in the house, their usual routine had been interrupted. Drew had taken his meals with Ice in her bedroom to spend time with his friend and encourage his recovery. With Drew sleeping in the bunkhouse, T-Bone and Gabe had seen more of him than Cassie lately.

The time apart had given her a chance to cool off and

consider her desire for him. She wanted him, wanted to be loved by him, but she doubted she'd be satisfied with only a night or two in his arms. How could she live with the man after having him intimately but knowing she could not have him totally? It wouldn't be fair to either of them, she told herself. He deserved a decent woman. He'd been through hell and back and he should have everything wonderful from here on. She just wished she could be that somebody wonderful.

The mare suddenly stopped, stared at her two-legged nemesis for a full minute, then reared and swung and trotted to the far side of the corral, tail swishing.

Drew chuckled. ''See what she did?''

''What?'' Cassie asked, knowing there must be more to what she had seen.

''She's showing her disrespect. She told me to get along and leave her be.''

''What will you—''

He held up a hand to silence her. The mare was looking at him again, her head swung around, tail still swishing. Drew moved forward. The mare gave a whinny, showed her blocky teeth, and trotted to the other corner, farther away.

Wonder what she said then? Cassie wondered. Drew sauntered forward a few steps, stopped, fingered the bridle in his hands, whistled softly. The mare's ears flicked forward.

''Easy, easy, easy,'' he chanted in a whisper in time with his footfalls as he approached the mare, not directly, but in a zigzag pattern.

The mare stood still, seemingly as transfixed as Cassie was. But when Drew was within reach of her, the gray horse whirled away. Drew whistled. The mare stopped.

Drew shuffled his feet in the dirt, turned on his heels, and walked away from the horse.

"Now what are you doing?" Cassie asked.

"Showing her who's boss. Horses have a pecking order, same as most animals. They travel together, like dogs, and migrating animals generally have leaders and followers. I'm making her see that I'm a leader and she's going to have to follow me."

Cassie shook her head. It was mumbo jumbo to her, but he'd saddle-tamed two horses with this same nonsense.

He pivoted toward the mare again and strode forward in a straight line. Reaching out, he grabbed a handful of mane and leaned into the horse, whispering in her ear. She twitched but didn't pull away. He let go of her, waved a hand, and she scampered toward the corner. He whistled. She stopped, looked at him, waited for him to join her again.

For the next half-hour Cassie observed the strange interplay. Whether he cared to admit it or not, Drew had a way with most animals, not just horses. Although he often told her that he wasn't interested in cattle, he had a vast knowledge of the bovine. He worried about them as much as she did. He was a cattleman, no matter what he said.

Who was trying to get him thrown back into prison or worse, killed? Who did he threaten? Who despised him? She knew so little about his life before he'd been imprisoned. Maybe she should ask around, starting with Gabe and T-Bone, both of whom had known Drew but had given her scant information about him.

Drew slipped the bridle over the mare's ears. Cassie sat forward, amazement flowering in her. He'd done it again. Somehow he had gained the horse's trust. The gray mare was now under his command.

Cassie smiled to herself, struck by the irony. She should understand this "nonsense" better than she did. After all, the man had gained her trust fairly quickly.

Drew led the mare around the corral, stopping, starting up again, then stopping. The horse obeyed, seemingly happy to do so.

Cassie wiped her sweaty palms on her leather skirt and laughed nervously. The man had magic in him. Pure, old-fashioned magic.

The crunch of wheels on pebbles broke through her reverie, and she looked over her shoulder to see a buggy she instantly recognized. She groaned.

"Who's that?" Drew asked.

"Viola Danforth," Cassie answered, giving him a sour smile. "The woman is nothing if not persistent." She dropped to the ground and brushed dust from her blouse and leather skirt.

"Hello, Viola," Cassie called, shading her eyes with one hand. "Did you bring some more food?"

Malice flickered momentarily in Viola's green eyes, then she smiled stiffly and displayed a big basket. "Yes, I did. I see that Mr. Dalton is here today. Don't let me keep you from your chores, Cassie."

For a moment Cassie was sorely tempted to remain steadfastly at Viola's side and spoil her plans to be alone with Drew, but then her childish jealousy would be on display not only for Viola, but also for Drew to see. She had no rights to him and certainly no right to be possessive of him.

But I am, she thought, angry with herself. *I'm pea*

green with jealousy and I wish I could order Viola off this land!

"Drew!" she called, waving him over. "Viola Danforth has brought you some dinner! Leave that mare and be neighborly, why don't you."

Not waiting for him to join them, Cassie started for the house. "Y'all can eat out on the porch, if you want."

"That would be perfect," Viola said, almost purring. "Thank you, Cassie.

Slamming into the house, Cassie exchanged a speaking glance with Oleta. She removed her gloves and hat and tossed them into a chair.

"She bring more food?" Oleta asked.

"Why, certainly," Cassie answered, not bothering to hide her irritation. "She figures we serve hog slop here, so Drew will swoon when he gets a taste of her vittles and he'll marry her to keep his stomach full."

"We do not serve hog slop," Oleta said, frowning. "He eats good. Everyone eats good here."

Cassie looked out the window. Drew and Viola were standing by her buggy, and Drew was looking into the basket Viola held out for his inspection.

"The woman is shameless," Cassie groused. "She's batting her lashes so much it's a wonder she isn't creating a whirlwind out there."

"I saw her making eyes at him at the barn dance."

"You did?" Cassie asked, looking over her shoulder at Oleta.

"*Sí.* She could not take her eyes off him, and she asked everyone who he was and what they knew about him."

"That he was in prison didn't seem to bother her."

"Oh, no. She was so . . . so *simpática.* She said it was

a shame that he had been locked up and he did nothing wrong.''

"Here they come." Cassie moved away from the window and spun toward the table. She grabbed up her gloves and hat, then put them back down, flustered and agitated. ''I hate this. I'm the one who is shameless, acting like a ninny.''

The squeak of boards on the front porch sent her gaze back to the window. Viola and Drew sat on the porch steps, and Viola spread out a checkered tablecloth. She was jabbering like a magpie, and Drew was smiling politely. He glanced toward the window, and Cassie darted back, but she thought he'd seen her spying on them.

Andy spoke in his baby gabble, and Cassie picked him up from the floor and sat in the rocker. She let him breastfeed while she rocked furiously and tried not to hear the occasional fit of laughter from Viola or the rumble of Drew's voice. Closing her eyes, she silently recited every rhyme and psalm she knew and then tried to recall bits of song lyrics. But part of her mind never relinquished the picture of Viola and Drew sharing a meal out on the porch. What did Drew think of the woman? Did he find her attractive?

Oleta busied herself with preparations for supper. She kneaded dough and peeled potatoes and onions.

''They are sitting in the swing now,'' Oleta whispered.

Cassie opened her eyes, then shut them again when she caught a glimpse of the two on the porch swing. Thank heavens, they weren't sitting close, leaving a discreet wedge of space between them. Cassie lifted one eyelid for a brief look and was relieved to see that Drew hadn't even rested an arm across the back of the swing.

Good. He should keep his hands to himself!

Andy fell asleep and Cassie buttoned her blouse, but she sat woodenly in the chair and rocked. She wanted Viola gone before she ventured outside again and faced Drew. When she heard the buggy pulling away, she released a long sigh and stood up.

"She stayed long enough," she said to Oleta as she carried Andy into the bedroom and placed him in his crib.

"Only a little over an hour," Oleta said.

An hour? Cassie glanced at the clock on the mantel, surprised that Oleta was right. It had seemed longer than that. A couple of hours at least.

Drew strode in, Viola's basket swinging from his fingers. He set it on the table.

"Did she forget that?" Oleta asked.

"No. We couldn't eat all of it, so she left it. Chicken and biscuits, freshly churned butter, and a jar of pear honey we didn't even open. We can have it for supper if you want."

"I don't want it," Cassie said, glancing disdainfully at the basket. "We've had her chicken and I don't care for any more."

"I thought it was tasty."

"Did you?" Cassie speared him with a pointed glare. "Then *you* eat it. Oleta has already started on supper, haven't you?"

"*Sí,* but I can—"

"So we don't need *her* leftovers," Cassie cut in.

Drew shrugged. "Fine." He withdrew the jar of golden pear honey and placed it on the table. "I'll take the rest of this out to the bunkhouse for the men. I know they'll enjoy it."

"You do that," Cassie sassed, then shoved past him out the door. She was in the sun before she realized she'd left without her hat and gloves. Grimly she turned to retrace her steps, only to find Drew approaching her. He was grinning, holding Viola's basket in one hand and her own hat and gloves in the other.

"Here you go," he said, extending them to her.

"Thanks." She snatched them from him.

"Don't mention it." He strode past her. "It would be a damn shame to toughen up those pretty hands of yours or blister that nose you aim at the sky like you're the cattle queen."

She felt her mouth drop open as she turned to stare at his back. "You've got me confused with another widow!"

Laughing, he shook his head and kept going, swinging the basket like it was a young lady's hand.

Cassie slammed her boot into the dirt in a fit of aggravation. Suddenly, she became aware of her stance—hands on hips, feet planted apart, nose in the air. She snapped her chin down and wedged her hat onto her head.

Cattle queen! She hoped Viola's chicken gave him a stomachache!

Ice was sitting up in bed playing solitaire when Drew entered the bunkhouse, Viola's basket in hand.

"Hey, there!" Ice grinned. "I see the sun's out. I thought you'd be up to your armpits in mud and steers."

"I will be by sundown." Drew pulled up a chair and sat beside the bed, placing the basket within Ice's reach. "A widow lady brought this by. Thought you and the boys might enjoy it."

Ice lifted the napkin and sniffed. "Fried chicken?"

Drew nodded. "And it's tasty."

"Widow woman?" Ice selected a thigh and sank his white teeth into it. "She tasty, too?"

Drew chuckled. "I wouldn't know, partner, but she's easy on the eyes."

"Yeah? Who is she?"

"Her name's Viola. She spotted me at the barn dance and decided to be neighborly."

Ice snickered. "Ain't that sweet. I bet Cassie blew smoke out her stack, eh?"

Drew ran a hand around the back of his neck and laughed, the sound rumbling in his chest. "Yeah, she—" A thorny thought pricked his jovial mood. "Why'd you ask that?"

Ice waved the half-eaten thigh in the air. "Don't keep riding that horse, *amigo*. It's me. Ice. You can talk man to man with me, eh? I know that you get hard when you look on that woman. I *know* this, so talk from your heart with me, *por favor.*"

Drew glared at the other man for a few moments before conceding the point and dropping his guard. "I think she was jealous."

Ice chuckled. "Good."

"Not good," Drew said, shaking his head. "She's too fine for the likes of me."

"You will hurt this woman—on purpose?"

"I don't want to hurt her. That's why I want her to find someone else."

"Hendrix."

"No." His heart hardened. "Not Roe. He's too old for her, and I'm not so sure he's not after her just to add this ranch to his. That would make him a mighty important fella in these parts.'' He tipped the chair back on two legs. ''Before his old man died, the Star H was twice its size, but Monroe Hendrix always cared too much about strutting his stuff and too little about the condition of his cattle.''

''He sold off some of his land?''

''Yes, to the north. He sold a third of it, then he sold off another third a few years later. He said he wanted to, but everyone knew that wasn't the truth. The truth was he needed the money, because his cattle had brought in low prices for three years straight. They were scrawny and sickly. They're better now, but it will take another ten years before he builds them up to where they'll take top prices at market. T-Bone told me that Monroe lost fifty head last year when he gave them some bad feed.''

Ice whistled and dug around in the basket for another thigh. ''Fifty head! So he would like to marry this ranch, you think?''

''And he'd like to bed Cassie. Anybody can see that.''

''Who can blame him?''

''Yeah, who can blame him?'' Drew let the chair tip forward, setting the front legs on the floor again. ''But he's not right for Cassie.''

''Does she know the bullet was meant for you, not me?''

The question jolted Drew, but he recovered quickly. ''That's how you figure it?''

''I thought maybe someone was hunting and mistook us for deer or bears, but we were making too much noise. No, I think someone was aiming for *your* back and didn't know until it was too late that I was wearing your fancy vest.''

Drew sighed. ''Yes, that's how I see it, too, but I told

Cassie different. I told her I thought it was a mistake.''

"You think it has to do with this cattle stealing?"

"I think I'd be a fool if I didn't."

Ice wiped his hands and mouth on the napkin covering the basket. *"Sí,* we must both be careful to watch your back from now on. You have any names for me? Quentin, maybe?"

"I don't think so, but maybe. It's keeping me up nights, that's for sure. I can't turn my mind off. Why me? Why is someone trying to get me thrown back into prison, Ice? Is it the same son of a bitch who put me in there before? I tell you, I don't know. I had plenty of time to think about it when I was locked up, and I never did figure it out."

"It's not drifters, not someone who is working this area and then will move on," Ice said.

"No. That's what I thought before, but not this time. This time there's no doubt that it's personal."

"I asked around, *amigo,* and you are not a popular *hombre* here among your home folks."

"They believe I'm a cattle thief."

"They think you must have bought your way out of prison. With cattle missing again, this will not be good for you, my friend. If enough people start talking about you, the law will come here."

"They've already been here. Cassie said the sheriff came by while we were taking the cattle back to Quentin."

"So it has already begun."

"That's right." Drew looked at Ice solemnly, but he saw a mischievous light lurking in the man's silver eyes. Although their subject was grave, Drew couldn't help but catch the man's mood and grin. "I'm a lot of trouble."

"*Sí*," Ice agreed readily, then laughed. "And you are wasting the day in here. Take yourself outside and get some honest work done."

Drew stood and set the chair back by the potbellied stove. "Yes, boss. Anything else?" he asked, moving to the door and flinging it open.

"*Sí*, tell your other boss that I like her fried chicken better than this cooked by Violin!"

Chapter 15

Viola's visit had left Cassie in a bad mood that she couldn't seem to shake. At supper she poked at the steak, mashed potatoes, gravy, creamed corn, and fluffy biscuits she'd prepared, taking over the cooking duties from Oleta because she had a burning need to impress Drew with her abilities.

Childish, she told herself, but was delighted when he made the appropriate sounds of praise as he tasted each item.

"Andy likes your cooking, too," Oleta said, smiling as she spooned potatoes and gravy into the baby's open mouth. Gravy dribbled down his chin and he giggled when Oleta spooned it up. He patted his hands, eager for more.

"You like Mama's food, sweet cheeks?" Cassie asked, planting a kiss on her son's blond hair. She smoothed his curls. "He's growing like a weed. Before I know it, he'll be riding horses and roping cattle."

"He took to walking like a duck to water," Drew said with a shake of his head.

"He's running us ragged, isn't he, Oleta?" Cassie asked.

"Sí. He is quick as a bunny." Oleta lifted Andy from the high chair. "It is nice outside. I'll take him for a walk with me. He likes to watch the chickens."

After Oleta left with the baby, Cassie touched Drew's arm. "I think Oleta has a beau."

"Who?"

"A ranch hand from over at Monroe's place. She met him at the dance. He's shy. His name is Ben."

"I thought she might strike up an acquaintance with Ice."

"No, Ice is too wild for her. Oleta is afraid of most men. She likes the quiet type."

"You think she's meeting him now?"

"Could be. She takes a lot of walks lately."

"But with the baby?"

"That way I won't be suspicious and ask a lot of questions," Cassie explained. "But I know what she's up to. I'm glad she's got someone, as long as he's good to her."

Drew glanced around the table, obviously looking for something.

"What do you need?" she asked, eager to comply.

"Where's that jar of pear honey Viola brought?"

Cassie's mood darkened abruptly. "Why?"

"I thought it would taste good on these biscuits. I put it on the table earlier."

"I know. I took it *off* the table."

He studied her for a moment. "You didn't throw it out, did you?"

"No." Surging up from the chair, she went to the cupboard, moved aside some tins and canisters, and reached into the very back for the jar of pear honey. She set it beside him with a thump. "There." Then she began stacking dishes and preparing wash water, keeping her back to him as much as possible. She wanted to pound him. Ungrateful buzzard! Asking for Viola's concoction to pour on her own perfectly prepared biscuits! She was a good mind to snatch the biscuits right off the table and toss them out to the chickens.

"Something wrong with you?" Drew asked.

"No," she snapped, despising him for even asking such a stupid question.

After a tension-filled minute, he shifted in his chair, opened the jar of pear honey, and sniffed it. "Smells good." He glanced at her. Was that a smirk in his eyes? "If there's anything that can sweeten the sour mood you've been in all day, I wish you'd do it."

Cassie faced him and gripped the edge of the cabinet behind her. "You mean that?"

"I surely do," he drawled, dribbling the pale golden syrup onto one of her delicious biscuits.

Before he could move a muscle to stop her, Cassie grabbed the plate of biscuits, including the one he'd poured Viola's slop on, walked briskly to the door, and threw them into the yard. The herding dogs that had been sleeping on the porch scrambled for the offerings, gobbling the rounds of bread like they were sirloin steaks.

Cassie kicked the door shut, went to the dishpan, and slid the empty plate into the water.

"Are you out of your everlovin' mind?" Drew demanded, rising slowly from the chair to glower at her. "Just what good did that do?"

"Made me feel better," she answered. "Sweetened my mood. If my biscuits aren't good enough for you without pouring that goo Viola made all over them, then

I'd just as soon let the hounds have them.''

Red color stained his neck and cheeks. ''You're jealous, that's all that's wrong with you.''

That, she couldn't admit to him, although she had already done so to herself. Giving in to her anger, she snapped the dish towel at him, making him flinch. She thrust her face up to his.

''I don't like to see any woman make a fool of herself over a man,'' she declared, and inside she cringed, because she could well have been talking about herself. ''Viola Danforth should be ashamed, flaunting herself, batting her lashes, and twittering like a bird at every word you utter! Makes me want to spit up my supper!''

He curled his upper lip. ''Jealous,'' he said.

''Dunderhead!'' She gave him her back again and stuck her hands into the soapy water. ''Watching you with her made me embarrassed for the both of you.''

''Nobody asked you to spy on us.''

''I didn't need to spy. You two were acting like fools out in the open for anybody to see you.''

''I can't talk to you when you're like this.''

''Then leave me alone.'' She aimed a black look at him over her shoulder.

He headed for the door, lifting his hat off the peg on the way out. ''What you need is to be honest with yourself and admit what's really got you so stirred up.''

''Look who's talking,'' she jeered. ''Just look who's talking. You don't let anybody know what you're feeling or thinking. You lie to everybody, including yourself. Strutting around and preaching about how you don't need no woman in your life when it's plain you need the loving of a good woman so bad you can't hardly stay in the same room with me for more than a few minutes without picking a fight or running up to the loft or to the bunkhouse.''

"I'm not the one acting crazy around here.'' He rammed his hat onto his head and escaped her.

Cassie wanted to go after him and apologize for her irrational behavior, but pride rooted her to the spot. She finished the dishes and heated water for a bath. To make room for the tub, she moved Andy's crib from the bedroom, placing it just outside her door, and dragged the copper tub to where the crib had been. She filled it, carrying bucket after bucket of water from the barrel they kept full beside the stove. She added two pans of hot water. A long soak would do her good, she thought, sensing the tightness in her muscles.

She undressed and slid into the warm water. Lathering herself with rose-scented soap, she took her time and enjoyed the ritual of bathing. When she was done, she lay back and closed her eyes.

Someone tapped at her bedroom door and she sighed wearily. "Yes, Oleta?'' she called.

She heard the door open behind her. "I am back with Andy. He is fast asleep.''

Cassie glanced around at the crowded room. "There isn't room in here for his bed and this tub.''

"Stay where you are,'' Oleta said when Cassie grabbed the sides of the tub, preparing to climb out. "I'll take him and the crib into my room.''

Cassie looked over her shoulder at Oleta and Andy. "Would you? Thanks. I was hoping to soak some of the soreness from my muscles.''

"Okay. Good night,'' Oleta said, backing out of the doorway.

"Good night, Oleta. Give Andy a kiss for me.''

Cassie closed her eyes again, and a curious sadness stole across her when she mulled over the past few days and her arguments and frustrations with Drew. What a couple of twisted hearts. They were lonely and lost, but they put up brave fronts. Her common sense told her to keep apart from him, but with each passing day that was becoming less and less tolerable. She was attracted to him in a way she had never been to any other man.

In fact, she hadn't believed it was possible for her to experience such an intense infatuation. Men had been part of her life since she was old enough to flirt—even before that—but men had never been much more than protectors or providers to her. They weren't objects of deep affection or tenderness. While she'd envied some marriages she'd seen, she hadn't envisioned such a relationship for herself. She couldn't imagine being starry-eyed in love or so devoted that she wanted nothing more than to please one man.

When A.J. had died, she'd been relieved and happy to face a future alone with her son. All she needed was Andy to love, she'd believed. But then Blue Eyes had ridden into her life and reminded her that a child could not satisfy every need or fill every nook and cranny of a woman's heart.

It was a bitter joke that A.J.'s eldest son should inspire her to dream of love. He was so unlike his father.

There was a tenderness in Drew that had been totally lacking in A.J. One had only to watch Drew with his horses to see that this man was in touch with his softer side. In her mind she could see his hand moving slowly along a horse's flank, hear his voice registering low and husky, feel the intensity of his gaze. She shivered and released the vision.

Rising, she stepped from the tub and grabbed a towel from the dresser top. She wouldn't throw herself at him anymore like Viola had done, but she wouldn't fool herself either by denying her attraction to him. She liked the feelings he sparked within her. The rush of blood, the breathlessness, the awareness of her female powers and of his male prowess—all were intoxicating! At first she had feared these symptoms, viewing them as weaknesses that could destroy her, but now she was relieved to experience them. She'd convinced herself that her past life had destroyed any chance for her to know mutual respect between a man and a woman. Any decent man wouldn't want her once he discovered she'd sold her body to the highest bidder. In a way she'd done that again when she'd answered the ad for a wife and arrived in Kansas to marry A.J. Dalton, sight unseen.

She hadn't expected love, just marriage and maybe a child or two. A.J. had been pleased, but he'd never trusted her and had certainly never loved her. He had loved to look at her and to have her around to show off, as he would a prize steer, but her happiness was not something he cared about.

The best, of course, had been Andy.

She remembered the first time she'd felt Andy move in her womb and how that was the moment she had vowed to give her baby everything in life she'd never had—a home, stability, and the knowledge that he came first with someone, that no sacrifice was too great, no danger too threatening, no challenge too daunting where he was concerned. He was her treasure, and she wanted to be sure he knew it, felt it.

Cassie ran a hand over her flat stomach, recalling a time when it had been huge and tight as a drum, full of squirming baby. Standing before the dresser, she looked into the mirror and remembered how wonderful it had been to be with child. Would she ever experience it again?

Lately a feeble flame of hope had ignited in her heart, and she had envisioned brothers and sisters for Andy. Siblings would be good for him. If it hadn't been for her own brothers and sisters, she would have been a terribly lonely child.

A little girl with blue eyes and russet hair, she mused. Or maybe a boy with dimples and the Dalton chin. Sighing, she allowed the images to swirl in her head like clouds across a sky as blue as Drew's eyes. . . .

The sound of the front door opening and closing veered her thoughts abruptly back to the present. When she felt the change in the air around her, the hairs on the back of her neck lifted. Oleta had not closed her bedroom door firmly enough, and it had crept open.

Tensing, she waited, not wanting to turn around until she heard Drew climbing the ladder to the loft. However, in the next moment she heard his footfalls coming toward her instead of away, and she spun around, one arm across her breasts to hold the small drying towel in place while she reached frantically with her other hand for something larger with which to hide her nakedness.

His hands covered her shoulders and she gasped as he spun her around so that she faced the mirror again. His reflected expression further shocked her. He was furious! But why?

"Who did this? Was it him?" he growled. "That sorry son of a bitch who sired me?"

She had no idea what he was talking about until she felt his fingers trace the scars crisscrossing her back.

"He beat you? Whipped you like you were his dog? If he were here now I'd strangle the bastard."

"No, no," Cassie said, finally recovering from her shock enough to speak. "It wasn't A.J. who whipped me." She saw the suspicion lurking in his eyes and turned sideways to place a hand on his arm. He was trembling, shaking with fury. "He didn't," she insisted. "It was someone else, before I came here."

Easing away from him, she reached for her robe and slipped into it.

"Who was it?" he asked, standing his ground.

"A man I worked for. He thought he owned me and he could do whatever he wanted to me. I left him and came here to marry A.J."

"What about that puckered scar on your shoulder?"

She had to think for a moment before she understood what he meant. Her hand went to the place and she felt it beneath her robe. "Oh, this. I've had it for years. I was shot by an arrow there when I was a child."

"My God!" His eyes widened. "Was it an Indian raid?"

"Sort of, but it was white men dressed up like Indians. They attacked my family's wagon." Suddenly she felt exposed, her scars revealed to him along with the ugly parts of her life. She inched back and pulled the robe tighter, folding it at the throat. "I know they're not pretty. But with my clothes on I'm passable."

He crooked a finger under her chin and brought her gaze up to his again. "You're more than that and you damn well know it."

She smiled, grateful for the compliment. Lifting her chin from the support of his finger, she looked away from him. "My body used to be fetching. You know, unmarked. But there's nothing I can do to hide the scars. I've thought and thought. I even tried to paint over them once. That was a horrible mess." She laughed lightly and pressed her fingers to the healing wound on his arm. "Now you're marked, too." Had she known even when she was dressing this wound that she would eventually end up in this room, wanting him?

"I hope whoever did that to you is burning in Hell."

"He is," she said, glancing up at Drew through her lashes. Tenderness softened the bold planes of his face, and Cassie's throat tightened. When he ran a fingertip down her cheek to the corner of her mouth, her knees began to shake and her heartbeats boomed in her chest.

"I've been out communing with the stars, telling them all the reasons why I shouldn't be with you," he told her, his voice low, raspy. "I can't for the life of me think of even one reason right now. Think of one for me, Cassie. Think hard before it's too late."

Her thoughts centered only on the gaping hole of longing in her soul. Stepping around him, she went to her open bedroom door. She looked back at him and saw the dawning of rejection in his eyes. Slowly she closed the door, then backed up against it and let her robe fall open, exposing the valley of her breasts, her stomach, the golden vee of her femininity, her shapely legs.

Her actions speaking for her, she saw fire ignite in his eyes, and in one decisive stride he was beside her and she was in his arms. He brought her lips within a fraction of his.

"This might be the biggest mistake of your life, Cassie," he whispered, his breath warm upon her face.

She looked deeply into his hooded eyes. "If so, I'm woman enough to get past it."

One side of his mouth kicked up in a rakehell grin before he covered her lips with his. His tongue eased into her mouth in an erotic rite of passage. Heat seemed to emanate from him and warm her through and through. Cassie drove all ten fingers through his thick hair and arched her body into his. He felt wonderfully big and male and powerful, but she knew she could tame him and have him purring like a kitten.

He lifted his mouth from hers. "Where's the baby?"

"In with Oleta."

"Good," he nearly growled, then spun her deftly about and down onto her bed. He feathered kisses down her throat to the swell of her breasts, where her heart fluttered like a wild bird. "You're beautiful, and I want you more than a saint wants heaven," he murmured hotly, his lips dancing on her skin.

"Then take me, Drew," Cassie whispered back to him, parting her thighs. "Take all of me."

"I'll probably disappoint you."

"You won't. You couldn't."

"You don't understand. It's been a while."

"For me, too."

His blue eyes probed her for a few heart-pounding moments, then he bent his head to her body and his mouth took one of her nipples into that warm, moist cave of sensation. Moaning involuntarily, she arched into him and her hands clutched his head, pulling him more tightly to her. Waves of pleasure swept through her, over her, drowning her. Colors exploded against her eyelids. His fingers—those long, clever fingers—chased her other nipple until it was as hard as a diamond and as hot as a coal.

Cassie located his belt and unbuckled it, then pulled his shirt free and ran her hands up under it to his heated flesh. His chest and back were hard and sculpted with muscle. She bit into his shoulder, nipping him lightly, gnawing playfully. He sipped in a breath and rolled onto his back. She straddled him and let the robe slide off her arms and pool at her waist.

"You're a damned goddess," he told her, his hands resting on her waist, his fingers nearly meeting at the small of her back.

"And you are my sacrificial lamb," she teased, un-buttoning his shirt with deliberate laziness. "In a little while you're going to be a mindless lump of manhood, putty in my hands."

"I already am." He sat up far enough to kiss her lips, then her pouting nipples. "What about you? You sure you're ready for me?"

"Oh, I'm ready. Good and ready." She'd unfastened his trousers and now shoved her hand inside and closed her fingers around him. He was ready, too. And a good deal more than she'd imagined. She widened her eyes. "Oh, my!" she whispered, the words carrying genuine awe.

He chuckled. "Yeah, that's *another* way I'm different from my old man." He rolled her onto her back, then peeled off his shirt. The boots and socks came off next, followed by his trousers and long johns.

Cassie was glad she hadn't doused the light. Standing before her in all his male glory, Drew Dalton was a sight to behold and one she would not forget—not ever. The chestnut hair on his chest was thick and arrowed to a thin line down to his belly button and past the nest of curls from which protruded his impressive, generously endowed, and engorged member. Cassie propped herself on her elbows and took in the sight of him. She swallowed nervously, smiled shyly, and held out one hand.

"You going to stand there all night like a frozen bull or are you going to put that to good use?"

He released a long sigh. "I just hope I don't . . . Damn, Cassie, it's been a helluva long time."

"Then come here and quit jabbering." She caught his hand and pulled him onto the bed with her. "Just relax and let it come natural."

"Umm," he murmured, his lips trailing along her jaw and then opening over her mouth. "You taste like a woman should taste. Sweet and juicy."

She nudged her midsection against his and wrapped her legs around him. He tongued her nipples again until she writhed with torturous anticipation. She felt herself grow heavy and moist, and she clutched his hips and urged him to join with her.

He braced himself on his arms, his biceps bulging, and the tip of him touched her. Flame to flame. She felt herself open to him, and then he was sliding inside slowly, carefully, stretching her, filling her. Her breathing grew rapid as her feelings intensified. Warmth flooded her, flowered within her, and she trembled from the incredible joining of their bodies. Man to woman. Soul to soul. She rocked against him and he groaned and pressed his face into the curve of her neck. It was then that she realized the depth of his anxiety. That he should care how she felt about this, and that she gained pleasure from it brought tears to her eyes.

Stroking his back and whispering encouragement into his ear, she assisted him in finding a driving, surging rhythm that brought them both quickly, joyfully to the edge of release. When he rose above her on stiff arms, the veins in his neck standing out, his eyes tightly shut, Cassie stared, momentarily mesmerized. But then he pushed further into her and touched off an avalanche of white-hot sensations she'd never experienced before.

Suddenly she was soaring and tumbling and shaking within and without. She held tightly to him, his body taking hers to a place of mindless rapture. She was vaguely aware of his own spasms of release; they were almost violent and longer than any she could recall. Everything about him was different from any other man, and her experiences with him and how her body had reacted to his could not be measured against anyone else.

When she came back to her own consciousness, she realized her throat was dry and rough from her heavy breathing and soft moaning. Her body was moist with perspiration and her limbs shuddered with tender spasms. She felt as if she were lying in the aftermath of a storm, ravaged but splendidly replenished.

Drew lay sprawled on top of her, heavy but no burden. She ran her fingertips lightly down his moist back and along his spine to the dimples above his hips. She kissed his shoulder and nuzzled his neck.

"Are you dead or alive, Blue Eyes?"

"Alive. More alive than I've ever been, I think." He raised his head to look at her. His face was partly shadowed, but his eyes were alight with twinkles. He shifted. He was still inside her and he was not in the least flaccid. "Feel that?"

Cassie sucked in a hiccuping breath. "I'll say. Hard to miss."

"That's all your fault."

"I'm glad to shoulder the blame."

"Ahh, Cassie." Her name rolled off his tongue and tickled her ear, warmed her heart. "I'm melting inside of you, darlin'."

He moved in and out of her and her body responded instantly, clutching at him, straining for him. She held on and let him take her to the edge and over again. They tumbled together, flying on feelings, soaring on passion, diving into desire so intense they both cried out in a chorus of unfettered joy.

When he finally pulled out of her, she curled her body into his and snuggled as close as she could get. He murmured sweet words to her and kissed the top of her head. His arms enfolded her like wings, encasing her in an embrace that protected and cherished. An embrace she had never known before. An embrace that squeezed tears from her eyes and fanned the tiny flame of hope in her heart.

Chapter 16

Everyone on the ranch would know what had happened between Cassie and Drew. There was no reason to keep it secret anyway. Cassie figured the others wouldn't be the least bit surprised. They'd probably wonder what took them so long.

Before the rooster crowed, Cassie slipped from Drew's arms and collected Andy from his crib in Oleta's room. She bathed and diapered him, then fed him before Oleta came into the kitchen. Sleepy-eyed, Oleta went to the stove and poured herself some of the coffee Cassie had brewed.

Thumps sounded in Cassie's bedroom and Oleta turned startled eyes on her.

"It's okay," Cassie said, cutting through her alarm. "Drew is in there."

Oleta's dark eyes rounded. "Ohh," she said, looking from Cassie to the bedroom and back.

Cassie felt her face heat up. She knew she was red as a strawberry, especially when more thumps came from the bedroom before the knob rattled and the door swung open to reveal Drew, shirttail out and hair mussed from sleep.

"Good morning," he announced cheerily, his gaze sparkling when it landed on Cassie. "A good, *good* morning!" Sparing only a glance for Oleta, he went to Cassie and dropped a kiss on her cheek, then another on Andy's forehead. "And how are we feeling this morning, hmm?"

She exchanged a teasing smile with him. "You're feeling your oats. What do you want for breakfast?"

"I already got what I want for breakfast," he teased.

"Stop that foolish talk," Cassie chided, embarrassed. "You want ham and grits?"

He cleared his throat and fixed a serious expression on his face. "Sounds good to me. I'll shave and clean up and check on the men."

That's more like it, she thought, glad to be settling into their morning routine. She diapered Andy again and set him on a blanket she spread on the floor. After giving him his favorite toys, she joined Oleta at the stove and stirred up flapjacks while Oleta fried ham and made grits.

"You want Andy to stay in my room from now on?" Oleta asked. "It's okay with me."

Cassie considered the offer. "Well . . . if you don't mind. Actually, I was planning on moving my things up to the loft someday, so Andy could have my room. He'll be a big boy before we know it."

"Or I could sleep in the loft," Oleta offered.

"No. I've already got my desk up there. I've had it in the back of my mind to use that space."

"*Sí,* but maybe you should not move your bed up there yet." Oleta forked big slices of cooked ham onto a platter. "Just because a man takes his boots off to wash his feet, does not mean he is ready to swim in the river.''

Cassie nearly dropped a plate she was setting on the table. ''Why, Oleta, where'd you get such wisdom?''

Oleta touched a forefinger to the corner of her right eye. ''I see things. I store them up here.'' She tapped her temple.

''That's good, and you're right. I won't be making any changes for a spell. I've seen a few things myself, and I know better than to think a man can be roped by a tangle of sheets. Nevertheless, I'd be much obliged if you would keep Andy in with you for the time being.''

Oleta nodded. ''He's a sweet baby.'' She put on the grits. ''The Star H lost ten head of cattle last week.''

''What?'' Cassie's blood chilled. ''Stolen?''

''No, they died.''

She slumped in momentary relief. ''What from?''

''Bad water, they think.''

''That's a shame. Sometimes I think Monroe doesn't keep a close enough watch on his business. Bad water, bad grain. That sort of thing seems to be happening too often at the Star H. Their stock is improving, I guess, but they lose too many head every year from stupid mistakes.''

''He has hired more men to watch over them.''

''I heard about that.'' Cassie glanced at Oleta. ''And where are you getting *your* information? Maybe from a certain young man named Ben?''

Oleta's lips curved into a pretty smile. ''Maybe.''

''You went out and met him last night, didn't you?''

''*Sí*, but I watched Andy. I would not let anything happen to him.''

''I'm not worried about that. I'm wondering why you

have been so quiet about this young man. Did he tell you not to say anything to anyone?''

''No, but I believe that when you try something new, the fewer people who know about it, the better.''

Cassie flipped the flapjacks, Oleta's sage advice ringing in her ears. The girl was young, but she knew a thing or two about men and women.

Drew came back into the house, whistling merrily. He hung his hat on the peg by the door and took his place at the table. Freshly shaved and smelling of lemon and lye soap, he tucked his napkin under his chin and waited for the two women to sit down with him.

Oleta murmured a prayer and passed Drew the ham.

''What's on the chore list today, boss lady?'' Drew asked, beaming at Cassie.

''I thought I'd let you and the other men sweep the land one more time for strays while I see to a few chores around the house.''

''Sure I can't help with your housework?''

''No.'' She passed him the platter of flapjacks. ''If you stay, I won't get any work done.''

''That's probably true, but you'd have fun. I guarantee that.'' He grinned and looked around the room, his brows knitted.

''You don't mind if I change things around, add a few pretty things here and there, do you?'' she asked.

He shook his head. ''Hell, no. Do what you want. This shack means nothing to me. I was never happy here.''

She considered that for a minute, studying him, thinking of all the dark days he must have experienced in this house. ''Maybe you should build another place.''

He looked at her, eyes sharpening. "What do you mean?"

She realized he was taking what she'd said all wrong. "I don't mean for you to clear out." She leaned toward him a little and lowered her voice to a whisper. "You surely don't think I'd be asking that of you after last night!" Sitting back, she let a smile pass between them before she continued. "I'm just saying, if this house is full of bad memories, maybe you should build yourself another one someday. One all your own with no ghosts hanging onto it."

He arched a brow in consideration, then grinned. "Maybe I should. Maybe I *will*. Someday."

She exchanged another smile with him, enjoying the glow of their new togetherness and the sharing of their ideas and dreams. Finally she cleared her throat and fastened her thoughts on more mundane items, like running the ranch. "You might ask T-Bone to fix that wagon axle while you and Gabe look for strays."

"The chuck wagon?"

She nodded. "We busted the axle last spring, and T-Bone keeps putting off the repairs."

"I'll send him out with Gabe while I fix the wagon. I'm good at things like that."

Cassie stared at him, a little surprised. He'd never shown an interest in such work before. He glanced at her and shrugged.

"I served some time in the blacksmith shop while I was in prison. The man there taught me a few things about ironwork besides horseshoes."

Again she was surprised, since his time in prison was another thing he rarely brought up. "So you worked at things in prison?"

"Yeah. We rotated, working in the blacksmith's, the laundry, out in the fields."

"They let you work in the fields?"

"Yep, in leg irons and with guards all around us on horseback. I liked working with the blacksmith best. He was a nice fella and a craftsman. What he could do with a lump of pig iron was pure magic." He ate in silence for a few minutes before picking up the conversation again. "He was what they call a trustee, a prisoner who has earned some freedom. He wasn't chained and was able to move around pretty much as he pleased. They locked him up at night, like they did everyone else, but Schotzie—that was his name—was able to move around freely during the day."

"He became your friend?" Oleta asked.

"No, I didn't make friends there. I was too full of anger and bitterness to be worth anything as a friend."

"Did A.J. ever write to you while you were in prison?" Cassie asked. "I only ask because it's odd that he never even mentioned your name to me."

"No, he didn't write. And it's not so odd that he didn't talk about me. I was dead to him."

"Just like that?"

He swallowed the last bite of flapjack with difficulty and pushed back from the table. "Just like that. He never loved me. We weren't like a normal father and son. We were competitors, him trying to keep his foot on my neck and me trying just once to grind his face in the dirt."

"Did he love your mother?"

"No." He stood up, pulled his napkin off his chest, and dropped it beside his plate. "I should get to work." He started to move to the door, checked himself, and stopped to lean down and give Cassie a light, lingering kiss on the lips. "I expect you to pine away for me today, boss lady."

She smiled into his eyes. "I expect your head is swelling so big your hat won't fit."

He chuckled and straightened from her. Again he started for the door but made a detour to sweep Andy up into his arms and give him a tickle. The baby laughed and squirmed in Drew's big hands. Watching them, Cassie swallowed back tears of joy and told herself not to wish for too much or she'd for sure ruin the little bit of happiness she'd found.

Later that day Cassie stood back from the front windows to admire the new curtains she'd just hung—blue and white gingham with wide lace ruffles. They'd been given to her as a going-away gift by her friends back in Whistle Stop. She set a vase of freshly picked marigolds, bluebonnets, and white mums on the low sofa table, shiny with beeswax and elbow grease.

She had shown the curtains to A.J., but he'd threatened to throw them down the well if she put them up.

"I won't have them lacy rags on my winders," he'd warned her. "The ones we got is fine, and you shore don't need to be puttin' on any airs."

But A.J. was long gone, and she could do as she pleased. Since his death she had worried more about the ranching chores than in fixing up the house, but today her mind buzzed with plans for painting the outside bright white and repairing the shutters and painting them green or red. Something cheerful, she thought. Something that gladdened the heart.

Oleta came inside, the front of her dress wet and her

arms gleaming with sweat and water drops. "I finished the wash. I'll hang it out in a minute."

"Sit down and rest. I'll do that." Cassie motioned to the windows. "What do you think? They're pretty, huh?"

"Oo!" Oleta touched a lacy border. "Where'd you get them?"

"I brought them with me from Whistle Stop. My friends bought the fabric and sewed them up for me."

"They make the room sparkle!" Oleta whirled in a circle, noting the other changes. "This looks like it's the home of a happy woman."

"That it is," Cassie assured her, resting her hands on the girl's shoulders and pressing her down into the nearest chair. "You sit for a spell. I'll hang out the wash."

"Where's Andy?"

"Having his nap, but he should be awake soon." Cassie put on a wide-brimmed hat and tucked her gloves in the waistband of her skirt. She went outside and eyed the two big wicker baskets full of wet clothes. She hoisted one and struggled to carry it to the four lines stretched from pole to pole.

The day was sunny and the clothes would dry quickly. She lifted one of Drew's shirts from the soggy pile, spreading it from shoulder to shoulder and imagining him filling it. That was one of the first things she noticed about him, she recalled, the breadth of him, the strength of his build.

But his strength was tempered by tenderness. She knew that personally now, although she had sensed it back then, too. Even when she'd argued with him, tried to order him off her land, she had never truly feared him. Something about him told her he would never raise a hand to her.

He'd begun being her protector within those first minutes, running off the two scalawags who had drifted onto her land again, looking for trouble. Wonder what had become of them? Were they still skulking around these parts?

After shaking out the shirt, she hung it on the line. On a whimsy, she selected one of her own blouses and pinned it beside Drew's shirt. Quite a contrast! His garment was twice or more the size of hers. She continued to inspect the clothes, mindful that she was trying not to think of how last night had or had not changed things.

In the hours before dawn, when she had lain awake in his arms, she had acknowledged the deeply rooted fear quivering within her, a fear that the heaven she had found would soon be stolen from her. She wished she could talk to someone, wished she had a mother to confide in and seek advice from, but there was no one. She shared much with Oleta, but she didn't feel close enough to the girl to bare her heart and expose her secrets.

When she had left Whistle Stop behind, she had sworn to herself that she would tell no one of her former life, not even her husband. Once she'd met A.J., she definitely knew better than to tell him she used to be a saloon girl. He would have treated her even worse if he'd known of her past.

Her decision to leave her old life far behind and never mention it to anyone had served her well. She was respected in the community of ranchers and treated like a lady in town. No, she wouldn't even confide in Oleta, although she didn't think the girl would ever tell anyone. It was better to keep the past in the past. She didn't want to take any chances, especially now that she and Drew had become lovers.

Lovers. Is that what they were?

She smiled. Only time would tell if last night would be repeated, but she felt confident he would seek her out tonight and the night after. He was hers for a while, and for that she was thankful. She'd ask for no more, but if he offered . . . would she take more?

Pinning the last pair of long johns to the line, she bent to pick up the laundry basket and spotted two riders approaching the main gate. She straightened, recognizing Monroe Hendrix as one of them. Drew emerged from the barn and greeted the visitors. The two men dismounted and shook Drew's hand. Cassie picked up the empty basket and set it on the porch. Drew was walking the men to the house, so she sat in one of the rockers and waited. She still didn't recognize the other person. Must be a new ranch hand. She hoped it wasn't a lawman bringing more trouble to her and Drew.

Monroe grinned and came up onto the porch to kiss her cheek. "Hello, there. You sure are looking pretty today."

"Thank you." Her gaze skittered to Drew, and her heart gave a little kick when she saw his dark scowl. "I'm feeling especially good today," she confessed, turning Drew's scowl into a smile meant just for her.

"I'm glad to hear it. Have you had any more trouble out here?"

"Not lately." She angled a look at him from beneath her hat brim. "How about you? I heard you lost a few head to sickness. Nothing contagious, I hope."

"No, no." Monroe hooked his thumbs under his belt. "They ate some bad feed or drank bad water."

"You've had trouble with that before." She didn't add that she thought he should learn from his mistakes. One of the things that perplexed her about Monroe was his inability to keep a sharp eye on his business. He left too much to his ranch hands, none of whom was especially loyal or reliable.

"These things happen." He shrugged. "But I'm not taking any chances from here on in. I don't like this rustling business going on right under our noses, so I've taken steps to catch the men responsible."

"Oh? How are you going to do that?" Cassie asked.

Monroe nodded to the other man. "Hired me a sharp-shooter to guard my land. He's one of the best Regulators in the country. Comes highly recommended." Monroe motioned him forward. "Let me introduce you to this pretty lady."

The man placed a boot on the first porch step and leaned in, giving Cassie her first unobstructed view of his face. Her blood turned to ice in her veins.

"Buck Wilhite, this is Cassie Dalton, my neighbor and friend," Monroe said, but Cassie could barely hear him above the roar in her ears.

Buck Wilhite! He reached out for her hand.

"My pleasure," he said, his familiar voice sending chills skittering across her skin as ugly memories from Whistle Stop crowded into her mind. He had been there. He had been a part of the horror, and he knew! He knew she had been a saloon whore.

Even as she extended her hand, she ducked her head, throwing her face into shadow under the hat brim. Her gaze jerked away from his face, which hadn't changed much during the years. The ominous black eyepatch, oily smile, ever-present scent of cologne wafting off his skin—all the same, all making her want to scream and run. He was her nightmare, the black shadow of her past seeking her out, blocking out her sunny future. From inside the house she heard Andy's cranky cry. She shook herself free of the icy grip of yesterday.

"That's my baby," she said, rising and moving quickly to the door. "I gotta go." *Gotta run. Gotta move.*

She darted inside. Her heart lodged in her throat, pounding furiously. Her knees shook so badly that she had to hold onto the furniture as she made her way into Oleta's room.

The girl was lifting Andy from his crib. She turned toward Cassie and gasped.

"What is wrong?" Oleta asked.

"I'm all right." Cassie sat on Oleta's bed. "I . . . I heard Andy."

"Shh, little man," Oleta said. "I will change your wet pants. I think he had a bad dream."

"Me, too," Cassie murmured, standing and moving like a sleepwalker to her own bedroom.

She sat at the dressing table and stared blindly into the mirror. All she could see in front of her was Buck Wilhite. What was she to do? Had he recognized her? He hadn't changed, but she had. Hadn't she? Inside she had, but what about outside?

Still staring in the mirror, she focused her eyes on her own image and saw what Oleta had seen—a white-faced woman with eyes so large they looked unnatural. Her mouth and chin trembled. She took off her hat and set it on the dresser. Shorter hairs curled at her temples and on her forehead. She was perspiring, although she felt cold, cold to the bone.

Lifting a hand to her ashen cheek, she noted its slight tremor. How could she have protected herself from this? She couldn't have, of course. She had had no inkling that Buck Wilhite would end up here in the same place.

"Is this my punishment?" she whispered, looking up, up through the ceiling to the firmament. "Because I did those bad things back then"—she swallowed a sob and forced herself to say the words she usually avoided at all costs—"sold myself. Is that why You've sent this mean man to tell everyone that he knew me when, that he could have had me if he'd offered enough money?"

When Andy was born, she'd been afraid that he would die for her sins or that his father would take him and make her leave. The possibilities had left her sleepless many nights. She had watched over Andy night after night, terrified that each breath would be his last, certain that this sweet joy would not last, would be taken from her because of what she'd done, what she'd been.

Then she'd worried that A.J. would discover her past and that he'd call her an unfit mother and make her leave without her son. She had envisioned scene after scene and imagined how she would keep her son, how she would kill A.J. if she had to, but she would not leave Andy behind.

None of that had happened, and she'd relaxed a little bit, until Drew Dalton had ridden into her life, throwing it into stark uncertainty again.

Now this. She'd gained Drew's trust, his respect, his loyalty, only for Buck Wilhite to appear like a specter, hovering over her newfound happiness, deathly sword in hand, ready to rip her world to shreds.

She stopped, suddenly realizing that she had risen from the dresser bench and was pacing furiously like a caged animal. She sat on the bed, her hands fluttering nervously, her stomach tying itself into knots.

What to do . . . what to do . . . what to do . . .

Maybe she wouldn't have to do anything. There was a slim chance that Buck hadn't recognized her. She thought back, squeezing her eyes shut to recall every detail of his face when she'd been introduced. Cassie Dalton. He'd displayed no sign of recognition. And why should he?

He had known her as Cassie Little. No, not even that. She had been Little Nugget to everyone back in Whistle Stop except for a few close friends. Little Nugget in her fancy gowns with her hair styled and her skin perfumed. Little Nugget flirting with every man who set foot into the saloon. Little Nugget who wore hats from Paris and gowns to match, who drank some and laughed too loudly and even smoked cigars at times, who cussed like a miner and danced like a chorus girl. He would never equate that gal with the woman he'd met today. A woman with a baby, who worked on a ranch alongside her hired men, who was respected by her neighbors, a widow trying to carve out a good life for her only child.

A tremulous smile touched her lips. "He doesn't know me anymore," she whispered. "I'll just stay away from him. No need for me ever to see him again."

That was true. She hardly ever ran into any of Monroe's saddle mates. She might see them at a distance once in a while, but that was it. Except for the occasional dance.

"I won't go to those until Buck leaves," she said, the sound of her voice lending her strength and purpose.

He wouldn't stay long. He was a drifter, went where the money was, and the cattle rustling scare would soon be over. Then Buck would leave and never come back. Then she could live free again and not look over her shoulder all the time. That's what she'd be doing until that day, looking back instead of forward.

She hated that! Balling her hands into fists of rage, she pounded the feather mattress, releasing her frustration and fear. But then she stopped and ran her palms over the mattress, that place where she had found new hope. She'd given birth in this bed and she had been reborn here as well. Last night.

Cassie eased onto the bed, curling her body, snuggling her cheek upon the pillow where Drew had laid his head. Last night had been the beginning, and today—oh, it could not signal the end so soon!

The pain tightened in her stomach, and she moaned and forced herself to dwell on her blessings. She stretched out, unknotting her muscles and releasing her pent-up fear. She would not give in to it. She would not bow or bend to it. She would be the shadow, skirting past Buck and never giving him a good look at her. He would never remember her because he would never see her! Not again anyway.

Simple. It was so simple.

She released a long sigh and told herself that she was safe again. Just as she'd been last night in Drew's arms.

"It won't be the *last* night," she whispered. "It will be the *first* night. The first of many."

A few minutes later, she heard the visitors mount their horses and ride away. A few minutes after that she realized she had curled herself into a tight ball again and was clutching Miss Tess. Hugging her doll like a child warding off the terrors of the encroaching darkness.

Chapter 17

❦

The only sounds in the room were the squeak of the rocker Cassie sat in and the ticking of the clock on the mantel. Looking up from the strips of leather he was braiding for a bridle, Drew saw that Cassie was still absorbed in the ranch ledger lying open in her lap.

He smiled, his gaze settling more comfortably on her. Always working on those ledgers. Guess she hoped to find answers there to problems that had nothing to do with numbers and everything to do with nature and other circumstances beyond anyone's control. But he admired her gumption. She was a fiesty one.

He was falling in love with her.

Quickly he concentrated on the leather in his hands as a tightness invaded his chest and shortened his breath. He needed to rein himself in, he thought, wishing it were as easy as pulling hard on leather straps until everything ground to a halt. Just stopped. Stopped falling. Stopped loving her. Stopped wanting her. Stopped.

Wasn't that easy, though. When he imagined not sleeping with her again or not waking up with her, a sharp pain pierced his heart. Even if he hadn't made love to her, he would want her. The days leading up to their first night of loving had been miserable, as miserable as the nights he'd spent in prison. Back then someone else had put him in prison, but with Cassie he'd put a lock on himself, on his heart, and that was worse.

"What did you think of that man Monroe hired?" she asked, not looking up.

He shook his head. "That's what you're thinking about?"

She glanced at him. "Yes. Why?"

"I was hoping you were thinking about me," he said, only half in jest. Something in her eyes prompted him to be serious. "I didn't think much of him, especially when he spit on Ice."

"He *spit* on Ice?" Her brown eyes widened with concern and she closed the ledger.

"He sure did, and I almost took his head off for it. I would have if Monroe hadn't pulled me off him and made a fast getaway. Dirty bastard."

"Why did he do that to Ice? Did Ice say something to him?"

"No." He laughed shortly under his breath. "It's a wonder Ice wasn't all over him in a flash. That boy has quite a temper."

"Ice always seems to be in a good mood," Cassie said. "When I think of him, I see him smiling."

"Yeah, he's pretty easygoing. I reckon that's what's kept him out of jail. He's got some brothers and cousins who are hotheads like him, but they're mostly locked up or on the run from the law. Ice can't stay mad and he doesn't much like trouble. He avoids it whenever possible."

"So do you."

He opened his mouth as if to object, then shrugged and smiled almost shyly. "Yeah, I guess so. Anyway, that Regulator fella asked Ice if he was Indian. Turns out Ice is. I never thought of it. To me Ice is Mexican, pure and simple. But that sharpshooter spotted it right off. Ice said his grandfather was full Blackfoot. That's when that bastard spit on him. Said a Blackfoot carved out his eye and he hated all Indians but especially Blackfoot."

"Did he say anything about me?"

"About you?" Drew frowned, wondering where this was leading. "No. If he had, he'd be a dead man for sure. What makes you think he'd say something about you?"

"I . . . I ran into the house. Andy was crying. I thought he might have said something about that."

"No, he didn't. I don't know what Roe's thinking of, hiring that man. I guess he wants to spill blood, and that's what will happen. That man will end up killing somebody. Most likely the wrong somebody, and Roe will be in a peck of trouble."

She set the ledger on the floor and crossed her arms tightly. "I wish he'd leave."

"Who, the Regulator?"

"Yes."

"Maybe you can sweet-talk Roe and get him to reconsider keeping that Regulator around here."

Her eyes were luminous in the lamplight. "Maybe I could."

He knew she was baiting him and he swallowed the lure without hesitation. "You want to drive me crazy, don't you?" He patted the sofa cushion. "Come here."

She slid out of the chair and went across to him, her

movements flowing like a river. He dropped the leather and took her in his arms. She was already in his head and heart, dwelling in those places like a fever. He kissed her softly and memorized the contours of her face with his fingertips: sandpaper caressing silk.

"If you want to sweet-talk a man, sweet-talk me," he said, speaking from the dark corner of his soul where jealousy reigned. "I don't want you to give Roe the time of day. Never again." He cradled her face in one hand and tipped her gaze up to his. "You hear me?"

"You can love me, but you can't own me."

The hard edge in her voice alarmed him more than what she'd said. "You think I want to own you?"

"Sounds like it."

"I'm having some fun with you, that's all."

"So it's okay if I rub up to Roe?"

"No, it's not okay," he said, his fingers moving to her throat.

"I'm having some fun with you," she whispered, seducing him with her voice and her doe eyes.

"This isn't fun."

"I agree." She turned her head to take the tip of his index finger into her mouth. Her tongue laved it, and a shudder coursed through him to his loins. "This feels dangerous," she added.

"It is."

"I tell myself I shouldn't . . . we shouldn't."

"I know." He kissed her hair, loving the smell of it, the feel of it against his cheek.

She leaned back in his arms. "Do you think about me being with your pa?"

He shoved the image from his mind. "No. I don't think of him."

"Yes, you do." She trailed a finger down his cheek, her short nail scraping the stubble. "Don't lie, not even to yourself. Lies will eat you up, darlin'."

He smiled briefly. "Darlin'. I didn't think you called anyone that other than Andy."

"I save it for special people." Her arms wound around his neck, and she pressed the side of her face to where his heart beat, hard and fast. "So you think of him. But I don't want you to let that thinking poison the times when we're together. Me and him didn't love each other. Not at all. I never felt anything with him."

"I don't want to talk about this." He ground his teeth and squeezed his eyes shut. "I don't want to hear this."

"All right. Shh." Her warm breath feathered his face and her fingers massaged his temples and slipped into the sides of his hair. "But if it begins to bother you—"

"It won't."

"It should."

"Why?"

She frowned and her pale brows met. "You know why."

"He's dead and gone, so let him stay that way." He stroked a thumb across her lips, sealing them. "No more words unless you want to call me your darling again."

"Darlin'." She blew softly against the side of his neck. "Kiss me like you love me."

"Like I love you? Hmm." He considered the request, then lightly touched his mouth to hers, rubbed gently, lifted away, smiled, then pressed his smiling lips to hers again. "There."

"Sweet," she said. "You're a sweet man."

"The hell I am." He kissed her hard then, stamping

her with his masculine need. "Let's sleep in the loft tonight."

"Up there? Why?"

"We can make more noise. We can roll around and buck and kick."

"I'm not one of your horses," she told him, pressing the heels of her hands to his shoulders and pushing away from him. "My bedroom is fine."

"No, it's not. Your baby and big-eared Oleta are next door. You think she's not listening to every sigh, every thump of the headboard against the wall?" He could tell that hadn't entered her mind until then.

"She can hear?"

"Why wouldn't she?" He placed his mouth against her ear. "But in the loft . . ."

"Okay. I'll get my nightgown."

"You won't need it." He stood, lifting her in his arms. She tightened her hold on him, her hands sliding across his shoulders and back.

"I will need one come morning."

"Will you shut up and climb that ladder?" He pressed her up against it. "Go on up. I'll stand here and watch your backside wiggle."

She blushed. "Keep your eyes to yourself, mister."

"Can't." He grinned and enjoyed the view. Her heart-shaped rear swayed from side to side as she climbed the ladder. When she reached the loft, she turned and glared down at him. "Put your eyes back in your head and get yourself on up here."

"Yes, ma'am!" He scrambled up the ladder and hooked an arm around her waist, spinning with her across the floor to the far corner of the loft, below which was the front porch. He turned her around to get at the buttons marching down her spine.

"What's this?" She stared at the blankets spread in the corner. "You moved your bed?"

"It's more private back here."

She looked around, noticing that he'd moved the furniture and crates into a semicircle around the roomy pallet. "What have you done?"

"I made a place for us."

"A love nest."

"Hmm, yes." He swept aside the curtain of her hair and kissed her nape. The dress was undone, and he slid his hands inside to cup her breasts. She sighed and leaned back against him, allowing him to gently knead her flesh and tease her nipples through the layers of her underclothes. She reached behind her and splayed her hands against the back of his thighs. Her hips squirmed, grinding on his most sensitive part, and he caught his breath and waited out the spasm of desire.

She was a bundle of surprises, this woman he held. Small and delicate, but big-hearted and tough-minded. And the way she touched him, her total absence of modesty! How he loved her lack of inhibitions! He was grateful that she didn't hide herself from him, didn't cringe when he touched her private parts or blush when she touched his.

And yet she was a lady in her gloves and hat, in the respect she demanded of others, in her daily behavior, surrounded as she was by men. No one ever forgot she was a lady.

"My lady," he said close to her ear. He turned her around and pushed the dress off her shoulders. He unlaced her chemise, resisting the urge to tear it off, and

eased the straps down her slim arms. A white droplet glimmered on the tip of her left nipple, and he gathered it with his tongue. She shivered. "Tastes sweet," he told her, then dipped his head and circled her nipple with his lips. He suckled her and she arched against him and moaned.

She melted to the bed of blankets and pillows and wriggled from her loosened clothes. She sniffed the air. "What's that I smell?" Her fingers moved over the pillows and found the flower petals he'd dropped there. "What is this?" She lifted the crushed blossoms to her nose, and her eyes shone in the light provided by the sputtering lamp, which he'd lit earlier and set on a crate. The wick was low and its fire barely burned.

"I wanted everything to be pretty." He swallowed and encouraged himself to continue to say what was in his heart. "Pretty like you."

She lifted one hand, her fingers white and slender, so graceful he thought of a bird in flight. "Drew," she said, making his name poetry. "Sit here beside me and let me undress you."

He sat down, and she rose to her knees and unbuttoned his shirt. She removed his belt, her gaze flirting with his, but her hands moving quickly and not straying from their task. Not until the clothes were puddled on the floor did those hands caress and stroke, massage and squeeze. They were like water on his heated skin, cool and liquid. They washed him in love and gentleness, in her feminine power and her womanly allure. He was a vessel for her, and she poured over him and inside him, filling him with sensations that flowed through his veins like a river of fire.

He lay on his back, sprawled, supplicant. She combed

her fingers through her hair and then tipped her head forward, and her hair swept down his chest and pooled around his throbbing member. Her lips touched him there. Every muscle in his body tensed involuntarily. No woman had ever done this to him. He didn't know what to think about it. Her lips stroked him there again, and thinking was no longer possible.

As his body quickened and hardened, she sat astride him and urged him to a climax that left him breathless and stunned. Her body slid against his. She rained kisses across his chest and tweaked his nipples to throbbing awareness.

"My beautiful man," she whispered against his chest where his heart thudded. "You're so big and powerful. I look at you and I want you."

"Lucky me." He meant it. He buried his hands in her hair and flipped her onto her back. Gazing at her round breasts, small waist, and flared hips, his mouth went dry. "How'd I get so lucky?"

Framing her petite face in his hands, he committed each feature to memory down to the dimples peeking out at the corners of her lush mouth. Then he claimed his favorite parts of her with his mouth—her small breasts, the curve of her waist, the indentations on either side of her knee, and especially the graceful sweep of her breastbone, which made him think of an archer's bow. He licked a path along that ridge, and she laughed under her breath.

"Just what do you think you're doing, licking me like I'm a piece of candy."

"I want to eat you up," he confessed. He pushed his hands up under her and cupped her hips, lifted them, and then placed himself between her spread thighs. He locked gazes with her for a few heart-stopping moments. He saw no fear, no uneasiness, no questions in her liquid brown eyes, and so he acted on instinct and lowered his mouth to her. He licked her. Like candy.

Her hoarse moans filled his head. He kneaded her buttocks and lost himself in her and in the incredible preoccupation of her body. Her giving, glowing body. He held her tightly, his mouth and tongue worshiping her, his mind reeling from the onslaught of such extreme pleasure. She quaked in his hands and against his mouth. She made sounds that weren't quite human, spawned by feelings not quite bearable.

While she was still trembling, he straightened from her and plunged deeply into her. She sat up and wound her arms around his neck. Her backside warmed his thighs, her breasts rubbed against his chest as she moved and he slid in and out of her.

She held onto him and bit lightly on his ear lobe. When he knew he was close, he drove into her, sending her over the edge again before he achieved his own release. Their bodies shuddering against each other, they moaned and spoke words of love and held each other tight, a handhold to keep anchored to earth, to time, to each other. Drew eased himself to one side of her, his body limp but his mind sharp. He had been with women, of course, but never like this, never with this abandon or with this certainty that the rewards would be intense and soul-stirring.

He gazed at her profile, the slightly tipped-up nose, the pouting lips, the round, determined chin. Her hair lay like pale gold ribbons across the pillow and around her shoulders. With each breath, a pulse ticked in her neck, disturbing the skin.

Rolling closer, he pressed his lips to that pulse and it quickened. The words—those words that changed everything between a man and a woman—smoked in his mind like a fresh brand, but he did not speak them to her. He could not. They would demand a response from her, and he didn't think she was ready to answer him. She had said as much.

No one would ever own her.

"You're so good to me," she said, turning her head to smile at him.

"But am I good *for* you?"

She knitted her brow and a sadness fell across her face like a veil. "We're good for each other."

He kissed her white shoulder, then put his hand there, momentarily mystified by the contrast of his deeply tanned hand upon her milky skin. He had told her he wasn't the marrying kind. She had told him she would not be owned. They were clear on this. So why did she look sad and why did he feel that sadness in the chambers of his heart?

"You're not happy."

"I am," she said, rolling onto her side and pressing her front to his. "You make me happy." She kissed him. "My darling." Another kiss. "My dearest." She smiled. "I've never talked to a man like this. I like it."

"I'm glad to hear it."

She pursed her lips and kissed the air between them. "You think other people do this?"

"Sure. That's how babies are made."

She slapped his shoulder. "That's not what—oh." Her eyes brimmed with something he couldn't name. "You think we've done that? Made a baby? What if we have?"

He lay on his back, words failing him. A baby. He'd always been so careful before, told any woman he was with that he wouldn't stay around to be a pa to some child. He didn't know how, wasn't interested in learning, in failing. But now ... a baby with Cassie. A smile poked at his lips. Lord! A child! Would that bind her to him? Is that what he wanted?

"It's okay." Her voice sounded distant. "Don't answer. I already know."

She had shifted onto her other side, facing away from him. He inched closer and placed an arm around her.

"I'd do the right thing by you," he said, striving to make her feel better, to ease her mind.

She was quiet. Quiet in his arms.

After a while, he sensed that she'd fallen asleep, and he was glad she'd relaxed, that what he had said had soothed her. His words had done nothing to pacify him.

He slept fitfully, dozing for minutes at a time, but never falling fully into the blackness of the night. Before dawn he kissed Cassie's shoulder and left the tangle of blankets. He dressed and went outside to feed the horses.

Ice was already pouring grain into the troughs. He glanced at Drew, then eyed him more carefully.

"You didn't sleep any?"

"Not enough." Drew stretched his arms above his head. "You ever think about settling down with a woman and having kids?"

"Sure. Is that why you couldn't sleep? Has she got you to thinking about raising babies?"

"She's a good woman."

"*Sí.* Wonder why she came here?"

Drew grabbed up a pitchfork and began cleaning one of the stalls. "She came to marry my old man."

"Yes, but what kind of life did she have that made this one seem so good to her that she would marry a man she had never seen?"

"I don't know. Women alone have it hard."

"What did she do before?"

"I think she worked at a depot restaurant."

"She doesn't talk about it?"

He shrugged. "Not much. I don't like to talk about my past either."

"A pretty woman like her—looks like she could have found herself a man where she was before."

"What are you saying?" Drew challenged.

Ice moved on, dragging the feed bag behind him, his gait still unnatural because of his healing injury. "Nothing, nothing. I am saying nothing."

"Good." Drew stabbed at the soiled hay. " 'Cause I came out here to work, not to talk." He grunted, releasing some of his frustration. "Talking does no good anyhow. No good." He thought he heard Ice chuckling, but he was out of sight by the time Drew could step from the stall to give him hell for it.

He attacked the hay again and found himself wondering about Cassie's life before the Square D. Had she come to his father a virgin? Had she come to the ranch in search of a home, or had she been running from someone?

Did it matter? Not really, except that he wanted to know everything about her. The more he knew about her, the more he could take with him when this fleeting happiness was gone and she belonged to another man. A better man. A man who didn't carry his past like a cross, who didn't bring trouble with him, wasn't tainted by prison and injustice and an inability to trust his own heart.

Of course, if there was a baby . . .

He shoved that thought from his mind, finding it too bright and beautiful to hold there for more than a moment.

Chapter 18

⌒⌒⌒

The shouting brought Cassie around from the vegetable garden she'd been weeding and to the front of the house, where she found Drew and Sheriff Nelson face to face in a yelling match. Both men were obviously on the verge of pummeling each other with the bunched fists now held stiffly at their sides. Blood caked one of the sheriff's shirtsleeves and dripped off his fingertips.

"I won't stand here and be called a thief," Drew said, jaw clenched and lips barely moving.

"I got a job to do and I'm doing it." Sheriff Nelson narrowed his eyes and his mustache seemed to bristle.

Cassie dropped her hoe and rushed to squeeze herself between the two men. "What in tarnation is going on here?" she demanded, planting a hand on each outthrust chest and giving a shove. "Back off so I can breathe!"

Drew obeyed first, then the sheriff. She kept her palms flattened against them, just in case.

"All right, then. What's going on? I could hear y'all bellowing all the way to the border."

"The sheriff says I shot him and that I'm a cattle thief," Drew said, his voice hard. "And I don't take that

266

from any man, not even if he wears a star.''

"Were you shot on this land?" Cassie asked, shocked.

"That's right," Sheriff Nelson said. "I was following a trail of cattle thieves and it took me to the Square D. I crossed onto the land and was shot."

"Well, it wasn't Drew. He's been around here all morning."

"The man was riding a black horse. Dalton's black stallion is lathered."

"Yes, he is, because Drew's been working him in the corral for the past hour. I've been watching him while I weeded the garden."

"Nobody needs to account for my whereabouts," Drew snapped. "My word should be enough, and I told the sheriff I had nothing to do with this ambush or any cattle rustling."

"You were in prison for rustling," the sheriff said.

The next thing Cassie knew, Drew's fist flew over her head and smashed into the sheriff's face. Then the sheriff grabbed Drew by the shirt, and the two men tried to fight without landing any blows on Cassie. Although Drew tried to push her out of the way, Cassie stood firm. Finally, in desperation, she turned toward Drew and let her fists fly. Her knuckles made contact with his jaw and his cheek. He grunted, and tears sprang to her eyes as sharp pain ran from her knuckles to her elbows.

"Oww!" She jerked off her gloves and examined her red fingers. "Look what you've done!"

Drew rubbed his jaw. A red spot bloomed on his right cheek where her fist had connected. "You hit me."

"That's right, and I'll hit you again if you don't rein in your temper." She looked at the sheriff and saw a twinkle of humor in his eyes. "Come inside and let me take a look at that bullet hole." She fired another glance at Drew. "You stay out here and holster your fists."

"He called me a—"

"I know what he called you. And I know he's dead wrong about you. We'll get this straightened out but not by fighting and screaming. Come on, Sheriff." Linking her arm with the lawman's, she escorted him onto the porch, where Oleta sat in a rocker and shelled peas. Oleta's dark eyes were round with fear, but she hadn't darted inside during the altercation. Cassie figured the poor girl was getting used to the occasional ruckus. Andy kicked and giggled in his baby swing.

"That son of yours is growing faster than chickweed," Sheriff Nelson said as he entered the house.

"He's walking and trying his best to talk," Cassie said, going to the cupboard for medicine and bandages. "Is the bullet in there?"

"I think so, but just wrap me up and I'll have the doctor in town dig it out."

"Fine with me. If I never have to mine for bullets again, it'll be too soon. You want to take that shirt off, or should I tear the sleeve?"

Hot color stained the sheriff's cheeks and neck. "Uh, go ahead and tear the sleeve. Shirt's ruined anyway."

Cassie bit her lips to keep from grinning at the man's modesty. Taking up a pair of shears, she clipped off the sleeve and angled Sheriff Nelson toward the sunlight that poured through the window. She examined the wound before trying to clean it.

"Shouldn't be too much of a trial," she said. "I can see the bullet."

"That's good. Guess my meat is tough."

"Your head is hard, too."

He peered at her from beneath bushy brows. "You think you know Drew Dalton? You think you know everything about him?"

"Nobody knows everything about him, but I know enough to be certain he didn't shoot you. He's been here all morning, I tell you. And he's never been a cattle stealer either."

"He was sent to prison—"

"He was proven innocent."

"What, *that?*" He flapped one hand in disgust.

"What do you mean? You're a lawman and you know his sentence was overturned."

"Give a fast-talking lawyer enough money and he'll get any sentence overturned. Every sheriff knows that. Him getting out of prison means spit to me. A judge found him guilty."

"And *another* judge said *that* judge was full of beans," Cassie said, her temper rising and making her hands shake. She straightened from the wound she was dressing and breathed deeply, trying to release some of her tension. "His own father stuck a knife in his back."

"When?" Sheriff Nelson gave her a sidelong glance. "I heard they came to blows many a time, but I don't recall hearing nothing about a knife."

"I don't mean he actually stuck him," she said with a labored sigh. "He didn't stand up for him when he should have. A.J. let Drew go to prison when he could have easily showed up in court and vouched for him."

"Ever wonder why? Lots of other people did and have since. When a father can't speak up for his own son . . ."

"It proves the father is a backstabbing coward. A.J.

knew Drew had nothing to do with the cattle rustling.''

"A.J. told you that, did he?''

She bent to the wound again, her stubborn streak widening. "No. Drew told me.''

"Uh-huh.''

"And knowing A.J., I believe Drew.''

"I heard you wasn't aware there was another son until Drew rode up pretty as you please.''

"Who told you that?''

"Monroe Hendrix. Is he a liar, too?''

"No.'' She finished bandaging the wound and turned to gather up the medicine and other supplies. "It's true that A.J. never talked to me about Drew, but A.J. was a man full of suspicions. He wouldn't turn his back on anybody. He thought the whole dagblamed world was out to take this land and put him in the ground. I never in my life saw anyone more eaten up with bad feelings for his fellow man.''

"Maybe he couldn't speak for his son because he knew his boy was as guilty as sin.''

"No.'' She shook her head. "I work side by side with Drew every day. I *know* him, I tell you. He is a man of honor. He would never steal cattle. Never!''

"Okay, okay.'' The sheriff held up one hand in surrender, then moved his injured arm, testing it. "That'll do fine until I can get to the doc's. Thank you kindly.'' He picked his hat up off the table. "But there is this other bit of trouble. Those tracks led to your land.''

"From where?''

"Cattle has come up missing from the Clover Leaf, west of here.''

"I know the ranch,'' she said. "How many head?''

"Twenty or so.''

"I haven't seen any strange cattle, but none of us have been far from the house for the past few days. We've been doing chores around here. Got our strays rounded up and branded and now we're fattening them for the trip to market." She looked out the window. Drew was in the corral, working one of the horses. "Where were you when you were shot?"

"That creek that runs—"

"Two Forks Creek," she interrupted. "Some funny things have been happening out there. I think whoever is doing this stealing must water his cattle there, and he makes sure they stomp all over the ground. It's always muddy along the banks. The drainage is bad. That creek floods every time it rains. Good place to make tracks."

"You think someone is trying to point the finger at you and Dalton?"

"I *know* someone is and doing a mighty fine job of it." She turned back to him. "You know the vultures have been circling ever since A.J. died. This is prime country. Cattle country. I'm a widow with a baby. If they can't get this land by wooing me or threatening me, then they'll steal it from me."

"If Drew goes back to prison, you'll still have this land."

Would she? she wondered. Could she go on without Drew beside her? Would she want to? She clamped down on the gloomy thoughts. "Why would he steal cattle? He isn't that interested in the ones he already wrangles."

"Habit? Habits are hard to break."

She stiffened and delivered a hard glare that wiped the smirk off the sheriff's face. "You can't do any better than that? You come here and accuse Drew Dalton of stealing cattle because it's his *habit?*'' She shook her head. ''Men have been shot for lesser things. Why, it's a wonder to me he didn't beat the living hell out of you instead of just calling you a few well-chosen words.''

The sheriff shoved his hat onto his head and made for the door, but Cassie stepped into his path.

''Just so you and me are straight on this,'' she said, standing tall, ''there is nothing anybody can say or do to make me believe that Drew Dalton would steal cattle. If you're not of a mind to find the cattle thief or thieves, then me and Drew will. His name has been muddied by this, and it looks like it's up to me and him to clean it up. That's fine. It'll be a tough job, but we're used to that. We'll manage.''

Sheriff Nelson cocked one bristling brow. ''You two are quite a team.''

She nodded. ''Me and Drew will saddle up and take a look at those tracks. If we find the cattle on this land, we'll round them up and drive them back to their range.''

''If you find them, you get word to me first.''

''So you can make an arrest?''

''No, not if your intention is to return the cattle.''

''Of course.'' She shrugged. ''The Square D doesn't need any cows other than our own. We've got some of the best bloodlines in the country, and we're particular about what we breed our heifers to.''

''You know, Mrs. Dalton, some men sprout from bad seeds. It ain't always noticeable at first, but it shows up later. They run with other bad seeds and they enjoy thumbing their noses at decent people. I noticed you got a new cowhand.''

''Ice. He's Drew's friend.''

"You know his last name?"

"Perez, I think."

"Uh-huh." He took a swipe at his mustache with the side of one finger. "I do believe he has two brothers in prison and one swung from a rope." He paused, and his eyes bored into Cassie. "Cattle thieves."

"So that makes Ice a cattle thief, too?" she charged. "When your pa was alive, I hear tell he made and sold moonshine all over this county. I guess that means you peddle it, too. Can I buy a bottle off you?"

He glared at her, then tugged at the brim of his hat. "Thanks again for the doctoring."

Cassie felt like a pillar of stone as she stood in the doorway and watched the sheriff move stiffly to his horse and ride away. Drew stopped working in the corral and stared at the sheriff until he was nothing but a dot on the horizon, then he slipped through the fence rails and strode to the house.

"Well? What did he say to you?"

"I told him we'd look for the cattle that's missing from the Clover Leaf Ranch. If we find them on our land, we'll send word to him."

"Then he'll arrest me?"

"No, not if we return the cattle to the Clover Leaf."

He spun away, muttering foul words under his breath, and stalked toward the barn. After a few moments Cassie muttered her own unsavory word and took a step after him.

"Mamamamama," Andy said, reaching out from his swing and grabbing handfuls of air.

"Listen to you." Cassie turned back and caught his little fists. She kissed them. "Yes, I'm Mama. I'm your doting mama."

"Mamama."

She laughed and kissed his rosebud mouth. "You precious angel, you."

"Dadadada," Andy said, then gave a shriek of delight and bounced in his swing.

Her heart nearly choked her, and her gaze went immediately toward the barn. Was Drew saddling up a horse to go looking for those stolen cattle? She wanted to be with him. Always.

"Oleta, I . . . I . . ." She glanced toward the girl. "I'll be back later. If the baby gets hungry, give him some juice."

The dark-eyed girl nodded and looked toward the barn. "Is there going to be more trouble?"

"No—yes." Cassie sighed. "Nothing I can't handle." She sprinted to the barn, her skirts flying, making her aware that she wasn't dressed for riding. She'd have to change. "Drew!" she called as she entered the barn, her breath whistling in her throat. "Drew Dalton!"

He stepped from a stall. "I'm here. No need to shout."

"Drew!" She rushed to him, rested her hands on his chest, and looked up into his shadowed eyes. She felt his reserve, his guarded heart. "I thought you were going to ride off without me."

"I was going to saddle two horses. I didn't expect you'd want me to go alone."

"Well, yes. I wanted to go with you." She frowned at his choice of words. "What's wrong? Are you mad because I hit you?" She stood on tiptoe and kissed his chin where the skin was slightly discolored. "I hurt myself more than you. My knuckles are still stinging." She stroked her hands across his chest. "Don't be angry. I didn't want you and the sheriff to come to blows. That would only have made things worse for you."

"Tell me!" He grabbed her by the wrists and gave her a shake. "Tell me which one of us you believe!"

"Which one?" She blinked up at him, her mind scrambling, then grasping at his meaning. "You! I believe you! How can you doubt—?"

"Doubt," he said, his fingers tight around her wrists. "If you have the slightest doubt, tell me now. We can't go on, not like this. If you have any question of my—"

"I don't!" She pressed into him, and he stepped back against the stall gate. The old wood creaked and groaned. "I've told you, Drew. I believe in you. Nothing has changed the way I feel. Nothing could. Certainly not Sheriff Nelson." She wanted to ask about Ice, but now wasn't the time. Not when he thought she might doubt him. Instead she pulled free of his grip and brought his face down to hers for a searing kiss that was meant to cleanse him of any doubt that she spoke the truth. Her heart's truth.

She felt the anger and resentment and frustration whirling in him like a funnel storm, and she wanted to give him release. Kissing him deeply, she combed her fingers through his hair, knocking off his hat. His mouth warmed under hers, and his hands cupped her hips, then slid up to her waist.

"Cassie, Cassie," he whispered against her lips. "God, how I need you!"

Their gazes met and then, as if orchestrated, skittered to the barn's loft. She looked at him. He looked at her. She nodded. He grinned.

They raced each other to the ladder. Cassie got there

first and climbed up ahead of Drew. She began unbuttoning her dress even as she turned toward him to watch him peel off his shirt and unbuckle his belt. Sunlight speared the loft and dust motes danced in the golden bars. The place was warm, almost too warm, and the smell of hay and dust and barn critters was nearly suffocating. She breathed heavily through her mouth, her gaze drinking in the muscled span of Drew's chest, the tautness of his waist, the readiness of his manhood. With a strangled cry she took a few running steps and flung herself into his arms.

Wrapped around each other, they dropped to their knees in the hay. His hands moved up under her skirt, caught at her underpants, and pulled them down and off her. Pushing up petticoats and skirts, his knowing hands located the bare skin of her thighs, and his mouth made love to hers.

Like the storm churning within him, his movements were swift, his hands and lips full of tumult. He joined with her in a jolting, shuddering surge. She clung to him, panting, and the world spun crazily and her body exploded from within. He thrust into her again, hips bucking, face buried between her breasts, hands gripping her hips and guiding her, controlling her.

"Cassie. My Cassie," he groaned.

She stared at the sunlight above her. Blood sang in her ears and her heart beat like a drum.

"No woman has ever believed in me like you do. No woman has ever wanted me like you do."

His confession was almost more than she could bear. She kissed the top of his head and wound the short curls of his russet hair around her fingers. She said nothing because no words could convey the joy or the pleasure she was experiencing because of this man.

Her man.

She ran her fingertips across the pink scar on his upper arm, the bullet wound she had dressed. "We're two of a kind, you know. We both have scars we carry on the outside and on the inside."

"What kind of man could whip a little thing like you?"

She flinched from the memory. "I—I don't want to talk about it now. Later, maybe. Not now. I'm feeling too wonderful."

He lifted his head. The storm had passed, leaving his eyes shining and his mouth smiling again.

"What are you thinking?" she asked, bringing one of his hands to her lips to kiss each blunt-tipped finger.

"I'm trying to recall any other lofts we could meet in. Christen, so to speak."

She brought his mouth to hers again, tasted his tongue, gave him hers. He caressed her thighs, her stomach. He nuzzled her breasts through her chemise. Slowly he pleasured her. Carefully he brought her to a trembling pinnacle of fulfillment. Lovingly he dusted her face with kisses. Wordlessly he cared for her.

In the loft that was too warm, too redolent, too dusty, Cassie realized that she could never love him enough. There were not enough hours or days or years, and there were not enough words or ways. In that loft, with the man cradled in her arms, she discovered that she did not love him as she did her son. She loved her child unconditionally. She loved this man with conditions, with the knowledge that there would be times when she might even regret loving him, when she might curse him and even come close to despising him. This was a love of one adult for another, permanent only in the moment, but feeling like forever.

But she would never, ever love him enough. She would die wanting one more fleeting moment with him, one more sun-golden moment.

She sighed and held him tightly, glad for the lessons she had once thought she would never learn, never be given the chance to learn. Such was life, she mused with a wistful smile. Such was love.

Chapter 19

"Did you find those stolen cattle?" Oleta asked as she sat at the kitchen table with Cassie.

The noon sun lit the room, warming it. Andy suckled noisily at Cassie's breast. "No. We saw their tracks and followed them. They cut across the west corner of the ranch and went on toward Abilene." She glanced out the window, looking for a rider.

"To market?"

"Hmm? Maybe. Who knows? None of this makes much sense to me." She winced when Andy's new tooth sank into her tender skin. "You keep gnawing on me and I'll be weaning you right quick," she warned him, and he giggled and gurgled around her nipple. "You little scamp, you. Sometimes I think he knows what I'm saying, Oleta." She sighed. "I suppose I should start weaning him, though."

"Some women let their children nurse until they are two or three years old."

Cassie shook her head. "Not this woman!" She noticed that Andy seemed to be finished, so she straightened her blouse and buttoned it. "I'm glad I could give him nourishment, but I don't want to keep him from growing and moving on, taking the next step and the one after that."

"You'll have more babies? Maybe with *Señor* Drew?"

"Uh . . . you never know," she hedged, then kissed Andy and carried him into Oleta's bedroom. She placed him in his crib and patted his chest until he drifted to sleep.

After stripping off the blouse she'd worn all morning, she put on a clean, white one that had a lacy collar and cuffs. When she joined Oleta again, the girl was preparing the butter churn. Oleta noticed the change of blouse and gave her a questioning look. Cassie went to the window and sighed with relief when she saw Monroe Hendrix riding through the gates.

"Is someone out there?" Oleta asked, sitting down to churn.

"Yes, it's only Roe." Cassie pulled on her black lace gloves. "I sent for him."

"Sent for him?"

"Yes, I sent Gabe over there to ask Monroe to stop by if he could." She felt the girl's measured regard. "I didn't want to ride over there," she said, telling a little white lie as she rubbed her backside. "I've ridden enough this morning!" She could tell that Oleta wasn't convinced.

"You still like *Señor* Hendrix?"

"Like him?" Cassie glanced at her, wondering where that question had come from, then she caught on. "Oh, you mean, do I fancy him? No. I never did. I just want to talk to him. It's private. Personal." She perched a perky straw hat on her head and opened the front door. "So there."

Monroe lowered himself from the big roan and directed his broad smile at her. "Hey, there, Miss Cassie! Gabe said you wanted to talk to me. I hope nothing's wrong, but if it is, I guarantee I'll make it right."

She held out her hand to him, something she knew he liked. He immediately took her gloved hand and brought it to his lips. "Won't you sit with me on the swing, Monroe? It's been too long since we've visited. I hope I'm not keeping you from your ranch work." She had learned early in life—too early some would say—how to sweet-talk men to get what she wanted. It came natural to her. She hoped it got her exactly what she wanted from Monroe.

"I have good men to work my ranch. They don't need the boss peering over their shoulders all the time." He settled on the swing next to her. Sunshine glanced off his shiny boots, spurs, and belt buckle.

"Have you had any cattle come up missing?"

"No. What about you?" he asked.

"No, but we heard that some were taken from the Clover Leaf."

"Yes, I heard about that. Wonder if they've been found?"

"No, I don't think so. They crossed our land, but their trail headed toward Abilene. They didn't trespass on your grazing range?"

"No. The word's out. Everybody around here knows I hired me a Regulator with orders to kill anybody who tries to steal my cows."

"Yes . . . umm . . . that's what I wanted to talk to you about, Monroe." She shifted her body toward him but kept her gaze averted, hoping to appear shy and reticent. "Hiring a sharpshooter isn't very neighborly. I think you have scared people, made neighbor fear neighbor, and that can't be good for our community. Can it, Monroe?"

"Why, Cassie, you wouldn't begrudge a man for protecting his property, now, would you?" He reached for one of her hands and sandwiched it between his.

"No, of course not, but having that man on your property has made everyone skittish. I sent for you because frankly I was afraid to ride onto your land for fear that man would shoot me." She leaned closer. "I don't like the looks of him, Monroe. I'm a good judge of character, and he makes my skin crawl."

"I don't know what to say."

"He hasn't said anything about me, has he?"

"About you? No. Why, if he said anything untoward about you, I'd skin him alive." Monroe patted her hand. "Don't worry. He's a professional. He doesn't shoot until he's sure of what he's shooting at. You can feel safe to visit my ranch any time you want. Same as before."

This wasn't working as easily as she'd hoped, Cassie thought, fidgeting on the swing and casting about in her bag of tricks for a different ploy.

"What do you really know about that man? He might be on the run from the law."

"He comes highly recommended. A fella I know in Texas used him to chase off some Indians."

"That's another thing. Drew told me that he spit in Ice's face just because Ice has a little Indian blood in him. What kind of man would do such a thing, Monroe? Just ask yourself that."

"So he flew off the handle. Every man does that from

time to time. He says an Indian cut out his eye. That's enough to make anyone hold a grudge.'' Again he patted her hand, placating her. ''If you were my responsibility, you'd have nothing to worry about ever. I'd protect you. You'd never be afraid.''

He always managed to steer their talks toward owning her, she thought with a slight frown. She tugged her hand from his with the pretense of straightening her straw hat and smoothing a few wayward curls off her cheeks and forehead.

''Why don't you join me for supper tonight? I'll send a buggy for you,'' he suggested.

''No, I can't.'' She fished around for an excuse and settled for a lie. ''Andy's fussy today. He's teething and I don't want to leave him.''

''Bring him with you.''

''He shouldn't be out. He needs his rest.''

''Oh, all right.'' A scowl darkened Monroe's features. ''You won't be doing him any favors by smothering him with your love, Cassie. You don't want the boy growing up to be prissy, do you?''

''Just because I stay home with him when he's running a fever won't make him prissy, Monroe.'' She sat facing front, distancing herself from him. The sweet-talking had fallen flat. So how would he like some good, old-fashioned harping? ''You don't approve of the way I conduct my business, and I can't say that I approve of the way you conduct yours.''

He turned rounded eyes on her. ''I beg your pardon?'' His tone was cool, even chilly.

A cautionary finger slipped down Cassie's spine. Experience with men, especially with angry men, had schooled her well. She knew when to back down to save herself from being slapped down.

"Oh, I'm sorry, Roe," she turned toward him again, batting her lashes and pursing her lips in a practiced pout. "I didn't mean that. I'm under a lot of . . . well, everyone is worried about these cattle rustlers, and now you have this awful man working for you—"

"He's not awful, Cassie. He's—"

"—a hired gun," she finished for him. "That's what he is. You're paying him to kill, to murder. Maybe he'll send one of our own friends to the bone-yard, and then how will you feel, Monroe? What will people think of you then?"

"If one of our friends is stealing cattle, it'll serve him right. And I imagine people will be glad I've gotten rid of the scoundrel." He peered into her eyes. "Are you upset because you're afraid someone you know—someone you are close to—will be killed or sent to jail?"

She reared back from him. "I am not. I told you I'm upset because I don't like having that kind of man in my community. And I don't like that you're the one who brought him here. Why can't you handle this on your own, like every other ranch owner around here? If your men are so good, so capable, why can't they work the ranch and protect your herd? Mine do, and I've only a handful. You've got a regiment over there at the Star H."

She knew she'd offended him, but she no longer cared. His fingering Drew as the culprit had offended her first. His face grew ruddy, and muscles twitched around his nostrils and mouth. Clearing his throat, he stood up from the swing.

"You don't know what you're talking about, Cassie.

That's one of the pitfalls of trying to be a rancher when you should leave such business to men." He jerked at his vest and coat, frustration in every movement. "Cattle rustling is serious, and I am treating it as such. Drew should know that, and he should have tried to make you see it. But then, he probably isn't interested in teaching you anything. The less you know, the easier it will be for him to take over this place and run it." He angled her a look. "Or is he already doing that?"

"We're partners. Equal partners." She stood up from the swing, but to no advantage. He looked down at her like a lord examining a disloyal subject. "We have an understanding."

"Understanding? What you *do* understand could fill a thimble and what you *don't* understand could fill the sky. Drew was always a wild one. I liked him, still do. But he was raised by a man who was as tough as an old boot and who didn't give a damn for anyone but himself. Drew's a chip off that block. He can be charming, yes. Like a snake. But he'll end up striking when it suits him. and he won't care who gets hurt. That's what *I* understand about him, Cassie. Has he turned your head? Do you think you'll tame him, change him, make a gentleman out of him?"

"I wonder what Drew would say if he heard your opinion of him?"

"He knows my opinion of him. Nothing I just told you would be a surprise to him. I've said the same things to his face. *We* have an understanding." He stooped to gaze at her directly. "Remember, I went to court and testified to his good character."

"You've changed your mind about him?"

"Bitterness can fester in a heart. He was sent to

prison, a hard-time prison. No telling what he went through while he was behind those walls. I haven't changed my mind about what kind of man he was back then, but I don't know what kind of man he is now after those long months locked up with animals.''

"I do. He wants to raise horses and live a quiet life. He isn't stealing cattle, Monroe.''

"I didn't say he was.'' He gave her an arch look. "But maybe he knows who is and he's keeping his mouth shut about it.''

"He wouldn't do that. He knows these ranchers and he—''

"Doesn't like any of them and they don't like him. What does he care if some of their cattle come up missing? *You* want a good name, Cassie. *You* want for you and your son to be respected in this community. Drew doesn't, and he never has. He's a loner and he likes it that way.''

The truth in what he said cut through her denial. Was it possible that Drew knew who was stealing the cattle? Could it be Ice, or buddies of Drew and Ice's?

"I see I've given you something to chew on. That's good.'' He placed a hand on her shoulder and bussed her cheek. "Good day, Cassie.''

"Thanks for dropping by, Monroe.'' She watched him mount his horse, and her fiesty spirit loosened her tongue. "Roe, let me give *you* something to chew on.'' She waited a moment, holding him in anticipation. "I won't set one foot on your land again until you send that black-hearted weasel you hired back to the hole he crawled out of. And don't you bring him onto my land again, or I'll shoot him for the scavenger he is.'' Then

she pivoted sharply and went into her house, slamming
the door behind her.

They had just had their midday meal the next afternoon
when the dog began to bark, signaling a visitor. Cassie
lifted Andy from his high chair and wiped his mouth with
a damp cloth as Drew went to look out the widow.

"Who is it?" Cassie asked.

"The sheriff."

The tense set of Drew's mouth and the coldness of
his tone reflected the same dread Cassie felt. She handed
Andy to Oleta and stepped onto the porch with Drew.

"Hello, Sheriff," Drew said, his face set in grave
lines.

"Had your dinner?" Cassie asked, attempting to be
cordial.

"Yes, thank you, Mrs. Dalton." Sheriff Nelson nodded and gave her a stiff smile that was gone in an instant. "Dalton, I want you to come into Abilene and
sign a statement about how you found Quentin's cattle
on your land and you returned them and how somebody
shot at you on the way back here."

"What good will that do?"

The sheriff tied his horse to the hitching rail and
moved to the porch steps. "I'll have your word in writing about what happened. Might help me figure out
who's stealing the cattle around here."

Ice strode from around the side of the house. "I will
go, too. I was there and I was the one shot."

"I was going to ask you—"

"I didn't say I would do it," Drew interrupted the
sheriff and glanced sharply at Ice. "I don't see any good
it would do and I've got work—"

"It won't hurt anything for you to do as the sheriff asks either," Cassie said, heading him off. She grasped his arm and squeezed. "We can do without you and Ice for a day, I reckon. Everybody wants the thieves caught, and if this might help the sheriff, then you've got to do it, Drew."

Drew tensed, and in his eyes she saw the flicker of rebellion, but then he faced the sheriff and gave a terse nod. "I guess, but it's too late to go now."

"We'll ride to town together, and you two could be back here by tomorrow morning if you sleep under the stars," the sheriff said. "Or you could stay in Abilene overnight and get back here by tomorrow evening."

"No use in staying in Abilene."

"You can if you want," Cassie said. "It will be chilly sleeping outdoors."

"We'll build a big campfire. We'll be fine." He patted her hand resting in the crook of his arm.

Staring up into his eyes, Cassie felt the rest of the world fade into insignificance. After a few moments, the sheriff cleared his throat, and Cassie remembered her manners.

"Can I get you a cup of coffee, Sheriff Nelson?"

"No, thanks. How long do you think it'll take for you to get ready to ride?" he asked Drew.

"I'm ready now, I guess. The sooner we hit the trail, the sooner we can get back home." He looked toward Ice. "You saddle the horses, and I'll get my bedroll and some vittles."

"I hope the gray mare doesn't foal while we're away," Ice said, already turning toward the barn. "It would be just like that cantankerous animal to do such a thing."

"I'll keep her in the barn and watch her," Cassie reassured Ice, then followed Drew into the house. Drew turned to look at her, and Cassie closed the front door and stepped into his arms. One corner of her mind registered Oleta's quiet exit with Andy.

"Damned pesky sheriff," Drew grumbled, his arms tightening around her. "I don't like leaving you now. Doesn't feel right."

"You should go," she said, rubbing her cheek against the front of his shirt, one she'd laundered and pressed with a heavy hot iron a couple of days ago. "Sign your name in blood and swear on the Bible, if that's what he wants, and it will make all this trouble go away."

"I doubt any of that will matter. I think the sheriff thinks he has his man and that man is me."

"Then we'll prove him wrong." She lifted her gaze to his and tucked her arms around his middle. "Be careful out there. Dress warm and take plenty of food and—"

His chuckle stopped her flow of admonitions. "I'll be back tomorrow, boss lady, and I know how to take care of myself. Been doing it for years."

"I know." She ran a hand down the front of his shirt. "But I'll worry anyway."

"You stick close to home and don't go riding alone. If you need something, send Gabe or T-Bone for it."

"I've been taking care of myself for years, too," she told him with a gentle smile that became sensuous. "I'll miss you something terrible tonight when I'm all alone in that bed and wishing I could wrap myself around you." She hugged him tightly, relishing the power in his body and the tenderness of his hands smoothing down her back to her waist.

"Lord help me," he groaned, then pushed her away from him. "You sure don't make leaving easy."

"It shouldn't be." She grinned and then went to the kitchen. "I'll pack your food and you see to your bed-roll."

She prepared more food than she knew he and Ice would need but wanted to err on the side of plenty. A lump formed in her throat, and she tried to dispel the vulnerability growing inside her with the advent of his departure.

He'll be back lickety-split, she repeated over and over again, but it did little to assuage her fears. When he joined her again in the kitchen, bedroll tucked under one arm, she couldn't pretend not to have tears in her eyes. When he saw them, he growled an epithet and embraced her.

"What's this? Hell, you're not sending me off to war or prison, Cassie."

"I know." She sniffed and stepped back from his arms. Wiping aside her tears, she fashioned a smile. "Go on, then. The sooner you leave, the sooner you'll be back."

He kissed her lips softly, then turned toward the bedroom. "Oleta, bring Andy out here," he called, and the girl emerged and handed the baby to him. Holding Andy high, he laughed up into the baby's grinning face. "Hey, there, boy, you keep your mama busy, you hear?" He lowered Andy and kissed him soundly on the mouth and then on the cheek. "When I get back, I think I'll teach this cowboy to ride."

"I don't think so." Cassie took him from Drew. "He's too young and you know it."

"Soon, though," Drew told her with a shake of his

finger. "Soon he'll be riding the range with us men."

"He's going to be Mama's boy for a couple more years at least." She kissed Andy's angel-soft hair and shared a speaking glance with Drew. That he would take a few minutes to say good-bye to her son filled her heart with sweet, sweet love. She could tell by the way Drew looked at her that he understood her fragile emotions. Finally he gave a short wave and opened the front door.

"I'm ready, Sheriff."

"Good. Ice is here with the horses."

Cassie moved out to the porch. T-Bone and Gabe stood nearby, worry clearly etched on their faces. The three men rode away, the sheriff flanked by the other two, and Drew looked back once and waved at Cassie and Andy.

Swallowing against the tightness in her throat, Cassie gave a sigh. "I guess we should get on with our work. Have you finished feeding the stock?"

"Yeah." T-Bone tucked his fingers under his belt. "We were gonna start building the new smokehouse today."

"Good. We'll need it up before winter sets in. I'll put on some other clothes and give you a hand."

"Does the sheriff think Drew took the cattle?" T-Bone asked, stopping Cassie in her tracks.

"No. He just wants Ice and Drew to swear to a statement about how they found the Quentin cattle and returned them."

"Wonder why? Ain't their word good enough?"

"I guess not." Cassie shrugged. "You know these lawmen. They like to have everything signed and sealed."

T-Bone turned and said something under his breath to

Gabe. The two men walked toward the lumber Drew had stacked a few yards away from the house.

Anxiety seeped into Cassie, jarring her nerves, and she couldn't shake the feeling that their troubles were only beginning.

Chapter 20

The house was uncommonly quiet as Cassie placed Andy in his bed and crept from the room. She avoided the loft, putting off sleeping alone for as long as possible, and went to stand by the front window. Pale moonlight barely lit the landscape. She wondered if Drew was asleep or awake and missing her.

"If he's awake, he'd better be lonely," she whispered with a wry smile. She looked up at the heavens and found cold comfort there.

Something had been bothering her all day. Something about T-Bone and Gabe wasn't right. She'd worked beside them most of the day, hammering together the frame of the smokehouse, but she'd felt like an interloper, a nuisance. She had caught the two men whispering heatedly several times, and when they saw that she'd noticed, they shut up. They were planning something. Something they didn't want her to know about. But what?

Tired of conspiracies and whispers, she put on her hat and gloves and went out to the barn to check on the pregnant mare. The big gray horse didn't seem in any distress, standing in her stall and munching on hay. Cassie ran a hand over the animal's swollen belly and felt the baby inside squirm.

"You about ready to pop, huh, girl?" Cassie said, and the mare made a low, snuffling noise. "I know I'm not Drew. I can't sweet-talk you like he does. Do him a favor and don't have this baby until he gets back."

She examined the mare and determined that she wasn't in labor. After brushing the horse and giving her some extra oats, Cassie fed the milk cows and goats and checked on the other horses in the barn. Dynamite's empty stall tugged at her heart and made her even more melancholy.

Turning away from the stall, she reached for the lantern she'd hung on a peg but stiffened when she saw a man standing only a few feet from her. Her heart jumped into her throat and she released a strangled cry, then fear bolted through her when she recognized him—*Buck Wilhite.*

She lowered her hand, leaving the lantern where it was, and tried hard not to let Wilhite see how unnerved she was in his presence.

"What the hell are you doing here?" she said, making her voice hard and unforgiving. "You've no business here." She looked past him. "Is Monroe with you?"

"I came calling all by my lonesome, honey lamb," he said, his tone like greasy velvet.

Honey lamb. That odd endearment sent her back, back to her girlhood, when she had been impressionable and a Montana lady named Miss Tess had given her the first pair of many gloves she would own. There had been a man in that Montana town where Miss Tess lived . . . a skinny man who had called young Cassie Little honey lamb.

Buck had called her that in Whistle Stop, too. Could he have been the man in False Hope, Montana, as well? Was it possible that this man was a bad omen, popping up in her life over and over again?

She stared hard at him, trying to remember things about him. He'd told Drew that he wore a patch because a Blackfoot had carved out his eyeball. A Blackfoot. Miss Tess had fallen in love with a Blackfoot named Storm—Storm something or other. She couldn't rightly recall.

She gave a derisive sniff. "You're chasing *false hopes* again," she said, setting a trap. When he narrowed his one eye and his head jerked back, she decided that he *was* her bad omen and she wanted desperately to shake loose from him once and for all. She wanted to be sure: she wanted to know that her hunch was true and that fate was playing a cruel game with her. "What's wrong with you? Why are you looking at me like that?"

He blinked and his mouth turned down at the corners. "You brought up bad memories, and I was feeling so good."

"What memories?"

"Of a town. False Hope. It's a dirty hole I was in once." He lifted one hand to touch the black patch. "Lost my eye there."

The world went gray, and Cassie thought she might faint. She reached out and wrapped an arm around a post to keep from pitching forward. Through a haze she saw Wilhite smile and move closer. His voice hissed in her head like a snake. She couldn't hear . . . couldn't understand . . . there was a drumming in her ears . . . a pounding in her head.

". . . looking right peaked, Little Nugget."

Suddenly her head cleared and the ringing and drumming and pounding stopped. All stopped. She stared at her nemesis and knew that he was pure evil, her personal demon.

He knew. He recognized her. She had never fooled him. She was the fool.

"You remember me," she said, her voice seeming to come from a far distance deep, deep inside her.

"Yeah. Who could forget you? Why, you're one of the prettiest little fliptails I ever did see. I offered to pay top dollar for you back in Whistle Stop, but Taylor was selfish. Didn't want anybody else touching you. He said he used to rent you out but that I didn't have enough money to buy even one minute of your time." One side of his mouth kicked up. "You don't charge anymore, do you, honey lamb?"

"No. That life is behind me." She inched backward, trying to figure out how to escape him. Should she scream? Would he let her dash past him? Maybe he only meant to taunt her, to frighten her.

"Hendrix said you married an old man and that he upped and died on you. Left you this ranch. Hendrix would surely love to get his hands on this spread—and on you." His one eye glinted in the lantern light. "Guess you know that."

"Why did he hire you?"

"To look after his interests."

"Seems to me that wherever you show up, misery follows. You brought nothing but blood and woe with you in Whistle Stop. If there was any justice in the world, you'd be dead.''

His brows arched. ''Why, if I didn't know any better, I'd say you don't like me.''

''I despise you, and I want you to get yourself back to the Star H.''

''Or what?''

''Or I'll call for my men, and they'll send you off packing lead, that's what.'' She tried to appear unflappable but felt her chin tremble. This time she knew better than to believe he hadn't noticed. Moving with speed, she started for the barn door, but he blocked her passage, and his strong hands closed on her upper arms.

''Where you going?''

''I'll scream.''

''You'll try.''

His mouth closed on hers, chopping off the scream she tried to make, and his tongue gagged her. She squirmed, trying to free her hands so that she could hit him. Instead she only managed to work the gloves off her hands and lose her hat somewhere at their feet. Memories of a life she had detested flooded her, and with them came her lessons of survival. She couldn't breathe, could barely move, so she went limp, forcing him to hold her up or let her crumple to the ground. He let go of her.

Scrambling, she tried to make it to the door again, but he snaked an arm around her waist and lifted her feet off the ground. Airborne, she was flung into a stall and landed in the hay with a thump that knocked what breath she had left right out of her.

Black spots floated before her eyes and her lungs burned. When she could breathe again, think again, Wilhite was on top of her and his wet mouth was making sucking noises on her skin. She pushed at him, kicked at him, bit him. He was her old life coming back to haunt her, and she fought him with all she had in her. Her breath rattled from her, and his weight, plastering her to the suffocating hay, made her dizzy. She screamed again and again in her head, but no sound emerged from her dry mouth and cracked lips except for her hoarse breathing when he lifted his foul lips from hers and allowed her a few gasps of hot air.

"Spread your legs, honey lamb," he murmured, his hands locking on her knees. "Let me at you. What you got on here, some kind of split skirt?"

With her lungs inflated again, she gained a measure of strength and hammered at his head with her fists. He cursed and caught her wrists. She drove her knee up and into him. He grunted and used his body to pin her down.

"We can do this rough, or we can do this nice," he rasped into her face. "But we're gonna do it. You've always been full of spirit, haven't you? You snuck up behind me back in Whistle Stop and split a bottle over my head. Remember that? If I hadn't left town quick like, I would have done this back then. I figure you owe me a good time after giving me that headache."

She struggled, only half listening, her mind working on how to escape, how to find an inch of advantage.

"I swear if you don't leave right now, you're a dead man. I'll kill you myself," she assured him, her voice coming out of her like ground-up glass. "I'll tell Drew about you. I'll tell everyone about you. I'll tell them that you're a murderer, that you kill innocent people and take money to do it. Nobody will care when I shoot you dead."

He smirked and clutched her head between his hands, squeezing until pain shot from one temple to the other. "Go on. Then I'll tell him you're a whore. I'm not the only one hiding a past, honey lamb."

A terrible maw opened inside her. She moaned, and hot tears flooded her eyes. Once again she was helpless and on her back, a position she had fought so hard against. After tonight she would never feel clean again or whole again or worthy of anything good again. Never. The futility of her existence sat like a stone in her heart, and she went limp with resignation, letting him have his way because she couldn't find any reason to fight anymore. She could not run fast enough to escape her past.

Then other voices intruded. Distant but growing near. T-Bone and Gabe! Wilhite heard them, too. He clamped a hand over her mouth and bore down on her to whisper in her ear.

"Another time."

His body peeled off hers like a snakeskin, and she stared up at a spider's web tucked in the corner of the intersecting beams above her. The wispy strands swayed in the night breeze, fragile but strong enough to endure winds and rain, freezing nights and blazing days. Like her.

Slowly she sat up and shook straw from her hair, brushed it off her clothes. She put on her hat and stood up, checked her clothing, buttoned her shirt and tucked it back into her skirt. A trembling permeated her body, but her will was strong and intact. Using it, she stepped from the stall and saw a wide, loose board swinging from a single nail at the back of the barn. Wilhite's means of entry and escape. She'd fix that tomorrow first thing.

She walked as steadily as she could toward the front of the barn, where Gabe and T-Bone spoke in hushed voices. She didn't like the sound of those whispers, didn't like the stealthy feeling she encountered as she approached them. They were saddling their horses.

"What's going on here?" she asked, their behavior superseding her own tremulous fears.

T-Bone and Gabe spun around, their eyes wide, their mouths moving, but no sounds emerging from them. Cassie ran her gaze over the horses, saddled and fitted for long rides.

"Is somebody going to say something?" Cassie demanded, propping her hands on her hips and glaring at them. "What are you two up to?"

Gabe looked imploringly at T-Bone. "You tell her."

T-Bone looked down at his scuffed boots. "We . . . me and Gabe here . . . we're clearing out."

Once again she was dizzy, and her breathing came in short gasps. "What do you mean? Where are you headed? And why?" For a moment she thought that Gabe was going to bust out and cry. He turned away and checked the belly straps on the saddles.

"We don't want to . . ." T-Bone cleared his throat. "We don't want to work for a cattle rustler."

Cold fury washed over Cassie, and she had to ball her hands into fists and cross her arms tightly to keep from striking T-Bone. "You *don't* work for a cattle rustler, but if you want to leave, then get, you yellow-bellied devil dogs!"

The events of the night shredded the last modicum of her civility. Staring at the shocked expressions of T-Bone and Gabe, she wanted to scream and kick and cry until all the anger and frustration writhing in her were spent. Instead she pushed her face close to T-Bone's and gave his chest a thump.

"You cowards! I thought you were going to stick with me through thick and thin. What happened? Did someone offer you better wages? Is Drew making you work instead of letting you laze around most of the day? You're the ones who talked nice about him when he first got here and told me to trust him, and now you're running out on us? Running scared, more like it. You afraid a bullet meant for him will hit you like what happened to Ice?"

"You got trouble here," Gabe said, his voice almost a whine. "The sheriff ain't looking at nobody but Drew. He's done made up his mind that Drew is the one."

"What if he has?" Cassie said, rounding on Gabe and making him retreat a few steps. "What's that got to do with how *you* think?" Suddenly she was weary and wanted nothing more than to be alone with her thoughts, to take a long bath and wash the stench of Wilhite's sickly sweet cologne from her skin, to kiss her son and sort through what she would do next. "Get," she said, her voice gruff. "I don't need any spineless cowards around me. You're nothing but sheep, following whoever is wearing the loudest bell."

Shouldering past them, she walked to the house, each step weighted, her knees wobbly and shaking. Once inside she stood by the window and watched. She didn't have to wait for long. Within minutes Gabe and T-Bone rode from the barn and across the flat land. They rode toward the Star H.

She sat in the rocker, where she had been sitting since two in the morning. A small-framed woman with pale blond hair spilling over her narrow shoulders, one hand gripping a gleaming Winchester rifle, the other gripping the arm of the rocker. Back and forth she moved, her gaze locked on the door, her ears tuned for any sound. She fairly quivered with anxiety.

When a mouse scratched at the corner of the fireplace, her gaze darted there. She assessed the noise and then returned her gaze to the door. She imagined the grinning, one-eyed man opening that door. She would lift the rifle, aim, and blow a hole through him. When she pictured this, she felt no triumph, no elation, only relief.

The one-eyed man had been trespassing on her life ever since she was a child. Maybe even before that, before she had memory, when he had both eyes. Perhaps he had even met her as an infant and called her honey lamb and had reached out to stroke her soft, round cheek and breathe upon her, marking her for life. She wouldn't be surprised.

Because he stalked her like a shadow, she had decided she could not dodge him or deflect him. If he came around her again, she would kill him and face her punishment. But even if he kept his distance, his curse was upon her, and she couldn't shake it. She would have to confess all to Drew. Buck Wilhite had given her no choice. Now that someone from her buried past had popped up like a mushroom to poison her new life, the word would eventually leak out about her days as Little Nugget. She wanted to be the one to tell Drew. She owed him that much. But once she told him of her former life, she would lose him forever.

Cassie heard the pat of Oleta's bare feet on the floorboards, and she stood and placed the rifle in its holder above the mantel. The rooster crowed. Another day. She yawned and flexed her arms, her shoulders, then went to check on her son. He was awake, and she lifted him from his bed and kissed him, held him, inhaled the scent of his silky skin.

"You're already dressed," Oleta noted.

"Been up for hours," Cassie said. "I couldn't sleep." *Wouldn't* sleep. Not with that one-eyed coyote skulking around and no Drew to protect her. "I'll wash Andy, and you can fix us some breakfast."

"Okay."

"Don't bother fixing extra for T-Bone and Gabe."

"Why not?"

"They left."

"Left?" Oleta blinked owlishly at her. "Where did they go?"

Cassie shrugged. "I don't know. They just left. They said they didn't want to work here anymore, and I told them to make tracks." Turning on her heels, she went into the kitchen and prepared a pan of warm wash water for Andy.

After throwing on some clothes, Oleta came bustling into the kitchen. She was obviously bursting with questions, but she went ahead and built up the fire in the stove and put a skillet on top, letting it get hot.

"But why would they leave?" she asked Cassie, spreading out her hands in supplication. "They like *Señor* Drew."

"I guess they don't like him enough. They think he's a cattle rustler."

"No, no!" Oleta placed her hands against her round cheeks and shook her head. "He is not! I can't believe T-Bone and Gabe would think this of him."

"Well, they do. The sheriff's visits spooked them, I

guess. Or they might have gotten offers over at the Star H. Wouldn't surprise me if they were working there right now.''

"*Señor* Hendrix would hire them when he knows they are your only cowhands?"

"Sure, can't you hear him, Oleta?" She fashioned a stern and condescending expression. " 'Now, Cassie, those two are good cattle men and they wanted to work here. Men don't like to work for a woman. I've told you that many a time, haven't I? Don't you see that you can't run this place? You need a man to help you.' Then he'd move in and try to kiss me or put his hand on my breast.''

Oleta smothered a giggle with a hand pressed against her lips. Her dark eyes danced.

"*Señor* Hendrix acts like he's trying to help, but mostly he tries to make my life harder than month-old bread." Having undressed Andy, Cassie stood him in the shallow pan she'd set on the side table and lathered his pudgy body with soap. He squealed and stomped his feet, sending water everywhere. "Stop that, you bad boy," Cassie said, laughing. "You just love to make a mess, don't you?"

Oleta laughed and kissed the top of Andy's head. "You will hire more men?"

"I don't know. I'll leave that to Drew, I reckon."

Oleta lifted a brow. "You have turned over everything to him?"

"No . . . I . . ." She shrugged. Once she told him she used to be a whore, she figured she'd be lucky if he didn't run her off the ranch.

"Something is wrong." Oleta, eggs in hands, turned from the stove and studied Cassie intently. "You did not sleep. Your eyes have no light in them, not even when you laugh. What has happened?''

"My two hands quit, that's what." Cassie busied herself with bathing her son, keeping her face down and averted from the girl's prying eyes. "I want two eggs this morning and flapjacks. My belly's growling."

Her belly *was* empty—empty like the rest of her—but she wasn't hungry. However, her ploy worked, because Oleta returned to her task of preparing breakfast. Cassie dried Andy's squirming body and dressed him in overalls and a red shirt. She put soft socks and shoes on his fat feet, kissing his soles and toes first.

No matter what happened to her, she had her baby. Her sweet, laughing baby. She smiled, trying to fill herself up with the love she felt for her son. But the emptiness persisted. She knew why. She had lost Drew. He didn't know it yet, but she knew, and the pain of that inevitable parting was almost unbearable.

They sat at the table to share breakfast, two quiet young women and a squealing, giggling baby with apple juice dribbling down his chin and pieces of soft-boiled egg and toasted bread decorating his bib.

After a while, Cassie sat back and looked at the dark-eyed girl who had become almost like a sister to her. Oddly, that realization struck her a blow, and she found herself wanting to talk to Oleta sister to sister.

"You ever do something you were really ashamed of, Oleta? Something that you don't want anybody else to know about? Something that at the time you just did because you couldn't see any way out of not doing it?"

Fear crept into Oleta's eyes. "I went to confession once and did not tell the priest about my papa . . . about him beating me and trying to t-touch me. That was the same as lying to the *padre,* wasn't it?''

''If that's the worst thing you can think of, then you don't have anything to worry about.'' Cassie pointed to the ceiling. ''God knew what your papa was doing already, and He provided a way of escaping him. Me.'' She smiled and reached across the table to squeeze Oleta's brown hand. ''I've done some very bad things.''

''You kill someone?''

''No, unless you can count my own self-worth. I killed that.'' She watched Andy cram egg into his mouth. ''I'm going to have to tell Drew about the bad things I did before I came here. When I do, I don't reckon he'll want to be around me.''

''He will make you leave?''

''Maybe. If he wants me to go, I'll go.''

''And I will go with you.'' Oleta sat straighter, her shoulders pulled back like a soldier's.

''You don't have to—''

''I *want* to!''

''After you learn about what I did—''

''I don't care. You are good to me. Have always been good to me. Whatever you did, if you ask God to forgive you, He will. I can do no less than Him.''

The girl's staunch friendship warmed Cassie's heart. ''I have asked for forgiveness. Many, many times.''

Oleta placed a hand on Cassie's shoulder. ''You only have to ask once. It is enough for God.''

''You don't have to leave. You should stay here and take care of *Señor* Drew.''

''He did not offer me his hand and open up his home to me when I was in need. You did. I will go with you and help you with your baby.''

"I don't know where I'll go, how I'll live."

"We will be fine," Oleta assured her. "Besides, *Señor* Drew might not want you to go."

"Don't count on that."

They fell quiet, and in the silence the pounding of hooves could be heard in the distance. Cassie stiffened. Oleta went to the window.

"It's them," she said softly. *"Señor* Drew and Ice. They are covered in dirt and look very, very tired."

"They've been riding since before sunup, I guess, to get here this early in the day." Cassie gripped the edge of the table and forced herself to her feet. "Guess we ought to rustle up some breakfast for them."

The thump of boots on the porch and the rattle of the handle preceded Drew's entrance. He filled the cabin with his very maleness, all brawn and brown and redolent of the trail and its cornucopia of scents.

"I'm home!" he announced, his gaze moving briefly to Oleta and then clinging to Cassie. "I'm home," he repeated softly just to her.

Her heart bloomed.

Andy pounded his fists on the table and gurgled happily.

"Hey, there, half-pint," Drew said, sparing a glance for the baby.

"Dada!" Andy said, clear as a bell.

Cassie's heart caved in on itself. Drew smiled and pink tinged his cheeks. He shrugged, clearly at a loss how to respond to Andy's name for him. Cassie could tell he expected her to embrace him or at the very least to tell him she was glad to see him again, glad he was safe and sound. Instead she turned away from him.

"How many eggs do you want?" she asked, already

cracking two at once and letting them slide into the hot skillet.

"That's it?" Drew said from behind her. "Aren't you even going to say howdy, stranger?"

Ice came inside, making the house seem smaller still. "Fry me up a dozen of those eggs," he said, sitting at the table. "I am so saddle sore the seat of this chair feels like eiderdown." He looked from Drew to Cassie to Oleta and frowned, obviously sensing something amiss. "What'd I do?"

"Nothing." Drew hung his hat on the peg. "Let's you and me wash up while these women cook. We shouldn't sit at the table with trail dirt still caked on our hair and skin."

"Right. Forgive me." Ice shot up from the chair and went back outside.

Drew stepped closer to Cassie and laid a hand on her arm. "You okay?"

"Fine. Just fine," she said, almost snapping.

"Hmm." His fingers slipped away. "We'll talk later."

She tried not to flinch from that promise but felt the constriction of muscle, the rebellion against destiny. She released her pent-up breath with his leaving. The eggs fluttered in the skillet, and hot grease leapt and landed on her hand, blistering the skin. She wiped away the greasy droplets, feeling no pain. The emptiness opened within her again, more agonizing than blisters or burns, more terrifying than any thoughts of being ousted from this ranch.

She had been empty inside for a long spell, but she'd come here to fill herself up, and she had. To the brim, she had. But thanks to a one-eyed snake, she'd sprung a leak and she could feel everything good draining out of her.

Damn Buck Wilhite! If she was going down, if she was sinking, by God, she'd take him with her. Straight to the bottom of Hell!

Chapter 21

"They just up and left?" Drew asked, dropping his fork into his empty plate.

Cassie had waited until he'd finished breakfast to deliver the news of T-Bone and Gabe's departure.

"This is hard to believe," Ice said, rubbing his chin, thoughtfully. "Very hard to believe."

"Well, it's true. They got antsy with the sheriff snooping around here, and I guess they began to think that where there's smoke, there's fire." Cassie gathered up the men's empty plates. "So there is a pile of work to be done and only us three to do it. You two had better get started. I'll join up with you after I've put Andy down for his nap."

"Hold up a minute," Drew said, catching her by the skirt. "What else is going on? You're acting mighty strange."

"We've lost our two cowhands," she repeated. "That's what's going on. Now, get on out there and get to work."

Drew directed a speaking glance at Ice. "You go on. I'd like to talk to the boss lady here private." He swept his gaze to Oleta. "Why don't you take Andy into your room and see to him? Cassie will be there shortly."

Oleta glanced nervously at Cassie and only moved to obey Drew after Cassie gave her a quick nod. Ice strolled to the front door and let himself out. Cassie jerked her skirt from Drew's fingers and placed the used dishes in the wash pan.

"It's just you and me now, so tell me what's on your mind," Drew suggested.

Looking at him, she realized that he thought she had wanted to be alone with him. She shook her head at the irony of it. What she *didn't* want was his company. She wanted to postpone what she must do—tell him about her life before she'd landed at the Square D.

"Isn't it enough that we've lost our last two workers?"

"I admit it's a blow, but something else is eating at you." He folded his arms against his chest. "I'm listening."

Lord, lord. She'd have to tell him. Couldn't keep putting it off. Not with him insisting that she spill her guts right here, right now.

Cassie crossed to the window and pushed back the pretty curtain. Her mouth felt as if it were full of cotton. *Damn Wilhite. Damn him to hell!* She gathered in a deep breath and prayed that she could get through this without sobbing and begging Drew to give her another chance.

What's that?

Her gaze sharpened. A horse and buggy. Company! Could it be that Roe had fired that snake Wilhite and had come to tell her so? Her heart fluttered with hope, then slowed. That rig didn't belong to Monroe.

"Are you going to talk to me?" Drew asked.

Cassie squinted against the glare of the sun and tried

to get a better look. She smiled. Viola Danforth! She never thought the day would come when she'd be overjoyed to see that woman again, but joy was exactly what filled her.

"You've got company!" she announced, already heading for the door to throw it open and wave grandly at the woman driving the rig. "Howdy, Viola! Drew, Viola is here to see you!" she sang out. "Climb on down, Viola. I hope you can stay a spell. Drew doesn't get a chance to entertain ladies very often. He just got back from Abilene. He'll tell you all about it."

Drew came out onto the porch and landed a glare on Cassie that felt like a fist. She edged away from him, still smiling but also trembling a little inside at his tightly checked anger. She reached back inside the house for her hat and gloves, then skirted past Drew.

"You've been to Abilene?" Viola asked, mounting the porch steps. "Has the new dry goods store opened up there yet?"

"Yes," Drew answered, still glaring at Cassie.

"Did you go inside?"

"Yes."

"Oh, do tell! I hear it's twice the size of Anderson's Dry Goods. Do they have dresses? Did you see any patterns? What about bonnets?" Viola looked from Drew to Cassie. "Am I imposing?"

Cassie blinked and tore her attention from Drew. "Imposing? Heavens, no! Drew, where are your manners? You haven't asked Viola if she'd care for a cup of coffee or tea. You two visit and don't mind me. I've got chores."

She left Drew in Viola's hands, feeling like a coward but glad for the reprieve. She knew she'd have to talk to him, but at least she had another hour or so before she revealed to him who she really was and endured his disgust and her own disgrace.

However, Viola's visit was far too brief. No more than thirty minutes passed before Cassie felt someone standing behind her. She was mucking out one of the stalls, and she whirled around, fearing for an instant that Buck Wilhite had returned. But it was worse. Drew stood there, a thundercloud of an expression on his face.

"You threw that woman at me," he said, his voice dark as pitch.

Cassie drove the pitchfork she held into the mound of clean straw. "I knew she wasn't here to see me."

"Yeah, but you always griped before when she came. This morning you almost broke your neck running out on the porch to greet her."

"I did no such thing," she protested weakly. "I had work to do, so I—"

He gripped her upper arms and gave her a shake sufficient to slip the hat off her head. "Enough of that bull! Talk to me, Cassie. What's wrong with you? How come you're throwing that woman at me and treating me like I've come home with lice?"

"All right. Take your hands off me. You're going to leave bruises."

His grip loosened. He brushed her arms lightly, as if apologizing for his brute treatment, then his hands slid away from her. His tenderness wrenched her heart.

"Has Viola left already? She didn't stay long."

He lowered his brows and tipped back his hat. "Forget her. I have."

Cassie swallowed hard. "She's a good woman, I guess. She'll make someone a fine wife."

He stared at her, *through* her, into her soul. Cassie shivered, feeling exposed. *No use putting it off any longer,* she told herself. *Out with it.*

"I didn't want to tell you this. I didn't want to tell *anyone* this."

"What?"

Tears burned the back of her eyes, but she kept them at bay as she faced him. A life full of hardships had created in her a place where she could stuff her feelings, her heart, her soul, keeping them apart from the pain. She did this now, leaving only a shell, a stone-faced woman, speaking in a lifeless tone about cruel twists of fate.

"I'm a liar and a cheat and no-'count for a good man like you, Drew," she said, noting his shocked expression but driving on while she had the courage. "Don't argue with me until I've finished, then you won't want to argue. I know you've wondered why I accepted your pa's proposal, why I came here to marry a man I never set eyes on before. Well, I did it because I wanted to start a new life. I wanted to bury who I had been and become who I always wanted to be—a lady. A real lady, not just a gal who wore fancy bonnets and pretty gloves and pretended to be as good as any other woman on the street."

Cassie peeled off her gloves and examined her un-marked hands. She sensed Drew's confusion but also his curiosity. Looking into his eyes, she girded herself for what was to come.

"Back in Whistle Stop I *was* a waitress." Was that relief she saw in his eyes?

"You've already told me."

"And before that . . ." She swallowed, her mouth dry,

her heart pumping hard. "Before that . . . I was a whore."

His face drained of color and he shook his head.

"Yes, I was. I worked in a saloon. This man . . . the man who whipped me . . . he owned me. Taylor, that was his name, made men pay top dollar for me. I was his special girl."

Drew continued to shake his head, and Cassie could no longer watch his silent denial. She stared at the toes of her boots.

"I was miserable, but I didn't see a way out until this woman, this wonderful lady I told you about before, she showed me the way. Adele Gold educated me, taught me to read and do my numbers, gave me a job as a waitress."

He was so quiet that she finally had to look up at him to see his reaction. What she feared was there on his face: the shock, the disbelief, the mounting disgust.

"So, that man, the one who owned you and sold you, he whipped you?"

She nodded, surprised that he had fixed on this. "Yes, in front of the whole town. He was going to kill me. That's when I got away from him. The friends I'd made rallied around me and protected me from him."

"Why tell me now?" He reached out and trailed his fingertips down her sleeve. "Is it because we . . . that is, you and me are . . ."

"Not because I'm noble or good at heart," she said, stepping back from him and from the hope in his eyes. He *still* wanted to believe that she was a decent person, a lady, a woman worthy of him. Bless him. "I'm telling you now simply because you'd find out sooner or later. Buck Wilhite will see to it."

He frowned. "Wilhite? What's he got to do with this?"

"He's a black-hearted hired gun who never goes any-where unless he's paid big money to kill somebody or cause heavy grief. Drew, I'm afraid he's here to hurt you, to kill you. Of course, if that's true, then that means Monroe Hendrix hired him to kill you, which makes no sense. I guess Wilhite is acting on his lonesome in this. Maybe he's jealous 'cause you're staying here with me."

"Why Wilhite?" Drew removed his hat just long enough to rake his fingers through his hair. "Why would he tell me something about you?"

Cassie ground her teeth, then forced out the confession. "He knew me back when I was called Little Nug-get. My pa called me that. Said I was his good-luck charm, his little nugget of gold." She released a sour laugh. "But I wasn't so lucky for him. I left him when I was fifteen and struck out on my own. Problem was, a young gal couldn't make decent money. The only way to get money was by being indecent. Eventually that's what I was." She swallowed the bile burning her throat. "Am."

"He's . . . been . . . with . . . you." The words were spoken with extreme difficulty, and Drew's face was deathly white.

"No!" Cassie reached out a hand but didn't touch him. The temptation to tell him about Wilhite trying to rape her here in this very barn was strong, but she resisted. Common sense told her that Drew would seek revenge, and his mindless rage would get him killed. "No, he hasn't, but he wanted to. Anyway, he knows me from back then, and he's told me that he's going to shout it to the four winds. Pretty soon everybody around here will see me for what I am—a lying cheat who used to sell herself. That is, everyone will know unless I pump a bullet into Wilhite and shut his big mouth once and for all.''

"You were a whore."

Those words coming from him tore chunks from her heart. Cassie nodded, the movement taking great effort. Her throat closed, blocking any further words. She'd said enough.

"Did the old man know?"

She shook her head.

"Anybody else know, other than Wilhite?"

Again she shook her head.

"A whore."

She cringed. "Drew, I want you to know that men have had my body, but I never let any of them touch my heart. Not until you. You're the only one I opened my heart to. If that means anything at all to you . . .''

He stared deep into her eyes for almost a full minute, his eyes growing darker and wetter by the second, and then he pivoted and strode from the barn.

Cassie sucked in a breath and her knees buckled. She rested her cold cheek against a splintered post and placed a hand above her breasts. Yes, something was still beating in there. But how could that be when Drew Dalton had just ripped out her heart?

After a while, she managed to drag her empty shell of a self into the house. She went straight to her room, shaking her head when Oleta inquired after her, and collapsed onto the bed. Pulling Miss Tess into her arms, she rocked back and forth, her tears wetting the doll's cloth body. She'd done this before, held this doll and wept and wished for a better life.

Miss Tess had always represented her ideal—a lady people respected. She'd felt like a lady when Drew had held her, caressed her gently, kissed her softly.

But "feeling" and "being" were vastly different. She'd never be a lady, especially not to Drew. He was so fine and proud. He'd expect nothing less in his woman. He deserved nothing less.

Stars peeked out from the twilight curtains, but Drew stayed put. Stretched out on a knoll of land near Two Forks Creek, his favorite spot on the ranch, he listened to Dynamite chomping grass, accompanied by a chorus of crickets and tree frogs.

Peaceful, he thought, but inside he felt little peace. Since Cassie's confession, his mind and his gut had been tied in knots and his heart had ached continuously. He couldn't go back to the ranch house and face her again until he had his feelings under control, until he knew what to think about this news she'd given him.

First off he'd been stunned, and then he flat hadn't believed her. But then he'd seen the pain in her pretty brown eyes, and he'd realized that she was telling him the unvarnished truth. After that he didn't know what to think or feel or say to her.

So he'd come here to this swell of land, a place he had visited many times in his youth when living with his father had become too much to endure. How many nights had he slept out here under a canopy of stars, wishing never to face his old man again?

He sure never thought he'd meet a woman who understood his upbringing, who could sense his deeply rooted resentment and the strange love-laced hatred he carried within his heart for his father. But Cassie knew. Her life had almost mirrored his own. She knew first-hand what it was like to be shoved around and treated like a mongrel. Her heart, like his, had been put through the wringer.

Those scars on her back she tried so hard to hide were nothing compared to the ones she hid inside. She deserved better, deserved *someone* better. After all, she'd come here to get away from trouble, and he'd dumped it on her doorstep. Trouble seemed to follow him, dog him, torment him. What was worse, he had forced Cassie to share it.

Nothing much he could do about that now, other than to clear up this cattle rustling nightmare as soon as possible. Then he'd do right by Cassie.

Hell, she would probably marry him just to give her son his fair share of the ranch. She might even marry him because she felt sorry for him or thought she loved him. But Drew wouldn't let her tie herself to him, denying herself the possibility of true happiness. She'd come here for a better life and she'd put up with a hell of a lot from his old man.

She'd put up with a lot from him, too. And she'd given him so much. He wanted her to have everything— a man who could be a good, loving husband to her and a fine father for her child. A man respected by people, who hadn't spent time in prison and come out hardened and bitter. He wished he could be that man, but that was a selfish wish. He'd never been taught how to be a husband or father. All he knew was that the feelings he had for Cassie were new and surprising, so much so that they scared him sometimes. Tenderness. That's what he felt toward her. Like when he saw a newborn colt. No, deeper than that. Deeper and richer. Was it plain old love? If so, there sure wasn't anything plain about it.

When he was with Cassie he felt himself opening up, no longer closed off from the world and stewed in bitterness and regret. But he didn't know how to love, how to show it or prove it or even wear it. Most of the time when he was with Cassie, he felt tongue-tied and clumsy. He expected her to laugh at him and at his awkward attempts to court her.

Dynamite moved closer and blew hot air into his face. Drew reached out and rubbed the horse between the ears.

"You ready to get back to your stall, boy?"

The horse pressed a velvety nose into Drew's palm, took another step toward him, and nudged his shoulder. Drew turned his head to look at the animal that had become his best friend. The stallion showed his teeth and lifted his head suddenly, ears pricked. Drew knew the signs.

In one motion Drew was on his feet and had his hand on the rifle strapped to Dynamite's saddle. From a distance came the bawl of cattle.

"Damn," he whispered, hoisting himself into the saddle. "Go to 'em, boy," he told the horse, and Dynamite set off toward the cries.

He might not like being called a cattleman, but that was what he was, Drew thought. He'd been raised around them, and those years of experience had taught him the bovine language. He could tell by the pitch of their lowing that they were unhappy. Cows didn't like to be driven after nightfall. They got spooked easily and shadows made them crazy.

Bursting through a thicket of bramble bushes, pin oak,

and pecan trees, Drew scanned the scene ahead of him. In the milky starlight some twenty or thirty head of cattle stained the landscape, moving jerkily, driven by three riders. Drew pulled the rifle from its sleeve and cocked it. He aimed carefully, figuring he'd get only one clear shot to stampede the steers. He'd have to make it a good one.

As he squeezed the trigger, the rider's horse reared, startled by a lunging bull, and Drew cursed viciously when in the next second the horse screamed and went down.

Sickened that he'd shot the horse instead of the rider, Drew spurred Dynamite into the fray as the cattle reacted to the sound of gunfire by breaking into a headlong race to nowhere. The drivers yelled and tried vainly to control the herd. They unholstered their guns and fired shots over their heads, trying to stop the stampede. Drew knew it was futile. The cows were making so much noise they wouldn't even hear the puny pop of the guns.

He headed toward the downed horse, hoping to capture the rider, if he hadn't been trampled to death. The cattle impeded him, keeping him on one side of the river of hides with the rustlers and the downed horse on the other side. Drew looked for a way to cross, but then he saw one of the rustlers pull the fallen rider onto the back of his saddle.

"Damn it to hell," Drew muttered, tugging on the reins, frustrated to be separated from the others by the surging cattle. The rustlers stared at him. One of them shouted, cupping his hands around his mouth, but Drew heard nothing above the bawl of the steers and the thunder of hooves.

In the darkness and with the dust rising thick as a

storm cloud, Drew could not see their faces. They wore black clothing and big-brimmed hats. He thought he saw the flap of cloth against their faces, so he figured they were masked again.

"Thieving bastards!" Drew shouted, although he knew they wouldn't hear him either. He shook his fist, thought about firing his rifle again, then decided it would be a waste of ammunition, since he could barely see through the dust cloud and he was afraid of killing another horse or hitting a steer. The cows were valuable, unlike the worthless pieces of dung turning tail and running in the opposite direction, leaving the cattle for him to control. Sons of bitches!

He set Dynamite to work, racing the horse alongside the herd, gaining on it little by little, dodging trees and leaping over rocks and other obstructions. Finally they came up even with the lead cows, and Drew positioned Dynamite to overtake them. Yelling and waving his arms and trying to make as much ruckus as possible to get attention and grab control of the herd, Drew acted instinctively to retard their speed and finally command them.

When the winded, blaring-eyed cows were subdued and milling in a circle, which Dynamite kept tidy by trotting around and around it, Drew breathed easier and realized he was shaking with a combination of fear and exaltation. Any man that close to stampeding cows had to know fear or he was an idiot, and there were certainly head-swelling rewards when a man could tackle a crazed herd and bring it to heel.

His pa had taught him how to harness a stampede. Say what you liked about the old man, but he'd known cows. Known them like his son knew horses. Down to the bone.

Drew pulled Dynamite to a stop and slumped in the saddle, breathing hard, while he pieced together the crime he'd stepped into. He saw something part the grasses a few yards from him and grinned when he spotted his herding dogs. "Hey, there, Lasso, Bubba, Dot!" he called to them. He whistled and set the dogs to working the herd while he and Dynamite returned to the place where he'd shot the rustler's horse.

The animal lay trampled and bloody. Dynamite shied, smelling death. Drew slid off the stallion and went to the fallen animal. Bending closer, he examined the brand shining on the hip. Just as he'd suspected. The horse was from the Star H. This was precious evidence, and he figured the rustlers would return for it.

Looking around, he saw a good hiding place for the dead horse some distance away. He wondered if he could use Dynamite to drag the carcass.

His ears picked up a sound, and he held his breath. He glanced toward inky shadows and knew he wasn't alone even before Dynamite pawed the ground and screamed a warning.

In the next instant he relaxed, recognizing the man who stepped into the open as friend, not foe.

Chapter 22

⚬━━⚬ ⚬━━⚬

The next morning Cassie felt as if life was playing tug-of-war with her. She'd been glad when Drew had come in for breakfast as usual, but she wanted to know what he was thinking now that he knew her deep, dark secret. In the next minute she hoped he'd keep his thoughts and opinions about her to himself. As long as they didn't talk about it, she could pretend that nothing much had changed between them.

"Guess you're wondering where Ice is," Drew said, glancing up from his plate. He'd put away three eggs, two slices of ham, six biscuits and gravy, and two cups of coffee. He used the last bite of biscuit to sop up the remaining gravy in his plate.

"Ice? I figured he was around, working the horses or something."

"I sent him to Abilene at first light." Drew sat back, pushing his empty plate to one side, and cocked a brow at Cassie's look of surprise. "Sent him for the sheriff."

Cassie swallowed, choked, and coughed violently for a few seconds. The sheriff! Was he going to have the lawman escort her off this land, now that he knew her for a whore? No wonder he was so quiet this morning, so calm! He had everything under control.

"Are you okay?" Drew asked.

"You need water?" Oleta inquired.

"Yes, water . . ." Cassie gasped for breath, then hammered Drew with a glare. "Am I okay? Of course I'm not okay! You tell me you've sent for the sheriff, and I'm supposed to sit here like a piece of stone? Why couldn't you have had the decency to talk to me about this first? I have a baby to consider, you know."

He drummed his fingers on the table and stared at her as if she were a Chinese puzzle. "I don't know what you're yammering about, Cassie, but I sent for the sheriff because last night I shot a horse I want him to see."

Oleta slammed the glass down on the table and sloshed water over Cassie's hand. "There was shooting last night? I heard nothing."

"Neither did I. Why are you shooting horses?" Cassie asked, drying her hand on her skirt before gulping down some of the water. Her head pounded and she felt queasy. She pushed aside her plate, although she'd eaten only a few bites of egg and biscuit. It was hard to swallow with her heart wedged in her throat and her stomach cinched into a tight knot of anxiety.

"I was trying to shoot the rider, but I hit the horse instead. Damn shame." He shook his head, obviously vexed.

"Whoa up there," Cassie said, placing a hand to her head. "Who were you shooting at and why?"

"Rustlers. I came up on three men driving cattle across our land last night."

"Oh, God," Cassie moaned, closing her eyes. "Not again."

"I couldn't see their faces, but I believe you're right about Monroe Hendrix. The horse I shot wore a Star H brand. So did the cattle."

Cassie shook her head, saddened and confused by the news. She had held out hope that Monroe might not be involved, but that hope was dimming. "But why steal his own cows?"

"I figure they herded the cows over here to make sure nobody suspected the Star H. I mean, if his cows are missing, then he's no longer a suspect."

"Maybe we should join in the game and herd some of ours over to his place," Cassie said with a touch of irony.

Oleta groaned, drawing their attention. She had paled and was making the sign of the cross. The girl whispered something in Spanish and groaned again.

"Hey, there, now, don't you be afraid," Drew said. "Nobody's going to hurt you. The sheriff will be here, and he'll handle this mess."

Cassie didn't think the girl was frightened. She recognized something else in Oleta—heartache. "Is your beau mixed up in this somehow, Oleta?"

"I don't know," Oleta wailed. "But he is acting funny, and he is friends now with those two men who made trouble here. And those two work for the one-eyed man."

"What beau? What men who made trouble here?" Drew slammed the flat of his hand down on the table, making silverware tinkle and almost upending a jar full of prairie flowers. "Would somebody speak plain English? I feel like I'm a rooster at a hen party and I can't understand a peck from a cluck."

"Oleta has been seeing one of the Star H ranch

hands,'' Cassie explained. ''But who are you talking about? What two men?''

''The ones who shot *Señor* Drew that first night,'' Oleta explained.

''Them?'' Cassie rested a hand above her heart. ''Those two sneaking coyotes? Reb Smalley and Dan Harper were their names.''

''*Sí, sí,*'' Oleta agreed. ''Those. They work for the one-eyed man now.''

''Buck Wilhite?'' Cassie asked, the name itself repulsive to her. ''Well, that *doesn't* surprise me. If there is trash around, Wilhite will collect it. I figured those two were long gone, though. You say your beau is running around with them?''

''*Sí.* I tell him that they are bad, but he doesn't listen to me. Ben has changed. He doesn't come to see me much anymore, and when he does, he gets mad at me for nothing.'' She stuck out her lower lip. ''I think he drinks too much now. Last time he came to visit, I could smell it on him. That and a woman's perfume.''

''I'm sorry, honey,'' Cassie said, patting the girl's hand. ''Sounds like you should break away from Ben before you really get hurt.''

''Monroe must be crazy to hire those men,'' Drew said. ''What's he thinking?''

''He didn't hire them. The one-eyed man did,'' Oleta said.

''Roe must be paying them, though.''

Cassie nodded. ''I don't like thinking that Roe is trying to ruin us, but with each passing day he looks more and more guilty.'' She sighed. ''That horse you shot could have been stolen.''

''I'm sure that's what Roe will say.''

"But you won't believe him," Cassie added.

"Like you said, he looks guilty."

Oleta dabbed at her eyes. "I should have told you all of this before, but I am afraid for Ben. What if he is the one stealing the cows?"

"Sounds like he's a follower," Drew said. "I'm aiming for the leader."

Andy, who had been playing with wood blocks, toddled over to Drew and yanked on his pants leg.

"Hey, there, little man." Drew reached down and hoisted Andy onto his knee. He began playing a game of "ride the horsey" with Andy, making the child giggle. "I hid the horse I shot. I want the sheriff to see it. I figure Roe will say it was stolen, but it'll make the sheriff suspicious of somebody else besides me, which will do me a world of good." Drew smiled at Andy, bobbing the laughing baby on his knee. "What I can't figure is why Monroe would be stealing cattle and making people think it's me. Besides, if it's true that he's the rustler, then that means he was probably the one who got me sent to prison. That makes no sense at all."

"He wants the cattle."

Oleta's simple statement was met with stone silence. Even Andy was quiet. Cassie and Drew stared at Oleta until the girl squirmed under their taciturn assault.

"You mean, the land," Cassie said.

"No." Oleta shook her head, then shrugged. "Well, the land, too. But land he has. Good cattle he needs. That's what Ben told me. He says the Star H cattle are sick."

"Sick?" Drew set Andy down, his attention captured by Oleta. "Besides the ones that drank bad water?"

"The herd is weak and winter is coming. Ben said it

will take a long time for the cows to be healthy.''

''Hmm.'' Drew sat back and drummed his fingers on the table again. ''What do you think about that, Cassie?''

''She's right. Roe lost a lot of cows last year. He says he only lost twenty or thirty, but I've heard different. Some say he might have lost nearly a hundred.''

''Damn,'' Drew whispered. ''That's a lot of beef.''

''Roe insists it's idle gossip,'' Cassie pointed out. ''I always felt he wasn't telling me the truth. He asked to buy some of my cattle after A.J. died, but I wouldn't sell. A.J. would never sell to him, either.''

''He asked Pa to sell him cattle?''

''Yes, but A.J. said he wouldn't turn over his top-quality cattle for Monroe to ruin. He said Monroe didn't know how to treat or raise cows. He told him right to his face that he grazed them on bad pasture and fed them cheap grain and that he didn't keep a close watch on his pregnant heifers and a lot of them died trying to calf. A.J. said that Roe wasn't interested in raising a good herd, so he was always trying to buy himself one.''

Drew chuckled. ''That sounds like Pa. I remember . . .'' He sat up straighter, as if suddenly prodded. ''Yeah, yeah, I remember that he tried to buy a few heifers and a bull from us.'' His voice took on more verve. ''A prize bull. Offered more money than I'd ever heard of, but Pa wouldn't sell. He'd sold some breeding stock to Roe a few years before that, and every last one of them had died before the next winter rolled around. Roe was so mad he was cussing a blue streak, but Pa laughed at him and told him he should try farming, because he sure didn't have the brains for ranching.''

''Could he be worse off than either of us thought?''

Cassie asked. "I figured Roe was doing fine over there in his big house. Anytime I ever went there for supper he served the best food on the prettiest china you ever saw. His clothes are always new-looking and he seems to want for nothing."

"Except for a herd to make a rancher proud," Drew noted.

Cassie nodded. "And we *are* in cattle country, where a man is measured by the size of his herd."

"Oh, is that how a man is measured?" Drew said, devilment lurking in his eyes.

"Oh, and don't forget that he had a hard time selling his young bulls," Cassie said. "He had to practically give them away."

"Yes, ma'am, I do believe we've been so busy looking for a jackass that we couldn't see the donkey standing right in front of us," Drew drawled. "We've been thinking that Roe is wanting this land, but Oleta has pointed us in the right direction. The land is icing, but our herd, that's the cake. He has ruined his cows, and they don't bring spit at the market. He doesn't have any money left to buy good cows, so he's stealing them. And since I'm already thought of as a cattle thief, I'm an easy target."

"But what about before, when you were sent to prison," Cassie said. "Was he behind that, too?"

"I don't know, but I wouldn't be surprised. The cows we lost were our best, and a couple of them were ready to calf. Then our prize bull vanished. I swore to Pa that I had checked those fences, but there were two places down, all the same. Somebody cut that wire and took our cattle and our bull. At the time Pa said he thought it was right strange that only our best were being taken."

"If A.J. thought that, why did he let you go to prison?"

"Other cattle from other ranches disappeared, and the sheriff realized it was cattle rustlers and not just broken fences. I halfway believe Pa thought I might have been in cahoots with the rustlers. He asked me if I was doing it just to rile him, to take his most prized possessions from him. Then he said I was stealing cattle to make up for the ones I'd let wander off because I'd been too lazy to mend the fences when he'd told me to." Drew ran a hand down his face in a weary gesture. "He grabbed at any opportunity when it came to hurting me."

"I know," Cassie murmured. Living with A.J. had been a colorless, loveless existence, but it had been better than being known as the town whore.

"I'm riding out to where I stashed that horse and make sure nobody bothers it," Drew said, standing.

"I'll go with you," Cassie added.

"No, you stay here. When Ice comes back with the sheriff, send them out to me. Ice knows the place."

"Okay." Cassie slumped in the chair, not bothering to see him to the door since he didn't seem to want her company. "Be careful out there. Remember that Wilhite can shoot the nose off a gnat half a mile away."

Drew made a comical face. "He's good, honey, but he's not *that* good. Anyway, I'll be careful."

After he was gone, Oleta elbowed Cassie. "He called you honey," Oleta said with a grin.

"It doesn't mean anything," Cassie assured her, rising from the chair to pick up Andy. She hugged him, and he squirmed and pointed down at the blocks he'd been playing with, wanting them instead of her. She fought off a cloak of self-pity, but still felt spurned.

"When he called you that, it sounded natural to me," Oleta said, ever hopeful.

Cassie let Andy slide down her body to the floor and his blocks again. "Sounds natural when he calls his horses that, too," she noted in a tone that could have soured fresh milk.

Approaching Monroe Hendrix's sprawling ranch house with the sheriff, Drew looked at the structure and the area around it from a new perspective. A lot of money had been poured into making this house to reflect prosperity, grandeur, and refined taste. Which was plumb silly in these parts, Drew thought. Nobody he knew was that impressed with Hendrix or his spread.

But now that he thought on it, Drew had to admit that Roe Hendrix had always been a bit of a peacock. He loved to wear nice clothes and flash his money roll. He considered himself a ladies' man and the best catch of the county, and he was the first to buy any newfangled machine on the market. No matter how much it cost or how useless it was to his ranching operation.

Running his gaze over the six fine carriages and buggies parked under a long canopy, Drew shook his head in derision. Now, why would any man need that many vehicles? Just for show. Same as the big, freshly painted house with its polished double doors and twin chimneys. He chuckled under his breath when they passed a chicken coop that some people would be mighty glad to call home. It was certainly nothing like the unpainted, wired-together coop back at the Square D. No, this coop was a miniature version of the big house. For laying hens.

The fence wire sparkled in the sun. All of it looked

new. The place was alive with movement. It seemed that
Hendrix had an army of men to work this ranch. Should
be one of the most successful operations in the state, but
it was far from that. Roe had spent whatever profits he'd
made on building himself a castle, on making an impression, when he should have spent it on his bread and
butter—his cattle.

They'd ridden out to see the dead horse, and the sheriff had agreed they needed to speak to Hendrix. Sheriff
Nelson had inspected the area and examined the tracks
and the stolen cattle. The steers, Drew had noted, were
underweight. One or two of them had glassy eyes. Not
exactly sickly cows, but not healthy either.

"One thing I was wondering." Sheriff Nelson looked
at Drew. "How did you drag that dead horse from where
it was shot all the way over to where you hid it in the
bushes?"

Drew shrugged. "I used my horse."

The sheriff ran his gaze over Dynamite. "Mighty
strong horse."

"And I had help."

"Ice, you mean?"

Drew pointed ahead. "Here comes trouble."

Buck Wilhite rode toward them, appearing out of nowhere. A long rifle rested in the crook of his arm. He
greeted them with neither a smile nor a scowl. He just
stared at them as if he were a prison guard and they
were his new inmates.

"What can I do for you?" Wilhite asked.

"You can't do anything for us," Drew answered, not
liking the man's question or his tone.

"We're here to speak to your boss," the sheriff said,

throwing Drew a disgruntled glance. "Is he at the house?"

"He didn't say anything to me about expecting anyone."

Sheriff Nelson leaned a forearm on his saddle horn and fixed a pleasant but somewhat peeved smile on his face. "Pal, I know you're just doing your job, but you surely noticed the star pinned on my shirt. I'm here to speak with Mr. Hendrix and I doubt if he'll object, so move aside. This is none of your concern."

Wilhite studied the sheriff, then Drew, before he gave an almost imperceptible nod and reined his horse around in a tight circle to lead them to the front of the house. Sheriff Nelson exchanged a speaking glance with Drew, and Drew knew they were thinking along the same lines: Roe was carrying the protection of his property a mite too far.

Monroe strode toward them from the direction of the stables, leading a fine-looking chestnut mare with white socks and a blazed face.

"Just the man I wanted to see!" he bellowed with a broad grin. "Howdy, Sheriff, how you doing? Drew Dalton, take a look at this piece of horseflesh and tell me what you think. I value your opinion."

Unable to resist the chance to admire a good horse, Drew slid from the saddle and walked to the mare. He ran a hand along her back, over her flanks, down her legs.

"A Thoroughbred," he said. "Built for speed."

"Indeed she is," Monroe agreed. "Superior, I'm told, to those horses you're breeding. What are they called?"

"Quarter horses," Drew said. "And one isn't any better than the other. They're bred for completely different things, is all.''

''How's that?''

''This is a racer, a runner,'' Drew explained. ''Quarter horses are quick, but they aren't distance runners. They go fast for about a quarter-mile is all. They're herding horses and the best cutting horses you'll ever see. They can cut fly specks from a can of pepper. Hell, I've seen saddle-bred men topple right off their backs, they turn so fast.''

''Oh.'' Monroe looked as if he'd lost some of his steam. ''Well, I'm thinking of breeding *this* kind of horse.'' He rubbed the mare's velvety nose. ''I like the looks of them.''

''They're pretty, and this one is a real beauty.'' Drew stroked her side. ''She's already been bred, I see.''

''Yes, bred to a champion.''

That's what he'd been told anyway, Drew thought. True to form, Monroe Hendrix was jumping into something without learning all he could about it first. He'd never bothered to learn cattle raising and now he was thinking he'd be a horse breeder when he didn't even know what kind he had decided to raise. Drew also found it interesting that Roe had chosen horses as his new endeavor. Maybe people were beginning to talk about the quarter horses at the Square D.

''Yeah, I've been meaning to have a good look at your herding horses,'' the sheriff said, interrupting Drew's thoughts. ''People in town have been telling me that you and that Mexican kid are raising some mighty fine stock. This stallion here''—he gestured toward Dynamite—''sure is fine. He'll throw off some pretty colts, I reckon.''

Drew held out a hand, and Dynamite came over to him, as loyal as a hound. He nuzzled Drew's palm and gently butted his shoulder.

"He's my pride," Drew said, stroking Dynamite's ears with open affection. "I raised him from a newborn, still slick from his mama's belly."

"Yeah, well, like I said, folks in town say you've got some of the best horses they've ever seen."

Drew beamed. So he was right. People *were* noticing, and that must have sent Roe into a fit of envy. So now Roe was going to be a horse breeder. Drew bit down on his lower lip to keep from laughing aloud.

"Speaking of horses . . ." The sheriff dismounted and removed his hat so that he could run a handkerchief over his balding head. "I just examined a dead one of yours over at the Square D."

Monroe's mouth went slack, and he stared at the sheriff, seemingly rendered speechless.

"I shot the horse by mistake," Drew said. "I was trying to plug its rider."

"Why the hell were you shooting at one of my men?" Roe asked, his face getting red.

"Because he was a cattle rustler, that's why. Him and two other men were herding your cattle onto my land when I surprised them. Your cattle are still on my side of the fence, but you can have them back any time you want."

"I'll be damned." Monroe shook his head and stared at his boots for a few seconds. "Two or three of my cattle ponies came up missing a couple of nights ago. I figured they must have wandered to a far corner of the property or maybe they were hiding in the tree lines. I didn't give much thought to it. Figured they would show up.'' He slapped a hand across his thigh. "Those dirty range rats must have stolen them—and my cattle, too!''

"Looks like you'd tell me about anything coming up missing,'' the sheriff said. "You know I'm trying to bust up a rustling ring.''

"You didn't notice you had cattle missing?'' Drew asked.

"No, but I would have.'' Roe cursed under his breath. "I'll have to double my efforts around here. I thought Buck would be able to patrol my property himself, but I guess he'll have to hire some more men to help him. After all, I've got a lot of acres to watch over.''

"I heard he'd already hired some men to help him,'' Drew said.

"Is that what you heard? Where'd you hear that?'' Roe asked, narrowing his eyes.

"I don't recall. Isn't it the truth?''

"The truth . . .'' Roe smiled. "The *truth* is that I think someone is trying to point the finger at me and thereby make himself look less guilty.'' Frost coated his smile. "I once stood by you, Drew. I sure would hate to think you'd repay me in this fashion.''

"Why, you—'' Drew lunged, seized by sudden fury, but the sheriff blocked his path. "You son of a bitch! I ought to drive you into the ground like a stake! You know I'm not stealing any cattle. You *know* it!''

"That's enough,'' Sheriff Nelson said, giving Drew a push away from Monroe. "You settle down and let me talk to Hendrix. You hear me, Dalton? Quit breathing fire. I'm in charge here.''

Drew nodded, his body taut, his temper barely checked. He wanted to peel Roe like a rattler, but he held his ground. He didn't have to look to know that

Buck Wilhite was close by and probably had him in his hair-trigger sights. Drew didn't want to give the one-eyed killer any excuse to add another brag to his collection.

"This don't look good," Sheriff Nelson said to Monroe. "If I was you, I'd round up every cowhand and do some talking to them. Could be some of your men are bad seeds."

"My men are not thieves," Roe said, puffing up like a mound of yeast bread. "I tell you, someone is—"

"And I'm telling you that you ought to be concerned about your horses being ridden by thieves," Sheriff Nelson said, cutting him off before he could say what would have been fighting words. "Talk to your men, then come into town, and me and you will have a visit about this. I want to know when your horses came up missing and if anybody saw anything suspicious that night. I expect your cooperation on this, Hendrix."

Monroe gave a stiff nod. "Everyone knows I'm doing everything I can to have the man responsible put behind bars." He gave Drew a long, hard glare before he led the Thoroughbred back to the stables.

Drew mounted up and pointed Dynamite toward home. Sheriff Nelson rode beside him in silence until they reached the place where the sheriff would veer off to Abilene.

"Listen to me, Dalton," he said, his tone kindly, like that of an uncle. "This is the time when you've got to be smart. Watch your back and keep your eyes peeled. If Hendrix doesn't show up at my office right soon, I'll send one of my deputies out here to get him. After I speak privately with him, I'll tell you what I think."

Drew studied the sheriff, taken by surprise at the

man's show of support. "Seems to me you're thinking the same thing I'm thinking." He looked over his shoulder at Star H land. "For a man who is worried enough to hire a sharpshooter to protect him from thieves, Roe sure was unconcerned when some of his stock came up missing."

The sheriff rolled himself a cigarette, then placed it between his lips and struck a match off his pants leg. "Yep," he conceded, blue smoke wreathing his head. "Some things are adding up and others just ain't. My pappy was a smart man, and he told me once not to trust a man who admires other folks' hossflesh too much." He squinted through the smoke at Dynamite. "I like that hoss, but that don't make me want to raise some like him. Monroe Hendrix has always got to have the best and be the best, even if he don't or ain't. He's like your pa that way, or so I'm told."

Relief trickled through Drew, but he cautioned himself not to put too much stock in the sheriff's faint show of faith. But it did lighten his load. He pushed back his shoulders, grateful for the small favor.

"A big part of me is hoping that Roe just isn't paying close enough attention to who he hires and what might be going on right under his nose," Drew admitted. "I'm beholden to him, you know. He spoke up for me at my first trial when my old man wouldn't bother."

"Yeah, well, all talk costs you is a little wind. See you in a few days, Dalton." Blowing smoke, the sheriff turned his mount toward town.

Drew watched him until he was out of sight, the man's words sinking slowly into him like a knife. What *had* it cost Roe to speak up for him in court? That gesture had put considerable more shine on Roe's character.

Maybe he'd been looking at this the wrong way all these years, Drew thought. Maybe Roe had gone to court for his own reasons that had nothing to do with Drew.

Like looking innocent and upstanding when he was exactly the opposite.

Drew set his spurs to Dynamite and raced the wind back home.

Chapter 23

As Drew walked the length of the front room of the house, his boot heels rang against the floorboards, punctuating his words as he described to Cassie the scene that had transpired earlier that day at the Star H.

"Why couldn't I see this all before? I rode up to that ranch house today, and the whole thing hit me like a lightning bolt. The place is all for show. New things everywhere you look and so many ranch hands, you'd think Roe owned every cow in Kansas. Sure didn't take any genius to see where his money was being spent, but I'd never paid any attention to that before."

Cassie looked up from the sock she was darning. "That's because Roe slapped blinders on you the day he stood up for you in court. He's clever. No doubt about that."

"Yeah, I guess you're right. Him standing up for me made me beholden to him. All the time I was in prison, I built him up in my mind as one of my few friends. I remember how surprised I was when he offered to appear in court."

"Why were you surprised?"

"Because I never thought we were that friendly. I never expected Roe to be that interested in what happened to me. I figured I'd misjudged him real bad."

"And as it turns out, we've both misjudged him real bad."

"Maybe."

Cassie laid the sock in her lap and looked at him squarely. "Maybe? You mean you still think he might not know anything about the cattle rustling?"

"It could be that Wilhite fella."

"The rustling started before he showed up," she reminded him.

"Or it could be those two skunks, Smalley and Harper."

"They don't have enough brains between them to carry out this scheme. Whoever is doing this is trying to get the Square D cattle and the Square D land and get you out of the way for good this time. If Roe is hurting for good cattle, he'd be desperate enough to try something like this."

"I guess."

"You hate to think that any of your neighbors would knife you in the back, but none of them was too concerned before, when you were packed off to prison, and none of them, except for Viola, was overjoyed when you came home."

His mouth quirked and he massaged the back of his neck. "You have a way of putting things, Cassie Dalton."

"I like to state things plain."

He sat on the sofa across from her. The night was a little cool, so they'd lit a fire, and the glow of it painted his face with gold. His eyes glimmered as if lit from within.

It would be the last fire this spring, Cassie thought. Summer was almost upon them. Drew would take the herd next week to market, if all went well. It was hard for her to realize that she'd only known Drew for two months. Seemed like a lot longer. So much had happened this—

"How old were you the first time, Cassie? If you don't mind my asking."

She glanced at him. "The first time?" she repeated before grasping his meaning. Her heart lurched. Oh, Lord. He was asking her about *that*. "Oh, you mean, when was I with my first man?"

"Yes."

"I was a few days shy of sixteen."

He linked his fingers and stared at them. "For pay?"

"No, for what I thought at the time was true love." She put her mending in the basket by her feet. "You want to hear about it, do you? All the details?"

"No, just what you think I should know."

She wanted to tell him that she didn't want him to know anything, not even that she'd been a whore before she'd married his father. But the cat was among the pigeons now and there was nothing left to do but to pick up the feathers.

"The man I told you about—Taylor—he courted me. I was doing laundry and working in a boardinghouse, barely making ends meet. The woman I worked for was a witch. She treated me worse than dirt. Taylor came and boarded there. He was new in town, just drifting, he said. He wore nice clothes and he had manners. He brought me flowers and a little box of candies. Chocolates all the way from Chicago!'' She smiled, remembering how special she'd felt. Like a lady.

''Where was this?''

''In California. Santa Clara.''

''How old was he at that time?''

''Twenty-five, I think, but I'm not sure. He was older and worldly.''

''And he had no business messing with a fifteen-year-old girl with no family to look out for her,'' Drew said, almost growling with outrage.

Cassie shrugged. ''Yes, but from where I was sitting at that time, I thought he was my hero, saving me from my terrible life. When he was ready to leave, he asked me to come with him.'' She laughed ruefully. ''He didn't have to ask twice.''

Pausing, she thought back to those early days when she had been so dreamily in love with Taylor and knew that what she felt for Drew was nothing like it. The emotions she experienced when she was with Drew were not dreamy; they were earth-bound, real, and solid. With Taylor, she'd been an impressionable girl, more scared than secure. With Drew she was a strong-minded woman, secure, scared only of disappointing him and making him regret his association with her.

''Where did you go with him?''

''To Texas first and then to Indian Territory. In Texas he worked as a bartender and got me a job serving drinks at the gaming tables. He was sweet to me then. A gentleman. He didn't even try to sleep with me until a few weeks after we got to Texas and then ... Well, he was paying for two rooms for us and told me he was running short of money. He said I could keep my room and he'd pay for it, but that he'd have to give up his. He said he'd stay in the stables out back.''

"And you told him you would share a room with him," Drew said.

"Yes." Cassie sighed. "Looking back, I suppose it was a dirty trick of his, but I didn't see it that way then. I didn't like it, though. Being with a man like that." Blood rose to heat her face and make her squirm in her chair. "I never liked it ... until ... well, until lately." She swallowed with difficulty and found she could not look at him, so she hurried on. "Then one night he told me that we were hurting for money real bad because he'd lost some at the tables. He said we'd be put out on the street if we didn't pay our rent the next morning, but he knew one way we could make some quick silver. He knew this man who would pay to ... uh ... pay ... to ..."

"I know, I know," Drew said. "So you did? That's how it started? Didn't you figure out that this Taylor fella couldn't think much of you to ask you to do such a thing?"

"It felt wrong, but I convinced myself it was right. Taylor had bought me pretty dresses and he had taken me away from that awful boardinghouse work. He told me I was beautiful and special. He had done so much for me, and I couldn't refuse this one thing he asked me to do. Besides, he swore I'd only have to do it once, that he would stop gambling."

"But he didn't."

"Yes, yes." She stood up, sending the rocker into motion without her. "I was stupid as a goose, and you could tell this story for me, it's all so humdrum. Before I knew it, I was seeing a man or two every week. Then

Taylor moved to Indian Territory and opened up his own place. He said I wouldn't have to be with any man but him because he couldn't stand thinking of another man laying hands on me.'' She moved closer to the fire, feeling a chill that seemed to settle in her heart. "But what he did was set me up as his high princess. Only the customers who paid top dollar were allowed into my bed. Most of them couldn't afford me, but once in a while some joker would come up with enough money to make Taylor forget how awful it was for him when another man touched me.''

"Wilhite never could meet the price?''

"Taylor would never let Wilhite have me even if he offered him a thousand dollars. Buck Wilhite worked for Taylor, and Taylor didn't want any of the people on his payroll sleeping with me. He said it was bad business.''

"Why did Taylor whip you?''

"I was getting uppity. I told him I was quitting him and going to work for his competition across the street. It was a brand-new saloon that had opened up, and the man who owned it had a good heart. He wanted me to quit whoring. He's the one who married Miss Adele.''

"Oh, yeah. The mail-order groom.''

"That's him.'' Cassie smiled. "He saved my life and my best friend's life.''

"Did he kill Taylor?''

"Yes.''

"I wish he were here so I could shake his hand.''

Cassie turned to face him, putting her back to the fire. "I'm not going to apologize about what I did back then. Love, or what can pass as love, can make people do crazy things. Every heart hungers for another, even a young whore's. But I got out and I'm staying out.''

"I didn't ask for an apology, did I?"

"No." She wrung her hands. "You haven't asked anything of me—yet—but it's coming. I know it's coming. I just want you to understand that I told you about me because I decided you should know, what with Wilhite making threats and all. But I don't want your pity or anything like that. And I don't want your charity. You have a right to look at me different now. I probably should have told you before . . . well, before you and me . . . got close."

He stood up. "I'm glad you told me."

"You are?"

"We should always be honest with each other." He lifted a hand and placed it alongside her face. "We've both been through hell and back, Cassie."

His touch, so gentle and warm, weakened her. She leaned into his palm and closed her eyes, her senses simmering. "Oh, Drew," she breathed his name. "Drew, Drew, I wish things were different." She inched upward and pressed her lips to his. At first he gave no response, but then he released a tortured groan, and his arms came around her and tightened as he deepened the kiss.

Cassie parted her lips, clutching madly at him and catching fire. His tongue dueled with hers, and his hands roamed her body, kneading her hips and breasts in wild abandon. She drove her fingers through his hair and wound her arms around his neck, clinging to him as their kisses lengthened and their passion soared out of control.

"God, Cassie . . . God!" His voice was ragged, rough. His eyes were darkly blue and haunted by ghosts she didn't recognize. "I want you," he bit out. "I could take you right here, over and over again, all night long."

She thought she might faint. She thought she might die if he didn't follow through on his words.

"But I won't." He pulled her arms from around his neck. "You've been used enough by men."

A whimper escaped her before she could stop it. Her pride was all that kept her from crumpling to her knees. She stepped away from him, anger and humiliation and confusion spilling through her like poison.

Someone landed on the porch and hammered at the front door. Gooseflesh broke out over her arms, and she reached for the rifle hanging above the mantel in an automatic reaction.

"Who's there?" Drew called.

"Ice!"

Cassie sighed and sat down heavily in the rocker. She felt as hollow as a dry well.

Drew opened the door. Ice stood on the porch, hopping from one foot to the other.

"She's going to foal," he announced, his voice pitched high with excitement. "I checked on the mare, and she's ready to pop out her baby any minute now."

"Holy smoke!" Drew grabbed his hat and coat off the peg. "How's she doing?"

"Pretty good, I think. Hey, that's what we ought to call her. Holy Smoke."

"Sounds right to me." Drew looked back at Cassie and struggled to punch his arms through the right holes in his coat. "You coming?"

She shook her head. "You go on."

"You sure?"

"Go on," she repeated.

He frowned before closing the door behind him. Cassie listened to the men's voices diminish as they hurried to the barn. She stared at the flames in the hearth and touched her fingertips to her throbbing lips, still tender from his drugging kisses.

Use her. Is that what making love to her was in his mind? She cringed at the thought.

"I can't stay here," she said, her voice sounding to her as if it had come from a great distance. "Not even for Andy."

Use her.

She shivered in revulsion. Obviously when he looked at her now, all he saw was a whore. No, she couldn't live here with him thinking of her like that. She loved him and always would, but she couldn't bear his low opinion of her. He had made her hope that she could be the woman in his life and that he could be father to her child, but it was not to be.

Lord, this was hard. She closed her eyes against the tears that threatened to overtake her. Nothing she'd suffered was any worse than thinking about leaving Drew Dalton.

At the door of the barn, Drew hung back. Ice stopped and whirled around, motioning him forward.

Drew shook his head and leaned against the outside wall. He bent over, propping his hands on his knees. The heartache was as severe as any injury he'd ever suffered. "Go ahead. I'll be right there. I need a minute."

"Why? What's wrong with you?"

"Just go on," he almost shouted. "Leave me be!"

"Okay, okay!" Ice held up his hands and retreated into the barn.

Drew sucked in cool air and blinked moisture from

his eyes. How the hell was he going to stay on here, feeling like he did about Cassie? He couldn't imagine being around her and not putting his hands on her, stroking her, loving her, pressing his mouth to hers. She was so sweet, so giving that she'd let him paw her, satisfy his hunger for her, but then she'd shown her true feelings when she'd let loose that small sound—a wounded animal sound.

He was like all the men in her life—taking and never giving unless he was sure to be well compensated. That's all she'd ever known of men. But he would change that.

His head came up and he straightened slowly. He pressed the heel of his hand to his thumping, aching heart. Yes, he'd change that. He would be the first man to give her something with no strings attached. He'd expect nothing of her, take nothing from her. In this way he would prove to her—*show* her—how much he loved her.

She meant the world to him, so he'd give her his world. He'd give her his ranch.

The ache eased around his heart, and he looked up at the starry heavens. A weight seemed to lift off him and rise up to the sky. He blinked away tears and sent a smile upward, then he went inside the barn to help Ice with the foaling mare.

The next day Drew stifled a huge yawn as he pulled himself up onto Dynamite's back and shifted his backside until he found it a good fit in the saddle. Dynamite turned his head and nipped at Drew's knee.

"Hey, stop that." Drew slapped the horse's rump, getting a trot out of him. "I know it's late in the day, but I slept in. Hell, I was up until past breakfast with that mare and her new baby. Prettiest filly you ever saw, Dynamite. She's going to have a deep gold-colored coat and white markings. Aw, she's special. She's got a lot of spirit. A real heartbreaker.''

He realized he was chattering away like a jaybird, so he ground his teeth together and focused his bleary eyes on the land before him. He looked over his shoulder and spotted Cassie bent over in the vegetable garden. What would she think about naming the filly Little Nugget?

He'd been disappointed when she hadn't come out to the barn to watch the filly being born last night. She probably thought it best if she kept her distance. She was probably right.

Looking up at the sun, he determined it was somewhere around two o'clock. Ice must be in the fields, loading up the wagon with hay to be taken to the barn. With only the three of them to do the chores, the work was piling up. But thank God he had something to occupy him other than his lusting for Cassie and his frustration over the cattle rustling.

He had learned patience while in prison, but those lessons were being tested. He'd told the sheriff he'd wait to hear from him, but he was finding it difficult to keep his word. He itched to confront Roe man to man, just the two of them. Wouldn't take him long to wring a confession out of Monroe Hendrix.

Once his name was cleared, he intended to talk to Cassie about the ranch and how she preferred that things should be handled. He wanted her to be happy. He wanted her.

Shaking his head like a fly-crazed cow, he vowed to place Cassie's happiness before his own.

The way she'd looked at him last night when Ice had knocked at the door and interrupted them . . . Drew closed his eyes in self-loathing, recalling how her eyes had shone with unshed tears and her skin had been so pale. Must have been the same look she gave men who plunked down a few dollars to have their way with her.

He hoped never to see that expression on her face again.

Dynamite had slowed to a leisurely pace. The morning had been cool, but the sun was high and hot, warming the air quickly. Heat rose in waves from the grassland, and Dynamite's coat was damp in places. Flies buzzed and bees darted from blossom to blossom. He squinted at the sun, then down at the green grass. They could use another rain.

Were those tracks? He recognized some as Square D horses. He'd shoed them himself and knew his own work. The other, though, he didn't recognize.

Something—maybe fate, maybe luck—made him look up in time to see the sun reflect off something shiny some distance away among an outcropping of brush and wild blackberry bushes. Drew slipped off Dynamite and led him over to the shade of a sycamore. He removed his rifle from the saddle sling, then left Dynamite with a command to stay put. Moving toward the bank of brush, Drew walked on silent feet. He saw a man's boots sticking out from under one of the bushes. The man was lying flat on his belly. A short sprint away his horse grazed, chomping on grass, the reins dangling.

Responding to a sixth sense that warned him to go slow and quiet, Drew approached the man from his right side. He stopped, hidden by brush, to examine the intruder. He wasn't the least bit surprised to see the black patch covering the left eye. Buck Wilhite. What the hell was he doing?

Wilhite's rifle lay beside him. He held something up to his face, but Drew couldn't make it out until Wilhite shifted slightly, readjusting his arms, and Drew saw that he was peering at something through a spyglass.

Crouching low, Drew moved off to one side of Wilhite and was able to view what the man was spying on. Ice!

Ice was working in the hay field, shirt off and brown skin gleaming with sweat. With pitchfork in hand, he slung mounds of hay into the wagon, unaware he was the center of attention.

Drew recalled how Wilhite had spit at Ice when he found out Ice was part Blackfoot. There had been venom there, enough to poison a man to the bone. Suddenly Drew knew that Wilhite wasn't just watching Ice. He meant to kill him.

Drew retraced his steps back toward Wilhite. The man was no longer looking at Ice through the spyglass. That instrument lay on the grass, its lens catching and casting the sunrays.

Propped on his elbows, Wilhite wedged the rifle more comfortably against his shoulder and took aim with his remaining eye. Drew covered the ground in six strides. He stepped down on the barrel of the long-distance rifle and rested the tip of his own .44 Winchester against the small of Wilhite's back.

"Take your finger off the trigger or I'll flex mine," he told him, watching a bead of sweat roll down Wilhite's nose.

Wilhite's lips curled back, but he released the rifle. Drew gave his shoulder a kick.

"Get up. Slow."

Wilhite rose first to his knees, then to his feet. "I should have finished you and that stinking Blackfoot when I had the chance."

"You're the one who shot Ice, aren't you? Did you think he was me?"

"He was wearing your clothes." Wilhite grinned. "Didn't matter to me who I shot, but it mattered to somebody else. I figured I'd get you another day."

"Who does it matter to? Your boss man? Roe Hendrix?"

Wilhite spat at the ground. "I ain't saying nothing to you. I don't talk to dead men, and you're as good as dead."

"Turn around and walk into the clearing," Drew said, following behind the man and watching for any false moves. When they were in the open, Drew fired his rifle at the sky. From the corner of his eye, he saw Ice whirl around. He motioned for Ice to join him. "Don't try anything," he warned Wilhite. "I have no qualms about filling you full of lead. None whatsoever."

Ice hopped into the wagon and strapped the two stocky horses into a creditable gallop. He'd been some distance away, but no hard target for Wilhite's powerful weapon. Ice used all his weight to pull back on the reins and stop the excited steeds.

"What's going on? Was he stealing cows?"

Drew shook his head. "He was aiming to shoot you dead."

Ice's face went still and his light-colored eyes seemed to glaze over as he glared at a smirking Wilhite. "I will cut out your heart!"

"Yeah, but first you will go for the sheriff," Drew

said. "After you help me truss him up. You can ride his horse. I'll drive back to the house in the wagon. Dynamite will follow us. I'll chain this dung heap in the barn, and he can wait there for the law."

"I say we hang him. To hell with the sheriff."

"Being in your barn again will bring back fond memories," Wilhite said.

"What's he talking about?" Ice asked Drew.

"Don't listen to him. He's trying to get a rise out of us. He's hoping we'll make a wrong move and give him a chance to run like a rabbit."

"Yeah, the last time I was in your barn I was getting some smooch off your pa's widow."

For a moment Drew thought the world had slipped out from under him. He measured Wilhite with his eyes, seeing past the smirking mouth to the blackness of his soul. Once this man had been human, but no more.

"You're lying!" Ice shouted.

"That's right." Wilhite chuckled. "I'm lying. Ask her," he challenged Drew. "I'm surprised she didn't already tell you about us rolling around in the hay that night. Ain't her skin soft as silk?"

"Let's hang him right here!" Ice demanded, shaking with fury.

Drew motioned for Ice to climb down from the wagon. "You got any rope?"

"Sí, I got some rope. Plenty enough to do the job." Ice jumped down, then rummaged in the back for a coil of thick rope.

Together Drew and Ice bound Wilhite's hands behind his back and hobbled him. Wilhite offered little resistance other than to curse at them roundly.

"Help me get him onto the wagon seat," Drew said.

Ice stared at him. "We're not going to hang him?"

"No. He's going to clear my name before he dies." Drew placed a hand on Ice's shoulder and lowered his voice. "I want him dead, too, but let's not be so quick to give the man what he's begging for. Believe me, my friend, there are things much worse than death in this world."

Ice thawed a bit and gave a terse nod. They hoisted their captive up onto the wagon seat. Drew whistled for Dynamite, and the horse came at a gallop.

"His rifle is over there in those bushes. Be sure and take it with you to the sheriff." Drew pointed to the thicket. "You ever line up dominoes, then topple one and watch the others fall?" He grinned at Ice and bobbed his head toward Wilhite. "Once we tell the sheriff what this man was doing, it'll be the same as giving that first domino a push. The others will soon be falling, my friend. Just you wait and see."

"I would like to tear this man limb from limb."

"I know, I know." Drew placed a hand on the hot-head's shoulder. "So would I, but then we'd only be making more trouble for ourselves. Now, get. I don't want this mangy coyote stinking up my barn any longer than he has to."

Ice retrieved the long rifle, but he couldn't pass Wilhite without baring his teeth and muttering darkly in Spanish. Hopping onto the back of Wilhite's horse, Ice kicked the animal into a ground-gobbling run.

Drew climbed up and sat beside Wilhite on the hard wagon seat. He unwound the reins from the brake lever and slapped them across the broad backs of the horses. The wagon rolled forward with a chorus of squeaks and groans.

Frowning, he thought of Cassie's failure to tell him that Wilhite had attacked her in the barn. He didn't doubt the man's story. It would be simple enough to check out, so there would be no reason for him to lie. Wilhite had jumped Cassie in the barn, and Cassie had kept her mouth shut about it. Probably because she didn't want to give Drew a reason to put his life on the line for her by calling Wilhite out for a gunfight.

Stubborn, willful, gutsy Cassie. Unwittingly Wilhite had given Drew yet another reason to love the woman.

"The sheriff won't do a damn thing to me," Wilhite said. "When I tell him that I was following the trail of a cattle rustler and you jumped me out of nowhere, he'll believe me. He sure won't believe someone who until lately was rubbing up against hairy butts in prison."

Drew backhanded him so hard that he sent him flipping over the seat and into the hay Ice had mounded in the wagon bed. He glanced over his shoulder and was glad to see Wilhite spit blood.

"Shut your mouth or I'll stuff it full of buffalo grass and horse manure, you sorry bag of wind." Drew hammered him with a blunt glare.

"Whatzamatter? Did I stir up some fond memories, pretty boy? You homesick for your boyfriends?"

Drew stopped the horses, planted one knee on the wagon seat for balance and planted one fist in Wilhite's face. The man fell backward with a grunt, then went limp. Out cold. Blood dribbled down his chin.

Satisfied, Drew sucked on his stinging middle knuckle and sat down again. He picked up the reins.

"Come along, boys," he said, the beast in him purring with contentment after that release of brute strength. "Step lightly." Then, pursing his lips, he whistled a merry tune.

Chapter 24

Since Cassie was nowhere in sight, Drew assumed she must be inside with Oleta and Andy, or around somewhere doing chores. He parked the wagon near the front of the barn and checked on Wilhite. Still out cold.

At the horse trough he filled a bucket with murky water and carried it back to the wagon. He grabbed Wilhite by the boots and pulled him none too gently out of the wagon and onto the ground. Then he poured the bucket of water directly into Wilhite's face and open mouth.

The man sputtered and squirmed, but with his hands tied behind his back and his feet bound together, he couldn't move out from under the sudden waterfall. Drew dropped the bucket, then reached down and grabbed fistfuls of the man's wet shirt, hauling him to his feet.

"Rise and shine, horse dung," Drew growled.

Wilhite coughed and ran his tongue across his front teeth. "You broke my tooth, jailbird."

"You're lucky I didn't break your neck." He yanked him toward the barn. "Get in there."

Owls fluttered in the rafters, startled by the scuffling and deep voices below. A barn cat streaked across the floor, hot on the trail of a mouse. Drew nudged his own prey toward an empty stall, or what he thought was an empty one. The gray mare and her long-legged baby filled it.

"Damn," Drew muttered. "I forgot I put them in here." He grabbed the back of Wilhite's shirt and directed him to the middle of the barn. "Stay there while I clear out a stall to put you in until the sheriff can collect you."

Wilhite shook his head, flinging water and mud from his hair and face. "Do you know you're living with a whore?"

Drew sent him a black look. "Shut up."

"No telling how many men have had her. Her whore name is Little Nugget. She fetched a high price for her favors."

"You want to talk? Tell me why you were aiming to kill Ice. He hasn't done a damn thing to you."

"He's an Indian and I hate Indians. Especially Blackfoot. I worked for one Indian in the Territory, and he almost got me killed. He was crazy. Them Indians are all crazy and dumber than dirt. I ain't got no use for them."

"I'm not Indian, and you said you wanted to kill me, too."

"Kill you or put you back where you belong—behind bars where you can't get in the way."

"In whose way?"

"Not mine." Wilhite grinned, giving Drew a glimpse of the tooth he'd chipped. "Your neighbors. They don't cotton to having a cattle thief living near them."

"I know what you've been up to, Wilhite." Drew went into the next stall, where a few bags of feed were stored, helter-skelter. He began moving them to one side so that he'd have room to shackle Wilhite to a post in the corner. "You hired Reb Smalley and Dan Harper, two thieves drifting through this area, and paid them to rustle cattle and make it look like I was doing the rustling. You got your orders from Monroe Hendrix."

"Yeah, you're one smart fella. Guess your smarts is what landed you in prison."

"I can understand why you keep wanting to talk about prison, seeing as how that's where you're headed." Drew glanced over his shoulder from time to time, but Wilhite wasn't moving. He stood erect, his one eye glinting with malevolence.

"Roe wants my cattle," Drew continued. "And my land. But mainly my cattle. My old man wasn't good for much, but he did know his steers, and he raised the best stock in the state. I never paid much attention to that until lately, when I was trying to figure out why Roe would be so desperate to pack me off to prison or watch me swing from a rope."

"I vote for the rope," Wilhite rasped.

Drew leaned down to pick up the final bag of feed, and out of the corner of his eye he saw Wilhite lean sideways to scratch his ankle. Biting flies, Drew thought, waving aside one that was trying to light on his neck. In the next instant Drew's mind registered that Wilhite wasn't scratching, but grabbing at something.

Tensing, Drew turned his head for a better view and found himself staring at the small gun that had been tucked inside Wilhite's boot and was now firmly in his hand. Wilhite chuckled, aiming the gun as best he could with his hands tied behind his back. His aim was good. Too damn good.

In the next instant Drew saw the end of his existence, and simultaneously he saw with certain clarity that the best thing in his life had been Cassie. His love for her filled him, absorbed him, lit him from within. He wished he had told her he loved her, told her that she was the first person he had ever truly loved. He wished he'd confessed his love for her son, his half brother, the baby he wished was his own.

Cassie. Her name blanketed his mind and erased everything that had come before, everything that was happening now. He knew no fear, only regret. Profound, drenching regret that he had not told her what she'd meant to him and how she had made him believe that he could be loved, that he could have a wife and a family of his own.

He cursed himself for not checking Wilhite for more weapons. A man hired to kill would most likely be armed to the teeth.

These thoughts swarmed on him in a blinding moment of time but arrived too late. Drew straightened slowly, wanting to leave this world standing up instead of crouched over.

The gunshot cracked like a whip, sending the animals in the barn into a frenzy. Horses reared, owls swooped, chickens squawked, a cat screamed. Drew stumbled backward, clutching his chest, rocked off his feet by the roar of the blast rather than its impact. That little gun sure had barked loud! He looked down at his hand and saw no blood seeping through his fingers, felt no pain. He'd been shot before, and it hadn't felt anything like this.

Wilhite fell forward, sending up a cloud of dust and dirt. His head struck the toe of Drew's boot. Blood poured from his cracked skull, staining the ground. Drew pulled his foot out of the way and looked up. He found himself staring at Cassie's pale face and the shaking, smoking Colt .45 in her hand.

"Good God, Cassie!" He sprang toward her and gripped her gun hand, pulling the warm weapon from her cold fingers. "Where'd you come from, honey?"

"I saw you . . ." She stared down at the man she'd killed. "It was like back in Whistle Stop. He was going to kill someone, and I hit him over the head with a bottle then. Should have shot him dead in Whistle Stop, and he wouldn't have brought trouble here . . . to you and me." Her brown eyes seemed oddly vacant. "He's like a black shadow following me, dogging my footsteps, disappearing for a spell only to turn up again when I thought I was rid of him."

"He won't be bothering you anymore," Drew said, draping an arm around her shoulders. "Let's go to the house."

"What about him?"

"I'll take care of him later. I sent Ice for the sheriff. When he gets here, I'll tell him what happened, how you saved my life."

"I did." She nodded, walking woodenly by his side. "He would have killed you, Drew. Killing is second nature to that man."

"I know." He hugged her closer, wanting to protect her, shield her from a life that seemed to heap too much woe on her narrow shoulders. Happiness over being alive flooded him, brought a mist to his eyes. He'd been given another chance! Another chance to tell Cassie that she was a miracle, that she had changed the rock in his chest into a beating heart. "I'm obliged to you," he said, and his voice sounded hoarse. He cleared his throat. "I mean it, Cassie. Cassie, honey?"

She went limp, and he scooped her up into his arms before she could fall to the ground.

"Cassie?"

Her eyes rolled back in her head and she fainted dead away.

Drew paced restlessly in the front room, pausing when Oleta came out of Cassie's bedroom and closed the door softly behind her.

"She is resting," Oleta said. "She came to and heard Andy crying, so I gave him over to her. He works like a cure on her. She will be fine."

"Yeah. That's good." He closed his eyes, experiencing a moment of drenching relief. "Cassie's tough."

"And tender," Oleta said, smiling, but her dark eyes were troubled. "Why did you bring the one-eyed man here?"

"He tried to kill Ice. We caught him, and I sent Ice for the sheriff."

Oleta moved to the window and looked out. "Is this them coming, you think?"

"No, can't be them already." Drew stood behind her and looked outside. Surprise bolted through him when he saw Ice riding up with the sheriff, a deputy, and between them Monroe Hendrix. "Well, I'll be damned! It is them." Satisfaction surged through him when he saw that Hendrix was in handcuffs, looking like he could spit bullets. A short distance behind them rode two others, men whose familiar faces earned a grin from Drew.

He stepped onto the porch, and Monroe began to bluster like a windstorm.

"You son of a bitch! You think because you've got two broken-down cowhands lying for you that I'm going to roll over and play dead? The hell I am!"

"Speaking of dead." Drew nodded toward the barn. "Your fancy sharpshooter is lying out there in my barn, dead as a beaver-skin hat."

"Wilhite? You killed him!" Monroe turned toward the sheriff. "You hear that? What are you going to do about it, let him get away with murder? What kind of lawman are you?"

"He didn't kill him. I did."

Drew whirled around to find that Cassie, pale-faced and haunted-eyed, had left her bed and joined him on the porch.

"Cassie, go on back inside. I'll handle this," Drew said, placing a hand on her shoulder, wanting to shield her from further ugliness. She swayed slightly, and Drew braced her with an arm around her waist.

"You should never have brought that m-man here, Roe. I warned you," she said, her voice strong with anger.

"Ice filled me in on how you caught him," the sheriff said. "What happened? Did he get away from you?"

"He had a gun hidden in his boot, and he was on the verge of murdering me when Cassie shot him." Drew squeezed her waist.

Suddenly Cassie stiffened, and Drew glanced at her to see that her face had gone still and her eyes were burning in their sockets.

"What are they doing here?" she demanded, pointing at the other two men. "You aren't welcome here anymore!'' she shouted at them, shaking a fist. "Get off my land and stay off!''

"Hold on there, Cassie," Drew admonished. "You don't know the whole story." He smiled at the two cowhands. "Gabe and T-Bone left here to help us, not harm us."

"They're lying, no-good varmints," Monroe declared, his face flushing scarlet. "Sheriff, you've got to see that these people are all in this together. They're out to ruin me. They want my land and my cattle."

Drew barked a laugh. "Your cattle? Hell, Roe, nobody wants your pitiful cows. And your land isn't all that great either. Plenty of it, but you've overgrazed it and you cut down so many of the trees, you destroyed your windbreaks. Most of your top soil has blown away."

"You've always been envious of me," Monroe charged, jutting out his chin. "Everybody in this whole county is envious of me. I'm a respected man and you won't be able to get away with this, Sheriff. The folks around here will be in an uproar when they hear how you're trying to pin this cattle rustling ring on me."

"What's T-Bone and Gabe got to do with it?" Cassie asked, eyeing the two men with open suspicion.

"We never believed that Drew was stealing cattle," Gabe said.

"Didn't believe it the first time and sure didn't believe it this time," T-Bone chimed in. "But this time around I couldn't sit by and let Drew go to prison for something I knew he hadn't done. Gabe fell in with me, and we decided to try and get hired on at the Star H, since we'd seen tracks and such that made us think that the Star H had something to do with the thieving going on."

Cassie looked from T-Bone to Drew. "Is this true?"

That she sought truth from him touched Drew deeply. He gave her a quick hug. "It's true, darlin'. Old T-Bone and Gabe have always been our friends. Always will be our friends."

"Why did you lie to me the other night?" she asked, looking at T-Bone for an explanation.

"If things didn't work out, if one of us got killed, you see"—T-Bone shrugged—"I didn't want you to bear the burden of that guilt."

"How long have you known that they weren't against us?" she asked Drew.

"Since the night I shot at those men who were driving Star H cattle onto our land. Gabe and T-Bone came riding up a few minutes later. They'd been following the rustlers. They knew the thieves were Harper and Smalley and that Ben fella Oleta knows. They helped me drag the dead horse to a place where I could hide it. I wanted to be sure the sheriff got a chance to see the animal for himself."

"Well, I'll be damned," Sheriff Nelson said. "I was wondering about that."

"Why did you keep it from me?" Cassie asked. "Didn't you trust me?"

"No, it wasn't that. We were . . . well, we were having our differences and—"

"You didn't trust me."

"No, Cassie, it had nothing to do with—"

"These two cow ropers are regular Pinkerton detectives," Sheriff Nelson declared, reaching out to pat Gabe on the shoulder. "They're going into town with me to sign sworn statements about what was going on at the Star H and how they saw with their own eyes Smalley and Harper stealing cattle and driving them onto Square D land.''

"They're liars," Monroe said, jerking and twisting at the cuffs binding his wrists. "If Smalley and Harper were stealing cattle, I sure didn't know anything about it. How can I be held responsible for something they did? I'm not their keeper!"

"You knew everything that was going on," T-Bone said.

"Cassie," Monroe implored, a slight smile curving the corners of his mouth, "you know I have no reason to steal cattle. I've been trying to help you since A.J. died. Tell the sheriff. Tell him!"

"All I know for sure is that Drew Dalton never stole a cow in his life." She hitched up her chin. "Sheriff, I killed Buck Wilhite, but I had no choice."

"Where'd you say he was? The barn? I'll take the body into town to the undertaker's."

"That's it? You'll take their word, but not mine?" Monroe demanded.

"You'll have a trial, and it'll be up to the judge to decide your guilt or innocence," Sheriff Nelson said.

"Want me to speak to your character, Roe?" Drew asked with a smirk.

"You go to hell!" Monroe shouted, and his horse skittered nervously. "Cassie, I'm disappointed in you. Very disappointed."

Cassie tipped up her chin, anger sparking off her like flint on steel. "And I'm disappointed in you!" She shrugged away from Drew's supporting embrace and glared at him. "And I'm disappointed in you, too! I thought you trusted me." She marched into the house.

Drew felt his mouth fall open. "Well, that's a fine

howdy and thank-you,'' he grumbled, totally baffled by her anger toward him.

"Dalton, show me Wilhite's body,'' Sheriff Nelson said, getting Drew's attention again.

"Sure, come on.'' Drew bounded down the porch steps. He'd deal with Cassie later, he thought, but changed his mind after a few minutes when he saw her riding away from the house. She was headed for Two Forks Creek.

"Sheriff, I've got something to attend to and I—I'll be back later,'' he said, waving aside further explanation. In the barn, he opened Dynamite's stall and didn't bother to saddle him. Grabbing the lead rope, he swung up onto the horse's back. "I want to see about Cassie.''

"Sure, go ahead,'' Sheriff Nelson called to him.

It was twilight and a few stars were blooming overhead. Drew pulled his hat down low as he urged Dynamite into a gallop.

Minutes later, he gathered handfuls of his mount's mane and yanked him to a halt atop the gentle rise he knew so well. A semicircle of knotty pines crowned the swell of land. In the distance he could see the sparkle of the creek among a grove of trees, willow and oak and birch. Cassie's horse grazed among them. She stood nearby as still as a statue. Coyotes yipped and barked in the distance. A cow mooed deeply, mournfully. A knot formed in Drew's throat as Cassie and the land seemed to meld into one, united in strength and beauty. He loved both fiercely. Cassie had to know. He had to tell her . . .

Cassie listened to the strange music of the coyotes and wondered what they were saying to each other. As she'd hoped, her anger and disappointment and guilt faded under the twilight sky in this place of peace and stillness. She breathed deeply. *Yes, yes, all fall away,* she chanted in her head. She needed to think, needed to sort through what had happened, what she'd done, what would become of her now.

"This is a favorite place of mine."

She smothered a cry of alarm and stared at Drew. Where had he come from? She hadn't heard . . . She saw Dynamite some distance away, silhouetted against the darkening sky.

"I come here when I want to think, when I want to be alone," Drew added.

"To be alone," she repeated, but knew it was futile. He wouldn't leave her alone now. She could tell that for once he was full of words and meant for her to hear them. "I used to come here sometimes, too," she admitted. "I think this might have been a homestead once." She walked to a thick patch of grass. "Daffodils and crocus. See? A woman must have planted them a long, long time ago. Women put flower bulbs around their homes or upon graves. Since there are no signs of headstones here . . ."

"Yes, I think there was a house here once. If you want, there can be one here again."

Cassie angled a glance at him. "You got something to say to me, Drew Dalton, say it."

He gathered in a big breath that expanded his chest. "I want to do right by you, Cassie."

Her heart beat furiously. Good Lord! Did he actually love her? Could it be? Had she figured him all wrong? She'd thought that he didn't trust her, so he couldn't love her. He hadn't confided in her about T-Bone and Gabe, and that had wounded her, made her believe that he would never give himself to her. But now! Now!

"I want to build a house for you right here," Drew said, walking off the land. "I'll build it exactly the way you want, and I'll give you and Andy half the land. You've earned it. I want you to have it, Cassie." He stopped to look at her. "It's the very least I can do. I care . . ." He swallowed with difficulty. "I mean . . . I . . . you mean so much to me, Cassie."

Cassie's heart trembled, and she inhaled a shuddering breath as her dream withered. He couldn't say the words. She meant a lot to him? So did his damned horse!

"A house and land, huh? You're the first man to offer me something for nothing, but I can't accept your gifts."

He frowned and propped his hands on his lean hips. "Why not? I thought that's what you wanted—for your son to get his fair share of this ranch."

"That's not *all* I want. For starters I want you to trust me."

"I do."

"Not enough to talk to me about Gabe and T-Bone!"

"Yes, and you never hold anything back from me, do you? You'd tell me if some lowlife jumped you in the barn, wouldn't you?"

Cassie gasped and staggered backward. "How—? Oh, he told you, did he?"

"He bragged about it." Drew reached out, his fingers gliding across her cheek. "He didn't hurt you, did he?"

"No. Scared me, but . . . nothing happened."

"I'm glad, and I'm glad he's dead."

"M-me, too, but I wish . . . I've never killed a man before and I—" She shrugged, refusing to surrender to the crushing remorse and guilt. "I'll be okay."

"You did what you had to do, Shorty."

The endearment pricked her heart, got her back on track. "I can't live here anymore, Drew. I can't live side by side with you."

He winced, then hung his head, throwing his face in shadow. "Look, I know I'm not a good father figure, certainly not the kind of man you want to have around your son. But with your own land, you'll find someone worthy of you, Cassie. And until you do, I'll make sure you and Andy never want for anything."

"That's not what I meant." She crossed her arms to keep herself from reaching out to him. "How can you stand there and believe that I have anything but respect and admiration for you?"

"Then what's the problem?"

"You. Me. We're both a couple of weaklings."

"Now that's the dumbest thing I ever heard. You've got more grit than a two-ton bull."

"Maybe, but I'm not tough enough to spend years on this ranch within grabbing distance of the man I love." She held up a hand before he could interrupt her. "No. You listen to me. Listen, while I can still talk without bawling like an orphan calf." She composed herself enough to continue. "I won't stand by while you find yourself another woman and wed her and give her babies. I'd rather lose the land and my son's rightful inheritance than put myself through that kind of hell. I'm sorry, but that's how it is with me."

"Did you say you love—?"

"Maybe you're disappointed in me," she said. "Guess I can understand that. I'm a gal pretending to be a lady when all I am is a former whore who came here to hide. I don't blame you for having second thoughts. But . . . you *care* about me?"

"Very much," he said, missing her point completely. "You've had some bad luck, but you're still a lady. Even when you were called—what was it? Little Nugget?"

She winced and nodded.

"I think that's a right pretty name. I'm even considering calling that new filly Little Nugget."

"It's a good name—for a whore or a horse."

He chuckled and took a step toward her. "Even when you went by Little Nugget, you were a lady."

She shook her head. "No, Drew. I was a saloon tart. A soiled dove. Nothing ladylike about that."

"It all depends on what you think a lady is, I reckon." He moved closer still, and his voice had dipped to a raspy purr that heated her blood and soothed her temper. "To me, a lady is a woman who makes me want to protect her and be good to her, makes me want to hold her, gentle and tender-like. A lady is a woman with airs. When you put on your hat and gloves and swing those hips and smile that smile, you've got airs, darlin', blowing every man in your path clean off his feet."

She couldn't help but grin. "You're a bag of wind yourself, Blue Eyes."

He took her face between his hands and made her look at him, square in the eyes. "Did you say you love me?"

Her lashes dusted her cheeks, then she nodded. "Yes, but I reckon you figure you deserve a woman who hasn't been used and thrown aside time after time."

"Haven't you ever heard that second-hand gold is as good as new?"

Tears burned her eyes, her throat. Her nobility wavered. "Like I said, if you got something to say to me, Drew Dalton, then for God's sake, say it!"

His smile was tender and reached clear into her heart. "I love you, Cassie, and I'm not letting you go." His lips brushed hers, soft and trembling. "And if you can still love me after knowing what kind of stock I spring from, after putting up with my bad moods and worse habits, then you can have me."

She was almost afraid to speak, but more afraid that if she didn't say yes quickly, she'd lose her chance. "I knew you loved me! Oh, Drew, I love you, too. So much that I think I might have died right here if you hadn't said you felt the same for me." She peppered his face with kisses until he laughed. "I love you! I love you! Oh, I've always loved you! Ever since I saw you, even though I was scared and thought I hated you, I guess I loved you that very moment. I was just too stupid to know it, because I'd never been in love before."

"Me either. I should have told you before now, but I didn't know how, Cassie. I've never loved a woman before you, and I didn't want you to feel beholden or sorry for me and stay just because of that."

"I was about ready to haul off and slap you," she said, smiling. "You can be right infuriating, you know."

"I know. Cassie . . ." He moved back from her. "I want you to know something, something real important."

"Uh-oh." She held her breath, afraid of bad news. His expression was grave, his blue eyes serious.

"I not only love you, I respect you and I will always cherish you," he intoned.

She caught her breath and blinked in amazement at him. "Now that you've started talking from your heart, I do believe you've become a regular Romeo! Oh, darling Drew." She sighed and pressed her lips to his. His arms lassoed her and his kisses seared her, branded her his.

"You're a saint to put up with a man like me. I know I'm tough to love."

"You're not too tough to love," she told him, caressing the bold planes of his face. "You're too tough to leave, so I'm staying."

He stamped her mouth with a kiss and let out a happy whoop of laughter. "We'll build a new house right here and make it ours! There will be only good memories in it for us, Cassie."

"The house we're in is fine, Drew."

"We'll need more room for all the children we'll have. Our sweet Andy deserves some brothers and sisters who will look up to him and pester him and love him. We'll give the old place to Oleta. It'll be a fine dowry for her to use in catching herself a husband."

"You've got it all figured out, haven't you?"

"Not really. All I know for sure is that when I was facing death there in the barn with Wilhite ready to shoot me, all I could think about was how much I love you and little Andy and how I wish I'd told you. Then, a moment ago, I felt that you and this land were joined. I couldn't be with one and not have the other."

"Oh, Drew." She gave a little sigh, then a laugh. "I just had a funny thought."

"What?" He caught her hands and swung them between their bodies, making her feel like a kid again. "Tell me."

"I was thinking that A.J. is turning over in his grave right now. I don't think he ever figured we'd find happiness together and would be planning a family."

He grinned rakishly. "Yeah, in a twisted way the old coot was our matchmaker."

Cassie tipped back her head and laughed up at the deep-purple sky. "Ain't that right and proper!" she said, still giggling.

"You're so pretty," he said, his voice dipping to a raspy whisper. He smoothed a hand over her hair and his eyes glimmered like stardust. "Suddenly I'm the luckiest man in the whole wide world. I sure never thought I'd be able to say that about myself."

"Look out, Drew, you're gonna make me cry." She sniffed, trying to hold back her tears.

"But you're happy, right? These aren't tears of sadness or frustration?"

"I'm happy," she assured him. "How about you?"

"Sweetheart, let me show you!"

With a joyful whoop, he swung her around in a dizzying circle. She laughed with him, her heart light, her spirits soaring. Stumbling, they fell and rolled down the knoll to where the spring crocus and daffodils grew, where the front steps of a house would be set, where two lives would join and flourish, and where two hearts found a forever kind of love for the very first time.

Dear Reader,

Each month, Avon Books publishes the best in historical and contemporary romance. So be on watch for these upcoming Avon titles.

For historical romance fans, there's Julia Quinn's Avon Romantic Treasure, BRIGHTER THAN THE SUN. The Earl of Billingham, a notorious Regency rake, must marry before his 31st birthday or lose his inheritance. He thinks he's found the solution to his problem in marriage to Miss Eleanor Lyndon. But Ellie is more than he'd bargained for. Is it possible for this rake to become reformed?

In THE WILD ONE by Danelle Harmon, Julia-Paige—and her baby—arrive in 1776 England from America to confront devil-may-care Lord Gareth de Montforte. When Julia informs Gareth that his late older brother is the father, Gareth impulsively marries the beautiful mother. But is he truly ready to settle down and become respectable?

The romantic Scottish Highlands is the setting for Lois Greiman's HIGHLAND BRIDES: THE LADY AND THE KNIGHT. It's 1516, and Sara Forbes is on the run with a very special baby. Soon, she finds herself protected by Sir Boden, an irresistible and brave knight. But can their growing love overcome his devotion to duty?

Looking for a contemporary romance with a touch of humor? Then don't miss Barbara Boswell's WHEN LIGHTNING STRIKES TWICE. Rachel Saxon, a modern career woman, is swept off her feet by Quinton Cormack and must decide if it's time to put *pleasure* before business in this sizzling love story by one of romance's most popular writers.

Remember, each month look to Avon Books—for the very best in romance.

Sincerely,
Lucia Macro
Avon Books